TWILIGHT HEALER
BARBARA CUSTER

I0554457

NIGHT TO DAWN

Night to Dawn Magazine & Books
P. O. Box 643
Abington, PA 19001
www.bloodredshadow.com
ISBN: 978-1-937769-35-2
Copyright by Barbara Custer:
First edition 2001
Second edition 2006
Third edition 2008
Fourth edition 2014

Illustrator: Dmitrijs Dmitrijevs
Calligraphy & design: Teresa Tunaley
Content Editor: Patricia Holley
Line editor: Gemini Wordsmiths

I dedicate this book to Anne Kaler, a college instructor who introduced me to writing, and all my fellow scribes who've supported me in my creative endeavors.

"Kenworthy always lived for the hunt, and Hades can't take anymore." The gentle way Elliott spoke reminded Alex of a doctor breaking bad news to a favorite patient. "Have you and your friend Leslie seen the bats?"

Alex nodded, licking his lips. A sense of foreboding ground into the pit of his stomach. "What will he do to us?"

"Hades plans to destroy all vampires. When he attacks, expect a slow, agonizing death."

"No ... I don't want to believe that." Alex slid his dry tongue over drier lips. "You and I have lived for over a century, but he must spare Leslie. Her father needs her, and she wants ..."

"Hades won't care." Elliott waved his hands. "He'll see Leslie as another vampire following in Kenworthy's footsteps."

"I should have known." Alex stood up without touching Hades's portrait. "Can Hades find us in the New World?"

"He'll find you no matter where you go." Elliott's words seemed to drop into the air like rocks into mud. "His bats will follow your scent. I don't know when or how he'll attack. Hades keeps his timetables secret."

Chapter 1

"Leslie, your negligence may cost Fitzpatrick his life. Right now, he's hanging on by a tiny thread." Daniel Crawford, Leslie's boss, folded his bulky arms across his chest. He spoke quietly, but his narrowed eyes betrayed a smoldering anger.

Leslie Taite sipped coffee while she sat before his mahogany desk. Her fingers trembled and she dropped her cup, spraying its contents on Crawford's blotter and gray business suit. Jumping up, she grabbed the cup. She strained her eyes, scanning the room for a towel to clean the mess, but her eyes saw nothing. "I'm sorry," she said in a weepy voice.

"I don't believe this." Crawford shook his head, wiping his jacket with a napkin. "Do you understand what's happened?"

"Oh, yes, I do." Leslie swallowed hard. She brushed the wisps of ginger hair from her reddened eyes. *Why did you choose respiratory therapy for a living? To heal people? That's bull. You're just seeking absolution for your Mom's death,* a phantom voice in her head scolded her.

"Are you going to fire me?" she asked in a small voice.

Crawford let loose a deep sigh. He gazed toward his phone, as if he thought he'd find his answer there. "I don't know how the lack of oxygen affected Fitzpatrick. If you're lucky, his family won't press charges. If you're luckier, he'll recover, and you'll get by with a written warning."

Leslie buttoned her lab coat and rubbed her arms. Crawford's olive oil voice sent chills up her spine. In the past, he'd delivered scathing criticism if she so much as farted off key. What surprises did he have in mind?

"So far, I only have Sarah's version." Crawford's smile didn't reach his slitted eyes. "Talk to me, Leslie. What happened downstairs?"

The shivers settled around her neck, and Leslie heard her teeth chatter. After dabbing her eyes with a tissue, she pulled out a wrinkled slip from her pocket, her assignment sheet. "Fitzpatrick had surgery for a perforated stomach ulcer last week. The other day, he became septic, and Dr. Saunders ordered a CAT scan to find out why. He said that Fitzpatrick's drinking and smoking history could cause complications."

Crawford leaned back in his leather chair, scratching his ruddy forehead thoughtfully. "Fitzpatrick did all right until his test. What went wrong?"

Balling her fists inside her pockets, Leslie stood and paced around the office. She paused by the shaded window, keeping her eyes on Crawford.

"The charge nurse Sarah and I brought Fitzpatrick to CAT scan. After I hooked him to the portable ventilator, she screamed at me to move the vent from the IV pump. I asked her where I should move it to. She shouted, 'Over there.' Her directions didn't make sense, so I asked, 'Where?' She waved her hand and yelled, 'Over there, Stupid!'" Leslie gazed at her boss, bracing herself for a scolding.

Crawford's face turned beet red, and his lips trembled, but he remained silent.

"The more she carried on, the more she confused me. So I put the ventilator where I thought it should go."

Crawford leaned back and covered his eyes. "You meant well, but Fitzpatrick's breathing tube dislodged. God only knows how long he went without oxygen." Straightening up again, Crawford folded his hands and regarded Leslie intently. His phone rang out loud, breaking a silence seemingly as long as death.

"Daniel Crawford, Respiratory Therapy," he said after snapping up the receiver. A long pause followed, and his gray eyes clouded over. "I see," he added softly. "Thanks, Sarah."

Leslie blinked, fighting an onslaught of tears. "Fitzpatrick didn't ..."

"He's alive, but unresponsive." Elbows propped against his blotter, Crawford counted on his fingers as he roll-called Fitzpatrick's symptoms. "He does not move or open his eyes, even when getting stuck for blood. His pupils are dilated. He does not breathe on his own. His contractured posturing indicates serious brain damage. Dr. O'Toole is seeing him now." Crawford paused and massaged his temples. "Fitzpatrick's wife knows what happened. She's threatening to press charges. She's already called her lawyer."

Tears formed in the corners of Leslie's blue eyes and rolled down her cheeks. "I'm sorry." She sank into her chair. "So sorry."

"Your tears won't make him better," Crawford said grimly. "The breathing tube dislodged during his CAT scan, a routine test. Do you know what lack of oxygen does to brain cells?"

Leslie nodded, blotting her eyes. Asphyxiation could turn a healthy person into a house plant, condemned for life to a respirator and feeding tube. Though Crawford's voice remained low-key, his censuring glare and tight-lipped frown accused her of criminal negligence.

Her brother Gerry had worn that look the day Mom died, she remembered. Emphysema had ravaged Mom's lungs, compliments of years of cigarette smoking. She'd spent her last years in and out of Betsy Ross Hospital, where Leslie worked now.

Leslie would never forget Gerry's frosty eyes or the anger in his voice when he badgered her with questions.

Never mind that emphysema was incurable. Never mind that, in the end, Mom had called the shots by swallowing a bottle of sleeping pills.

Leslie buried her face in her hands and sobbed loudly. For the moment, she forgot about her boss. Instead, she thought about the numerous complaints she'd endured about faulty equipment and botched procedures, especially the times she tried to draw blood. She'd palpated the radial artery and wedged it against the bone, the way she was taught, but the needle always missed its mark. *"Get out, you vampire!"* one patient shouted. *"Get someone who knows what they're doing."*

She thought about Bill Saunders, her mother's doctor, who'd supported her decision to attend respiratory school, even after he saw her Apticom test scores. He even convinced Crawford to give her a job. *Your stupidity may cost Bill his career,* the phantom voice continued to scold. *What about that, Leslie?*

"Assuming Fitzpatrick's wife sues, my track record won't help," she managed after a pause. "And the way I have trouble catching on ..."

"Leslie." Crawford's eyes, pale and resolute as steel, met hers levelly. "The courts won't care about your past mistakes. I suggest that you keep your mouth shut. Bringing up your mechanical difficulties will only give the Fitzpatricks' lawyers ammunition."

"OK." Leslie lowered her eyes. "What happens next?"

Crawford dragged his fingers through his sweat-drenched hair and studied his notes. "If Fitzpatrick snaps out of his coma, his wife may drop the charges. As you pointed out, Fitzpatrick didn't take care of himself. That will help our case. Realizing that you didn't mean any harm, I could let you off with a written warning."

Leslie gasped and felt her throat go dry. Why was Crawford acting so nice? "Suppose Fitzpatrick doesn't recover?"

"If he remains comatose for an extended time or dies, I'll have to let you go," Crawford said quietly.

"You've got to believe I'm sorry," Leslie repeated. "The way Sarah kept yelling, I couldn't think straight."

"I understand that," Crawford said in an edgy voice. "Unfortunately, Fitzpatrick has two girls, ages six and nine. Your inability to think may have robbed them of their father."

Crawford stood up, his way of ending their meeting. "For now, you're suspended, pending the outcome of Fitzpatrick's treatment. You may get a second chance. But you'd better think hard, Leslie, before practicing respiratory therapy here or anywhere else. How will you live with yourself if your mistakes cost someone's life?"

"I hear you," Leslie mumbled, bolting from the office. She fled to the lot, where she'd parked her rusty blue car. Jamming her key into the ignition, she jarred the engine into an angry roar and sped out of the lot in a cloud of blue smoke.

She hurried down Cherry Street, a four-lane thoroughfare surrounded by battered tenements, nested in the bowels of Northwest Philadelphia. Night blanketed the buildings like a shroud. Thunder blasted overhead, and rain splattered on the windshield. Its dampness penetrated the windows, sending shivers through Leslie's body.

Dr. Wolf had diagnosed her learning disability, and aptitude tests didn't lie. What made her think she could work with complicated machines and formulas, especially with human lives involved? *Your father,* the shadowy voice whispered. *After Mom died, he insisted that you go to college. Gerry, Shelly, and Warren made it through school, he'd said. Why not you?*

"School." Leslie's voice came out in ragged gasps. "Dad, you meant well, but you're not the one coping with motor and perceptual deficiencies."

Thunder blasted like fireworks, cutting into her thoughts. She turned right on Sunset Lane, an S-shaped road, lined on both sides by woods. Rivulets of rain flooded her windshield, making the trees look like sickening blobs.

She would have given anything for a job near home, instead of her present commute that included miles of unlit roads. But hospitals had downsized, and jobs for new therapists had become scarce. As it was, Crawford had hired Leslie only because of Bill's recommendation. She didn't dare live in an area where gangs and criminals ran rampant. Given her learning impediment and the poverty of offers, she had to settle for any position, even if it meant driving across Pennsylvania.

Leaning against the seat, Leslie rubbed her throat where two scabs had formed. She'd cut herself on some rose bushes, and the healing sores itched terribly. She started to think about Alex, one of the few friends she'd made at Betsy Ross. Alex lived on Mill Road, just off Sunset Lane. *I wonder if he's home. Maybe I could stay at his house until this storm passes.*

She'd met him weeks ago at Saunders' office. Her coworkers considered Alex important because he wore a three-piece suit and carried a briefcase. He had approached Leslie with a smile, and later asked her out to a night club for dancing. He insisted that she consider him her friend, even after she told him about the trouble she had mastering procedures at work. Either he wore blinders, she concluded, or he didn't understand the score.

What would she tell Alex? That she got suspended because her carelessness had caused her patient to suffocate? That his family will sue the hospital? No respectable man would want anything to do with her.

With a weary sigh, Leslie clicked on the radio, hoping that music could take the edge off her shivering. Instead, a newsflash cut in. "A woman's body was found in a dumpster off Forrest Road. The police have no identification at this time. They found no signs of foul play, except puncture wounds in the throat. An autopsy showed that her body was exsanguinated."

"Exsanguinated?" Leslie echoed, shuddering. Another reason she hated working at Betsy Ross was that at least ten similar casualties had turned up recently near the hospital. That, and an injured coworker, Fred, her good buddy. She'd never forget his gut-wrenching cries the night she found him bleeding in the alley.

"Authorities have launched a full scale investigation, but they have not named any suspects." The radio voice continued.

At the word "suspects," Leslie snapped off the radio with trembling fingers. *What if Fitzpatrick's wife went to the police?*

Moments later, orange construction signs surfaced from the misty shadows. Leslie knew from past trips that parts of Sunset Lane had been scraped for resurfacing. Straining her eyes, she scanned the road for potholes, but could only make out puddles, grass, and mud-covered pavement. She eased her foot off the gas pedal.

The street curved on a downward slope, and she felt the car slide. "Shit!" she cried, pumping the brake. The Ford zigzagged, did a three-sixty, and skated down a ravine.

The trees below seemed to rush at the car. Crunching of metal followed as her hood crumbled like an accordion. The steering wheel plowed into her chest, causing pain to explode inside. Her head rammed into the windshield. Only dimly aware of her throbbing pain, Leslie stared at the colors flowing in sickening shapes before her. Waves of dizziness washed through her. Seconds later, she plummeted into darkness.

Chapter 2

When Leslie came to, she found herself in a hospital bed. Two IV needles lay buried in her arm, and nasal prongs fed her oxygen. Her head ached terribly, and her chest felt as if a heavy weight laid on it. Maybe a two-ton weight. Her breath came out in short rasps. *I'm having a heart attack,* she thought. *I'm going to die, and no one can do anything about it.*

But that didn't sound right. She'd just turned twenty-eight, an unlikely age for someone to suffer from heart problems. Aware of intense pressure on her bladder, she snapped on a light. Looking down, she saw that a Foley catheter was collecting her urine.

She cried out, tears running down her face, as stabbing pain tore through her chest. The dim light illuminated the words "Property of Betsy Ross Hospital" on her IV pump.

"Beige blinds," she murmured, casting her gaze toward the window. Leslie mopped the sweat from her face with her blanket. The cardiac unit had pink blinds. She remembered this from her job orientation.

To her left, she spotted a bedside commode, sink, and a mirror. She wanted to inspect her injuries, and the semi-closed drapes offered privacy. Fingers gripping the side rails, she pulled herself upright. Her legs dangled over the side. Somewhere through her cloud of pain, she heard clattering on the window pane.

A bat hovered outside the window, its webbed wings and claws tapping the glass. Spiked teeth protruded from its mouth. Its flickering tongue dripped blood down its gray hairs. Its red eyes focused on Leslie with a reptilian watchfulness, making her feel like a mouse gazing into the eyes of a cobra.

"I can't move with that thing staring at me," she muttered. Gripping her IV pole and drainage bag, Leslie struggled to her feet. Waves of dizziness rolled through her, causing her head to reel. Her right leg buckled. *Call a nurse, for God's sake,* her mind screamed.

The call bell dangled out of reach.

Bracing herself against the wall and pole, Leslie hopped on her left foot to the sink. Her right foot flopped and thumped on the linoleum. Her head and chest throbbed with each hop. What felt like rusty nails dug into her chest with each intake of air. Sweat trickled down her face. When she wiped her forehead, her fingers brushed against silk tape and gauze.

Silk tape and gauze? How did it get on her forehead? Elbow braced on a wall arm support, Leslie groped along to the sink. She felt for the light switch beside the mirror. The light revealed a white turban covering her head. A mop of red curls peeped through the bandages. Thin ribbons of blood trickled from her bruised lips.

"Oh, my God!" she gasped.

"Leslie, what are you doing?" Leslie craned her neck.

The speaker, a blonde nurse, ran to the sink. "You're not allowed out of bed."

"I felt the bandages and had to see how badly I'd gotten hurt." Leslie swallowed hard, staring at her visitor. Something about the woman's narrowed eyes coated her stomach with unease. "Who are you?"

"Sarah." The nurse's voice dripped with sarcasm. "I'm the one who cleaned up your mess last night."

"What mess?" Leslie winced as Sarah yanked her shoulder. "Stop! You're hurting me."

"If you want to kill yourself, do it somewhere else." Sarah eased Leslie into bed. "I'll be damned if I get sued because of a shit like you."

Leslie rubbed her arms, trying to soothe the goose bumps. "I don't even know you."

"Very funny," Sarah snapped. "Now shut up. Ow!"

Tapering fingers closed over Sarah's arm and yanked. The owner's milk-pale skin and spare frame made him look frail, but his piercing gaze intimated that those hands could tear through limb and bone. "A professional never talks down to her patients," he said. "She advises, but she never condescends."

Sarah's cheeks bleached ivory. The anger fled from her eyes, chased by utter terror. "Um … of course, sir. I was just leaving."

Hugging herself and shivering, Leslie watched Sarah scurry to the exit. Who was this man? He sounded like a teacher or manager. Maybe Sarah's boss. "Thank you," she said, smiling.

The stranger's green eyes glimmered like gemstones. He draped the blankets over her shoulders. "I promised not to let you face your problems alone."

"You did?" Leslie's ragged breathing echoed through the room. The stranger's chestnut curls and angular features looked familiar, but she couldn't recall his name. "Do I know you?"

The man's eyes opened wide as saucers, betraying surprise and disappointment. "We danced at Neptune's Orchard."

"Neptune's Orchard?" Leslie stared at him, thinking that he'd confused her with someone else. She didn't recall dancing at Neptune's Orchard or anywhere else since college. "Who are you?"

"Alex Wallach."

Leslie detected a European accent. It sounded familiar, but she still couldn't place him. "Do we work together?"

"No." Alex lowered his eyes. "Maybe … never mind, we'll talk more when you're feeling better." He turned toward the door.

"Alex, wait!" Panic seized Leslie, causing her to shake and hyperventilate. Her voice sounded cracked and dusty. "What if that maniac comes back?"

Alex turned toward Leslie again, his satiny, icy hands reaching for and cradling hers. "Sarah won't hurt you. I personally guarantee it."

His silvery voice took the edge off Leslie's shivering. She almost forgot about her injuries, but not quite. A spasm wreaked her chest, causing her to double over. Tears flooded her eyes. "God, I hate this. What happened to me?"

"During the storm last night, your car hydroplaned and slammed into a tree. My driver and I brought you here."

"Then you saved my life."

"I did my best." Alex eased her against the pillows. "Try to get some sleep. I'll stay with you."

"Please do." Leslie closed her eyes. Colors floated in sickening shapes under her lids. Only dimly aware of her throbbing headache, she thought about her job and the two years of training she'd endured to get her degree.

Her family held a graduation party, she recalled. Even Gerry, who belittled her achievements, had wished her luck. Her fiancé Tom bought her … where was Tom? Did he know about the accident?

****

Rat-a-tat. *Rat-a-tat!* The noises stirred Leslie awake. The bat hovered outside her window, guarding her room like a sentry. Its wings stretched across the lower pane. Moonlight streamed into the room, throwing ghostly shadows on the plaster walls. Her eyes scanned the room for Alex's chair. Empty. Any second, the panes would shatter, and the bat would swoop down on her.

Her door creaked inward, and light flooded the room. Two men wearing white lab coats entered, whispering in hushed voices.

Silvery gray hair crowned the short man's chubby face. He carried a chart and clipboard.

Leslie recognized his companion as Bill Saunders, her mentor and family doctor. Studying his tanned face, she saw why Alex had looked so familiar. Thick, wavy brown hair crested his angular features and green eyes. Except for his tanned complexion, he almost looked like Alex's twin, right down to his aquiline nose and thin lips.

"Hello, Leslie," Saunders said, smiling. "I'm sorry for waking you so early."

"Don't apologize." Leslie inhaled deeply, feeling relief trickle through her body. Another protest from the rusty nails near her rib cage followed. Hugging a pillow against her chest, she struggled to a sitting position. "I'm hurting badly, Doctor. What happened?"

"You took a nasty hit," Saunders said. "Three broken ribs and a concussion."

A deep sigh escaped the pudgy man's mustached lips. "The concussion required emergency surgery. Your friend brought you here in time to avoid complications. In most cases, by the time the patient reaches the hospital, the train's already left the station."

"The train ... what?" A sick feeling rose in Leslie's stomach. She'd learned the score on severe head injuries during her training. If the patient lucked out, he or she recovered and squeaked through life with a walker or cane. In most cases, severe concussions spelled years on life support machines. "I'll never work again."

"You almost didn't survive," the older man said.

"But you made it." Saunders's soothing voice offered a reprieve. Almost like Alex's, but without the accent. "You'll work sooner than you think."

"I hope so." Leslie gazed toward the older man. "I already thanked Alex for saving my life. That goes for you, too, Doctor ..."

"O'Toole. Joseph O'Toole. Don't mention it."

"Dr. Saunders, I didn't know you had a brother." Leslie still thought about the resemblance. "Alex treated me quite ..."

"They only look like brothers." O'Toole pulled up a chair. "Know where you are, Leslie?"

"Betsy Ross Hospital, where I work as a respiratory therapist." Leslie closed her eyes, hoping to ease the throbbing. "My mother died, and my father lives with my brother Warren. Alex Wallach brought me here after the accident. How's that for alertness and orientation?"

O'Toole and Saunders exchanged looks. "Not bad." Saunders smiled, but his voice sounded edgy. "Who's the president of the United States?"

"Clinton." Leslie shrugged. "Why?"

Leaning forward, O'Toole shone a light in her eyes. The glare made her squint. "How long have you worked here?"

"Long enough to qualify for health insurance."

O'Toole chuckled. "Time goes fast, Leslie. Let's try this one again. What's today's date?"

"I'm not sure." How long had she worked at Betsy Ross? The rattling at her window made it hard to think. She counted on her fingers. "March, 1993. Crawford hired me in October 1992, and I've worked here six months."

O'Toole scribbled something on his clipboard. He glanced toward the window and started. "Holy ... what's that thing doing on the windowsill?"

"Beats me." Leslie cringed against her pillows, shuddering. "That bat, or whatever you call it, gives me the creeps."

"I can see why." Stepping to the window, Saunders lifted the blinds. A horrible flapping sound followed. "What an ugly-looking brute. It doesn't look like any bat I've ever seen."

Hugging the blankets against her chest, Leslie peeked toward the window. The rosy fingers of dawn streaked the sky. The bat hovered in mid-air a moment, then soared away into the shadows.

Saunders pulled the blinds shut. "Whatever it is has gone. I'll notify Maintenance, in case the critter makes another visit."

"Good idea." O'Toole wiped his ruddy face with a tissue. "Let's get back to you, Leslie. I heard that you took a short walk. How did you feel?"

"Awful." Leslie eyed O'Toole, but his poker face didn't offer any hints. "My right leg gave out when I put weight on it. It was like my muscles had gone on vacation. I'd better find a desk job."

"Not necessarily. As your brain cells heal, you should notice more mobility. Physical therapy will strengthen your muscles." O'Toole spoke in a monotone voice, as if he'd stuck his nose in a book. "The harder you work at your exercises, the sooner you'll walk."

He paced around the bed. "What makes respiratory therapy so important to you?"

"Well ..." Leslie coughed explosively. More waves of pain followed. "My mom died of emphysema, and I want to help patients like her. I hate to quit my job before I've even started."

O'Toole furrowed his eyebrows. "For the record, Leslie, you've worked here two and a half years."

"No way!" Leslie rubbed her eyes and yawned. "I just made probation."

Reaching into his jacket, Saunders produced a newspaper. "Look at the date."

Leslie reached for the paper with shaky fingers. The date, "March 20, 1995," leaped at her from the front page. "Oh, no!" she moaned, covering her eyes.

"It's not the end of the world." O'Toole's voice softened. "We expected some memory loss."

"Some?" Leslie pressed her fist against her quivering lips. "I lost the last two years."

O'Toole edged toward the door. "Try not to get upset. I'll order some Xanax to help calm you."

"Not so fast. Sarah said she cleaned up my mess. Why?"

"Ask Sarah," O'Toole said before closing the door behind him.

Leslie swallowed hard, choking back her noiseless sobs. "What Sarah said ... I can't remember any of it. Why not?"

Saunders paced around the room and stared out the window. "You don't work in a friendly environment. People here will blow up if you look at them crooked. I believe that the stress here added to the trauma, causing your amnesia. Joe feels the same way."

"I see." Saunders's gentle demeanor and willingness to explain emboldened Leslie to continue asking. "Sarah said if I wanted to kill myself, I should do it on someone else's shift. What did she mean? What mess did I leave her?"

Saunders cleared his throat. "I can't say because I wasn't on call. Sarah behaved inappropriately."

A professional never talks down to her patients. "Really?"

"You don't bring your hostilities to the bedside. One of my patients, for example, beats his wife. I hate his guts, but I can't let him see that when I'm treating him. I'll speak with Sarah."

"Doctor?" Leslie's voice trembled. "Was my bedside manner any good?"

"My patients speak highly about you." Saunders laid his slender hands on her shoulders. "Neither Joe nor I would help if we spoon-fed you specific details. You've suffered through multiple injuries and major surgery. Concentrate on getting better. Your memories will return when you're ready to accept them."

The gentle way he spoke made Leslie believe that he wanted to help. Her shivering eased. "Dr. O'Toole won't even look at me. He couldn't wait to leave. Either he hates me, or he's hiding something about my condition."

"Joe keeps negative feelings to himself. You may have minor impediments, but I believe that you'll return to work."

Leslie managed a weak smile. "I hope you're right."

"I'll tell you what's bothering Joe and me." Saunders opened the blinds again, showing the dilapidated buildings against a hazy sky. No sign of the bat.

"Go on," Leslie prodded.

"During your surgery, Joe heard a ruckus outside the window. A school of these bats, like the one we saw, crowded at the window, rattling the panes." He turned toward Leslie, shaking his head. "The maintenance men can take down one, but if a cluster of them nest in the courtyard ... well, people better look out."

Chapter 3

Drusilla Corbi clawed up the ravine, eyes blinded by tears and face coated with mud and wet leaves. Her tattered dress swam around her bony frame. She hadn't eaten for two days, and her head ached terribly. Her surroundings started to blur. She had spent those days hiding from the soldiers.

Her flight began in Adria's market square, when she helped herself to some bread. Ten steaming loaves beckoned from the shop's window. Surely the baker wouldn't miss one. Its cheese-flavored chunks melted in her mouth as she savored each morsel.

Clattering footsteps sounded from the hall. Wooden thongs. Arms hugging her leftovers, she raced outside to the cobblestone street.

"Stop, thief!" the baker shouted from his doorway. "Someone, call the constable."

Moments later, hoof beats punctuated his cries. Officers riding black horses chased her through the streets. Drusilla zigzagged around carriages, then down a back alley. Crouched in a ditch covered over by leaves, she watched the soldiers ride by. *All this fuss over a stolen loaf of bread.* Adria's governor considered theft a capital crime, no matter the amount. One could barter produce for goods or take on work to meet obligations, but begging or stealing warranted the death penalty—hanging.

She hid in the woods, making do with berries or other fruits. At night, she slept under rocks and leaf piles, always keeping an ear out for hoof beats. Was her hunger was causing to her to have visions? She was having many the last few days. What would people think about them, especially the one where Fitzpatrick ...

Drusilla sagged against a tree, exhaling deeply. Who was Fitzpatrick? Where did his healers get their talking boxes? Perhaps the gods knew.

The images bubbled through her mind like a boiling stew: Drusilla working around boxes that beeped and flashed numbers in shining colors; Drusilla wearing pink trousers and a white overcoat. The other workers wore similar clothes. They shouted at her in a strange accent, accusing her of causing Fitzpatrick's brain damage. They said that he needed a feeding tube.

Feeding tube? That didn't sound right. People ate using spoons or forks. Besides, she never heard of women wearing trousers, or inanimate objects talking. What would the gods say about her visions?

Collapsing in the shade, Drusilla wiped the sweat dripping from her scraggly red hair. Another headache starting as a whisper built in crescendo to intense throbbing. *It's the coca. I should quit smoking it.*

She'd been promising herself to quit for the last ten years, since her parents said they couldn't keep her. Anyone wanting to know how Drusilla survived only had to look at her gaunt figure, bruised limbs, and the latticed scars on her back. Once Mamma and Papa decided they couldn't afford her upkeep, life became an endless parade of slave bosses and starvation wages.

Drusilla's shoulders shook with sobs. By now, she felt sure, the coca had affected her judgment, making hiding difficult. Judgment aside, her lack of skills limited her choices of employment. She spent the last month disguised as a lame person, begging for money and filching food when she thought no one was looking. After a few days, someone always caught her, forcing her to start over in a new town.

With a weary sigh, Drusilla gazed at the trees stretching ahead. What made her think she'd escape? When the soldiers found her, she'd ride the noose, unless hunger killed her first.

Hugging her shredded cloak around her, Drusilla sprinted through the forest. She'd keep on going until she reached a new town or dropped dead, whichever came first. The darkening sky blurred her surroundings. Brambles and thorns scratched her face and tore her already ripped clothes. Her sunburned skin peeped through the holes in her linen dress.

Hours later, Drusilla emerged into a clearing. Ahead of her, a building thrust up from the grass in great masses of stone that shone like silver in the moonlight. Its windows, tall rectangular expanses of stained glass, gazed at Drusilla as if they knew, and were moved by, her plight.

A temple. Drusilla wept tears of relief. *Most temples offer food and lodging to travelers. This one might provide me a refuge from the soldiers.*

Flapping of wings impinged on Drusilla's consciousness. Something gray was soaring through the moonlit sky. A bat. A hungry bat, judging by its gleaming red eyes and clicking, sharp teeth. It charged at Drusilla like a soldier on his horse.

Drusilla bolted to the temple, arms shielding her eyes. Her piercing cries echoed through the clearing. The bat swiped at her hands; its moist breath caressed the back of her neck. Its bite slammed agony through her right forearm.

"Help!" she screamed. "Someone, help me!"

Arms wrapped around her forehead, Drusilla dashed to the temple's oak door. She glanced over her shoulder. The bat nested on a tree branch, chewing on a wad of pink flesh that dangled from its mouth. The crater in her left arm spilled blood down her cheek and left a trail on the grass. The bat's ravenous-looking eyes and slavering mouth threatened a second attack.

"Hello," she cried, banging on the door. "Anyone home?"

Only the flapping of wings answered her.

Drusilla ripped a mud-stained tatter from her skirt. It would stop the bleeding. She knocked again, praying that someone would open the door.

"Someone help me!" Her voice quivered, and tears streamed down her cheeks. "Don't let me die out here."

Silence. The bat now circled slowly, its glowing eyes seeming to taunt her.

"Forget it." Drusilla sobbed. "I'll die of rabies anyway."

Rabies? Where did she hear that word? Certainly not in Adria. The people in her visions used "rabies" to describe a disease from an animal bite.

"Oh, Mamma!" Drusilla collapsed on the doorstep and braced herself for agony. "Why couldn't you and Papa keep me?"

Why blame your parents, a phantom voice whispered. *They didn't force you to smoke coca.*

Squealing noises from behind cut into her thoughts. The oak door swung open, showing a marble room lit by torches.

Drusilla's sobs faded. Tears halted, she ran inside and slammed the door shut.

"Thank you," she whispered. Her voice trailed off; no one was there to hear her. With bulging eyes, she took in the slate fireplace, marble floor, and velvet furniture. The crackling fire threw ghostly shapes on the wall tapestries, brass staircase, and rear hallway.

"Hello?" Drusilla called, hands cupped around her mouth. "Anyone here?"

Again, no answer. Drusilla rolled her eyes. Who left the fire unattended? Sparks could ignite the drapes or furniture, and burn the place to ashes.

With an empty shrug, she headed past the stairs. The rear hallway led to a kitchen, dining area, and what looked like a day room. Paintings of war scenes decorated the curved ceilings. It wasn't a temple after all, she concluded, gazing at the coat of arms and pearl-handled daggers hanging on the walls. Maybe a local squire owned the house. She knew that if she was caught trespassing, she'd be shot on sight.

But the faintness rolling through Drusilla reminded that she hadn't eaten for two days. She lurched to the kitchen in a sidestroke motion, inhaling a spicy aroma. Inside, cheeses hung from the ceiling, and a keg filled with wine sat by the window. Sweetmeats laced with cinnamon called to her from the wooden table. "Goat cheese and wine," Drusilla murmured, licking her lips. "My favorite."

After a moment of consideration, Drusilla helped herself to a cheese slab and a glass of wine. The wine slid down her throat, warming her stomach. She forgot about the soldiers. She forgot about the bat. She forgot about everything except the cheese's tangy flavor.

"I see you're enjoying yourself," a male voice called from the doorway.

Whirling around, Drusilla threw up her arms. Her shaking hands bumped the glass, spraying the veined floor with wine.

"I've frightened you, haven't I?" The man ambled inside, regarding her intently. His eyes glistened like silver coins. With his bisque complexion and black overcoat, he looked like he'd spent time in a monastery.

Drusilla met his gaze, mesmerized by his high cheekbones and glowing eyes. His voice lacked harshness. Still, he caught her stealing, and maybe he'd disarm her with kindness before summoning his foot soldiers.

"I'm sorry, Sir. Really, I am." Her voice broke, and fresh tears misted her eyes. "A bat attacked me, see?" She held out her wounded arm. Already, blood was seeping through the soiled bandage.

"Don't worry." His muscular, cold hands rubbed hers. "I know the difference between a thief and someone who needs a friend."

"Friend?" Drusilla's voice came out in hoarse sobs. The gentle way he spoke made her think everything would turn out OK. "Are you a god?"

"In an oblique sense." He smiled, showing unusually long teeth. "Hades gave me my powers ... indirectly."

"I see," Drusilla heard her voice say. His eyes seemed to drill into her very soul.

"Let's not bother with labels, titles, or beliefs." Her host smiled again. "What should I call you, pretty lady?"

"Drusilla Corbi." She swallowed hard. "And you?"

"Kenworthy Mason." Fingers cold as icicles pressed against her cheeks. "My friends call me Ken. You look so alone. I recognize such pain because I've endured it since Hades tried to destroy me."

"Destroy you?" Drusilla's eyes opened as wide as saucers. "Why? You seem like a kind person."

"Before my change, I called myself Lazlo Magnus. I used to rule this district under the Magnus dynasty. Persephone, Hades's wife, and I became lovers. She was going to become my First Lady. Hades never accepted that. Persephone despised him and only married him out of duty."

Skeletal fingers of terror crept up Drusilla's spine. She understood that public officials owned mistresses, but no one dared toy with any god, least of all, Hades. Why was Ken confiding in her?

Ken rested his hands on her shoulders. "I'm telling you this," he said as if reading her thoughts, "so you'd understand his motives. Hades doesn't care about affairs between mortals, but he loves his wife."

Drusilla's voice came out a faint croak. "What did he do to you?"

"Hades said that since I found Persephone so attractive, I should be with her always ... in Tartarus." His voice saddened. "While I was asleep, he set fire to my house. By the time I escaped, the flames literally tore away my skin. I ran, not stopping until I collapsed on a village street. A sorcerer named Titus took me in and put herbs on my burns. He said he could save me by casting a spell of immortality. Know what 'living dead' means?"

Drusilla nodded, thinking back to her childhood. Her parents had made her stay in at night because of the vampires, or living dead, roaming the fields. Then she thought about the way her slave bosses had beaten her, using chains and heated rods. Surely, this man couldn't do any worse.

"Hades left me alone after my change." Ken smiled. "Titus never realized that he'd given me a gift."

Drusilla stared at Ken, mouth gaping, fear and awe combined. Did becoming one of the living dead protect him from Hades's wrath? Did Ken appeal to another god for help? Eyes glued to his translucent face, she listened to her clicking teeth.

"*Undeath* enables me to read people. I know your hurt runs far deeper than those skin tears." Ken draped his arms across her shoulders and ushered her to the couch. "Your parents put you on the street."

Arrows pierced Drusilla's heart. Face buried in her hands, she let out muffled sobs. "They couldn't afford to keep me."

Ken pried her hands loose. "You tell people that, but you wonder if they abandoned you. Why haven't they contacted you?" He shook his head sadly. "Alas, you looked for answers in your coca plants. Those herbs will drive you mad."

"They make me forget things."

Ken looked her in the eye. "Such as what?"

Drusilla pressed her hand against her trembling lips. Dare she confide in this stranger? Maybe he'd understand, given his own problems, and besides, she had nowhere to go. "Without money, you take any work you can get. People who owned estates hired me, promising decent living conditions. They lied. Sometimes I worked twenty hours a day. If I displeased the master in any way, he'd beat me. Most nights, I went to bed with bleeding welts."

Her nail-bitten fingers traced the burns scarring her arms and shoulders. "Between jobs, I slept in the street without a blanket or coat. I never knew where I'd get my next meal. I want to forget how I almost died of starvation."

Ken laid his hands on her shoulders. His piercing gaze made her fidget. "Have you left out something?"

Drusilla lowered her eyes. "Sometimes I dream that I'm working around sick people," she said after a pause. "These people are attached to beeping boxes called machines. They call me a healer ... respiratory therapist ... but I keep hurting the people I'm supposed to help."

Drusilla stood up and paced around the room. "Most of the other healers scream at me, call me these awful names. The ones who talk nice act like they're tossing a bone to a dog."

She giggled and plopped on the sofa again. "The machines I dreamt about don't exist. Maybe the herbs have made me crazy."

"No," Ken said quietly. "You saw a parallel world."

"What?"

Ken eased himself into the cushions beside her, smile tucked in place. The feel of his sinewy muscles against her thigh generated an inner heat. "The world as you know it exists in two dimensions," he said. "Each of us has a double in the parallel world."

"Parallel world?" Drusilla echoed. The shivers worked toward her bones. Was this man crazy?

But Ken's glimmering eyes and soft voice radiated confidence. Maybe immortality gave him access to this other world. "According to my dreams, my double wore silks and studded clothes, but she didn't look happy."

"I've seen your double," Ken said, "and you're right. She's not happy. People in her world use machines on their jobs, complicated machines that challenge the average intellect. Your twin, Leslie, has a learning impediment which makes mastering these machines almost impossible."

Drusilla scratched her head thoughtfully. Understanding dawned when she studied Ken's face. She recognized it as one she'd seen in her visions. "Leslie's master looks like you. I heard him accuse her of causing someone's brain damage, whatever that means. She may lose her position."

"Don't count on it. Leslie makes up for her lack of ability with determination." Ken's eyes, bright as moonlight, misted slightly. "Watching her from a distance, seeing her daily struggles ... I can't help but love her."

Drusilla twirled her hair between her trembling fingers. "Does she love you?"

"I never told her how I feel." A faraway look crossed Ken's features. "She'd never understand our world, a world lit only by fire. Her people employ electricity and machines to do their work. They buy clothes ready-made and ride horseless carriages called automobiles."

"Auto ... what?" Drusilla tried to imagine a carriage without a horse, but couldn't. "How do you know?"

"A year ago, I fantasized a world where people could fly, and I imagined a door opening into this world. A door materialized, and I found myself in this flying machine with people wearing strange clothes. They called the machine an 'airplane.'" The smile returned to his thin lips. "Hades doesn't know this dimension exists."

"Guess not." Drusilla felt so hypnotized by his glowing eyes, she'd believe anything.

"As you pointed out, I resemble her superior." His voice grew mournful. "Once, I approached her on the street and made small talk. She acted polite, but she looked at me with utter loathing. So I understand your loneliness." He brushed his lips against her forehead.

Second choice, Drusilla thought, her eyes watering. *Why can't anyone love me for myself?*

"A healer might wean you from those herbs," Ken said, stroking her wavy hair. "He can't ease your pain, but

I can make your memories seem like distant nightmares."

He draped his arm across her shoulders. "I'll show you how to find the secret door between the two worlds."

"Who cares about this other world?" Drusilla asked. "I've got enough troubles in mine."

"We should speak with Leslie." Ken's eyes wavered, and his voice grew distant. "Right now, I see her in bed, badly hurt. Somehow, an automobile accident caused her mind to cross with yours. Maybe she can help us figure out what happened."

"My twin?" None of this made sense. Ken was only acting kind because she reminded him of this stranger. Still, she had found an ally, someone valuable when you were running for your life. "When do we go?"

"After I've changed you." Ken opened his eyes again and gazed at her. "Power will be yours for the asking. Especially in this new world, because the people there won't acknowledge the supernatural."

Power? A smile worked its way to Drusilla's blistered lips. This stranger might rival her for Ken's affection, but power would give Drusilla an advantage. Before she could ponder the issue further, Ken scooped her into his arms and headed upstairs. He laid her on a silk comforter.

"What will you do to me?" Drusilla gaped at his teeth—two of them, pointed, glistening in the candlelight.

"Love you and share my gift with you." After stripping his robe, Ken crawled into bed. Icy fingers ripped through her dress tatters.

Drusilla tensed as his tongue slid down her cheek. "Will this hurt?"

"No. All that came before." His tongue probed the recesses between her chin and throat. She barely felt the pin pricks. Head pressed against his shoulders, she listened to her heartbeat in her ears. Her surroundings dimmed, and she felt herself float.

Chapter 4

While picking his way through the bones littering Tartarus's fields, Hades stepped over the writhing bodies of ten men convicted of murder. They squirmed on the black grass, their sores weeping foul-smelling blood through their tattered clothes. After these men died on the gallows, Minos and other Judges of the Dead sentenced them to daily torture—stabbing, beating, anything to cause ungodly pain. Hades ignored their sour stench and the maggots crawling from their sores, but he swatted the blood-sucking flies caught in his robe.

Slow, deep rage stirred inside Hades, forcing him to clench his fists. Watching the men squirm and listening to their piercing cries brought up images of his enemy Lazlo: Lazlo lusting after Persephone, Lazlo killing people and drinking their blood, Lazlo teaching others to kill. Lazlo now went by the name Kenworthy; it wasn't the first time he'd changed names to avoid capture. Hades longed for a wolf to rip his enemy apart, or a disease to cause slow, excruciating death. But Kenworthy, nee Lazlo, would never face death or judgment.

Kenworthy was a vampire.

With a deep sigh, Hades walked up the grassy slope, past the river Styx. Its waters, once clear, had turned rusty from the blood of condemned prisoners. Every now and then shrill screams punctuated the deathly silence.

As he watched, a reed ferry pulled out from the opposite shore. Its captain was bringing him the newly deceased people waiting for judgment. But other business came first. Hades continued up the slope to a building made of black rocks, situated near a field of pink and white flowers. His palace, from which he ruled his underworld.

"King Hades." A bearded man stepped from the shadows and bowed. It was Minos, his chief judge and servant.

"What do you want?" Hades glared at him. Already, he felt a question coming, and he hated questions. Questioning his decrees was a prelude to blatant disobedience.

With shaky hands, Minos pulled out a papyrus scroll that was tucked inside his robe. "Julian, the one who was drinking your nectar and eating your ambrosia, showed immense sorrow before his death. In this diary, he wrote that he regrets his actions. Perhaps you'd like to read it and reconsider his sentence."

"I certainly shall," Hades said, lowering his voice. He managed a smile. "I might lighten Julian's sentence if the document proves his sincerity."

After accepting the scroll, Hades tore it into tiny pieces and let them fall on the grass. "My word is final, no matter how many half-baked pleas you get. Don't dare question me again."

"You know best, sir." Hades turned away, and Minos stared with dark, hateful eyes at his back.

Every time Hades passed his servants, he sensed their fearful eyes on him. For years, the dark tumors of rage had infected him, and the least offense caused him to explode. Hades never understood what made him so angry. Perhaps it started after the Three Fates exiled him from his home in Olympus. Perhaps watching Kenworthy flirt with Persephone stirred his anger. Whatever it was, the rage nested in his heart. Years in the Underworld had taught him to pick out timid servants like Minos, people he could bully into following orders.

The loneliness that lodged inside Hades, making a home the way a tenant would, wedged like a sword as he entered his palace. The halls rang empty without his wife Persephone. She'd gone above ground to visit her mother, not that she cared about him when she was there. At home, she rarely spoke, and when she did, conversation never went beyond stilted politeness.

Hades went to his drawing room, where he kept his ebony throne. The throne faced an oblong table surrounded by ten empty chairs. Soon, he'd meet his messengers, the bats who were spying on Kenworthy. He knew this because his mind sensed the whereabouts of all his servants, including the messengers.

Fluttering of wings sounded from behind him. Two bats, Phetheus and Lydia, soared through the open window. Phetheus flapped his wings before settling on the table. Lydia drifted in, giving Hades a wide-eyed look.

The bats had important news. A smile worked its way to his face. "What do you have for me?" he asked.

Phetheus flapped his wings again. "Lazlo took a wife named Drusilla," he said. "He changed her into a vampire."

Hades exhaled, trembling at the rage smoking inside him.

"Drusilla went to his home begging for food," Phetheus continued. He spoke in an unintelligible twitter, but for Hades, the words came through loud and clear. "I tried to stop her, but Kenworthy got to her. I also found more of his kills in the woods. He's teaching Drusilla to hunt."

And drink blood. "Was she receptive?"

"She worships him like a god," Phetheus said. "I overheard them talk about an alternate world they plan to visit."

Lydia began digging at the table with her claws.

"What's making you so nervous, Lydia?" Hades asked, staring at her.

"I saw this alternate world." Lydia paced up and down the table. "The other messengers and I were feeding outside, when a huge wind swallowed us. I, too, saw Drusilla, only she was lying on a stone road. Her horseless chariot had run into a tree."

"Horseless chariot?" Hades started and looked at Lydia. "Even gods need horses for their chariots."

"Everything looked different ... the buildings, the streets, clothes people wear." Lydia rolled her ruby eyes. "The man who found Drusilla called for help by using a magic box. Two other men came along and lifted her into another horseless carriage. The other messengers and I followed them to a building. Healers in white rushed her to a special room, where they cut her head with saws. Whatever they did helped, because she survived. These healers called her 'Leslie.'"

"Leslie," Phetheus repeated, shifting his gaze between Lydia and Hades. "Lazlo ... Kenworthy talked about this woman named Leslie. He said that Leslie was Drusilla's dimensional twin."

"Does Leslie's world have a name?" asked Hades.

"They call her village Philadelphia," Lydia said. "The people there use inanimate objects to do their work. Their fancy herbs cure diseases that would kill Adrians. Leslie doesn't know it, but vampires exist in her world, too. The man who found her is immortal. He called himself Alex."

"Maybe Alex is another fake name for Lazlo," Phetheus said. "He said that he loved Leslie and wanted to help her."

"Not possible." Lydia glared at him. "This man didn't look like Lazlo, and besides, Lazlo was with Drusilla when Leslie had her mishap. I'm sure of it."

"Does any of this make sense, King Hades?" asked Phetheus.

Hades nodded, fighting the tears brimming in his eyes. He knew about the alternate world. Olympus was part of that world, centuries ago, when he and the other gods ran their own court. That ended after the Three Fates forced them to give up their palace. Later, the Christians drove them away with their crosses, exiling them to Adria, the earth's alternate universe.

"Lazlo changed his name to Kenworthy after becoming a vampire," Phetheus said. "He won't rest until he bleeds this new world dry."

Hades nodded again, shuddering at the tensing muscles in his back. His fists clenched and unclenched. "I'll bet he sent Alex to start his foul mission."

"I doubt it," Lydia said. "Sometimes I hear Alex cry when he thinks no one is looking. At night, he keeps vigils ..."

"Silence!" Hades slammed his fist on the table. "No vampire deserves pity."

He got up and stormed around the room, shoving chairs and kicking rocks aside. Moments passed, and then he turned toward Lydia. "I bet he's thinking about turning her into a vampire."

Lydia looked at Phetheus, then at Hades. "He never said anything about it. He just watched Leslie while she slept."

"Lazlo and Alex work together." Hades sighed. "Lazlo thinks he's fooled me, and he's laughing at me, while he sets up shop in the new world. I don't like this at all."

Phetheus and Lydia exchanged nervous glances. "I suppose not, King Hades," Phetheus said.

"I must destroy Kenworthy and his followers," Hades said. "They kill relentlessly because they think they can't face judgment. I let it go for years, not caring to toy with the supernatural, but enough is enough."

"What will you do to them?" asked Lydia.

"I haven't decided yet." Hades shuffled to the window and gazed out at the darkness. "Fire will destroy vampires, but innocent people might get hurt."

He turned toward his messengers. "Phetheus, watch Lazlo and Drusilla. Lydia, go back to this new world and follow Leslie."

"I can't," Lydia said. "The healers barred her room with strong glass. Alex and family members are guarding her."

"People do go to bed, Lydia, and vampires feed." Hades gave her a censuring look. "So pay attention, especially when Alex visits. If he offers her immortality, do what you must to stop him, even if you have to destroy Leslie."

"How can I?" Lydia cried. "If I get near Leslie, her screams will alert everyone."

"Aim for the vessel beneath her chin," Hades said, smiling. "One slash and she'll die before anyone can help her."

Chapter 5

Alex Wallach tiptoed through the tiled hall, trying hard not to overhear the nurses' conversations or read their thoughts, but their voices came through loud and clear. A ward clerk paged someone overhead. A nurse transcribed orders. The tension on the floor sank through his brain like teeth.

He spotted room 414, five doors past the nurses' station. Leslie's room. Droning voices sounded behind the closed door—Bill Saunders reassuring Leslie that she was getting better, that she would return to work. The loneliness that had circled Alex since her accident, circling the way bats circled a body in Adria where he'd lived as a boy, fell upon him.

Leaning against the wall, he licked his lips. His drag-on burned his throat with fire, and the loneliness that had haunted him since Kenworthy ushered him into the vampire world aggravated his blood lust. He tried to distract himself by staring at Leslie's keys. He found them in her car after the ambulance whisked her to the hospital. Eyes gazing at the heart-shaped ring, he searched for a key to her suppressed memories.

A man wearing a lab coat atop a navy suit emerged from Leslie's room. Bill Saunders was Leslie's doctor, and to hear her speak about him, a hero. Alex considered Bill his friend. He'd sold him blue chip stocks and bought him drinks at Neptune's Orchard. But Bill was screening her visitors, including him. *Given the staff's censuring stares and Leslie's fragile condition, maybe she needed a watchdog.*

"Alex." Smiling, Bill extended his white-sleeved arm for a handshake. "Who died?"

The keys dropped. Alex retrieved them and met Bill's gaze. "What did you say?"

"You look like you lost your best friend."

"Leslie and I were getting close before her accident." Alex lowered his eyes, hating the desperation in his voice. "Now she doesn't even know me."

"She knows you saved her life," Bill said. "Believe me, she's grateful."

Alex swallowed hard, fighting the lead weight of despair. He hugged his gray cloak around his shoulders. "I don't want her gratitude."

Bill regarded him, his green eyes hard and resolute. "Don't push her, Alex. Leslie's facing major issues, and she needs all the support she can get." His voice softened, offering a reprieve. "When she regains her memory, your rescue will reinforce her positive feelings toward you, and your relationship will grow."

"How long will that take?"

"I don't know." Bill rubbed his chin. "Joe and I believe emotional trauma caused her amnesia."

Shouting echoed from the nurses' station, two doctors and a nurse arguing. Their narrowed eyes and heated voices told Alex that they'd carried an ongoing feud. "The squabbles here won't help."

"Tell me about it." Bill shook his head. "I already reprimanded a nurse for her behavior toward Leslie. We get the staff that no other hospital wants because of the bad neighborhood. It hurts to watch Leslie because she really tries to help people. Did she ever talk to you about her job?"

Alex rubbed his neck. The burning eased somewhat. He suspected that Leslie suffered the same intense loneliness he did. Bloodlust tormented Alex, making him avoid social gatherings; people shunned Leslie because of her limited abilities. At the hospital, he'd overheard the staff call her stupid and incompetent. Who could say which of them suffered more pain?

"Once," he said, looking at his feet.

"If she remembers your good times, she'll recall the ugliness here. Do you understand that?"

Alex nodded. "Why does she insist on working in this snake pit?"

Bill shrugged. "She owes fifteen thousand dollars in school loans, and Betsy Ross provides her only source of cash. She blames herself for her mother's suicide, and thinks that working in the health field will set things right."

"Survival guilt." Alex affected a deep sigh. The dark tumors of loneliness welled up again, threatening to crush his heart. "How can I help her?"

"Talk about pleasant things. Reminisce over past dates, but don't mention her job or anything else that would upset her."

"She deserves much better."

"Keep telling her that. Maybe one day, she'll believe it." Bill smiled and patted Alex on the shoulder. "I know you'll say the right thing," he finished before heading down the hall.

Alex tucked the keys into his back pocket. Slowly, he cracked the door.

Leslie lay propped against her pillows, appearing to be asleep. Thick curls poked like roses from her bandages. Already, he felt heat building in his groin.

She reminded him of Elizabeth.

The oldest of eight children, Elizabeth had grown up on Adria's farms. She had the same blue eyes and fiery red hair that Leslie did. Her kind voice and compassion toward her siblings invited his love. When he joined the army, her words of endearment buoyed his spirits before each battle until the day her body washed up from the Athyr River. He never expected suicidal intentions to lodge behind her gentle laugh.

"Alex." Leslie's eyes fluttered open. She sat up and swung her legs over the side of the bed.

"Leslie, wait!" Alex cried, rushing to her side. "I'll get a nurse."

"I can't stay here." With a shaky hand, Leslie wiped the sweat dripping down her face. "That bat spooks me."

Alex glanced toward the window. A bat perching on the sill stared back. An Adrian bat. He recognized its ruby eyes and pointed incisors. Somehow, the bat had crossed the time dimension between Adria's world and Philadelphia. "Son of Hades," he murmured, shivering. Remembering that Leslie could hear him, he added, "I see."

"I don't blame you for being scared." Leslie pointed to the window. "Look at its teeth. Dr. Saunders said that he never saw anything like it. Have you?"

Alex heaved a long, skeletal sigh. *Go ahead, Alex, level with her,* a voice inside yammered at him. *Tell her how your god Hades created those bats to spy on immortals like yourself. While you're at it, give her gruesome details about life at Betsy Ross before her accident.*

"Maybe it escaped from a zoo." He tapped the pane. The bat shrieked and rammed against the window. After closing the blinds, he turned toward Leslie. "No bird or animal can penetrate this glass. You know that, don't you?"

"I do." Leslie smiled, but her voice sounded edgy. Leaning forward, she massaged her right leg. "My leg feels like cooked spaghetti. If that bat comes after me, I'm up shit's creek."

"I've sailed up that creek myself." Poking between the blinds, Alex stared at the moonlit sky. *Undeath* wore many faces: the tears in Leslie's eyes, the harassment by her peers, and her accident. "Don't worry, this glass is sturdy."

Moments later, plodding footsteps echoed from the hall, followed by sliding metal and men's voices. An elderly man limped through the open door, leaning on a walker. He breathed through pursed lips. A stench of rotting vegetables drifted from his scrawny body, suggesting incipient infection.

An auburn-haired man wearing dungarees, a T-shirt, and multiple tattoos on his arms ushered the older man to a chair. His son, Alex presumed. The scar snaking across the young man's left cheek and the glint in his eyes said that he'd gotten into his share of fights. After the older man settled in, he swaggered to another chair and propped his sneaker-clad feet on the radiator.

"Dad?" Leslie pressed her fist against her lips and shrunk against the covers. "Oh, my God, Daddy! What happened to you?"

"Well, Leslie," the older man spoke in a slurred voice. "It's a long ..."

"He's fine," the younger man cut in.

"The hell he is!" Tears rolled down Leslie's cheeks, and her lower lip trembled. "He lost so much weight. He can hardly breathe. Don't dare lie and tell me he's fine."

The auburn-haired man—Warren, Alex recalled from past conversations with Leslie—glared at his father. "I told you to stay home."

Alex avoided their gaze, not caring to get caught in a family quarrel. Instead, he focused on Leslie. "Your dad had a stroke and pneumonia," he said, cradling her hand in his. "He'll have to watch himself."

"I see." Leslie's eyes became huge and vulnerable. "How did you know?"

Alex gazed at Leslie, the machinery by her bed, and the room. Her reddened, tearful eyes and erratic heartbeat warned that the wrong answer could provoke a relapse. "You told me about your father before your accident," he said at last.

"How could I ..." Leslie coughed hard and clutched her chest.

"I'd better find a nurse," Alex said, rising to his feet.

"Please sit." Bracing a pillow against her chest, Leslie grabbed a white cord. "This button will disburse pain medicine when I need it." She pointed toward her relatives. "Daddy, Warren, meet Alex. He fished me from the car wreck."

"Hello," Warren grunted.

"You saved my daughter's life." A tear dripped down her father's ruddy cheek. "I don't know how to thank you."

"You just did, Mr. Taite." Alex smiled.

"Christian will do," her father said. "The Mr. business makes me feel old." Turning to Leslie, he rubbed her shoulder. "Don't worry about me. I'll get better."

"I don't remember you being sick." Leslie's voice croaked like that of an old invalid. Alex longed to assure her that everything would turn out well, but he knew that her father's illness offered only a preamble to her troubles.

Warren jumped up and paced around the room. His fists balled inside his jeans' pockets, and his gray eyes narrowed. "Guess you forgot about the grisly murders, too."

"Murders?" Leslie's eyes widened. "Such as what?"

Alex stared at Warren, catching his eye as he headed to the window. Eyes locking, he lulled the young man into hypnosis. *Watch what you say around Leslie. Do not upset her.*

Warren's head bobbed up and down, as if pulled by a string. Alex released his control. Warren rubbed his eyes and started. "Nothing involving our area," he said. "Dr. Saunders called today and said that you're doing well."

Christian's mouth broke into a toothless grin. "You've got a hard head, Leslie. You'll get your memory back in no time."

"I hope you're right." Reaching toward Christian as far as the IV poles would allow, she managed a hug.

Warren chuckled. "Feeling better?"

"I think so." Leslie eased herself against the pillows. Her voice lost its edginess. "Dad, you need to start eating."

"Dad can't swallow or cough up his spit," Warren told her. "That's how he got pneumonia. Saunders prescribed a soft-to-chew diet."

"In other words, I have to eat baby food." Christian grimaced. "Alex, where did you meet Leslie?"

"At the hospital." Alex kept his eyes on Leslie. "I work here as a financial consultant, and Bill introduced us. When she had her mishap, I was headed to the hospital. I saw her car plow off the road."

Warren whistled. "Talk about acts of God."

"Will you continue to see her?" asked Christian.

Alex managed a smile. "I'd like to, if she'll let me."

"I'll let you." Smiling, Leslie clapped Christian's shoulder. "Dad, don't give him a hard time."

Christian laughed a coarse laugh followed by gasps and wheezes. "I'm too old for that." He clasped Alex's hand with hard gnarled fingers. "You're freezing. Why aren't you wearing gloves?"

"I forgot them." The lie came easily after years of practice.

"Come and see Leslie any time you want. She'll stay at my house after she gets her walking papers."

"I'd like that," Alex said, licking his lips.

"Hey!" Warren cried, peeking through the window blinds. "Look at that bat. Where did it come from?"

Leaning back, Leslie crossed her arms over her head. "Beats me. Dr. Saunders said that an army of them crowded the window during my surgery. Alex thinks it escaped from a zoo."

Alex rolled his tongue through his mouth, gagging on the dryness. Why would Hades send so many bats across the border?

"Doesn't surprise me." Christian grimaced. "The bosses here keep this place like a shit house."

"If you say so." Alex rubbed his arms.

"During my stay here, a nurse came to my room stinking of beer." Christian lowered his voice. "When you lay down with dogs, you get up with fleas. Be careful, Leslie. Those bums treated you like a ...”

“Another worker.” Warren nudged Christian with his elbow. “Dad, you've had enough. We'd better go.”

“Yeah, yeah, yeah.” Christian's lower lip jutted out in a pout.

“Come on, Dad.” Warren ushered Christian to his feet. “Alex, nice meeting you.” Leaning over the bed, he pecked Leslie's cheek, as did Christian.

After her father and brother left, Leslie burst into giggles, jarring another violent cough. “Dad and Warren make me laugh. They fight because they're so much alike.”

“I noticed.” Despite his intense thirst, Alex felt a smile play on his lips. “I'd sell tickets to see them go at it with these nurses.”

“Especially Sarah,” Leslie agreed. “Mind if I ask you something?”

Alex glanced toward the door. “Ask away.”

A gleam crossed Leslie's eyes, and she cleared her throat. “I know that some people here made my life miserable. You seem like a good listener. Did I confide in you?”

“You talked about your father,” Alex said, clicking on the television. He flipped through the channels, hoping some program would catch Leslie's attention. “But you never mentioned work.”

“Are you sure?” Leslie persisted.

Alex rested his hands on her shoulders. He could hypnotize Leslie into forgetting Betsy Ross, but he dared not because of her head injury. “Even if I knew something, I wouldn't tell you. Friends don't tell friends hurtful things.”

“In other words, Dr. Saunders told you to keep quiet.” Leslie's eyes blazed. “That's ridiculous. Do you understand what it's like to meet strangers who claim to know you? What it's like to lose time? I feel like I've wandered into a black hole.”

"I understand because I've met soldiers with amnesia after the war. Forcing a memory won't help unless you can handle it."

"Yeah, right." Leslie crossed her arms over her chest.

Alex stood up and paced around the room. "One day, Leslie, the past won't matter. Why don't you forget about work and concentrate on getting better?"

"I'd like to divorce this hardware." Leslie ran her fingers along her IV tubes and pumps. "OK, if it will make you happy, I won't hunt for skeletons from my past."

Alex kissed Leslie on the forehead. "I should go," he said, heading to the door. "But I'll stop by tomorrow night."

At the nurses' station, more hushed whispers drifted from the desk. Sarah was arguing with a male nurse.

"I'm not changing Leslie's dressing," she shouted.

"I can't do it for you," the young man said. "My patient's going bad."

"Someone wrote me up, thanks to Miss Taite. The next ..."

"Excuse me." Alex smiled, staring into her eyes. "I believe we spoke the other night. Let's go for a walk."

Sarah's eyes became glazed sapphires. "Sure," she murmured in a dreamy voice.

He ushered Sarah through the Forrest lobby outside to her blue car. She let out a whimper when his teeth grazed her skin. By the time Alex's dragon slithered away, well sated, Sarah lay unconscious in her car seat.

When she woke, Sarah wouldn't remember what happened, but she'd stop hassling Leslie. Alex ensured this by hypnotizing her. He also knew that he'd broken a cardinal rule that his mentor Elliott had preached during their years together: you don't feed near your neighborhood or work station.

"*Undeath*," Alex whispered, feeling Sarah's warmth infuse his veins. "Leslie, I could show you so much happiness."

What will you do to Leslie? Change her into a vampire?

Tears trickled down his cheeks, and he let out a breathless sob. At the lobby, he stopped in the men's room to check his clothes. All intact, except the crimson stains on his teeth. So much for the New World's theory about mirrors and vampires.

"You don't deserve Leslie," he told himself. "If you cared about her, you'd walk away before it's too late."

Except that he knew in his heart of hearts that it was already too late.

Chapter 6

When Leslie woke, moonlight shone through her window blinds, dancing ribbed shadows on the walls. The rattling noises at her window had stopped; perhaps the bats found new haunting grounds. After snapping on the overhead light, she pushed herself to a sitting position and swung her legs over the bed.

The effort cost about 1000 kilowatts of pain. Her head throbbed, and razor blades of agony twisted inside her chest with each breath. She'd spent the last three days in Physical Therapy, trying to awaken her dormant leg. It dangled like a tree ornament. The dizziness threatened to topple her with any quick move; this morning, she'd refused to attempt any exercises.

A tray lay on the table before her. Lifting the lid, she surveyed its contents: mashed potatoes; pureed chicken and squash.

"This stuff looks like vomit." She grimaced. Hands gripping its sides, she moved to lift the tray. As she did so, another 1000 kilowatts of pain knifed through her incision. Her hands splayed. The tray clattered to the floor, spraying pureed chicken and squash.

A nurse rushed in, clutching her chart. "Leslie, can it!" she shouted, eyes flashing. "You've caused enough trouble."

Leslie furrowed her brows. The woman's name tag said, "Ruth Simmons, Registered Nurse," but her dark, wavy hair and ruddy complexion didn't look familiar. Another hostile stranger from the past.

"It was an accident. I'm sorry."

"Yeah, right." After scooping up the broken dishes, Ruth laid the tray on the windowsill. "Don't expect me to call the kitchen for another."

"Who said I wanted that shit?" Another spasm wrenched Leslie's chest. Pillow tucked against her incision, she crawled underneath her blanket. "Get out."

Ruth yanked aside the blanket and stuck her face in Leslie's. "You threw that tray, didn't you?"

"It was an accident," Leslie repeated, massaging her temples. "No wonder my dad hates this place. Bums like you made him miserable."

"You want to talk about bums?" Ruth's gray eyes narrowed. "Before your accident, you screwed up royally with your Singer Sewing Machine method for drawing blood gases. You insisted on using broken equipment on my patients."

"I did not!" Leslie cried, shaking. Or had she? According to Betsy Ross's staff, a lot happened during the last two years.

"Watch who you call a bum," Ruth said in a measured, quiet voice.

"Or else what?" asked a man's voice. It was Dr. Saunders. Leslie hadn't heard his footsteps. Few people did because of his crepe soles. Sometimes he seemed to materialize from nowhere. He stood at the doorway, giving Ruth a censuring stare. "What's going on here?"

"Leslie threw that tray at me," Ruth said. "She needs restraints."

"That's enough." Saunders's square jaw tightened. It looked like he'd swallowed a fishbone. "You may go. I'll talk to you later."

Ruth backed toward the door. "Doctor, I ..."

"I said that's enough." Saunders tossed his clipboard on the windowsill and looked Ruth in the eye. "Consider this a warning."

Slumped against her bed, Leslie hugged herself,

shivering. Her hands shook, and she felt her mind slip. She took deep breaths, fighting to regain control. "I'm sorry," she heard her small voice say. "I got an awful pain when I tried to move the tray, and I dropped it."

"You shouldn't lift those trays with your incision," Saunders said quietly. "Next time, ask a nurse to help you."

"Every time I use the call bell, the nurses yell at me. Ruth said that I tortured people when I drew blood gases, and that I used defective equipment." Leslie drew in a deep breath. "Did I perform that badly?"

Saunders stood over her bed, regarding Leslie. "Let me put it this way. If you do 99 out of 100 medical procedures well, the people here will focus on the one with complications. Your boss hates spending money. He insists on repairing his blood gas analyzers rather than buying new ones. You can only use what you've got."

"Guess so." Leslie blew her nose and sniffled.

"As for blood gases, everyone has different thresholds of pain. Most people complain after enduring multiple blood draws. But I received compliments about you, too. You can take that one to the bank." Saunders smiled. "But that's enough shop talk. I hear you gave your therapists a hard time."

Leslie crossed her arms over her chest and stared out the window. "I hate it here. Please send me home."

"I can't do that." Saunders's voice rose a notch. "You've just made it out of ICU. You're still getting transfusions and IVs. You can't dress without help. How will you care for yourself at home?"

"If I stay at Dad's house, Warren can cook my meals. Visiting nurses can do my IVs." Leslie's eyes focused on Saunders. "Come on, Doctor, it's been done."

"Not this time. Warren works long hours at his newspaper and he's got enough responsibility handling your dad." He leaned toward the bed to check her IV drips. "You don't remember it, but your therapists helped your dad to walk. Give them a break."

Leslie thought about the white-coated people who coached her through therapy. "They look like strangers to me. Mom warned me not to take candy from strangers."

"I know these therapists, and you trust my judgment, right?"

"Yes, but their exercises really hurt."

"I know," Saunders said. "I promise they will hurt less when you get stronger. Once you can do simple tasks, living with your father might work. Until then, you've got to play ball with your therapists." Saunders rubbed his head and looked at the chicken-squash mixture streaking the floor. "Pureed food again? I ordered you a regular diet."

"Ask the kitchen people. They keep sending it."

"I'll get someone to clean this mess, too. Boston Market opened shop across the street last year. If I get you a platter, will you eat it?"

"Sure." Leaning on her side, Leslie nudged open her bedside drawers. Empty, except her cosmetic bag and a bath pan. "Where's my pocketbook?"

"Don't worry about the money." Saunders smiled. "After treating your mom and dad, I consider you family."

Treat your patients like family, a phantom voice whispered. Saunders's voice.

"I'll be right back," he said, heading to the door.

Leslie watched Saunders as he went out the door. *Treat your patients like family,* his voice echoed in her head.

She was in ICU, setting up BIPAP, a breathing machine that delivered positive pressures through a mask. Saunders ordered it for an older man with sleep apnea. The machine's pressures and oxygen output kept fluctuating, no matter how she adjusted the knobs. Her patient's oxygen saturation dropped, setting off panic alarms in her head. Something—she couldn't remember what—kept her from asking for help.

Saunders, who heard the alarms, came in to check. After glancing at his patient and the machine, he adjusted the mask. "You need tighter straps for that mask," he said. "Otherwise, BIPAP won't do him any good."

Leslie shrunk against the window, head lowered. "He's not getting the oxygen, either."

"He is now. Oxygen readings will always fluctuate with BIPAP." Saunders paused, his eyes widening. "Hey, you're shaking. Are you OK?"

Leslie shrugged and said nothing.

"No one needs to hear about this," he said, patting her shoulder. "Relax and treat your patients like family. You'll do better."

"CODE BLUE, ICU! CODE BLUE, ICU!"

The booming intercom snapped Leslie back to the present. Leaning against the pillows, she closed her eyes. Someone had a cardiac arrest, and she couldn't do anything about it.

Sometime later, a knock sounded at her door. A stout man in green scrubs ambled inside, carrying a Boston Market bag. His blonde hair and pale face glistened with sweat. It was Fred Mayes, a coworker. He'd coached her through job orientation, and he'd visited every day since the accident. More important, he smiled, really smiled, instead of humoring her with a plastic grin.

"Hi, Leslie." He hurried to her bedside, panting, and laid the bag on her table. "Dr. Saunders got busy with the code. He told me to give this to you."

A spicy aroma wafted from the bag, causing Leslie's stomach to rumble. Instead, she focused on her visitor. Beads of perspiration dripped on his scrub shirt. His eyes looked red and puffy.

"Have a seat," she said. "You look tired."

"Think I will." Easing himself into a chair, Fred blotted his face with a napkin. "Go ahead and eat. Don't mind me."

Leslie lifted the plastic lid covering her dish. Roast chicken, cranberry sauce, diced potatoes, and decaffeinated coffee. Every drink was decaffeinated, per Dr. O'Toole's orders. "Thank you," she murmured, inhaling deeply. "That kitchen slop made me feel like a piece of shit on a rainy day."

Fred burst into gales of laughter. "You said it."

"What's happening with the code?"

"Not much." The laughter died in Fred's throat. Leaning back, he wiped his forehead again. "How are you really feeling? Are the nurses treating you OK?"

Leslie gulped, fighting the lump that rose in her throat. She did not answer.

"That bad, huh?" Fred dabbed at his forehead again. His downcast eyes betrayed lingering sadness.

Leslie nodded. "Doctor ... I mean, someone said that Crawford refuses to buy new equipment. That surprises me. During my interview, he seemed to love spending money."

"Don't worry about Crawford. You've got enough on your plate."

"Translated, Saunders warned you not to mention the days of yore." Leslie nibbled on a chicken leg and chased it with coffee. "Thing is, I need health insurance. If I'm about to lose my job ..."

Fred shifted in his chair and cleared his throat.

"According to the nurses, I've done terrible things." Leslie laid down her fork and regarded Fred. "Bad enough to warrant dismissal. No job, no health insurance. So if Crawford fired me, please tell me."

"Crawford said he's going to cut some deal with you."

"Did Crawford and I get along well before my accident?"

Fred stood up and shot a glance up and down the hall. After closing the door behind him, he wedged a folding chair between his own and the door. "That's better," he said, turning toward Leslie. "Crawford isn't your main problem."

Icy fingers of dread crept up Leslie's spine. "I can't think of anything worse than losing my job."

"Maybe I should spare you History 101, like Saunders asked." Fred leaned back in his chair and looked at Leslie. "But you deserve the truth because you saved my life."

"I did?" Leslie took a deep swig of her coffee. "If I rescued anyone, please tell me about it."

"During the last year, ten people were found dead near the hospital—exsanguinated." Fred cocked his ear toward the door. "Betsy Ross beefed up on security, and now the lobbies and parking lots are crawling with cops. You'd think that the killer would avoid the hospital, right?"

Leslie nodded, then shrugged.

"You get to feeling safe because you hope the officers will protect you. If you're lucky, you never have to find out any different. I wasn't so lucky."

Fred dragged his chubby fingers through his moist hair. "Three months ago some guy jumped me in the alley behind the Forrest building. He had broad shoulders and teeth like a wolf's. He dragged me behind the bushes and tore into my throat. Now I won't leave the building without an escort."

He unbuttoned his top and leaned toward Leslie. *Oh no, here it comes,* her mind screamed, as he yanked his collar sideways. *I don't need to see this.* Thick scars looking like punctures rippled across the fleshy mound under his left ear.

"Oh, my God!" Leslie dropped her fork.

"Lucky for me, you followed because I'd forgotten something." He traced his fingers down his neck. "You did great, Leslie, using your scarf to stop the bleeding. You never left my side, even after they brought me to the emergency room. Thanks to you, I managed to keep it together."

Leslie looked at Fred, trying hard not to notice his scars. "I don't recall any of this. Did the police catch the creep?"

"Nope. That monster drank my blood." Fred nodded, confirming this to himself. "I never provoked him, but something about me didn't sit right, so he decided to lunge and attack."

"Did he see me?"

Fred nodded, his ragged breathing echoing through the room. "When that maniac saw you, he got this weird look. It was like he knew you. He took off like a shot. I still have nightmares about him."

A groan escaped Leslie. She blotted the tears forming in her eyes. "I don't know what to say."

"I don't mean to upset you." Fred's tone softened, but still edged with fear. "You needed to know so you can make informed living arrangements. Get someone to stay with you here at night."

Leslie nodded. "I think I can work out something with Alex and my brother. Thanks for leveling with me."

"It's the least I could do. I ought to stand lookout for you, but frankly, the sight of my own shadow makes me jump. You ..."

Heavy rapping sounded at the door. "Leslie," shouted a man's voice.

"Come in," Leslie called.

"I can't." The knob twisted and turned. "The door's stuck."

"Shit," Fred muttered through clenched teeth. "It's Crawford." Jumping to his feet, he yanked the chair loose. The door flew open and slammed against the plaster wall.

A man wearing a gray tweed suit strode into the room. Chestnut hair slicked with cream crowned his reddened forehead. His thin-lipped scowl matched his narrowed eyes and stony face. *He'd make a lousy ad for Brylcreem,* Leslie thought, fighting the hysterical giggles rising in her throat.

"Fred, what are you doing here?" Crawford demanded. "They needed you at the code stat."

With trembling hands, Fred straightened his scrub shirt. He groped through his lab coat pockets. "No one paged me."

"It doesn't matter. When someone calls a code, you run."

"I did. When I got there, Dr. Saunders told me to bring something to Leslie."

Crawford's shiny eyes shifted from Fred to Leslie. "I'll bet he did."

Leslie wrapped the blankets around her, shivering. "Dr. Saunders bought me dinner," she ventured timidly. "Fred was only trying to help."

"I don't pay Fred to run errands," Crawford said in an acid voice. "Get back to that code, young man. NOW!"

"Yes, sir." A blush worked its way through Fred's pudgy cheeks. He skittered to the door.

"Thanks for everything, Fred," Leslie called after him.

After Fred left, Crawford closed the door. "Sorry about that," he said, turning toward Leslie. His lips curled into a wolfish grin. "Sometimes I let the pressures of running a department get to me."

"I understand." Leslie huddled under her covers, still thinking about Fred and his neck scars. "Do I still have a job?"

"God saw fit to give you a second chance at life." Crawford leaned against the wall, smile tucked in place. "You've learned a painful lesson, so I took the disciplinary notes from your file."

"Disciplinary notes?" Leslie echoed, watching her boss. He'd worn a tweed suit during her training period too. Always black or gray, as if he'd dressed for a wake. "What did I do?"

Crawford let out a low, deep chuckle. "Relax, Leslie. I can afford generosity. Fitzpatrick drank like a fish. The booze ruined his liver and brain. Therefore, his lawyers have a weak case."

Leslie furrowed her rust-colored brows. None of this was making sense. "Do I know Fitzpatrick?"

Crawford's head jerked. His hands shook, and he avoided eye contact. "Don't worry about Fitzpatrick. When Dr. O'Toole nods his OK, you'll return to work with a clean slate."

"I appreciate your help." Leslie tucked her legs under her tray table. Crawford's oily voice intimated that he'd planned another agenda. "I want to remember my mistakes so I don't repeat them."

"You won't." Crawford smiled again, the snake-advancing-on-a-mouse smile. He edged toward the door. "Bringing up the past will only hurt you."

"Mr. Crawford ..." Even as she mouthed the words, he bolted down the hall.

She brushed her hands over her face. Her skin felt cold and clammy. What had she done?

Glancing at her bedside table, she spotted a newspaper left by Warren. She flipped through its pages without reading anything. Instead, she kept seeing Crawford's reptilian eyes. And Fred's haunted look, when he revealed his scarred neck.

Chapter 7

About two days later, Drusilla opened her eyes and found herself nested in Ken's sinewy arms. Something sticky coated her tongue. Her surroundings glowed with an eerie brightness, without candles or moonlight, revealing rose-colored silk sheets, a brass headboard, and porcelain walls.

Drusilla swallowed and licked her lips, hoping to ease her thirst. Her mouth burned, as if someone had jammed a lit torch down her throat.

She stood up stiffly, focusing on an oblong mirror by the door. Hugging the sheet around her, she took slow, tentative steps. The cool marble floor chilled her feet, but the dizziness she'd felt was gone. She walked without lurching or swaying.

The mirror revealed a scrawny woman with bony arms poking like twigs between the sheet's folds. Tangled red curls surrounded her bleached, freckled face. Blood congealed around her mouth and neck.

The sheet draped over her left shoulder, Drusilla tied a knot, forming a sari. She checked her back for injuries, expecting to see burn marks and scars, souvenirs from past beatings. Her cream-colored skin showed no blemishes at all.

Understanding dawned when Drusilla noticed the cobra fangs that replaced her eyeteeth. Ken had made her into something inhuman. Her parents would despise her. Any hope she had for a reunion, which faded with each passing year, had become a fantasy. Drusilla wept noiselessly, dripping tears on her sheet.

Moments later, Ken's gentle arms cradled her shoulders. "You must hate me," he whispered. "Even those who embrace the change grieve their lost humanity."

Drusilla gasped. "What have you done to me?"

"I've given you new life." He folded her against his chest and stroked her hair. "No mortal can hurt you now."

"But you've turned me into a ..."

"An immortal." Ken rubbed her back. His musk scent tickled her nostrils, easing her shivering. "Without my gift, you would've died of hunger."

Drusilla nodded, her breath heaving.

"You've seen your last sunrise." Cupping her chin in his hand, Ken tilted her face toward his. "A small price, given what you've endured, don't you think?"

Drusilla chewed on this a moment. As a housemaid, she'd worked sixteen-hour days. Sometimes her masters requested her "companionship" if their wives became ill or pregnant. Refusing merited ten lashes with a knotted whip. Dropping a plate got her fifteen. Spots on the furniture earned five lashes, sometimes more.

Her more sadistic masters used chains instead of whips. One even singed her hair and shoulders with a lit candle. Between jobs, she slept in deserted caves, and took coca to dull her hunger and fear. It almost worked until she had her visions.

"The sun stopped rising for me a long time ago," she managed in a faint voice. "When my parents said they couldn't keep me."

"I know." Ken looked her in the eye. "Now you have hypnotic powers over mortals, including those who have hurt you."

Drusilla let out a breathless gasp. "Is that why you called Titus's spell a dark gift?"

Ken laughed hideously, a cackle sounding like rattling bones. "I found many reasons to call Titus's spell a gift after I discovered this other dimension. Hades doesn't know this world exists."

"How can you say that?" Tremors edged into Drusilla's voice. Outside, a gusty wind blew tree branches against the house, clawing like skeletal fingers. "Hades knows everything."

"Hades created these bats, like the one that attacked you, to spy on immortals. If he knew about this world, he'd send them across the border after me. That hasn't happened." Ken pulled Drusilla close, massaging her arms, as if trying to rub away her fear. "Any time you feel overwhelmed by your bodily changes, consider this. The next time a slave owner forces his attentions on you, you can say no, and he'll listen."

Drusilla's shoulders sagged. She backed away, keeping her eyes on Ken. "How did you know about that?"

"When we first met, scenes from your past revealed themselves, as if you were acting in a play. I read your childhood memories, your recent experiences, even what you ate for breakfast last week. Human minds are open books for people like us. You'll understand when we go hunting."

"Hunting?"

Ken nodded, grinning. "Feeling thirsty?"

"A little." Actually, her mouth felt bone dry, but the last ten years had schooled her to minimize unpleasant sensations.

"That won't do." Hands cradling Drusilla's shoulders, Ken walked her to his closet, a walk-in room laden with silks and crinolines. Reaching inside, he pulled out a green lace dress studded with sequins. "Put this on," he told her. "You shall learn to hunt and kill."

"Kill what?" Drusilla held the dress at arm's length. The silvery gleam in Ken's eyes and his hungry look left a sick feeling in her stomach. "Wild life?"

Ken gave a low, deep chuckle. "Very funny, Drusilla. Now get dressed and wash your face. You'll want to look your best."

"I've never killed anyone." Drusilla rubbed her arms, trying to ease the chills. "Can't I take blood from animals?"

"You could," Ken said reflectively, "but animal blood tastes bitter, and you'd become so weak you'd drop. Human blood has something that gives us life."

Drusilla paced around the room, hugging the dress against her chest. She paused by a wall tapestry of a sunset. "I guess it won't hurt if I just take a little bit."

Ken stepped beside her, watching her. "Now, why would you want to do that?" he asked. "When your victim's blood rushes out in a gush, you'll want to drain him dry. Don't look at me like that. Titus's gift has made us gods."

"That doesn't make killing right."

"Doesn't it?" His shimmering eyes discouraged argument. "Humans would slaughter us if they got the chance."

"I suppose you're right." With a weary sigh, Drusilla put on the dress. Dipping a cloth into a water-filled bowl, she wiped her face.

"Think about your life before I changed you. Did your slave masters heed your pleas for mercy? Did Mamma and Papa consider your feelings before putting you on the street? Do they even speak with you?"

Dropping her cloth, Drusilla collapsed into a chair and wept loud, choking sobs.

Ken sat beside her and pulled her close. "I don't mean to sound cruel," he said, his voice conceding compassion. "But these people didn't respect your right to live. Why do you care what happens to them?"

A smile surfaced on Drusilla's face. "You've made a good point."

Ken motioned her to the door. "You're only doing what comes naturally to people like us," he finished quietly.

Fingers clasping his hand, Drusilla followed him up a cement stairwell. He led her through his living room, past the fireplace. The fire had burned out, but her sharpened senses enabled her to see as though it were daylight.

Outside, a crackling wind whipped her cheeks. Casting her gaze skyward, she made out glowing ruby eyes nested between the tree branches. They belonged to the bat that attacked her the previous night. She shuddered against Ken's cloak.

"What's making you so nervous?" Ken smiled, sounding amused.

"Look at that thing," Drusilla said in a faint voice. "It wants me."

"Bats eat human flesh, but they won't touch immortals," Ken told her. "Believe me, they know the difference."

"Why does Hades use bats for his spies?" Drusilla leaned her head against Ken's shoulder. "They can't talk."

"Hades understands their twitter." Ken brushed his lips against her forehead. "He threatened to destroy me if his bats catch me taking innocents."

"We should hunt animals," Drusilla said, trembling. "I'd rather that than risk the tortures of Tartarus."

"When the bats aren't watching, we can have any man, woman, or child. I know because I've lived this life for two centuries." He trailed his finger across her cheek. "Let's find some dinner."

"I hope you're right." Arm hooked around Ken's waist, Drusilla slid through the gnarled branches and tree trunks. The limbs blocking their path snapped like twigs. Moments later, the forest thinned out, and she made out a string of shops jammed along a cobblestone street. It was the market square, where the soldiers had chased her.

"We can't go here," she cried, pulling back. "The soldiers caught me stealing. They're looking for me."

"Their weapons can't hurt you. They won't even recognize you." Ken laughed again and patted her shoulder. "We should have them for dinner."

Lowering her eyes, Drusilla gazed at her studded dress and thought about the tatters she'd worn during her flight. She giggled. "That's right. I forgot about my clothes."

Ken slowed his pace and glanced over his shoulder. "Lower your voice. That bat is following us. He'll tell Hades everything he hears."

Drusilla stopped by a tavern. Ahead, hordes of shoppers milled about, bartering animals, food, and clothes. Some slipped past her into the bar. Their scents toyed with her nostrils, smelling sweeter than any bakery. "Hades doesn't like us drinking blood, does he?"

"He'll tolerate it if we go after thugs and undesirables." Ken's gray eyes darted right and left. "His opinion won't matter when we move to the New World."

"But that world uses fancy machines." Drusilla stepped aside as a horse-drawn carriage rolled across the path. "I can't imagine learning to work them."

"I'll show you what you need to know. You'll love it because the people there don't acknowledge our existence." Ken hugged her close. "Their officers would laugh if I told them the truth about myself."

What world existed without belief in the supernatural? Adria's shopkeepers strung garlic over their windows. Its citizens wore chains bearing statuettes of Hades as protection against vampires. Drusilla once owned a similar pendant before thugs stole her jewelry. "What else can hurt us besides sunlight?"

"Fire. Don't worry about it." After steering her through the maze of stores, Ken led her to a dirt alley behind a tavern. He pointed to two men sprawled against a stone wall. "Supper's waiting."

"What?" Drusilla gasped. "How did you find them?"

"I followed my nose," Ken replied, "like you will one day."

"You think so?" Drusilla grimaced at the horrible stench of sour liquor and urine floating from the sleeping men. The holes in their clothes revealed dirt-crusted skin. Flies buzzed around their faces, nesting in sores that wept creamy pus. "Forget it. These people stink."

"Drusilla." Ken laid his hands on her shoulders. "When you master basic hunting techniques, you'll drink the caviar of blood. Until then, hone your skills on people who won't be missed, especially when the bats are watching."

He pushed Drusilla to her knees. "Take him."

Drusilla bent over the unconscious man. Hands gripping his shoulder, she rolled him onto his back. The man groaned, but his eyes did not open. A cloying scent assaulted her nostrils. The smell was strongest around his chin, where the vessel throbbed with a steady beat. Eyes rolled back and teeth gaping, she punctured his throat.

A crunching sound followed, and a sweet taste filled her mouth. His life force slid down, its warmth blossoming inside her stomach like a rose. She licked and swallowed, until she felt Ken's hand on her shoulder.

"Stop," he said firmly.

"What?" Drusilla straightened up, clearing the blood dripping from her lips and chin. She gazed at the bleached bodies at their feet. Ken's flushed face told her that he'd fed, too. Ecstasy surged through her, and with it came a new respect for life. What made her so skittish about drinking blood?

"He's dead," Ken said, gazing up and down the alley. "Blood from a corpse will kill you. Whenever you feed, listen for your victim's heartbeat. When it stops, leave him be."

Drusilla's jaw sagged. "Why?"

"Something bad gets into a person's blood when they die." Ken's voice saddened. "I once saw a vampire drink from a corpse. Afterward, he doubled over, writhing in agony that would make your whippings seem like love taps. He withered to a skeleton within hours and died by the next sunset."

Drusilla nodded, rubbing her arms. "Anything else?"

"Always look over your shoulder and listen for the bats, especially before you take nourishment."

"I'm still thirsty." Drusilla licked her lips.

"That doesn't surprise me. We'll hunt again later, but now ..." Ken lowered his voice. "We bury our kills."

"Where?"

"In the woods." Ken pointed down the alley toward a dirt path. "Walk quietly and follow me. No one will notice you."

Flipping a body over his shoulder, he crept down the path. Drusilla followed him, hoisting her kill like a bag of flour. She kept glancing over her shoulders, but the trail appeared deserted.

After burying the bodies between two oaks, Ken cradled Drusilla in his arms and planted a kiss on her forehead. "You learn fast. Later, I'll show you how much I appreciate that."

Drusilla traced her tongue over her teeth, catching stray drops of blood. "How much will I need to survive?"

"How much and how often depends on the individual," Ken said. "When the bloodlust gets you, you might need six lives or more to quench your thirst. Don't deprive yourself."

He started back up the trail that led into town. The moon spilled silver over the grass and tree tops. Gazing at their shadows, Drusilla imagined them as walking spirits. "I'll take as many as I need."

"That's right. Love what you are, Drusilla."

"I do." Drusilla paused in mid-step and turned her head. She heard crackling of torches, hoof beats and laughter. Someone on the market square was having a party. She knew that such parties ran into the wee hours of the morning. "I should call on one of my former masters."

"I agree." Ken's lips curled into a sunken grin. Drawing Drusilla close, he guided her through the market square.

About two miles past the market square, they happened upon a sprawling mansion made of brick and ocher, surrounded by plots filled with roses, tulips, and wild flowers. Drusilla inhaled deeply. Their floral scent threatened to overwhelm her senses.

Tears slid down her cheeks when she saw the roses. She'd planted them five years ago, when she worked for the owner, Sir Ambrose. Her problems began when she'd sprained her ankle on the steps. Sir Ambrose had caught her sitting on the porch, leg propped on a stool. He'd beaten her so badly that she had to take her meals standing up for the next two weeks.

The familiar, sweet aroma drifted from the porch, nudging her back to the present. Her sandal-clad feet swished in the grass, followed by a gunshot.

"Who's out there?" Sir Ambrose's voice bellowed. Seconds later, a bearded man wearing a blue silk robe emerged from the door, brandishing a pistol.

"Sir Ambrose, do you remember me?" Drusilla ambled to the porch, crooked grin tucked in place. She trod on the tulips, grinding her sandals into the dirt. "I'm Drusilla, the one you whipped because you thought I'd soiled your furniture."

"My flowers!" Ambrose cried in a hoarse voice. His lips flared, showing his yellowed teeth. Finger curled around the trigger, he waved his gun. "You lazy whore. Leave before I kill you."

Drusilla burst into raucous laughter. "You can't kill a dead person." Taking a running leap, she lunged at Sir Ambrose.

The gun fired. Even as the bullet whizzed past her shoulder, Drusilla pinned Sir Ambrose to the grass. His gun clattered against the porch steps. It only took seconds to find his pulsing vessel, and minutes to bleed him dry. Just as she finished burying him, she heard clapping behind her.

"Well done." Ken stepped from the shadows and locked her in a bear hug. "Tomorrow night, we'll dine in the New World."

"The New World." Drusilla stared at the moonlit sky. The stars overhead glittered like diamonds. She'd never seen anything so beautiful. "Will we live there?"

"Yes. I plan to open a business there so we'll look respectable."

"Do we care?"

"We'd better. I intend to earn enough money to keep us in silks forever, and forever is a long time. Besides ..." A dark shadow crossed his gaunt face. "A clean front may ensure our survival."

His eyes, glowing white in the darkness, rolled up at her. "The New World offers plenty of nourishment," he said, cradling her face in his hands. "Just watch that the bats don't follow you when you make your crossover."

"Otherwise, Hades will punish us." Drusilla sighed, rubbing her hands.

"Hades could make ashes of us if it crosses his mind to do so." Ken's hands dropped to her shoulders. "Do you understand that?"

Drusilla nodded, trembling. She'd heard enough stories about Tartarus to last an eternity. Hades had condemned one soul to suffer ungodly thirst in a desert. Others were chained to a rock, torn apart by Hades's three-headed dog, bats, and other Underworld creatures.

"What about my dimensional twin?" she asked after a pause. "Leslie and I should talk. She could help me understand my visions."

The smile on Ken's face evaporated, replaced by a thin-lipped frown. "Watch what you say around Leslie."

Drusilla gazed into Ken's eyes and saw a protective look—the same look her masters wore when referring to their wives. "Why?"

"I told you that Leslie won't understand our life." Ken's eyes flashed with anger mixed with sadness. "She caught me feeding on her peer worker. Luckily, she didn't see my face. She screamed bloody murder. I never saw such terror in anyone's eyes, but she kept her wits together to help the young man."

Drusilla leaned against a tree and looked at Ken again. His face still had that protective glance, one that she didn't like at all. Suppose he later decided that Leslie could handle his world after all? No, Drusilla would make sure this didn't happen.

"You're right," she said, smiling. "Leslie doesn't need to hear my troubles."

"Leslie has much love to give. She will sympathize with your former hardships." The tension faded from his voice. "Just leave out the supernatural aspects. When the time is right, we'll visit her together."

"I'm looking forward to it." Drusilla leaned against a tree and twirled her hair around her fingers. She could imagine Ken being attracted to Leslie's syrupy disposition. He might charm Leslie and convince her to join his world. But Drusilla promised herself to find Leslie and eliminate her before that happened. First, though, she'd teach Leslie about real suffering.

Chapter 8

After struggling into her dungarees and beaded silk shirt, Leslie limped to the bathroom to inspect her injuries. The mirror revealed a C-shaped incision over her forehead, lined by red stubble. Her freckles stood out like raised dots on her face.

The nurses' censuring eyes and hushed whispers haunted her like shadows. Conversations with them seldom went beyond "yes" and "no." She longed for a real smile instead of the stilted grins that didn't touch their eyes.

You've learned some painful lessons, Crawford had said. What lessons? Leslie could only speculate. No one volunteered answers. During her three-week hospital stay, she worked at her exercises until her muscles throbbed. She started to do her own self-care. When Saunders signed her discharge papers, he assured her again that her memories would return when she was ready to accept them.

"I'm ready now," Leslie said aloud. "How do I apologize for something I can't remember?"

"Don't apologize," a male voice boomed from the hallway. It was Warren.

Leslie hobbled out of the bathroom and packed her clothes in a plastic bag. In a more benign environment, the nurses would help with packing, but Leslie counted herself lucky to get her medicines on time. Warren paced around her room, hands hitched in his jeans pockets and lips puckered in a frown.

"I was thinking out loud," she said.

"Just thinking out loud?" Warren propped his elbow against the door and sighed. "Mom spent her whole life apologizing to people. Do you remember what happened to her?"

Shuffling to a window, Leslie peeked between the blinds. A maze of decrepit buildings loomed large against the foggy sky. "I'd give anything to recall what happened last month."

"Maybe Dad and I can help you. Ready to go?"

Leslie nodded. After easing into a wheelchair, she hugged the bag against her chest. Warren steered her through a corridor littered with stretchers and machinery. The path was barely wide enough to accommodate her chair.

"Look at this mess," she said. "One day, someone will get hurt."

Warren stopped at a steel-gray elevator. Leaning against its button panel, he rolled his eyes. "Some of the attitudes here need rearranging, too. Where are the security guards? Where are the escorts?"

"Probably hiding." Leslie grimaced. "Welcome to Betsy Ross."

The elevator doors opened like a gaping toothless mouth. Warren pushed the button marked "B," the basement. Its tunnel led to the hospital's garage.

The basement corridor reeked of rotting tomatoes. The stench intensified around a garbage truck parked by the garage entrance. A sliver of fear nagged at Leslie, causing her muscles to tighten. Casting her gaze, she noticed feet wearing sneakers poking between the filled trash bags.

"Warren," she cried, biting back a scream. She pointed with a shaky finger. "Look."

"What the fuck?" Warren rushed to the truck, retrieving gloves from his pockets. He donned them and lifted out the bags. Underneath, a man wearing dungarees and a sweatshirt lay sprawled in the bin. Bloody gashes covered his throat. To Leslie, his injuries looked like Fred's scars. She shuddered.

"Damn it all." He shook his head. "I've got to call the police and my editor. He'll want pictures, a report ... the whole nine yards."

"The hell with your editor." Leslie held her nose, gagging on the stench. "Get me out of here."

"All right." Warren wheeled Leslie past the sliding doors. "Wait in my car."

"Gladly." Leslie shifted her gaze toward Warren's car, a beige Plymouth parked by the rear pillar. "I think that man's killer attacked my coworker Fred. Maybe he left the body as a warning to me."

"Well, nothing like this ever happens near Dad's, so you ought to be OK." Taking Leslie's arm, Warren helped her into the front seat. "All the murders happened near this shit house. No wonder everyone acts so weird. When you recover, Leslie, find another job, even if it means digging ditches for a living."

"With legs like mine, I'll need a desk job."

"Whatever." After stowing her bag into the trunk, Warren reached into the glove compartment for his cell phone, camera, and notepad. "Sit tight. This could take a while."

"Sure." Taking a deep breath, Leslie leaned against the vinyl cushions. She gazed right and left, hoping to find some reassurance that she'd work again. The chair remained between the Plymouth and a truck, its footrests swaying in the breeze. It looked like a relic of her career, once loved, but now in ruins.

"Could you return that chair to the lobby?"

"Let the nurses come and get it themselves. I'll be damned if I do any favors for those shits."

****

Warren returned sometime later, head lowered, hair moist with perspiration. After mopping his face, he dumped his equipment in the rear seat and plopped behind the wheel. He jammed his key into the ignition, stirring the Plymouth into an angry roar. Burning rubber, he sped onto Cherry Street.

He cruised past dilapidated row homes and tenements. Leslie didn't remember seeing so many broken windows and graffiti. Their crumbling porches scattered splintered timbers on the street. Obscenities plastered their boarded doors. People wearing vacant stares and tattered clothes squatted on the front steps.

After they passed the tenements, Warren turned right on Sunset Lane. Mile after mile of trees and shrubbery flew by. Leslie made out construction signs and ravines, where Alex said he'd found her. She hoped that riding by the scene of her accident would jar memories; instead, she stumbled into a blank wall.

"Shit!" Warren cried, slamming his brakes. "Fucking idiot didn't use his turn signals."

Looking up, Leslie watched a twelve-wheeler ahead of them turning left without using his signals. Warren's fists gripped the wheel, knuckles turning white. "Warren, what's wrong?" she asked.

"I hate finding a body at your hospital," Warren snapped. "Wait until Gerry reads about it."

"Will he care?"

"You bet," Warren said between clenched teeth. "Especially if he plays the hangman. Your accident merited a family conference. He's staying the night."

Leslie cringed against her seat, her mind whirling. The car's heater delivered blankets of warm air, but chills wreaked her body. She felt cold because she dreaded fights with Gerry. She felt cold because Fred's attacker might learn Dad's address and deliver another warning. Maybe even go after her directly.

"In case you don't remember," Warren added softly, "Gerry looks for someone to hang when something goes wrong. Anyone but himself. He dumped on us every time

Mom went to the hospital."

Leslie rubbed her arms, trying to soothe her goose bumps. A dull ache erupted behind her forehead. She remembered all right. Her brother Gerry, who headed a corporation of lawyers, arrived at family gatherings in his three-piece suit, toting his alligator briefcase and an ego to match. His visits began with subtle digs and built in crescendo to scathing accusations. "Who will ride the noose this time?" she asked in a small voice.

"Probably me, but you never know. If he starts anything with you, I'll wrap his fucking rope around his neck."

Leslie stared at the miles of blacktop stretching ahead. The healing incision caused her scalp to itch. She sat on her hands, willing herself not to scratch. According to her doctors, scratching might damage or infect the incision. "Does Gerry approve of my working at Betsy Ross?"

Warren dragged his fingers through his moist hair. "During his human moments, Gerry coached you on self-defense. Murders aside, you never talked about your job. You were too bummed out over some guy."

A dull ache settled in Leslie's heart, determined to make its home there. "I remember my engagement to Tom. We met at Meadowood College, where he teaches history. He hasn't visited me since the accident. Did we have a fight?"

"You could say that." Warren's eyes held a scared look. "You said that Tom thought you were retarded."

"Maybe my Apticom test scores frightened him." Leaning back, Leslie thought about her clinical training. Despite hours of studying each night, she barely squeaked by with C's. She shivered at the crawling sensation on her skin. "Dr. Wolf warned that I'd need hours of coaching and tutoring to succeed at my job. Did Tom leave me because my mistakes hurt a patient?"

"I don't know." The tension evaporated from Warren's voice. "You stopped giving details ever since Gerry came down on you."

Warren's statement jarred Leslie out of the present and back to her freshman year in college, when she'd taken her Apticom test. That day, snow came down in huge pellets, announcing the arrival of winter and freezing temperatures. Dr. Wolf, her psychologist, had been reassuring when she explained Leslie's scores. She kept talking about the Big Game Plan that would help Leslie succeed.

Leslie almost believed that things would work out until she reached her father's home. Gerry and her father were sitting in the kitchen, drinking wine, when she shuffled inside.

"Dad ... Gerry," she began, "I got my Apticom test scores. I know now why I'm having trouble with my grades."

"Have a seat." Her father reached for a bottle of Moselle. "You look like you need a drink."

Gerry smiled at her, a weird, skeletal grin. "What's your problem?"

"I need tutoring." Leslie took three deep breaths. The fact that Gerry hadn't started shouting encouraged her to keep talking. "When my instructors explain equipment, they should spell out details as if they were teaching a six-year-old. Dr. Wolf also found problems with finger coordination and math, but I can compensate with tutoring ..."

"Cut it!" Gerry's smile dropped off his face. He gave Leslie a withering glance. "Stop it right there. Your explanation sounds like glorified laziness."

"Let's talk to Dr. Saunders," her father said. "He'll know what to do."

"Dr. Wolf will say anything to collect her fees." Gerry's rising voice sounded like a harsh whip cracking in a silent room. "Meantime, Leslie, you waste the taxpayers' money frittering your time in school. After your loans run out, you'll drop your marbles and run home to Dad." He shook his head. "You're a disgrace to this family."

The coldness in his voice turned Leslie's cheeks red and made her eyes water. Shame gnawed away at her heart. What made Dr. Wolf think that strangers would give Leslie a break if her own family didn't believe her? No matter how Wolf made the scores look, even if she emblazoned them in gold, people wouldn't understand. As far as Leslie was concerned, winter would last forever.

"Like I said, your accident merited a family conference," Warren repeated, his voice invading her thoughts. "Gerry wants to put on his show."

"Great." Leslie closed her eyes, trying to blot out the image of Gerry's stony face.

Moments later, Warren pulled into a gravel driveway behind two other cars. Leslie hobbled up the sidewalk. Hands braced against the picket fence, she surveyed the property. Pink azaleas surrounded her father's two-story flagstone house. Marigolds lined the cement walkway and front steps.

"Azaleas." She inhaled their scent. Every time she turned, her right leg buckled, reminding that mobility was tenuous. "Mom's favorite."

"Do you remember your visits here?" Warren asked.

"I remember buying new dresses for my dates with Tom and making probation at work. Beyond that, I keep drawing blanks." Eyes lowered, she shuffled to the door. A heavy feeling settled in her stomach. "Gerry thought I lied about my Apticom scores. How will he handle this?"

"People don't fake brain surgery." Warren laid a hand on her shoulder. "Even Gerry knows that."

The wooden door swung inward, leading to an eat-in kitchen. A ceramic basket filled with white and red roses sat on the table. Her sister Shelly stood at the sink, dressed in black corduroys and a sweatshirt, peeling potatoes. She'd worn her auburn hair loose during her visits with Leslie at the hospital; but today, her hair was pulled back in a tight braid.

The aroma of turkey caused Leslie's mouth to water. For the moment, she forgot about Gerry. Leaning forward, she sniffed the flowers. "These roses smell fresh. Who brought them?"

"Gerry," Warren told her. "It's part of his show."

"Of course, he wants to look good." Lifting her right shoulder, Shelly gave Warren a wink. "He and Dad are having their powwow in the den."

Warren cocked his ear to the hallway, then shook his head. "Dad's talking about the way I mistreat him. He's so full of shit."

Rubbing her arms and shivering, Leslie hobbled through the dining room and peered into the den. Her father wept over his desk, head resting against his wrinkled forearms. She longed to hug him, to still his restless heaving, but Gerry stood by the desk, his narrowed eyes discouraging any approach.

"Warren keeps this place like a shit house," she heard her father say in a muffled, shaky voice. "That bastard goes out and brings his girls home. Every night, I hear his bed springs creaking. He turned my house into a brothel."

Turning his back towards Leslie, Gerry laid a pudgy hand on Dad's bony shoulders. "Tell him it's your way or the highway," he said in his courtroom voice. "Want me to talk to him?"

Something nudged Leslie's shoulder, soft as a kitten's paw. It was Shelly's gloved hand. "You don't need to hear this," she whispered. "How about helping me fix Dad's supper?"

"Good idea." Leslie followed Shelly to the kitchen. On the counter top, a blender and food processor stood by the sink. Five plastic bottles bearing her father's name lined up like soldiers by the blender. "I don't recall Dad needing so much medicine," she said. "Guess I'd better learn his new care plan."

"It's not difficult," Shelly said. "You simply puree everything. No rice, no corn, or things like that."

Perching on a chair, Leslie watched Shelly grind the turkey into a mixture resembling baby food. Images bubbled from the deep recesses of Leslie's brain, and she saw herself filling plates with mashed hamburger and pureed vegetables. The aroma of stewed tomatoes issued from the pot on the stove. In her mind's eye, Dad ranted about the food, swearing that his dinner looked like something that had dropped out of a tall cow's ass.

"Shelly, Warren." Leslie burst into peals of laughter. "I remember something about Dad. I remember ..."

A deafening crash cut into her voice, followed by flapping of wings. Leaning against Shelly's shoulder, she limped to the den. Web-shaped cracks skated across the window by her father's bed. Outside, a huge bat like the one she'd seen at the hospital banged the glass, spraying the powder-blue rug with shards. Its webbed, membranous wing squeezed through the splintered opening.

Screaming, Leslie turned on her heels. She forgot about cooking for Dad. She forgot about her reunion with Dad and Gerry. Right now, she needed to run. Instead, her leg buckled, sneaker snagging against the rug, spilling her to the floor.

Warren's muscular hands hauled her up by the armpits. "Hang on," he cried, dragging her into the hall bathroom. "I've got you covered."

Inside, he eased Leslie onto the toilet seat and leaned against the door, gasping for breath. His face turned beet-red and shone with sweat.

Obscene flapping and twittering shrieked from the den. Heavy objects thrown, then a bull roar.

Silence followed, and then an authoritative voice said, "OK, everyone, I've got him."

Warren cracked the door and helped Leslie to her feet. Gerry hovered by the desk, brandishing a pistol. The bat lay at his feet, thrashing with its wings and claws.

Blood from its wounds formed a crimson puddle on the carpet. "Are you OK, Leslie?" he asked.

"Yes, thanks to Warren." Leslie swallowed hard and managed a weak smile. "Where's Shelly?"

"She ran upstairs." Gerry kept his eyes lowered, gun trained toward the bat. "I didn't know you were here."

"You and Dad seemed busy, and ..." Her eyes dropped to her father, who was still sitting at the desk, and the shoes scattered on the floor. She leaned against the wall, fighting waves of dizziness. "My God, Dad, did that bat hurt you?"

"That thing couldn't touch me," her father said, laughing raucously. "I threw my shoes at him."

"Dad would've killed him if I didn't." Gerry smiled a sardonic smile that coated Leslie's stomach with unease. The gleam in his eyes hinted that he'd scored a power play. Squatting by the bed, he poked the bat with the barrel. The creature lay still. "I've never seen anything like this."

"I did," Warren said. "At Leslie's hospital."

Leslie hobbled to her father's bed, giving the creature a wide berth. "Dr. Saunders said that these bats tried to break through the OR's window during my surgery. Thank God for Plexiglas."

"Why would ... never mind." Adjusting his wire-rimmed glasses, Gerry turned toward Warren. "Get some Plexiglas for that window. Better yet, replace all the windows with Plexiglas. Those bats seem hostile."

"Great idea," Shelly spoke up, emerging from the stairway. A smile worked its way to her parchment-pale face. "Nice save, Gerry."

"Thanks." Gerry patted her on the shoulder. "I'll take this critter to the police. Animal Control will want to check for rabies."

"Gerry, sit." Shelly waved her hand. "I'll talk to the police. You enjoy your visit with Dad."

Leslie stared at the splintered hole, listening to her ragged breathing. What if a bat broke into the house while she was asleep? She hugged the blue bedspread around her, hoping to ease her shivering.

After donning plastic gloves, Shelly wrapped the bat in newspapers, then laid it in a plastic trash bag. The bag dangled from her hand like a dirty diaper. "Save me some turkey," she called, hurrying to the door.

Warren eyed the glass fragments on the rug. "I'll board up that window."

****

During dinner, Leslie sat through a fiscal report on her father's medical expenses, a dossier on Gerry's latest case, and a psychoanalysis of Warren's boss. She listened to it all, while she filled up on turkey and mashed potatoes.

Every now and then, she glanced at her father. His loose cough and labored swallowing threatened imminent aspiration. Pain like a rusty nail quivered through her rib cage. She took an Oxycodone.

Afterwards, she proceeded to the den and curled up on the bed. According to Warren, Dad used that bed because he couldn't navigate the stairs anymore. Head nested in the pillow, she drifted to sleep.

Sometime later, she felt Gerry's hand shake her shoulder. "Do you want some dessert?" he asked.

"What's that?" Leslie sat up and rubbed her eyes.

"Pumpkin pie. Warren's making coffee. Decaffeinated coffee." A strained look crossed his chubby face. "You look exhausted."

"I'm all right," Leslie assured him. "Just a little tired. I'll pass on the coffee and have ginger ale."

"Stay put," Gerry said. "I'll get it for you."

Moments later, Gerry's harsh voice bellowed from the kitchen. "Warren, you slob!"

"Now what?" Leslie struggled to her feet.

In the kitchen, Gerry leaned against the open refrigerator door, pointing toward an open drawer. His fingers shook, his face reddened, and his hazel eyes burned like smoldering coals.

Warren stood at the table, hand gripping a knife half-buried in a pumpkin pie. His head jerked. "What's wrong?"

"Look at what I found." Reaching inside the drawer, Gerry lifted a plastic box of strawberries with his thumb and forefinger. The fruit inside had rotted to a deep shade of lavender. "Even dogs live better."

More samples followed. A loaf of moldy bread. A bowl of spinach crawling with fungus. Brownish-black bananas.

So much for Gerry's attempt at humanity, Leslie thought, wringing her hands. His glistening eyes and tightened lips warned that he was just getting started.

Warren kept his voice low, but his fists balled inside his pockets. "I thought that Shelly cleaned the refrigerator," he said.

"You think Shelly's your maid?" Gerry's voice reeked with contempt. "What kind of bastard are you, to make Dad eat and sleep in filth?"

Leslie rubbed her temples, feeling the throbbing roar in her head. "Gerry, I don't think now is ..."

"You're no better," Gerry cut in. "You're so worried about your amnesia; here's one for your missing pages. You never kept track of Dad's medicines. You left the kitchen a mess when you cooked. Dad got ptomaine poisoning from things you've served him."

"What things?" Leslie blurted. "I don't remember any of it."

"Then you'd better try because Dad's living in squalor." Gerry opened and closed the oven and cabinet doors. "Food crumbs on the floor. Crud in the sink and oven. No wonder you've got bugs."

Leslie staggered to the living room, hands clapped over her ears. She tried to drown out the sound of Gerry's shouting, the anger in his voice.

"We never discussed your accident," Gerry persisted, keeping at her heels. "You'd do anything for sympathy, wouldn't you?"

"What?" Leslie jerked against the wall.

"Dr. Saunders said that some trauma before the accident caused your memory loss." An icy glint crossed his eyes. "Know what I think? You faked amnesia to avoid responsibility for your actions."

"What actions?" Leslie's head ached terribly, bringing tears to her eyes.

"Stop badgering her!" Warren shouted, charging in with clenched fists. Gripping Gerry by the collar, Warren yanked him toward the kitchen. "Damn it all, you want to blow steam, get the fuck out of here."

"I can't deal with this." Rooting through the living room closet, Leslie reached for her coat. She crept outside through the back door to an alley that led into trees. To hell with the bats and recent murders. She made getting out of Gerry's face her first priority. Every few seconds, she glanced over her shoulder, but neither Warren nor Gerry followed.

After exiting the alley, she headed up an S-shaped trail, past gnarled oaks and bushes. Potholes dented the soil, causing her to lurch in a sidestroke motion. She braced herself against the tree trunks. The beads and sequins on her shirt glittered like gemstones in the moonlight. A cool breeze brushed against her cheeks.

She used to love camping in these woods, especially when things got too hot between her parents. Before Mom's emphysema, her father couldn't accept that sometimes things went wrong, and he made Mom his scapegoat. If Mom bought anything without his permission, he'd let loose a barrage of curses. Going out without leaving a note might merit a slap on the head.

Leslie shivered, rubbing her arms. More than once, Dad used his fists, but his verbal temper left Mom in tears. Like the time he announced to his friends that he'd married the stupidest woman in Pennsylvania. She'd never forget the cruelty in his voice or the wounded look in Mom's eyes.

A numb feeling worked its way up her right leg, but Leslie pressed on. She smiled at the trees that surrounded her like old friends. Tom and she used to have picnics here. They'd bring a basket of fried chicken and wine, and afterwards make love in the grass. But that all ended when ... what? Why did it end?

The full moon cast a silvery glow over the paths and tree tops. Hands braced against the trunks, Leslie limped further up the path, eyeing the branches and fallen logs. For a moment, she thought about the body in Betsy Ross's garage. Then a shadowy voice inside assured her that Dad's neighborhood was safe, and she stopped worrying.

Still, she needed a place to rest. Where could she lay? Certainly not on the grass because the dirt and bugs would infect her incision. She spotted a tree with hefty V-shaped branches, sturdy enough to support her weight. Maybe she could sleep there if the birds flying overhead didn't disturb her.

What about those bats, the ghostly voice whispered. *What if they attack you here? They could chew your incision. How about that, Leslie?*

Liquid fear ran through her soul. What was she doing in the woods, when a clean house waited to protect her? Why would she play Nature Girl with a busted skull and ribs? Maybe by now, Warren convinced Gerry to leave, unless Dad insisted that he stay. It was, after all, Dad's house.

"Alex should reason with Gerry," she said aloud. Leslie couldn't put her finger on it, but she noticed that something about Alex made others putty in his hands.

He'd persuaded Sarah to leave her alone. She'd sell tickets to watch Alex and Gerry go at it.

Several yards farther, she came to a clearing and spotted a house flanked by cement pillars. Wrought iron curlicues lined its roof. Its stained glass windows reminded her of a church. She didn't recall seeing this house. Another missing page. Did she and the owner know each other?

The numbness had now reached her thigh. Leslie hopped on her good leg, stumbling from tree to tree. Thorns from the bushes tore at her blouse, scattering its beads on the trail. She prayed that whoever lived in the house owned a phone so that she could call Warren.

The oak door stood ajar. After loping to the porch, Leslie sagged to her knees. "Hello," she called. "Anyone home?"

There was no answer.

Hands groping for a switch, Leslie snapped on a light. She crawled into a sitting room with a slate fireplace and velvet furniture. "Hello!" she called again. "May I use your phone?"

Silence.

Perhaps the owners went out and forgot to lock the door. Leslie scanned the room for a phone, but saw none. She crawled on plush, patterned rugs through a hallway that led to a kitchen, dining room, and what looked like a den. No phones. She'd have to wait for the owner, or for her leg to feel better so she could walk home herself. After climbing onto a sofa, she rested her head on a cushion and drifted to sleep.

Sometime later, a door creaked open, stirring Leslie awake. She sat up, rubbing her eyes.

A woman wearing an ivory, beaded dress strolled into the room. Her ice-blue eyes glittered between a map of freckles. With her fiery red curls and heart-shaped face, she could have passed as Leslie's sister. *My twin,* she thought crazily.

But the woman's skin had a waxy pallor. More to the point, her face wore the look of a person who enjoyed the pain of others.

The woman smiled, showing her teeth. Very white and sharp, especially the two at the top of each side. Her eyeteeth. What looked like tomato juice dribbled down her chin and specks of maroon peppered her lips.

"You," the woman said in a chilling voice, poking her finger at Leslie. "You're the one."

Screams came and died in Leslie's throat, only seconds before grayness closed in on her.

Chapter 9

His right arm curled around a leather sack filled with roses, Alex gazed at the unconscious soldier at his feet. The young man lay sprawled in an open field, surrounded by other dying Adrian and Lyonnesien soldiers. His navy tunic and pearl-handled dagger told Alex that he'd fought for Adria before the enemy's swords felled him. Soon, the vampire of war would claim them all, leaving behind widows and orphaned children. The soldier's right cheek dangled like a potato peel, revealing gleaming white bone. Jagged gashes oozed blood that congealed over his shirt tatters. His eyes were black marbles, their pupils engulfing the iris. Fixed and dilated.

Leslie had once said that "blown pupils," as she put it, meant approaching death. This soldier exuded a pungent stench. Past experience with victims had taught Alex that this odor meant imminent death. But the cloying scent from the young man's wounds beckoned to Alex, inviting him to feed. After glancing over his shoulder, Alex yanked the man's collar, exposing a pulsing vessel under his chalky skin, and he began to drink.

After he finished, Alex wiped his face with a handkerchief, rose to his feet, and gazed at the sky. The position of the stars told him that it was midnight in Adria. According to his crystal watch, it was 7 p.m., Philadelphia time. By now, he assumed, Leslie and her folks were finishing supper. He'd surprise her with his roses, the mixture of reds, pinks, and yellows crowded in his sack.

Hugging the bag against his chest, Alex trekked to his home in the outskirts of town. No taxi or chauffeur waited for him; people traveled by horse or foot on dirt and cobblestone streets. A fifteenth-century people, Adrians did not own electricity, running water, or other modern conveniences.

People on horses and in canvas-lined wagons passed Alex, not seeming to pay him any attention. He lived in a fieldstone two-story, a palace compared to the splintered, wooden shacks that his Adrian neighbors inhabited. His porch door opened to a living room filled with gold-embroidered furniture and oil paintings. Silver candelabra lined his flagstone fireplace and end tables.

Standing before the fireplace, Alex turned his dark overcoat inside out, checking for bloodstains. He doused himself with cologne and changed into a cotton shirt. He preferred cotton because it lasted and sold cheaply. He wanted to look his best before traveling to Leslie's world.

After he finished dressing, Alex squeezed his eyes shut and conjured the image of an oak door. Oak reminded him of happier times, when he'd lived on his parents' farm and courted Elizabeth. He tuned out extraneous noises ... horses hauling wagons, the wind blowing through the trees.

Moments later, he opened his eyes. He faced a wooden door, standing between his sofa and tub chairs. The door swung inward, leaving smoky outlines for a doorway. Still concentrating, Alex glided through this doorway to Leslie's world, right there in his living room.

Only immortals crossed time dimensions. With practice, they could guide humans and animals across the border. He considered choosing another location besides his house to exit Adria, but there was no telling where he'd find himself after making the crossover.

Alex emerged into his Philadelphia living room, with a sofa with gold embroidery portraits. Only now, ceramic lamps replaced his candles, perched next to his television and phone. Outside, he heard the squealing of tires instead of hoof beats.

He checked the roses. Sometimes plants wilted during a crossover; this time, they remained intact. Now, he'd summon Willard, a servant and former soldier. Lyonnesien swords had mauled Willard's legs, rending him incapable of fighting. Since the attack, Willard jumped at sudden moves and loud noises. Moved to pity by Willard's condition, Alex hired him and brought him to Philadelphia. Willard's duties included chauffeuring, housekeeping, and anything that Alex couldn't or wouldn't do himself. "Willard," he called, pacing from room to room.

A young man wearing dungarees and a plaid shirt lay sprawled in the den's leather recliner, eyes shut, mouth open, hand dangling over the side.

"Willard." Alex stood before the chair. "Get up."

Willard's sky-blue eyes flew open like window shades. With a deep yawn, he stood up and stretched his wiry arms. "What's up?"

"I want to visit Leslie," Alex said. "She's staying with her father. Her pain medicine makes her sleepy, so I want to get there before she retires for the night." He handed Willard a scrap of paper. "Her father's address."

"Sure." After running a comb through his blonde hair, Willard donned a sweater and limped to the door. Alex followed him to the garage. He opened the car door for Alex, and then scooted behind the wheel. The engine flared into a startled roar, and Willard pealed onto Mill Road, a crumbling path of a street.

Leaning back in his seat, Alex rolled down the window and inhaled deeply. A gentle breeze brushed his cheek, bringing with it the scent of grass and flowers.

Moments later, Willard took the Schuylkill Expressway toward the Roosevelt Boulevard. The boulevard stretched to the outskirts of Northeast Philadelphia. He doglegged onto Johnstown Avenue, a side street winding through woods.

The wind changed directions, chasing the floral aroma, and replacing it with a fetid stench. The woods, only miles from Leslie's father's house, reeked of animals long dead and decayed. Alex sniffed deeply and stared out the window like a soldier watching for the approach of the enemy.

"Willard, pull over."

They came to a screeching halt. Willard spun his head, blue eyes darting. "What's the matter?"

"I'm not sure." Alex scrambled from the car. "Wait for me."

Alex proceeded down the trail, listening hard, and followed a scent. The smell was worst around the trees opposite the lake. His shoes slid against the ground, greased by wet leaves.

Someone with a head injury could get themselves killed, he thought. Like Leslie. Despite intense physical therapy, she walked with a pronounced limp. Maybe she'd never make a full recovery.

Alex rounded the lake's curve, went off the path, and squeezed through the crooked trees. The stench became sickeningly strong, reminding him of blood that had gone bad weeks ago.

Two sneaker-clad feet poked behind a bush. Tearing aside the branches, Alex unearthed a man dressed in bloodstained sweats. Blood clotted over the gashes below his chin.

"Human killers," he whispered, clenching his fists. He read about the murders and heard about the brutal attack on Fred Mayes, Leslie's coworker. "Bloody hypocrites, calling my people monsters."

On closer inspection, he saw that the wounds had jagged edges, like the kind made by sharp teeth. Fang marks. After rolling the man sideways, Alex lifted his shirt. He expected to see mottled skin on the back, caused by pooling of blood. Instead, the moonlight illuminated smooth, parchment skin, a sign that someone had drained the man's blood. Alex let out a ghostly sigh.

Too close to Leslie for comfort. Many vampires chose victims who couldn't run or defend themselves. Like Leslie. Worse, Leslie never acknowledged the existence of vampires, except the emotional kind that worked at Betsy Ross. Even when she saw Fred's wounds. She swore that some nutcase slashed Fred's throat. Once, Alex tried to discuss *Undeath* with Leslie, but his explanation went over her head the way the hospital's medical procedures did when she tried to learn them. She'd never believe that Adria existed, or that the bats migrated to Philadelphia from another time dimension.

Closing his eyes, Alex conjured Leslie's face. He imagined Leslie laughing with her family over dessert and coffee. Instead, his mind's eye conveyed her weeping and clutching her head. She limped through a crooked path, stumbling over fallen logs, lurching against gnarled oaks. He couldn't pinpoint her direction, though, because he'd never traveled through these woods.

Probing further into her head, he saw an image of a man dressed in a three-piece suit, clenching his fists. There was shouting, but the words came out garbled. "Even dogs live better! Left the kitchen a mess ... we never discussed your accident."

"What about the accident?" Alex wrinkled his brows. Judging from the harsh voice, he deduced that turbulence of some sort had hit the Taite home, sending Leslie to the woods in tears.

****

The image of Leslie's tearful face bumped Alex out of the present and back to the weeks before her accident. After gentle persuasion, he convinced Leslie to join him at Neptune's Orchard for drinks. On their first date, she arrived at the club wearing beaded lace and satin; face layered with rouge, and ordered "virgin" drinks. "I never drink when I'm working the next day," he remembered her saying. She smiled, but her voice exuded unspoken fear.

At the hospital, she smiled and made jokes, but he kept hearing undercurrents of tension in her voice. When Leslie thought no one was looking, she'd sit hunched in a chair, biting her nails. Her eyes, sapphire pools of unshed tears, said that something destroyed her confidence.

It wasn't until the week before Leslie's accident that Alex learned of her nightmares, and the reality that had created them.

That night, Alex had agreed to meet Bill at his office to discuss portfolio changes. Instead, he found Bill's door locked. A note taped near the doorknob said, "Alex, ICU needed me. Be right back."

Alex shrugged. He knew that emergencies happened in Bill's line of work, and so he walked to the chairs by the elevators to wait. Moments later, an elevator's door slid open; Leslie bolted to the hall, gasping for breath. Her freckled face shone with sweat, her hands shook, and her eyes brightened with tears.

"Bill," she said, gazing at Alex, but not seeing him, "those ventilator changes you ordered on Roberts ... she coded, and Sarah filed an incident report. She said ..."

"Whoa, there, Leslie," Alex said, getting up. "You've got the wrong guy. Bill isn't here."

"Where did he go?" Leslie shouted, banging on Saunders's door. Her voice cracked. "I've got to talk with him."

"He went to the ICU." Alex pointed to the note. "Did you try paging him?"

"Yes." Leslie slumped against the door. "He didn't answer."

Alex gazed at her attentively. Instead of the plastic smile and made-up face, he saw a terrified young woman. "I think he's tied up with a very sick patient," he said. "What's the matter?"

"Everything!" Leslie snapped, meeting his gaze. Her voice softened. "I'm sorry, Alex. You don't want to hear my troubles."

Alex leaned against the chair, licking his lips. "Why not?" he asked. "You look like you could use a friend."

"I barely made C's in college, and without tutoring, I can't ..." Her voice broke, and she burst into choking sobs.

Alex folded Leslie into his arms, rubbing her shoulders. He walked her to the chairs. Easing her to a seat, he laid her head against his chest. Her cries smoked with pain, and, he feared, self-loathing. After her weeping subsided, he handed her a box of tissues.

"Thanks for letting me cry," Leslie murmured, blowing her nose and wiping her eyes.

"Something here frightens you," Alex said. "I've noticed that. But Bill speaks well of you. Maybe he can help you find another job."

Leslie gave him a vacant stare, the kind that reminded him of a soldier with battle fatigue. "No one's hiring. I need tutoring to catch on, and no one here wants to provide it. Besides, I can't think when people yell at me." She sniffled. "People who learn quickly can't understand, but that's the way it is."

"You seem reasonably intelligent," Alex said, reaching for her hand. "You wouldn't have gotten the job otherwise. Right?"

"It's complicated. I have to do a procedure fifty times to become proficient; management and staff expect you to learn it after five tries. I made a mistake; I have to pay for it."

"Bill told me that you've got heart." Alex draped his arm across her shoulder. "You chose your career wisely, but you made your mistake practicing it at Betsy Ross."

"Tell me about it." Leslie sniffled again and blew her nose. "Someone's always getting stabbed near this damned hospital. Every afternoon, I go to work wondering if I'll make it home alive."

"No one blames you. You shouldn't walk to your car alone."

"Fred walks me to my car. We've stuck together ever since his go-round with that madman."

"At least you've got one ally." Alex glanced at his watch. "I don't think we'll see Bill tonight. Want me to drive you home?"

"I guess ... I suppose I could leave my car here and take the train to work tomorrow. But first, I have to give shift report."

"I'll wait."

Alex followed Leslie several floors down to a conference room filled with people in white lab coats. Staff respiratory therapists. He stood outside the door, watching and listening while two therapists—a blonde woman and a bearded man—bombarded Leslie with accusations. Leslie swallowed hard, as if a fishbone caught in her throat. Her lips moved, but no words came. The haunted look in her eyes would stay with Alex forever.

After her report, Leslie shuffled down the hall, head lowered, eyes tear-streaked. Despite her thick overcoat, her body trembled like someone with severe palsy.

"I'm sorry you heard that," she said after they got onto the elevator.

"I'm sorry you went through it," Alex said. "You're shaking." He draped his arm around her and pulled her close. They headed to the lobby, and then outside to his car. "Let me take away those chills."

Leslie's head jerked. Her eyebrows arched.

"I'm talking about Neptune's Orchard," he said quickly. "Dancing. I'd never do anything you didn't want."

They rode down Cherry Street in silence. Leslie's trembling subsided. Willard drove on, eyes focused on the road, never asking a question. Alex paid him well for his silence.

"Have you seen a healer ... doctor ... about your problem?" Alex asked after a pause.

"My psychiatrist, Dr. Wolf, recommended tutoring and friendly surroundings." Leslie leaned against his shoulder, hugging her coat around her. "Crawford and whoever's stabbing those people won't allow me any peace.

If Bill didn't take my part, Crawford would've canned me long ago." She shook her head. "How can I expect you to understand something that doesn't make sense to me?"

"I know more than you think." Alex turned Leslie toward him. "Look at me, Leslie."

Leslie met his gaze. Her blue eyes became blank. Alex drew in an airless breath, savoring her sweet scent. He kissed her on the mouth, tentatively at first, then ardently. His tongue glided down her chin to her throat. She moaned as his teeth punctured her skin. Listening to her heartbeat in his ears, he licked and swallowed.

When he pulled away, Leslie stared at him in shocked silence. Her eyes, bulging like soup plates, still wore their distant look. She dabbed her throat with a tissue, then gazed at the blood dripping from her cuts.

"Why did you do that?" she asked timidly.

"Because you're a beautiful woman." Alex stroked her thick curls. "You remind me of someone I loved a long time ago."

"I never expected this." Tears trickled down her cheeks. "What if you'd nicked an artery? You could've killed me."

"I'd change you into something else before letting you die." He wiped her cuts with the tissue. The bleeding stopped. "Small exchanges of blood won't hurt you."

"Have you gone mad?" Leslie's lips quivered as she struggled to get out the words. "You can't ... you aren't supposed to drink human blood. It's not normal. You could catch a disease." She tried hard to find her therapist's voice, and failed. Alex kept his eyes locked with Leslie's.

"People like me don't catch diseases. One day, you won't, either." Alex unbuttoned his shirt, exposing his ivory chest. Flicking open a penknife, he made an incision above his left nipple. "It's your turn."

"To do what?" Leslie questioned between sobs.

Staring into her eyes, Alex saw desire mixed with fear. "Drink," he whispered. "Just a taste. It won't hurt."

"No." Leslie's head wobbled back and forth. "I don't want to." She stiffened against his arms, breath coming out in ragged gasps.

Alex brushed away the wisps of hair that had fallen into her eyes. He longed to make love to her. He longed to wake up in her arms. He longed to feel her soft, silky body against his. "I care about you, Leslie. Do you believe that?"

"I believe you do, but this … this is wrong."

"I know your society considers blood drinking taboo, but we're not monsters or sexual deviants. We're just sharing our own communion." Arms caressing her head and shoulders, Alex pulled her close.

"No," Leslie murmured, but she placed her lips over his incision and drank. She drank and gagged on the bitter taste of his *undeath*. Yet, she smiled when he eased her against the cushions.

"What are you?" she gasped.

"Whatever you need me to be." Alex wiped the blood from her lips. "We're tied, now. You don't have to endure Betsy Ross alone. If anyone tries to hurt you, just think my name. I'll come."

"OK," Leslie said in a monotone.

"I want you to sleep. When you wake, you'll recall scraping yourself on some rose bushes, and that I treated your cuts and drove you home. You won't consciously remember our exchange, but your subconscious will urge you to call me whenever you're in trouble."

"OK." Leslie nestled into his arms. She closed her eyes, and moments later, she fell into a deep sleep.

****

And so his rescue the night of her accident had been no coincidence. Leslie had summoned him, without realizing she was doing so. She called out to him again tonight, and Alex felt compelled to answer.

Twilight Healer

He pushed his way past the gnarled trees, sniffing, trying to catch her scent. Moments later, he heard Leslie's shrieks—heard them with his mind. A mental picture formed: Leslie crawling through a flagstone house. Leslie slumped on the floor, writhing in pain.

Looking down, he noticed footprints. Something glittered on the ground, nested between the grass and leaves. A green sequin shining like a gemstone in the moonlight. Another sequin, this one red. He followed the trail of sequins and footprints to a flagstone house surrounded by cement pillars.

A foul odor drifted from an open window. The door stood ajar, leading to a gloomy hall. Inside, the smell became nauseating: a mixture of sweat, stale blood, and rotting tomatoes. After tiptoeing through the hall, Alex made out velvet furniture and a slate fireplace. A peacock-blue jacket lay across the couch. It was Leslie's coat. Warren had brought it to Leslie the night before she left the hospital.

"Leslie?" he called. "Are you here?"

Silence.

Looking down, he spotted Leslie's sneakers. They sat beside the couch. Ribbons of blood trailed along the velvet rug to the hallway to his right, ending abruptly at the kitchen door.

Chapter 10

Leslie floated through a gray mist. The whisper of the woman's footsteps faded; everything went silent. The numbness and pain didn't seem so awful. Nothing seemed bad except the pointed teeth and hungry look in the woman's eyes, until what felt like a hammer rammed her on the left side of her chin.

From far away, she heard the woman's laughter, then slurping sounds. The breeze on her face,

(OH! OWWW! How it hurts, it HURTS, my jaw what did you do?)

and her eyes snapped open. Blood was dribbling from her nose, pooling on her neck and the sofa cushions. Her jaw seemed to burn in rivers of fire. Only dimly aware that she was sobbing, Leslie gazed at the woman in the white dress. She saw the fangs, still nested in the woman's hideous smile, and the gray dots spiraled up before her eyes again. The woman sat on the sofa facing Leslie.

(My jaw, she busted my jaw!)

She was licking maroon stains from her right fist. Leslie refused to give in to the grayness. Instead, she pushed herself up on one elbow ... oh, how it hurt, it was like being stabbed with knives—and faced her attacker.

"Oh, my God," she heard herself murmur.

The woman's voice, laced with what sounded like a thick European accent, wafted through the cloud of pain. "I wouldn't run if I were you," she said, smiling.

And if you try, her smile said, *I'll pulverize you.* It gave the message loud and clear without any accent.

Leslie looked up at the overhead chandelier. Spiked crystals like fangs hung from its brass plate. "I'm sorry," she blurted between swift, harsh breaths. "I didn't know anyone lived here."

The woman sidled forward; pressing her leg against Leslie's hip, chilling like a cold beef slab. "You're the sorriest woman I ever met," she said amiably.

Too much. The gray dots again, the woman's voice fading into an eerie tunnel. Leslie waited for the sensation to pass, then continued. Her rattling teeth drowned out the sound of her whimpering. "I got sick ... dizzy. Your door was open, and I thought I'd rest."

"That doesn't surprise me." The woman smiled again. "We know each other well, Leslie. Quite well."

God, she knows my name. Another hostile stranger like those bitches at Betsy Ross. Only this one uses her fists. Looking at the woman, Leslie sensed emptiness, a black hole. Her host's vacant stare hinted that she'd become unhinged from the familiar landmarks of her life. Her pupils were dilated black marbles. Leslie recognized that look. It was the look of someone high on drugs. It was--

Don't look at her eyes, a voice inside screamed. Leslie flipped her head sideways. She paid for the movement with a thousand kilowatts of agony. "I don't remember meeting you."

"I'm Drusilla Mason. You give sick people breathing herbs, right?"

Leslie gulped, choking on the coppery taste of blood. The pain was now radiating to her head. "I'm a respiratory therapist," she said. "I banged my head in a car accident, and the last two years became blank. Did we work together?"

"In a way," Drusilla said. "Your lost years became mine."

"I don't understand." Grabbing a tissue from her pants pocket, Leslie blotted her nose. The tissue came away soaked with blood.

"Don't be coy, Leslie," Drusilla said in a steady voice. "You threw yourself at my husband."

"You've got the wrong person. I never chase after married men. You can take that one to the bank."

"His name's Kenworthy." Drusilla licked her lips, clearing the blood off her chin. "Somehow, you got his attention. He married me because I look like you."

Leslie swallowed again, tasting more blood. The grayness dissipated, leaving behind terrible throbbing in her jaw. "I don't remember anyone named Kenworthy either," she said, struggling to a sitting position. "I'm talking amnesia here."

"I don't know about amnesia, but you look awfully nervous," Drusilla said in a sugary voice. She got up and paced around the room, keeping her eyes on Leslie.

Damn straight I am, Leslie's mind screamed, *because you busted my jaw. You've gotten into bad dope, Drusilla, something that made you crack, and there's no telling where the pieces will fall.* "I didn't mean to intrude," she said, fighting the tremors in her voice. "Please don't ..."

"Don't hurt you? You have no concept of real suffering," Drusilla sneered softly. "Frankly, Leslie, I think you lack manners. Here you lie, bleeding on my couch, and staring at me as though I were garbage, the way my masters used to look at me. I find that very offensive."

ALEX! ALEX WALLACH! WHERE ARE YOU? Leslie looked down at the blood that was now soaking the cushions. Her blood, which was still dripping from her nose. *You rescued me from the bitches at Betsy Ross, why not this monster? Why not Drusilla before she kills me?* She got no answer, of course, but images rushed through her head, memories of her and Alex. Alex comforting her near Saunders's office. Alex swabbing alcohol on her cuts. She'd scratched her throat on some rose bushes before her accident, but she still felt the scabs. Then a voice floated from her subconscious.

How did you really get those scratches, Leslie?

Not scratches, but love bites ... the sound of drinking. *"We're tied,"* she remembered Alex saying. *"If anyone tries to hurt you, just think my name."*

But that didn't sound right. People did not drink blood or communicate by thought. Alex wanted her to telephone him. "I wish I could fix whatever you think I've done," she said, reaching for her sneakers and coat. "But I can't. I'd like to go, but I need help getting home. May I use your phone?"

Drusilla swept the room with eyes that burned like smoldering coals. "I don't have a phone," she said coldly. "Find your own way home."

In the next instant, Drusilla's foot, clad in a shoe with a spiked heel, lashed out, torpedoing Leslie's left hip. Ungodly pain like ground glass shattered through Leslie's side. The room spun around her, and she felt herself fall in slow motion. She got a look at the bloodstains on the velvet rug; a glimpse of the light playing on the gold-lined patterns embroidering the velvet. The lines merged, forming skull faces. The gut-wrenching screams she heard came from her throat.

"I used to beg for mercy when my masters chased me with their whips. They never listened. You look just like them with your shiny clothes and painted face." Drusilla's cherry-red lips curled into a sunken and rather horrible grin. "Where you're going, you won't need shoes or a coat. Get up."

Leslie wanted to—badly needed to get up and run. But the shattered fragments in her pelvis ground against each other, flashing sharp, hot, terrible agony. Sprawled on her side, she looked up at Drusilla, who now stood over her. "I can't," she cried, her voice sobbing. "You've broken my hip."

Folding her arms across her chest, Drusilla gave Leslie a piercing gaze. "Perhaps you'd like to wait for Kenworthy. Big mistake. He won't find you so desirable after I finish with you."

Leslie tasted hot salty tears mixed with the blood. She thought about Warren, her dad, and Shelly, and how they'd welcomed her home with a family dinner. *The Last Supper,* she thought crazily. What made her run into those trees?

"You want to kill me?" she sobbed. "Go ahead."

"Now, why would I do that?" Drusilla twirled her red curls with a manicured finger. "The fun's only beginning."

"If Kenworthy cares for me, like you say, he'll be furious."

"Kenworthy will never know. I can get away with anything because I'm an immortal. Know what that means?"

Leslie huddled on the floor, shivering, though beads of sweat formed on her skin. Signs of incipient shock. The pain came and went in waves. Nothing Drusilla said made sense, but she'd rather talk than get beaten. "It means that you're a ghost."

Drusilla resumed her pacing, still watching Leslie. "Kenworthy and I are vampires. Plain and simple."

"Damn!" Leslie clawed at her neck, where she felt intense itching. Had Drusilla–

"Relax. If I bit you, you wouldn't live to remember it."

Leslie lifted her gaze to Drusilla's face. The black hole loomed large, threatening to swallow her. "Certain diseases cause craving for blood, but vampires don't exist."

Oh, yeah? The voice inside yammered. *Drusilla's teeth look very real. And, while we're at it, how did you really get those neck scabs?*

"Where I live, blood drinking is a way of life," Drusilla said. "I grew up in Adria, a very old country belonging to the gods. You cross dimensions of time to get there. Humans can't make the trip unless escorted by immortals."

96

Leslie rubbed her arms, trying to ease the goose bumps. Her surroundings took on a nightmarish quality, but the pain made everything real. Reaching into her pocket, she pulled out her rosary, a present given by the hospital chaplain.

Drusilla's fist reared out and snatched the rosary. "Idiot!" Her voice seethed with contempt. "Religious symbols don't hurt me."

"I guess not." Leslie squeezed her eyes shut, praying for rescue or death. She opened her eyes again and turned her head. Stabs of pain muttered through her cracked jaw. "You say that my memories became yours. What did you mean?"

"My mind absorbed your memories ... birthdays, holidays, work days, as if I'd lived them. I remember your father's stroke and the way he hassled his healers, even though I never met him."

"Was I a good therapist ... healer?"

Stepping back, Drusilla howled with laughter. Moments passed, and then she composed herself. "I'll tell you what you want to know after we go for a walk."

Grabbing Leslie by the armpits, Drusilla hauled her to her feet. Jolts of pain flared through her battered hip. Her right leg buckled. She bawled, fresh hot tears rolling down her cheeks.

"What? You want more?" Drusilla yanked Leslie again, bony hands wrapped around her left arm. Sharp burning followed, accompanied by the sound of Leslie's arm tearing from its socket the way a drumstick tears from a turkey. "Want me to break your neck? I could do that very easily, you know."

"I can't take any more," Leslie screamed. "Go ahead and kill me."

"In due time." Drusilla hoisted Leslie in her arms like a sack of potatoes. "You lived a soft life, hiring machines to do your work. I saw them in my visions before Kenworthy made me a vampire."

"What kind of visions?"

"I saw you walk into a sick room with a zombie-look on your face. You pushed some buttons on the machine, the one that killed the person you were paid to cure. A man wearing fancy clothes said that your carelessness cost lives." Drusilla shook her head. "I felt sorry for you until I saw the lust in Ken's eyes."

"I did all that?" Leslie dangled in Drusilla's arms, longing for the grayness to return and dull the pain. "Did you see me show anyone kindness?"

"You invented enough lines to fool Adria's governor," said Drusilla. "I saw it all, right up to the time your horseless carriage hit the tree. Tell me, Leslie, have you seen any bats? Big white things with red eyes and teeth?"

Leslie nodded, shivering. "My doctors saw them, too."

"Hades made those bats spy on people like me and Kenworthy." Drusilla's voice sounded tinny and distant. "Those bats transferred memories between us."

"How?" Leslie asked in a faint voice.

"Their powers enable them to transfer memories between dimensional twins like you and myself. Everyone in your world has a twin in Adria."

Leslie shook her head. "I don't get what you're ..."

"Be quiet," Drusilla said sharply. "I must concentrate."

Leslie's mouth snapped shut. She watched Drusilla close her eyes. As she watched, a thick limestone door overhung with skeletal branches appeared before them. The door creaked open. When Drusilla opened her eyes again, she headed through this doorway to the front door of the house. Stepping outside, she followed a narrow path that wound through shrubbery. Moments later, she paused by a lake.

"Take a good look," she said.

Leslie craned her neck. The moon splashed silvery puddles on the water and scattered leaves. A damp wind seeped through her bloodstained clothes, chilling her to the bone. She heard rustling noises behind them, perhaps the snapping of twigs. "Someone's following us," she said.

Drusilla cast furtive glances over her shoulder. "You're only hearing things." She smiled, but her voice sounded edgy.

That was when a woman's screams cut through the trees, blood chilling cries sounding almost inhuman. Drusilla let out a skeletal laugh. "Hades's bats must be enjoying their meal. A school of those bats can pick a body clean."

"I believe it." Leslie stared ahead, quivering.

The screams issued from a cave nested in the shadows. Its entrance, shaped like an inverted V, was surrounded by clusters of rocks. The structure reminded her of the boulders she'd seen in the mountains as a little girl, when she traveled with her family. "A bat almost ... never mind."

"Almost broke into your father's house?" Drusilla laughed again. "I can read your thoughts. Lucky for you and Papa, your brother carried a gun. Want to see what made that girl scream?"

"No, but I'm sure you can't wait to show me."

Drusilla nudged her, and now Leslie's shoulder burned like white iron. The agony went through her body. Shattered bone chips grated her hip and jaw. Sweat trickled down her face in spite of the chilling wind slapping her cheek.

"Our officials chain criminals someplace where the birds and people like me can get to them." Drusilla ambled toward the cave's rocky opening. "That girl you heard was caught dipping into the butcher's money box. Stealing is a capital offense."

The bone fragments shifted in Leslie's hip. She bit back a scream. "Where I live, murder is a capital crime."

"If I spare you, you'll sing to your officials and complicate things for me." Drusilla smiled again, a crooked, malignant grin. "Besides, I'll enjoy watching the bats tear your flesh."

"Drusilla." Leslie turned toward her. Grayness was setting in until dirt got into her nostrils. She sneezed heartily, jarring her broken bones. The ten-thousand kilowatts of agony that followed jolted her back to reality. She tried telling herself that death offered reunion with her mother, but she kept thinking about her father. Who would cook his soft meals? Certainly not Warren. He hated cooking.

After spitting more blood, she gasped for breath. "I'll die before your bats find me. Please leave me alone so I can make my peace with God."

"Better make your peace with Hades. He'll damn your soul to Tartarus. Listen and you'll hear the condemned beg for his mercy."

Listening hard, Leslie made out a cacophony of cries sounding like people caught in a burning building.

Stooping low, Drusilla stepped inside the cave. Her feet made horrible crunching noises. The stench of carrion caused Leslie's stomach to churn. Bile rose in her throat, and she swallowed hard to keep from vomiting.

To her right, a young woman lay tethered to a rock, writhing against her ties. Her screams had faded, replaced by barely audible whimpers. Dirt and mud coated her face, skeletal limbs, and torn clothes. Something gleamed in the moonlight, only a few feet from the beaten woman. A human skeleton, fully gutted, lay propped against the rocky wall, suspended by chains around its wrists and ankles. Even in the darkness, Leslie saw tufts of pink flesh and gristle clinging to its ribs. Flies formed dark clouds over the body. She opened her mouth to scream, but her cracked, roughened voice afforded only faint, crowing noises.

Bending over, Drusilla laid Leslie on the ground next to the skeleton. "The sun will come up soon," she said, glancing toward the archway, "so I can't watch the fun. But I'll check on you tomorrow night." With a peal of laughter, she slithered into the shadows.

Leslie kept her head flat, eyes turned away from the skeleton. Razor blades of pain shot through her hip and shoulder if she so much as wriggled. Her left arm dangled like a battered ornament. Even if she could run, where could she go? Miles of forest surrounded the cave.

"Damn you, Gerry," she muttered, listening to her wheezing breath. "You said I caused Mom's death. Think I've had enough punishment?"

"Leslie," called a distant voice. It sounded like Alex. "Where are you?"

Leslie's eyes blinked, and her shoulders sagged. She couldn't have heard any voice. It was her desperation talking.

"Leslie!" Louder this time. Then Alex ran into the cave, still screaming her name over and over. Leslie was aware that his eyes glimmered like emeralds above his powder-white cheeks. She thought he looked like an angel.

"Alex!" Fresh tears pooled in her eyes. Her voice was barely audible over her wheezing breath. "Alex, I'm not going to make it."

"Leslie, why did you run to the woods?" His voice came out in choked sobs. "Were you contemplating suicide?"

"Gerry and I had a horrible fight." Leslie wiped her eyes with her good hand. Alex's face swam in and out of focus. "I thought ..."

"Never mind." Alex caressed her face, brushing back her curls. "I found you in time."

Leslie shook her head. "Not this time. Will you tell my father that I love him and that I forgive him about Mom? Please?"

"You can tell him yourself after I've brought you home."

Leslie stared at Alex's face, the tears in his eyes, his anguished voice, and then she understood. He wanted to save her badly, but he didn't have access to a car or medical supplies.

"Alex, listen carefully," she mustered between hoarse coughs. "This girl, Drusilla, who looks like me ... she beat me up. I think she's the one the police want. She said she loves to kill, and she accused me of chasing her husband, Kenworthy something or other. She ranted on about vampires and second dimensions. Do something to stop her from hurting others."

Alex knelt by her side and draped his cloak over her shivering limbs. "Drusilla ... or whatever she calls herself ... sounds dangerous, but she has it right about the world existing in two dimensions. You never saw a cave like this near your father's house. Doesn't that seem strange?"

Leslie nodded, shuddering. "But vampires and second dimensions don't exist. She's gotten into drugs, that's what."

Alex blotted Leslie's face with a hanky. "I think you know differently."

"I guess I do," Leslie managed between clicking teeth. "But I don't want to believe it because Drusilla said that only vampires can travel between dimensions without help. You came here to find me, so that makes you ..."

"One of them." Alex lowered his eyes. "I tried to tell you, but you weren't ready to hear me."

"I remember you comforting me in the hall near Bill's office. You took me for a ride, and then you ..." Leslie blinked her eyes and shook her head. "It doesn't matter now."

Cradling her shoulders, Alex looked her in the eyes. "Yes, it does, Leslie. Your injuries are grave, and Adria doesn't have sophisticated medical equipment. Even if I get you to a hospital in time, this woman won't rest until she kills you." His voice softened, and tears fell down his cheek. "Immortality offers your only chance for survival, and I can give you that."

"Immortality?" Leslie fixed her gaze on Alex and noticed his teeth for the first time. Two of them, pointed, just like Drusilla's. But his voice whispered kindness and sadness. "You act more human than many people I know. Maybe vampires come in different breeds."

"No, it's the same breed. But we have free will." Alex hiked his shirt sleeve. "People might say that if I really cared, I'd let you die a natural death. Maybe they're right. If you join me, you'll live by twilight forever."

Leslie met Alex's gaze. Her thoughts about Drusilla and the pain faded. Instead, she saw a man who was trying to save her life. "I'd rather Dad saw me by twilight than not at all. Another death in the family would kill him. Will this change affect my quality of life?"

"Not at all. The keen senses you'll develop may even improve it." Alex tilted her face toward his. "Will you join me?"

"I want ..." Leslie's mind went blank. She felt the wind again, a high, roaring wind inside her own head. "Yes, I'll join you. Will I have to do anything complicated?"

"No. We'll have to exchange blood, a lot of it to make you immortal. Once your heartbeat stops, your body will change."

Using his teeth, he sliced his right forearm, and then held the wounded area to her lips. Leslie gagged on its bitter smell.

"Drink." He stroked her cheek. "Think of this as medicine."

"Medicine." Leslie parted her lips. She licked and swallowed, trying hard to ignore the acid taste. Only faintly aware of the pinpricks in her skin, she focused on his eyes. Their emerald glow washed through her consciousness, filling her with serenity. Moments later, all time and space slipped away, and the darkness waded in.

Chapter 11

Ear pressed against Leslie's chest, Alex listened to her fluttering heartbeat. Moments later, her head slumped. Her face became ashen. Her eyes rolled backward, and her heartbeat flickered to a stop.

Having watched past transformations, Alex expected Leslie to rise in two to four days. Already, her head incision fused into smooth skin, and the bruises on her face started to fade. When she woke, her dragon would demand nourishment.

Muffled sobs impinged on his thoughts. Shifting his gaze, Alex sighted a woman in the shadows, curled like a salamander, wrists and ankles chained to a rock. A mental picture flashed before him—the woman filching money from a storekeeper's cash box. The prisoner didn't look older than twenty-five. Her coarse, agonized breaths spoke of intense pain and forthcoming death.

"Human monsters," he muttered, brushing his fingers across her tearful cheeks. People said what they wanted about vampires, but at least *Undeath* gave him a ticket to the New World, where poverty didn't warrant execution.

Two bats flying through the cave landed beside Leslie.

"Scat!" Alex hollered, waving his hands at them. The bats fluttered toward Leslie, sniffed her face, then soared into the night. Reaching into his cloak, he pulled out a wineskin from his inner pocket. He knelt by the chained woman.

Distrust slid over her glazed eyes. She cried pitiably for help when Alex slit her wrist. He sighed, tears spilling down his cheeks while her blood drained down the spout. After he finished, she lapsed into unconsciousness.

Soon, the bats would eat her alive. Alex caressed her forehead, turning her face toward his. "Sleep," he murmured in their native tongue. "Become impervious to pain."

Looking up, he saw the rosy fingers of dawn streaking the sky. Without shelter, the sun would roast him and Leslie to cinders. He longed to find the woman shelter from the bats, but Leslie came first. That meant transporting her back to Leslie's world before sunrise. Right there at the cave.

After gathering Leslie into his arms, Alex conjured his wooden door, then made his crossover. He found himself in the woods near Johnstown Avenue. After heading up the trail and rounding a curve, he saw his car parked behind a rose bush.

The car door opened; Willard's pale face poked through the crack. His widening eyes spelled awe close to horror. "Son of Hades!" he cried, lips trembling. "What happened?"

"Kenworthy brought another vampire, Drusilla, to the New World." Alex stepped back while Willard opened the rear door. Hugging Leslie against his chest, he plopped into the seat. Swirls of her fiery red hair draped over his right arm. "Drusilla attacked Leslie, then left her in a cave to die."

"Why?" Hands making nervous, eager gestures, Willard leaned against the fender and looked down at Alex. His facial scars creased like snakes in his wan skin. "Is Leslie ...?"

"Leslie will become like me." Alex caressed her swollen cheek. "It was the only way I could save her."

Willard's thoughts drilled through Alex's brain. He listened to Willard's clicking teeth and shivering.

"Obviously, you don't approve." Alex's green eyes, shiny and resolute, met Willard's. "Leslie hasn't reached thirty, but she has seen more grief than most people do in a lifetime. She's had to look after her sick father. Emotional vampires terrorized her at work. She almost died in a car wreck. Instead of offering support, her family blamed her for the accident. She had enough, Willard, so she ran away from home. Drusilla attacked her in the woods."

Alex glanced at his watch. Crossing over to Philadelphia bought him another five hours of darkness. "Know what I think? Leslie wanted to die. She almost got her wish. You still have a problem with what I've done?"

"Leslie might not like it," Willard said.

"You think so?" Alex looked Willard directly in the eye. "What about those people who died by exsanguination? Leslie almost became the next victim. Besides, she chose to join me."

"Oh," Willard said in a small voice. He began to fidget, shuffling one foot against the dirt, then the other.

"Get in and drive," Alex ordered. "I'll look after Leslie. She'll sleep with me in my chamber."

"OK," Willard said in a flat, resigned voice. He flopped behind the steering wheel. "You need me to do anything?"

"I'm going back to Adria to find out more about Kenworthy, but my trip will have to wait until sunset." Alex traced his finger along Leslie's jaw. The swelling had receded. "Watch Leslie, Willard. Guard her with your life."

Willard nodded, keeping his eyes focused on the road.

"I expect Drusilla to return to the cave. When she finds Leslie gone, she'll probably search Adria's township first, then Philadelphia. She'll question Leslie's relatives, and their answers might lead her to our home."

"I'll watch Leslie," Willard said in a weak voice. "She seems like a nice person. Anything else?"

"Leslie needs clothes." Alex fished Leslie's heart-shaped key ring from his coat pocket. He didn't expect to need it so soon after the accident. "Take these keys and go to her apartment. I'll give you the address when we get home. Bring pants, shirts ... whatever you can carry."

"No problem." Steering hard, Willard swung onto a ramp that led to the Schuylkill Expressway.

"Drop the clothes off at my chamber. When Leslie wakes, she'll find a place for them. After I've rested, I'm heading to Adria to speak with Elliott."

"Elliott?" Willard echoed in a feeble voice.

"Yes, Elliott." Alex fingered Leslie's chin. Her skin felt cool as marble. Ghostly shadows flitted through the car, illuminating her bisque face. "My old friend. He might know something about Kenworthy's plans."

Willard's hands gripped the wheel, his knuckles turning parchment. "You shouldn't. Hades won't like what you've done."

"In other words, you don't like what I've done." Alex shook his head. "Come on, Willard, act like a grown man."

"I can't help it!" Willard blubbered. "When Leslie wakes, she'll want ..."

"Willard." Alex mustered as much patience as he could. "Don't you trust me to leave provisions for her?"

"Maybe." Willard dragged his shaky fingers through his moist hair. "I don't want to hear about it."

"Then do as you're told." Alex sighed, exasperated. "When Leslie wakes, she'll remember her attack. She may even recall the events before her car accident, and she'll feel too terrified to contemplate hurting anyone."

"What do I say if she asks me about her change?"

"Tell her that I'll answer her questions," Alex said. "Keep your conversation light, and you'll do fine."

Leaning against his seat, Alex lifted Leslie's shoulders onto his lap. He gazed into her lifeless eyes in silence.

****

At home, Alex carried Leslie to his bathroom and

began the arduous task of bathing her. Her wounds had healed, but blood and mud matted her hair and clothes. He peeled off her torn shirt and dungarees, exposing a bruise the size of a frying pan. The sight of her lumpy hip and jaw brought tears to his eyes.

"Leslie," he whispered in a cracked and dusty voice. "I promise to make everything all right."

Leslie lay limp, her blue eyes staring vacuously at the ceiling. By the time Alex finished soaping her, the bath water had turned rusty. He drained and refilled the tub. After toweling her dry, he clothed Leslie in one of his flannel robes.

The living room grandfather clock struck six. Alex slipped into a silk robe. After cradling Leslie and the wineskin in his arms, he crept to his sleeping quarters, hidden in his basement.

He had to credit Elliott with teaching him about secret rooms and passages. Without Elliott's instruction, the day time would have made him easy prey for vampire hunters. Elliott explained that a vampire's home offered his best defense during the day sleep, and so Alex installed wall panels using rectangular boards of equal measurements. No visitor ever guessed that one panel hid a door. Two silver candlesticks poked from the panel facing the stairs. Alex pulled on the right candlestick, and the door slid open, revealing a brick hall.

The door swung shut, cloaking Alex in darkness. He walked down a flight of stairs, carrying Leslie in his arms. The steps led to a room barely large enough to accommodate a night table and double bed. He tucked Leslie under the bedspread. After laying the wineskin on the table next to a note to Leslie explaining his whereabouts, he crept into bed and laid his head on her chest. Moments later, he drifted to sleep.

****

When Alex woke, three filled green trash bags lay wedged between the bed and door. Leslie's bruises had faded, along with the swelling. Except for some atrophied muscles in her right leg, her body appeared intact. Would she hate him or embrace her new life? Her face, remaining still as death, offered no clues. He'd have to wait until her change was complete.

Upstairs, Alex donned a green tunic with matching trousers and boots. He found Willard in his living room watching a baseball game.

Willard looked up and gave him a hard, suspicious stare. "Dr. Saunders called. He said it's urgent."

Alex felt bands of tension close around his throat. His dragon wanted to feed, and hearing about Bill didn't help. It didn't take mind reading to figure out that Leslie's family panicked after she ran to the woods. Of course, they called Bill. They probably called the police, too.

"Tell Dr. Saunders that I'm out of town, and ..."

Faint rustling outside his window caught his attention. Rushing out to his porch, Alex glanced up and down his driveway. Nothing. He searched the rose bushes surrounding his home. Harsh wind slapped against his face. The bushes near his house were scraping the siding. After deciding that nothing else caused the noise, he went back inside.

"Willard," he called before conjuring his wooden door. "I'll return in a few hours."

Moments later, Alex crossed over to Adria, tuning out the baseball game, wind, outside traffic and other New World sounds.

****

Instead of going to the market square, Alex hiked up a dirt road that bore left toward the Athyr Mountains. He leapt over rocks and logs, and slithered through gnarled branches, covering more distance in one hour than a mortal managed in three. After the forest thinned, he approached what used to be an old temple with crumbling flagstones and open windows.

Charred remains of pews and statues lay scattered on the stone floor. He and Elliott had burned out the temple's interior to conceal the underground maze of ballrooms and apartments belonging to the vampires.

Nothing's changed, Alex thought as he headed down the stairs by the altar. Downstairs, the opulence overwhelmed his senses—the crystal chandeliers, porcelain floors, and brass trimmed walls. He savored the aroma of the blood-filled kegs lining the marble tables. Perhaps Elliott and his companions were anticipating a harsh winter.

Moments later, Alex happened upon a man in white sitting on a stool, painting a mountain scene. It was his friend and mentor, Elliott. His thick-set brows, salt-and-pepper hair, and round face reminded Alex of Dr. O'Toole, Leslie's surgeon. But O'Toole's eyes betrayed arrogance; Elliott's eyes invited trust.

After laying down his paintbrush, Elliott met his gaze. "Andrej!" he cried, jumping to his feet. "How good ..."

"Alex, Elliott." Alex held a finger to his lips. "Always Alex. If Kenworthy finds out that I've escaped ..."

Elliott nodded. "You took your chances coming here, but I'm sure you have compelling reasons." Grabbing his easel and paints, he waved his hand. "Let's go to my apartment."

Elliott's apartment looked toward the hall, a six-room suite filled with oak tables and silk-covered chairs. Alex couldn't help admiring the animals sculptured on the porcelain walls; the white marble floors streaked with veins of gold.

"Make yourself comfortable," Elliott said.

Alex eased himself into a seat, swallowing hard. His tongue stuck to the cottony insides of his mouth. Leaning over a keg by the wall, Elliott dipped two pewter mugs inside and handed one to Alex.

"Thank you," Alex murmured. He drained the cup in three swallows. "Crossing dimensions always gets the dragon roaring," he said while Elliott provided a refill. "I'll get to the point. Kenworthy made a home for himself in the New World. One of his followers tried to kill someone I love."

"I see." Elliott rubbed his bearded chin. "Did you know that Kenworthy has taken a bride?"

Drusilla, who looks like me ... she beat me up. Alex's shoulders slumped. "No, but that doesn't surprise me."

"Her name's Drusilla." Twisting sideways, Elliott lifted three paintings that were propped against his chair. He handed them to Alex. "I've never met her, but I've captured her image on these portraits."

Leaning against his chair, Alex studied each canvas before laying it face-down. In one, soldiers with whips chased Drusilla through the market square. Her freckled face and red, curly hair made her look like Leslie's twin. In another, Drusilla tore into someone's throat, fangs dripping blood. In the third canvas, Drusilla stood waving her fists at a woman in dungarees, cowering on a blood-stained rug. The victim was Leslie.

"You've painted a monster!" Alex cried, his green eyes rolling wildly. "She's the same killer who attacked my Leslie. How did you know?"

"I paint my visions as I see them. My psychic powers manifest themselves through art." Elliott leaned back in his chair. A faraway look crossed his chalky face. "Someone told me that Drusilla's parents forced her to live on the street. She got caught stealing."

"And now, she's letting out her anger by attacking the weak." Alex felt old and tired. "People like Leslie. For all Drusilla's powers, she envies Leslie because she's got family."

Elliott nodded. "Knowing Kenworthy, I'd say he promised her a seat in the gods' court if she became immortal."

Alex massaged his temples. "Drusilla can't hurt Leslie now, at least, not directly. I granted Leslie immortality."

Elliott's gray eyes narrowed. "You did what?"

"I couldn't let her die." Alex shuddered at the unhealthy dread rising within him. "Leslie reminds me of Elizabeth; if you met her, you'd see why. She cares about me, and I believe that our love will grow."

"You are smitten, aren't you?" Elliott leaned against his chair and drained his mug. "Do you remember what happened the year after Elizabeth died?"

Alex propped his elbows on the table, chin resting in his hands, and braced himself for a lecture. "Kenworthy locked me in his courtyard, expecting the sun to roast me. But you rescued me and coached me on using my powers. And then I met someone."

"Delia," Elliott said, smiling. "She, too, reminded you of Elizabeth. Remember what happened?"

Alex nodded, shivering. Though Delia had died almost a century ago, he still pictured her rosy face, flame-colored hair, and gentle laugh. "Our relationship soured after I made her one of us. She wound up hating me. One night, she said she was going for a walk. She never came home. The next evening, I found her rings buried in an ash pile near my garden."

"I remember that." Elliott took both mugs and refilled them. "How did Leslie feel about changing life?"

"Leslie knew she was approaching death, and she worried about her sick father. She wanted to survive, so she agreed to undergo the change."

"I see." Elliott folded his hands in a steeple position. The words rolled forth from his mouth like a dirge. "I assume you explained the concept of immortality."

"I did."

"Our aversion to light."

"Of course. Leslie said she'd rather survive by twilight than not at all."

"What about our need for human blood?"

"I think so." At least, Leslie heard the word "vampire," and knew the legendary dietary requirement. But reading about the thirst and experiencing the craving were two different things. Head bending forward, Alex covered his eyes.

"Ah, that's what I thought." Elliott let out a ghostly sigh. "Once she sees the effects of her craving, she may prefer death."

"I couldn't let her die," Alex stated emphatically.

"I understand that," Elliott said. "Will Leslie take to this life? Maybe. Her cultural background may give her a unique take on her bodily changes. She may even thank you for trying to save her life. I suggest you handle her with kid gloves."

"In the end, she might still hate me." Alex buried his face in his hands. "What does Kenworthy want with the New World? He and Drusilla left a string of bodies through Philadelphia."

"Where?" Elliott jerked his head.

"A city in Leslie's world." Tears worked their way down Alex's cheek. "Without immortality, Leslie would become the next victim. I'm hoping that her new powers will enable her to do things that she'd previously considered impossible. She has a learning impediment which interferes with her work, and it's ruined her confidence."

"You can't predict how Leslie will act after the change." Elliott's voice saddened. "Perhaps she will consider immortality a gift. More likely, she'll panic. She may attack someone important. She may even try to destroy herself."

"My butler is watching her." Alex finished his cup. Though its contents stilled his dragon, Elliott's words left a cold feeling in his stomach.

"Leslie's feelings might not matter anyway." Elliott reached for another portrait from the pile near his chair. Fingers splayed along the painting's edges, he propped it on the table. "Take a good look."

Alex studied the painting attentively. In it, a man wearing a long, black robe sat on an ebony throne. His eyes blazed like hot coals, reminding Alex of a snake coiling to strike. His fingers curled around a lit torch, illuminating walls made of black rocks. A bat perched on his shoulder.

Terror pierced Alex's heart like a sword. "Oh, no," he cried, his shoulders shaking with harsh sobs. "That's Hades!"

"Kenworthy's blood feasts made Hades very angry," Elliott said. "I hardly go out anymore. I keep telling myself that he can't get to me here."

"Kenworthy became immortal over two centuries ago. He's always boasted about his dark gift and Hades let him live. Why should Hades destroy us?"

"Kenworthy has started his own coven of creatures who can't die." Elliott laid his white-sleeved hand on Alex's shoulder. "He coached Drusilla and other followers to take innocents. Hades went along with it when Kenworthy took thugs and undesirables, but the destruction has gotten out of hand."

"Kenworthy also bragged about his affair with Persephone." Alex leaned against the table, shoulders drooping. "He locked me in his courtyard because I refused to take a healthy young mother."

"Kenworthy always lived for the hunt, and Hades can't take any more." The gentle way Elliott spoke reminded Alex of a doctor breaking bad news to a favorite patient. "Have you and your friend Leslie seen the bats?"

Alex nodded, licking his lips. A sense of foreboding ground into the pit of his stomach. "What will he do to us?"

"Hades plans to destroy all vampires. When he attacks, expect a slow, agonizing death."

"No ... I don't want to believe that." Alex slid his dry tongue over drier lips. "You and I have lived over a century, but he must spare Leslie. Her father needs her, and she wants ..."

"Hades won't care." Elliott waved his hands. "He'll see Leslie as another vampire following in Kenworthy's footsteps."

"I should have known." Alex stood up without touching Hades's portrait. "Can Hades find us in the New World?"

"He'll find you no matter where you go." Elliott's words dropped into the air like rocks into mud. "His bats will follow your scent. I don't know when or how he'll attack. Hades keeps his timetables secret."

Elliott got up and motioned toward the door. "Go home and tell Leslie that you love her. You two might have a few years together. But if Kenworthy's killings spread to the New World, Hades's attack may come sooner. Much sooner."

Alex shuffled to the door. Just as he went out, he felt Elliott's hand on his shoulder. "I wish I had better news. But I consider you my friend, and friends don't lie to each other."

"I know."

Head bent and eyes brimming with unshed tears, Alex went up the stairs. Somehow, he'd prepare his answers and an apology before Leslie regained consciousness. How could he apologize to someone he'd drafted into a nightmare?

By the time Alex made it home, the sky paled to deep lavender. Crossing over to Philadelphia would buy another six hours of twilight. As he hiked up the dirt path leading to his house, Alex noticed that all of his windows were broken.

"What the Hades?" he muttered, cracking open the front door.

Inside, he found candlesticks scattered, battered lamps, and furniture ripped to shreds. Feathers and bat droppings coated his hardwood floor. In his dining room, his hutch's glass doors and the plates inside had shattered to pieces. He let out a shrill wail of grief from deep in his soul.

I've got to tell Leslie. Alex concentrated hard, trying to ignore the glittering shards and the stench of the bat dung. A few moments passed, and he made his crossover. A broken television and shattered lamps faced Alex in his Philadelphia living room. Stuffing poked through holes in his sofa's ripped cushions. Fine scratches dented his end tables. Glass from the windows lay scattered among bat droppings on the floor, glittering like diamonds. Two dead bats lay in a pool of blood by the bathroom.

Worse was the fetid stench that warned that someone had gotten hurt badly, maybe even killed. What if Hades made Leslie his first casualty? Tears rolled down Alex's face.

"Leslie!" he bellowed, racing through his house.

Chapter 12

Rat-a-tat, rat-a-tat.

Hades tightened up at the sound and gazed toward his palace. At his feet squatted Cerberus, his three-headed dog, snarling and slavering over a young man tied in thick robes and chains. A farmer known for his foul temper, the prisoner fed his wife and visitors to his animals. He paid for his crime on the gallows. After his death and arrival at Tartarus, Hades ordered Minos to chain the prisoner to the gate, where Cerberus could sup at leisure. At this point, Cerberus's teeth were gnawing up his right leg, leaving behind naked bone.

Rat-a-tat, rat-a-tat. Despite the farmer's earsplitting screams, Hades still heard the scratching. Phetheus, his bat messenger, was tapping the rocky window near the door. "King Hades!" he called. "We must talk. It's urgent."

Hades looked up at Phetheus. The look in his messenger's eyes hinted of dreadful news, something involving the vampires. The familiar rage reared in Hades's head, causing his hands to shake. "Go to the drawing room," he said. "Wait for me there."

After checking his prisoner's ties, Hades rushed inside the palace. At the drawing room, he found Phetheus pacing up and down the wooden table.

"You look upset, Phetheus," he said in a leaden voice. "What happened?"

"Drusilla spread Kenworthy's destruction to Leslie's world," Phetheus said. "She tortured Leslie and left her for dead."

Hades furrowed his thickset brows. "Then I shall prepare to meet Leslie at the river. Charon will bring me the new arrivals soon."

"Leslie did not die." Phetheus glanced toward the window. "Her friend Alex rescued her. I think he did something to her so that she could summon him by thinking his name. Before Leslie lost consciousness, he offered her immortality. She accepted."

"Phetheus." Hades drew in a deep breath. His mind refused to process what he suspected was true. "One needs large exchanges of blood to make a vampire. Drusilla's feeding wouldn't leave Leslie enough blood to effect the change."

"Drusilla broke nearly every bone in Leslie's body," Phetheus said, digging grooves in the table. "But she didn't feed. So Alex managed to turn her. I know because I smelled *Undeath* in Leslie."

Cancerous throes of rage swelled, tightening around Hades's throat. "She's better off dead," he gasped. "Lydia was supposed to watch her. Where is she?"

"Lydia's dead, King Hades. Leslie's brother shot her."

"That stupid fool!" Hades clenched his fists, knuckles turning ivory. "I warned her to use discretion."

Phetheus slowed his pacing and met Hades's gaze. "I followed Alex to the New World, and later to the crypts in Adria. When I left, he was speaking with Elliott. Elliott called him 'Andrej.' Does the name sound familiar?"

Hades nodded, his fingers gripping the chair back. He recalled hearing Kenworthy boast that he locked Andrej in the courtyard. He'd expected Andrej's arrival at Tartarus after sunrise. It never happened. Somehow, Andrej had risen like a phoenix, taken a new name, and moved to a distant land. "Alex forced *Undeath* on an innocent woman. He and Kenworthy went to the same school of evil."

118

"Leslie joined him willingly," Phetheus said. "Her father's sick, and she feared that her death would destroy him."

"Maybe so," Hades conceded, crossing his arms over his chest. "But her *Undeath* will kill him quicker."

"Alex told Elliott that she had a learning impediment. She's a healer by trade, and this impediment interferes with her duties. He thinks that her new powers will compensate for her limitation."

"And Elliott gave Alex his blessing." Images of Elliott and Alex caught in a burning pit flashed before Hades's eyes. He imagined their bloodcurdling screams, the stink of their flesh cooking in the flames. Leaning against the table, he burst into gales of laughter. "I give these creatures credit for their creative stories."

"I think Alex is telling the truth. According to Lydia, Leslie's healers called her 'stupid' and other awful names. Her experiences—some of them very painful—became part of Drusilla's memory. This made Drusilla angry and dangerous. So the other messengers and I want to hold a ceremony to give Leslie back these memories."

"That sounds reasonable." Hades smiled indulgently. "While you're at it, give Andrej my calling card. I'll deal with Kenworthy and Elliott."

Even before he finished speaking, Phetheus sailed out the window, headed on his mission. The rage simmering inside Hades threatened to boil over. He stormed around his drawing room, throwing chairs and cursing out loud.

Soft footsteps pattered from the hall. Persephone emerged through the doorway, her auburn hair and ivory silk gown flowing tent-like around her shoulders. "Stop it!" she shouted. "What's the matter with you?"

"Don't dare try to order me around." Hades shook his fist. "Lazlo ... Kenworthy must be destroyed. His kind will burn if I have to demolish all of Adria. First, I'll set fire to the crypts, then I'll ..."

"You're no better." Persephone's blue eyes flashed with indignation. "You've ruined Lazlo in his undeveloped youth simply because he knew how to love me. No wonder he sought desperate measures to survive."

Hades turned his head, his eyes clouding with unshed tears. The hatred in her voice dug through his heart like claws, but he'd die before letting her see him cry. "You belong to me, Persephone. I will not tolerate anyone, much less a mortal, trifling with you."

"What am I, some trophy for your palace?" Persephone's voice harshened. "Why did you choose fire to take Lazlo? Because you like torturing for sport? The way you feed prisoners to your dog speaks volumes about your cruelty. That poor farmer! I can't stand to watch Cerberus eat him alive."

"Then don't. That farmer committed ghastly crimes. What kind of monster do you think I am?"

"Just a monster," Persephone said coldly. "No special kind."

"Kenworthy and his breed left behind widows and orphans," Hades said in a tired voice. "Don't you think I should punish them?"

"If you set fire to their villa," Persephone persisted, "these widows and orphans will die, too. Do you want that?"

"Sometimes the good die with the bad."

"Then do what you must," Persephone cried, wringing her hands. "I wish I understood what makes you so bitter."

What made him so bitter, he wondered? Finding Persephone in Kenworthy's arms? Being exiled from Olympus? More than once, he tried to give Persephone answers, but her tight lips and the quiet contempt in her eyes discouraged any explanation. With a soft, despairing sigh, he hugged his robe around him and trudged outside and up the black grassy trail.

Harsh wailing called to him from the river Styx. It was Sir Ambrose, a former slaveholder. He thrashed in the water, wrestling with two bats. The creatures tore away his hands, leaving bloody stumps for arms. Though darkness enveloped Tartarus, Hades made out glistening bone between the skin tears and blood. Before his death, Sir Ambrose had beaten up his servants, especially Drusilla; Hades punished him by feeding him to his bats.

"What's the matter, Sir Ambrose, can't swim?" he jeered. "When the mighty fall, they fall hard."

Tears forgotten, he laughed raucously and hurried up the grassy slope. More screams bellowed from the shadows: a man sinking in quicksand; a woman groping for her missing limbs. To his right, an older man pushed a huge boulder up the slope, only to have it slide from his grasp and crash to the rocky terrain below. Hades preferred walking to traveling in spirit form so he could observe his prisoners.

At the upper light, Hades faced rows of crumbling markers. The setting sun left behind a bruise-colored sky. The crypts lay halfway between the cemetery and Adria's market square. He assumed his spirit form and flew through the gnarled trees.

The trees thinned, revealing a crumbling flagstone temple. Hades resumed his human form and slid past the charred pews and down the cement stairs. These steps led to a marble hall lined with brass doors—the vampires' sleeping quarters. At the entrance, he conjured up an invisible barrier, impervious to the vampires, but not himself. He walked on tiptoe, prepared to take them by surprise.

Moments later, the doors creaked open. People wearing silk robes stepped out to the corridor. The moonlit sky invited them to seek nourishment. Two men headed up the steps, chattering about their plans for hunting. Their smiles flashed pointed teeth.

At the doorway, their smiles faded, replaced by cries of stunned pain.

"What's wrong?" Hades called, breaking his silence at last.

A man dressed in white turned toward Hades. Blood flowed from gashes on his forearms, dyeing his sleeves red. Hades knew that vampires wounds normally closed within minutes, but the shield he created rendered them incapable of healing.

The man lurched through the crowd, dribbling a bloody trail. He stared at Hades with increasing panic. "Why must you torment us?" he croaked.

Hades felt something probe his head, soft as a kitten's paw. The man was trying to read his thoughts. "You value immortality so much," he said, chuckling. "I thought I'd indulge your taste. You shall spend eternity at my home."

"I need blood to survive," the man pleaded in a small voice. "I never meant to hurt anyone."

"Your intentions don't matter anymore." Hades waved his right hand. Bolts of blue exploded around the man's sandal-clad feet.

Screaming, the man collapsed, mouth drawn in a rictus of pain. His neck tendons stood out like corded ropes. The fire whispered up his calves with agonizing slowness, controlled by Hades's will. An onlooker tried to smother the flames with a blanket. It didn't work. The fire exploded into menacing brightness, engulfing man and blanket, giving off a pungent odor. When the flames died, ashes lay at Hades's feet.

"Would anyone else like to challenge me?" he asked.

Silence. The onlookers stared with vacuous eyes.

"Wise decision." Hades smiled. "Where's your leader?"

"Elliott's sleeping in that chamber there," a woman in green replied, pointing to the end of the hall. "Please don't hurt us. We didn't ask to be what we are."

"That's true," he allowed. "Kenworthy made it his mission to procreate a society of vampires. With that in mind, I'll give you a quick, easy death."

He extended his arms, waving them back and forth. Streaks of silvery-blue knifed from his hands, igniting the wooden furniture. White sparks rained off his fingers, landing on the vampires' clothes. The vampires fled like leaves before a raging wind. Their murmurs became shouts and bird-like shrieks.

Within minutes, the conflagration exploded into a flash of brilliant white light. Its crackling drowned out the sound of their screams. The air reeked of smoke and charred flesh. Yet the flames parted, allowing Hades access to Elliott's apartment. Being a god gave him power over fire.

The last door whispered inward, and Elliott stepped outside. His salt-and-pepper hair dripped with sweat; his gray eyes bulged in their sockets. His lips moved, but no words came forth.

"Go back inside, my friend," Hades said, grinning. "You and I must talk."

"No, no, no." Elliott shook his head. "This can't be real."

Hades hooked his arm around Elliott's shoulders and walked him inside to a chair. "I assure you, Elliott, this is real," he said. "What does Alex plan to do with Leslie?"

"What!" Elliott cried, covering his eyes. "Who told you about Leslie?"

"I'm omniscient." Hades smiled.

"Alex loves Leslie," Elliott blubbered, his lips quivering. "He's trying to help her overcome a learning impediment."

"Come on, Elliott, don't lie to me." Hades knew that Elliott would protest, but he took perverse pleasure in watching the vampire leader squirm. "He's using her impairment as an excuse to get a hunting partner."

"Leslie's had it rough." Elliott let out harsh, choking sobs. "Take me if you want, but let her and Alex go."

"Your people will invent creative excuses to procreate." Hades shook his head, fighting the bile that rose in his throat. "I expect that Alex's New World bride will take a unique approach to *Undeath,* and he'll come to you for advice. Maybe he'll even introduce her to you. You shall give them my warning."

"What should I tell them?"

"You needn't say anything. Let your appearance deliver its own message." Hades roared with laughter. Taking Elliott by the arm, he yanked him to his feet. "Come, Elliott, let's go to your bedchamber. We've got work ahead of us."

Chapter 13

For what could have been hours or days, Leslie floated through a misty fog. No stabbing pain or headache troubled her. She felt the forces of her bodily change guiding her through the mist, pushing her into oblivion.

Sometime later, the dreams started. In one, she was once again working as a respiratory therapist, in Betsy Ross's ICU. A ventilator sounded a shrill alarm. Two co-workers—Diane, a freckled blonde, and John, a dark-bearded man wearing gold-rimmed specs—followed her to the patient's room. There was a palpable look of anger on their faces. Diane and John tried to explain how to troubleshoot the ventilator, but they kept using technical terms that Leslie didn't know. She stared at them, trying to understand their language. *Forget it, stupid,* John shouted. *Diane and I will handle it ourselves.*

The dream faded, replaced by another. Leslie was now giving Mrs. Baker a treatment. The bright colors illuminated every line on Baker's withered face; her glazed eyes, toothless grimace, even the mole on her left cheek. Baker, who'd had a tracheotomy, spewed copious amounts of secretions. Leslie aspirated a mucus plug the size of a bullet.

Baker's face turned blue. Her heart monitor went flat, a sign of cardiac arrest. Sarah, Baker's nurse, bolted into the room. *Get out!* She shouted at Leslie. *You've done enough damage.*

She guessed she had. But she'd tried so hard. Her

shift was almost finished. After donning her coat, she ran out to the parking lot. Tom, her husband-to-be, was supposed to give her a ride home. *You've got no business working in this neighborhood,* he'd once told her.

Tom, she screamed, flinging open the car door. He listened while she described her failure with Baker. She expected hugs and words of support. Instead, his tense voice whispered a rumor of loathing. *How can you be so careless? We're talking about human life.* He gave a deep, mournful sigh, as if looking at Leslie made him sorry to be alive. *I envisioned you as a blossoming rose. Instead, you've withered into a dried-up weed. I'm calling off the wedding.*

Tom's figure drifted out of focus, and Leslie found herself staring down at a pavement coated with blood—the alley behind Betsy Ross Hospital. Fred lay scrunched against a trash bin, blood pouring from a gash in his neck. A man in black kneeling over Fred looked up at Leslie. The attacker's face reminded her of Crawford, but then he was running, fleeing to the street before she got a second look.

Using a scarf, Leslie formed a compress to stop the bleeding. Police officers and paramedics swarmed the area; someone lifted Fred onto a stretcher. Reporters surrounded Leslie and bombarded her with questions while she placed an oxygen mask on Fred's face. Crawford stood watching from the street corner.

Your job's intact, he later said with a crooked grin. *That save with Fred and the publicity you've garnered bought you another chance.*

The images kept marching through Leslie's head when she awoke—family birthdays, Christmas celebrations; Dad's stroke, and the resulting fights with Gerry; her first meeting with Alex. She recalled Neptune's Orchard and its glittering strobe lights when she and Alex waltzed. The night she'd confided in him at Bill's office, she saw no loathing or disgust; merely his gentle voice and the feel of his satiny ice lips brushing her cheek. She knew then that she wasn't dreaming; all of this had really happened.

With a burst of excitement, Leslie jumped to her feet. "Dad! Warren!" she shouted. "I remember everything. I'm going ..."

Her mouth snapped shut when she realized that she was standing and yelling in an empty room. A closet-sized room without windows or lights. Yet, her surroundings glowed with an eerie brightness, enabling her to make out a spindle bed, end table, paneled walls, and filled trash bags by the door. It wasn't her father's house after all. Whatever gave her that idea?

Instead of her jeans and glitter top, she had on a plaid robe that draped to her ankles. Her mouth burned, as if someone jammed hot coals down her throat. A sweet scent drifting from a wineskin on the table toyed with her nostrils.

Hands gripping the bed board, Leslie took one tentative step, then another. No headache or rib soreness troubled her, not even a twinge. No dizziness threatened to topple her when she walked. She traced her finger along her scalp, expecting to feel scabs and tenderness, but her skin felt silky smooth. She inspected her arms and legs. No bruises or cuts. She understood then that she'd become something other than human, and that the world as she knew it had changed, but she refused to contemplate the specifics. Not yet.

A scrap of paper beckoned from the table. Leslie snatched it up. "Dear Leslie," it read, "this nourishment should hold you until I get home. Wait for me. I will explain everything. Love, Alex."

"Nourishment?" Leslie peeked inside the wineskin. Its outside looked like goat skin. A cloying scent burst from its contents—bright, crimson fluid.

More horrific memories came to mind: Drusilla's fists pummeling her face; Drusilla dragging her to a cave in Adria, a prison littered with human remains; Alex telling her that she could survive by becoming immortal like himself and Drusilla.

Kenworthy and I are vampires. Plain and simple.

"Alex wouldn't turn me into anything bad," Leslie assured herself, her voice dry and raspy. "He saved my life."

She licked her lips, longing for a cup of cinnamon-flavored coffee, the kind she used to drink for breakfast. Instead, Alex provided this "nourishment." Leslie inhaled, sampling the aroma. It was almost as sweet as cinnamon-flavored coffee. She assumed that he'd taken the blood from an animal.

She lifted the wineskin to her lips. The liquid slid down her throat, quenching her thirst, and tasting sweeter than any gourmet coffee. It wasn't until she'd finished that she heard her teeth clicking around its rim. Leslie trailed her hand across her mouth. Her fingertips felt two long, pointed teeth, like the kind Drusilla had.

"Oh, no," she wailed, sinking into the bed. She burst into tears. "Alex, what have you done to me?"

Undeath. As in *Dracula* and other horror movies. Still, the fact that she didn't feel an urge to kill offered hope. Maybe none of this was happening; maybe she was still in the hospital, having the grandfather of hallucinations. But her better mind knew this wasn't true. The room's eerie brightness, her newly-sharpened teeth, and the taste of blood left a bitter dose of reality.

Sobbing loudly, Leslie tore open a trash bag and fished out black cotton pants, matching flats, and a pink silk blouse. Shelly had given her the blouse last Christmas, she remembered now. But this thing inside her! She needed answers yesterday. Either she'd wait on Alex or find out for herself.

With trembling hands, she tried the steel gray door. A click sounding like grating bones followed, and then the door swung outward toward a brick hall. The corridor led to a cement staircase. No lamps or candles lit her way, but her newly developed eyesight enabled her to make out ceiling cobwebs, chipped railing, and roaches scuttling through the cement cracks.

What would Gerry say about the bugs? She imagined his reddened cheeks, narrowed eyes, and the smoke flaring from his nostrils. The caricature image caused Leslie to bray with hysterical laughter.

The laughter died in her throat when she reached the landing, and discovered a sealed panel. No doorknob or key beckoned. Perhaps Alex locked her in the basement to die. But that didn't sound right. Immortality precluded death, and besides, Alex wanted her survival badly enough to justify taking desperate measures.

"Help!" Leslie banged against the panel. "Someone let me out of here!"

The panel flew open, catapulting her into a room lined with shelves. It looked like a basement. Moonlight streamed through a tiny window overhead, spreading silver over the floor tiles and furniture. A horrible, fetid stench emanated from another staircase.

Leslie crept up the steps. The smell intensified, reminding her of a patient with end-stage cancer that she'd worked with, someone who should have died weeks before his time, but didn't. Hand pinching her nose shut, she reached for the door handle, expecting to find something ghastly.

She wasn't disappointed.

Crunching sounded beneath her feet—jagged glass. She found herself in a living room. Shards poked from the windows like teeth. Glass fragments scattered like diamonds on the hardwood floor, burglars' leavings. Leslie felt her feet slide, and she grabbed a chair back for support.

"Shit," she muttered, glancing at her foot. What looked like bird manure clung to her shoe. The droppings splattered the living room floor and end tables. "Nice assessment," she added, donkeying another dry laugh.

A ceramic lamp lay on its side; underneath it was a dead bat. It looked like the ones she saw at her hospital window. Even in death, its ruby eyes seemed to follow her every move. The glass shards trailed to a kitchen, where windows were shattered like eggshells. Chairs lay on their backs. The scattered knives and crimson skid marks on the linoleum told her that someone tried to defend himself. She also knew that whoever, or whatever, trashed the house would return, and she didn't want to be around when that happened.

"I'm calling the police." She glanced around for a phone. One sat on the table near the dead bat. She snatched up the receiver, giving a sigh of relief when she heard a dial tone. Halfway through dialing, she hung up. What would she say? The police might ask questions that she couldn't answer, not that they'd believe the truth.

Warren will know what to do, she decided, dialing her father's phone number. "God, I hope ..." She paused, aware that she'd used the name "God" without any adverse effect. No pain, not even a twinge, like what she'd seen on TV.

"I hope Warren and Gerry didn't kill each other." She leaned against the wall, cord twirled around her fingers, listening to the phone ring.

"Hello," a gruff voice said. Gerry's courtroom voice. Leslie held the speaker against her mouth, but said nothing. She could almost predict her oldest brother's reaction. He wouldn't ask if she was OK. He wouldn't say he was worried. He'd say, "There you go again, crumbling when someone questions you. Grow up!"

"Hello." Gerry's voice edged with irritation. "Who's calling?"

With an empty shrug, Leslie laid the receiver back on its cradle. She'd have to keep trying until Warren answered. Just as she headed to the door, she heard faint moans. A man's voice faintly called for help. It sounded like Willard, Alex's driver. Leslie remembered meeting him the week before her accident.

"Hello?" she shouted. "Who's there?"

No answer.

"Hello?" Leslie called again, hands cupped around her mouth. She wandered into a corner room furnished with a desk, chair, and television. The groans were loudest around a door behind the desk. "Willard, is that you?"

"Go away," Willard cried in his thick accent.

Leslie tried the doorknob. Locked. Then she remembered Drusilla bragging about her strength, how she lugged Leslie like a rag doll.

"OK, Willard." She rattled the door's lock. Simple and somewhat worn. "Here goes."

After taking several steps back, Leslie dove into the door, left shoulder forward, knees dipping. The door popped with absurd ease, opening into a bathroom. There was a lip too small to be considered a step between the bathroom and outer room. Leslie struck this with the edge of her shoe. In the past, she would have gotten hurt. But her hands instinctively reached for the sink, breaking her fall. Immortality had given her the reflexes of a cat.

Willard lay curled on the floor tiles, back against the tub. Blood wept through the tears in his plaid shirt and jeans. Deep gashes on his face and arms exposed glistening bone. His body radiated a putrid odor. The stench reminded Leslie of her cancer patient, especially when he'd suffered recurrent infections.

"Go away," he pleaded again, covering his face.

Under normal circumstances, Leslie would run. But Willard needed medical attention, and her training taught her first aid. *What will you do about it,* her inner voice demanded. *Let him die?*

"No way," she said aloud. "Willard, do you remember me? Tell me what happened."

"Hades sent his bats to warn you."

Leslie spotted some towels draped over the tub's ledge. Using them as compresses, she wrapped them around Willard's arms. His body stiffened, his fists clenched, and his teeth chattered every time she touched him.

She wants to feed on me. His thoughts burned into her head. Stepping away, she glanced down at Willard. The words gained a stronghold in her brain when she looked into his eyes. "I don't know anyone named Hades."

"Hades is a god," Willard said in a quaking voice. "He hates vampires because they don't die. His enemy Kenworthy populated Adria with vampires, including Alex. Hades plans to destroy all of you." His voice grew shrill. "Alex said that you'd sleep another day."

"Kenworthy and I never met." Standing before the sink, Leslie glanced at the mirror. A freckled, ivory-complexioned face looked back. Her pointed teeth sparked in the dim light. "You've confused me with the wrong entity. Vampires can't think about anything except killing. They can't see their reflections in the mirror, and they can't tolerate references to God. I, to the contrary, can."

"Leslie, you're talking about a myth. Real vampires ... never mind." He curled up, arms folded across his chest. "I wish you'd slept another day."

Leslie affected a deep sigh. "Well, I didn't. I'll figure out this vampire thing later. Right now, I'm taking you to a hospital."

"Hospital?" Willard arched his thick brows. "How ... how are you going to do that? You can't drive."

"I don't know about that." Another sigh. "It wouldn't be wise to move you, though, badly hurt as you are. So I'm calling an ambulance. The paramedics will drive and they'll know what to do for you."

Willard shook his head. "I'm not going anywhere until Alex gets home. He'll know what to do."

"By the time Alex gets here, it may be too late to help you," Leslie said. "I know because my job is to work with sick people. If Hades, or whatever you call him, hates people like me so much, he won't forgive me for letting you die in Alex's bathroom. I promise I only want to help. Will you let me do that? Please?"

"All right. Just let Alex know where we're going."

With a cursory nod, Leslie sprinted to the living room. After scribbling a message on notepaper, she dialed 9-1-1. A deep sigh of relief escaped her lips. Vampire or not, her instinct for helping people remained intact.

****

At Betsy Ross, Leslie watched the paramedics wheel Willard into the emergency room. The sounds of beeping monitors, humming ventilators, and scratching pens bombarded her from all directions. She'd never minded the noises before, but the *new and improved* version of herself felt overwhelmed. Hands covering her ears, she followed the stretcher into a cubicle by the nurses' station. A husky, blonde woman in green marched in to take Willard's vital signs.

"Hello." She smiled, but didn't introduce herself. Her ponderous breasts bobbed as she leaned forward to check Willard's blood pressure. Even through the thick scrub fabric, Leslie could tell she wasn't wearing a bra. Thick ruby lipstick and layers of cherry blush gave the look of a circus clown.

Jenny. Leslie sighed, shifting her eyes sideways. *She hassled me every time I worked the emergency room. Gets worse by the second.*

"Can you give me your name, sir?" Jenny asked.

"Willard." His eyes fluttered. "The birds ... bats ..."

"What birds?" Jenny prodded.

"They broke into the house."

Jenny gave Leslie a questioning look. "Can you understand him?"

"These huge gray bats clawed him real good," Leslie said. "I was there when it happened. I think he's got an infection."

Jenny's plump face wrinkled into a frown. "Dr. Atkins will decide that for herself. Is Willard your brother?"

Leslie swallowed something dry in her throat. The thirst was returning with a vengeance. "No, he works for someone I know."

Jenny reached for an IV set up. She stretched Willard's arm across a table. "Last name?"

Leslie gazed toward the bed. Willard's eyes had closed, and he was snoring. "Willard," she prodded, nudging his shoulder. "You've got to help us out here. What's your last name?"

"Udjvaris ... ow!" he cried, as Jenny punctured his arm.

"What kind of insurance does he have?" Jenny persisted, lips tightened, eyes focused on Leslie.

"Shit." Leslie rubbed her throat, trying to ease the burning.

She gazed at Willard again. Fresh blood seeped through the pads on his shoulder. His wounds reeked of rotting vegetables. "The hell with the insurance," she said. "Willard's terrified, and he's bleeding like a pig. Shouldn't you concentrate on, you know, treating him?"

Placing her hands on her ample hips, Jenny lifted her face. "You've got nerve," she said through clenched teeth. "When I paged you stat during a cardiac arrest, you took your sweet time getting there and ..."

"Jenny." Leslie's eyes focused on Jenny's neck, where a vessel throbbed, radiating a sweet aroma. A red haze closed in on her, and fantasies of blood-drinking swam through her head, thoughts that had never crossed her mind before. "Do me a favor. Will you SHUT UP and DO YOUR JOB!"

"Jenny, we'll get the demographics later," a young man spoke up. Dan, a relief nurse. Leslie remembered working with him in the ICU. "Call Dr. Atkins. I'll look after Mr. Udjvaris."

"Whatever," Jenny snorted. She stormed to a phone. Leslie lowered her head and waited for the urges to pass. Arms propped on the bed rails, she looked down at

Willard. "I'm going for a walk," she said. "The people who work here don't like me very much."

Willard shifted on the bed. The shakiness and chattering that she'd noticed earlier stopped. "Alex told me that the healers ... peer workers made your life miserable. He told the truth. They might poison me."

"That won't happen," Leslie said, hoping she sounded more confident than she felt. "There are laws against that sort of thing."

****

Arms folded across her chest, Leslie proceeded to the lobby. The grandfather clock by the elevators struck nine. A tentative smile crept into her face. Her coworkers were doing their treatment rounds now. Fred had once said that a smart therapist spent all his time doing treatment rounds, even if he wasn't seeing patients. Treatment rounds meant staying out of Crawford's way.

How will her powers affect job performance? Can hypnosis put agitated patients at ease? Will her sensitive ears detect aberrant breathing and maybe even help her troubleshoot equipment?

For starters, her change meant asking Crawford about working the night shift. It meant wearing rouge and approaching everyone with a tight-lipped smile. At all times. No more working days or early evenings. "I'll try a test run," she told herself. "Listen to breathing and do mock ventilator set-ups."

She stepped onto the elevator and pressed the button for the first floor. Before getting off, she scanned the hall. Empty. Her flats made loud, clacking noises against the linoleum. After glancing over her shoulder, Leslie tip-toed inside the respiratory offices. She passed the conference room, Crawford's office, and a dirty utility room.

The storage area sat in the hall's rear. Inside, six Bennett 7200 ventilators lined the wall like soldiers. She had used the 7200 on Fitzpatrick. With her memory now intact, she could recall his blue-tinged face after he exited the CAT scanner. A tear slipped down her cheek.

Ask yourself how you'll feel if your mistakes cost a patient his life, Crawford had said afterwards. She'd made a bad choice when she picked her college major; like most bad choices, respiratory therapy seemed like an ideal option at the time.

After attaching a test lung to a 7200, she flicked on the switch. The machine flashed the words, "safety valve open," then let out a shrill whistle.

"Damn!" Leslie cried, silencing the alarm. The machine pumped the amount of air set on the dial, but its harsh roar sounded like a defective vacuum cleaner. Leslie spent the next half-hour testing the other ventilators. She heard the same whistles and bells, but the machines put out accurate volumes of air. The pitch changed when Leslie kinked the tubing. Her new ears magnified every noise, even when she dropped the tubing.

Swishing footsteps sounded from the hall. Crepe soles, like the kind belonging to her coworkers. After snapping off the machine and light, she ducked behind the ventilator. The door opened; Diane rushed in and headed toward the shelves. After helping herself to a bag of plastic tubing, she left.

Leslie waited a few minutes, then tiptoed to ICU, Fitzpatrick's ward. The nurses huddled at the desk, conferring with two doctors. No one looked her way.

Fitzpatrick's room stood furthest from the station. A glance at his chart showed his "do not resuscitate" orders. Leslie's throat went dry, and guilt pierced her heart. Turning toward his room, she forced one foot before the other, determined to relive Fitzpatrick's tragedy and the circumstances that had created it.

Fitzpatrick lay in bed, face shiny with sweat, blank eyes focused on the ceiling. No wince or sharp intake of breath occurred when Leslie squeezed his hand. His arms, swollen like stuffed sausages, warned of incipient heart failure. Even from the doorway, she heard his chest rattle and wheeze. She grimaced at the stench of decay and felt her heart splinter within her.

"Mr. Fitzpatrick, I'm so sorry for what I did to you," she whispered. "I wish I could make it better." Make what better? Apologies wouldn't heal his brain damage. Apologies wouldn't ease his family's grief. With a sick feeling, Leslie concluded that she'd lost her humanity years ago, when her mistakes hurt the people that she'd tried to help.

Shoulders trembling with noiseless sobs, Leslie shuffled to the exit. She promised to give herself a week to see if her powers compensated for the learning deficit. Either she'd pass muster or she wouldn't.

Just as she reached for the door handle, the door swung inward, banging her shoulder. A man wearing a gray suit stared at Leslie, eyes bulging. It was her boss. His face, white as parchment, dripped with sweat.

"Leslie!" His lips quivered as he struggled to get out the words. "My God! Your brother Warren called today, telling me you were dead."

Chapter 14

Night faded by the time Drusilla left the cave, affording only an hour to make it to shelter. Shelter was Ken's home, though he said he loved sharing it with her. He even bought her a diamond ring and introduced her to everyone as his wife. Drusilla expected him to propose marriage, a brief civil ceremony perhaps. It hadn't happened.

Kenworthy put the township under his spell. His charm and power were addicting, and addictions led to other addictions. Like the things his money bought, the blood feasts, and ability to do what she pleased with mortals.

In particular, Leslie Taite.

Looking back on the evening, Drusilla thought that the loathing in Leslie's eyes and the expensive-looking clothes reminded her of a particularly vicious slave boss. The images radiating from Leslie's mind revealed her father, a sickly old man hacking and wheezing; her friend, a healer wearing tailored suits and carrying a fat wallet. Kenworthy admired Leslie, though she didn't know it. This last image stirred Drusilla into a burning rage, the kind that urged her to kill.

While Drusilla sashayed through the trees, memories of her own childhood tugged at her, memories of a time when she, too, lived with loving relatives. In the stony doorway of her parents' cottage, she put aside the knowledge that her mother's embrace and siblings' laugh had become history.

A cool mist brushed Drusilla's cheeks as she climbed

a slope, waking the child within her, the forgotten one buried under her slave masters' whippings. She remembered wearing a plain cotton frock and working in the fields with her father. Back then, she didn't need coca. She spent her free time lying on the grass, gazing at the azure sky, fiery curls spread around her face. She tried not to notice her family's threadbare clothes or their meager meals. But her parents' hushed whispers and pointed fingers gave away too much for comfort.

Looking upon her younger self, gazing through that child's eyes, Drusilla saw why she hated Leslie so much. Fate had given Leslie a loving family, something she'd never have. This realization brought tears to Drusilla's eyes. Her fists clenched, their fingernails drawing blood from her palms.

Moments later, Ken's home beckoned to Drusilla, a friendly giant waiting to shelter her. She dashed through the marble halls, chased by the sun peeping over the horizon. "Ken," she called, heels clacking against the veined floor. "I'm home."

There was no answer.

Stepping through a doorway to her right, Drusilla entered what looked like a dining room—paneled walls, a beige slate table trimmed with gold, and cushioned chairs. Ken said that he used it as a conference room. Lifting out a panel, she headed down the steps toward his bedchamber.

His brass bed was empty; someone had folded over the silk covers. Then she remembered that he'd spent the last day at his New World home. He said that he was transferring funds between banks. Drusilla didn't know what "banks" meant, but his woolen black suit told her that he was meeting somebody important.

She contemplated the night she'd gone hunting and came home to find Leslie napping on the sofa. A burst of excitement rushed through Drusilla as she recalled Leslie's contorted face and pitiful whimpering. She crawled into bed and drifted to sleep with a smile on her face.

****

When Drusilla woke, her throat blazed with thirst. She considered going back to the cave to see if Leslie was still alive.

"Forget it," she said, getting up. "I want healthy blood." A crooked and rather wicked grin surfaced on her parchment face. "I'll hunt in the New World."

The marble floor felt deliciously cool and smooth under her feet, a welcome change from the dirty tents and cellars that reeked of urine. She rooted through her walk-in closet, filled with satin and woolen dresses. Only the wealthy afforded such clothes.

She selected a black shirtwaist studded with rhinestones. After powdering her face and combing her hair, Drusilla went upstairs. Because the New World still had six hours of daylight, she decided to kill time by browsing through Ken's gallery.

Paintings of Ken's family lined the wall between the tapestries. His relatives looked stunning, with flowing blonde hair, oval faces, and aquiline noses. Persephone's portrait hung by the door. She wore her auburn hair tied in a braid; bisque complexion, and sky-blue eyes. Drusilla recalled seeing a woman looking like Persephone in Leslie's memories, but she couldn't place her name.

It occurred to Drusilla that no active memories lingered in her consciousness. She recalled describing visions of talking machines and mishaps with equipment, but she didn't recall living those memories now. Perhaps the bats had gotten Leslie. When someone died, their thinking processes stopped, including, Drusilla presumed, the transferred memories.

Something shiny lay on Ken's roll-top desk. It was a twelve-inch knife with the letter "M" engraved on its platinum handle. Ken's "good-luck" knife. He said that the knife used to belong to his father. Drusilla ran her finger along its razor-sharp blade. Its silver gleamed in the moonlight.

"Family heirloom, huh?" She tucked it into her side pocket. "Maybe it will bring me luck."

Arms propped against the sill, Drusilla watched the position of the stars and moon. At midnight, she conjured the image of a platinum door, her gate to the New World. After she crossed over, she proceeded to the forest.

A syrupy smell wafted from a cement road coated with tar. At first, Drusilla shivered when she saw the horseless carriages—automobiles—whiz past her. But the scent stirred her craving to life.

Moments later, she sighted a woman in hot pink trousers and shirt running along the street. Her blonde ponytail dangled over a neck that glistened with sweat. Her vessel throbbed, exuding the aroma, and inviting Drusilla to feed. Drusilla imagined her waxen fingers snapping the woman's neck like a twig.

Drusilla broke into a trot until she caught up with the woman. Thinking about the beatings she'd endured on Adria's estates, she worked up tears and quaking sobs.

The woman stopped quickly, almost whacking her head against a tree branch. She gave Drusilla a wary look. "Excuse me," she said. "Are you lost?"

"No." Drusilla squinted and more tears came. Probing the woman's mind assured her an easy kill. No live-in friend or lover. Her siblings lived far away. Her parents might question her death, but heart problems and other ailments would prevent them from making an investigation. "I'm looking for an officer."

"You live around here?" the woman asked.

"Back there." Drusilla pointed to the woods. "My name's Drusilla."

"I'm Claire." Her breath came out in short huffs. "Why do you need an officer?"

"My friend's hurt." The thirst became unbearable; Drusilla fought hard to contain her excitement. "A wolf chased us through the woods."

"A wolf?" Claire laughed, but her breath came out in ragged, little gasps. "We don't have any wolves here except the two-legged kind."

"Maybe it was a large dog." Drusilla wiped the tears from her cheeks. "Whatever it was, it chased her up a tree and tore a chunk out of her leg."

"Oh, dear!" Hand braced against the branch, Claire craned her neck, casting her gaze. "Some dogs can get nasty. Where's your friend?"

"Back there." Drusilla pointed to a grove of trees. "She's bleeding hard, and the dog's watching her in case she falls. He growls and snaps if I get too close."

"She must feel terrified." Claire's eyes darted around the trees. "But I don't hear any screaming."

"She didn't scream. She's just sitting on some branch all white-faced with a funny look in her eyes."

"Maybe she's in shock. I know a thing or two about first aid. Let me take a look at her. I can call for help on my cell phone."

With Claire close behind, Drusilla proceeded through the maze of trees. At a clearing, she happened upon a hole in the ground surrounded by stones. It looked like a well, a convenient place to store her leftovers.

Claire walked a few paces further, scanning the trees with a flashlight. "I don't see anyone or hear barking. Do you know where we are?"

Was that fear she sensed in Claire's voice? Her eyes dropped to the thrilling pulse of Claire's vessel. She felt its steady beat, coaxing her craving into full bloom. Fist clutching Ken's knife, Drusilla stepped behind Claire. "She climbed that large oak to your right. The top branch. See it?"

Claire raised her light, its beam casting bright circles on the gnarled branches and leaves. "No one's up there, Drusilla. I'm afraid you've gotten us lost."

While Claire spoke, Drusilla reached for Ken's knife. Yanking Claire's ponytail, Drusilla pulled her neck taut and slashed her throat.

Claire's voice came out a muffled scream. Her eyes filled with terror. She writhed only seconds before collapsing against Drusilla.

Spinning Claire like a top, Drusilla squatted to catch the spurting blood. She inhaled its sweetness as it gushed down her throat. When Claire's heartbeat stopped, Drusilla stepped back and watched the blood pour onto the grass. She then hauled Claire by the armpits across the grass and tossed her into the well.

The clothes inspection came next, always done after feeding. Blood soaked her gown. She felt through her pockets for the knife. It was gone. She sifted through the grass hoping to see its silvery-white blade gleam between the fallen leaves. Crouched on her knees, she also peered into the well. Her eyes saw nothing.

A sick feeling gnawed at her stomach. What if the wrong person found that knife? Like maybe an officer. Hadn't Ken warned her to use discretion? Besides, the knife was a family heirloom. Losing it would make him angry. She wouldn't tell him, at least, not yet.

Instead, she walked home, whistling to herself. Her soiled clothes went into a trash can. She tossed Leslie's coat and sneakers into the living room fireplace, and threw a lit match onto the pile. While the clothes burned, she took an oil bath, donned a pink lace gown, and reclined on the master bedroom's four-poster bed.

Sometime later, the front door squealed open, and Ken came up to the bedroom. His face had the ruddy glow of a vampire who'd gorged himself. Grimacing, he slammed the door shut. "Son of Hades," he murmured, wiping his eyes. "It stinks downstairs."

"I'm sorry," Drusilla cried, jumping to her feet. "I was disposing of evidence." She rushed up to Ken and gave him a hug. "I missed you."

"I missed you, too." Ken looked down at her, smiling, his eyes gleaming like gemstones. "You look like a cat that swallowed a bird."

"I swallowed a big bird," Drusilla said, opening his shirt. She walked her fingers down his hairy chest. "How did your visit go?"

"I bought an apartment complex. New World property is a good investment."

"I suppose so," Drusilla humored him. Nothing about the New World made sense so far except the hunting trips.

Ken burst out laughing. "You fed pretty well while I was gone, didn't you?"

"Of course." Drusilla pulled him close. "Now I can show you my love."

"Sounds tempting." With an arm hooked around Drusilla's shoulders, Ken stared at her with glistening eyes. "First, I want to hear about your adventure. Obviously, your meal wore sneakers. The stench nearly made me sick."

"The sneakers belonged to a woman who ran for sport. I lured her into the woods, saying that someone there got hurt. She satisfied me nicely." Drusilla watched Ken's moon-glow face, scanning his emotions. Lately, he seemed distant, and she wanted—needed—his approval badly.

"I made sure the bats weren't following us." She burst into giggles. "I tossed her remains into a well."

"Wait a minute." Ken started and backed away. His eyes became feral and sharp, missing no attempts at shielding emotions, no matter how slight. "What did she look like?"

"She was thin and blonde, and she wore pink trousers." Drusilla shifted her eyes. "Why?"

"You're talking about Leslie." Ken's thin lips wrinkled into a frown.

"Her name was Claire. Don't worry, I was ..."

"Liar!" Ken circled the room, fists clenched. Without warning, he yanked Drusilla by the hair and shoved her against a bureau. Its brass handles rammed her back, sending bolts of pain through her spine. "I called Leslie's father, posing as her boss, to ask about her recovery. He said she ran away and got killed. I found red hair on the sofa and rug. The look on your face confirms my suspicions."

The white heat of rage welled up in Drusilla's throat, making her long to strike back, but she could not twitch a muscle. "So what?" she mumbled instead. "No one cares about Leslie, least of all, her peer workers."

"Think again," Ken said in an authoritarian voice. "She's got two brothers; one a newspaper reporter with connections to the police. The other works for a prominent law firm. Besides, she's got spirit, unlike you. She's looked after a sick father and coped with limited skills; yet she made it through college."

"She hates our kind." Drusilla cringed against the wall, dreading the harshness in his voice. "You said that she could never love you."

"That doesn't justify your actions." Hands gripping Drusilla's shoulders, Ken shoved her against the closet, splintering wood. His eyes blazed like smoking, black coals. "Granted, Leslie and I come from two different worlds, and I look too much like her boss. But I can still help her. What did you do to her?"

"I beat her up and left her in a cave." Drusilla's voice came out in trembling sobs. "She must be dead by now."

"Maybe not." Rooting through a drawer, Ken fished out a navy tunic and trousers. "I'm making her one of us."

"What?" Drusilla struggled to her feet; chin lifted, and shoulders squared back, glaring at Ken. She'd be damned if she'd share her powers with Leslie. Then again, given her stupidity, Leslie might walk into a sunrise or something equally disastrous. Her lips curled into a twisted smile.

"Don't laugh!" Ken shouted, jerking her arm. Spinning Drusilla to the door, he gave her arm a twist.

Drusilla screamed as he pulled her muscles like taffy. "Let go of me."

"I don't find this funny at all," Ken said between bared teeth. "We've got two hours before the sun rises in Adria. Go back to that cave and find Leslie."

"I told you, she's dead," Drusilla protested in a feeble voice. "I know because I don't get any more visions of her life."

"You'd better pray you're wrong." Ken's voice chilled like ice. "If not, I'll decide on a suitable punishment for you."

"Right." Drusilla focused on her door to Adria's dimension, trying hard to swallow her feelings of anger and hatred. Ken didn't want her; he loved Leslie. Once Leslie became a vampire, he'd make her his bride. Drusilla knew this as well as the loneliness gnawing at her heart.

Moments later, she found the cave, the one where she'd left Leslie. Two skeletons lay chained to the wall— one freshly bloodied, with tufts of pink flesh and gristle. A half-dozen bats formed a black cloud as they picked at the bones. She also noticed a dried pool of blood near the skeletons, where she'd left Leslie.

Leslie's body was gone.

Chapter 15

Fists balled in her pockets, Leslie stepped into the hall, eyes on her boss. Crawford skittered several feet back, horror-stricken.

"Warren said I was dead?" She tightened her lips, fighting back a giggle. She couldn't help taking pleasure in watching Crawford cringe. In fact, she found it hilarious. "Are you sure?"

"Diane took the call. Your brother screamed in her ear, blaming your death on our hospital." Crawford hugged his clipboard like a teddy bear. "My God, you look like a ghost."

Leslie glanced at the wall clock and started. She'd spent a long time here, too much time. The dryness gnawed at her throat again. "I haven't pulled any Lazarus numbers," she said, smiling.

"What are you doing here?" Crawford's eyes swept the hall, his pupils jumping like frightened rabbits. "Why aren't you home with your family?" Backing along the tiled hall, he stumbled over a laundry bag. His gray-sleeved arms flew out, gripping the side railing for purchase. His clipboard clattered to the floor, spewing the beige linoleum with papers.

Squatting on her knees, Leslie gathered his papers. One of them listed tonight's assignments. Each critical-care therapist worked two intensive care units. Another assignment involved floors in the Forrest and Tower wings, enough work to occupy three therapists.

"My brother had to cover a fire, so I spent a couple of days with my friend Willard." Leslie lowered her eyes as

147

she handed him his papers. She hated lying, but she rationalized that Crawford invented more lines than a telephone directory. "Some bats flew into the house and cut Willard badly, so I came here with him in the ambulance. I can't have Warren thinking that I died."

Crawford leaned against the wall, arms folded against his chest. His shivering subsided, and the frightened-child look evaporated, replaced by his I'm-the-boss smirk. Reaching forward, he straightened Leslie's shirt collar.

Leslie felt herself stiffen as his ruddy fingers brushed against her skin. He'd often prefaced his disciplinary sessions by comments on her appearance. *I'm better than you,* his smug look said. *Better dressed, more educated, and more intelligent.*

"Want to use my phone?" he offered.

"Yes, please." Swallowing hard, Leslie walked to his office. After calling Warren, she'd pitch for the night shift job, then scram.

To her dismay, Crawford had to run to keep up with her. "Whoa, there," he panted. "I thought you couldn't walk."

"I heal fast," Leslie said, smiling.

"I'll say." Rooting through his pockets, he fished out his office keys. "Use my private phone. Do you remember how to dial out?"

Leslie nodded. She stood before his mahogany desk, facing two leather chairs. Chills shuddered up her back as she recalled the times she'd cowered in them, listening to his tongue-lashings.

Crawford plopped at his desk, head bent, and eyes focused on a thick folder. Her file. Certain forms went to Personnel after an employee died, and her "resurrection" left Crawford with more paperwork. After closing the door, Leslie dialed her father's number, praying that someone besides Gerry would answer.

"Hello," answered a low-pitched voice. It was Warren.

"Warren, I'm alive," Leslie blurted.

"Warren gasped. "*What!* Who's this?"

"Leslie. Someone made a terrible mistake. Will you tell Dad that I'm OK?"

"Wait a minute." Annoyance crept into Warren's voice. "No one heard from you for over two days. Why didn't you call?"

"After I ran away, a creepy woman attacked me in the woods." Eyes focused on Crawford, Leslie lowered her voice. The silver gleam in his eyes warned that he would use whatever he overheard against her. "She lives up the street from you and Dad. Alex was looking for me, and he found me in time. He brought me to his house because he thought that this woman might come after you or Dad."

A long, deep sigh followed. "Oh, God! Did he call the police?"

"I don't think so." Hand cradling the receiver against her ear, and back toward Crawford, Leslie walked the phone to the window. "Warren, this isn't your typical cop-versus-bad-guy situation. The police can't do anything."

"They'd better do something with the fucking taxes I pay. Some broad with a heavy accent called, saying she found you dead. She hung up without giving me her name or number, so I called the police. No bodies turned up at the morgue, and they couldn't trace her number. Guess who caught the shit from Gerry when it hit the fan? Yours truly. Why didn't Alex call Dad or something?"

"I don't know."

"He's playing a head game, that's what. Both him and Tom. Where do you meet these turkeys anyway?" Warren let out a tired groan. "Did he call Saunders? You've got follow-up visits and stuff."

Leslie glanced at her boss. He was smiling with bright malice. "I think he did."

"Shit," Warren muttered. "Maybe I should believe in the tooth fairy, too."

Leslie drummed her fingers on the cold windowsill. "Warren, there's more. You deserve the truth, but I'd rather tell you in person."

"Leslie, how ... how bad is it?"

"I'll need time to figure out the answer to that one. Besides, I'd rather visit when Gerry isn't there. He wouldn't understand."

"He doesn't understand squat. Where can I reach you?"

"I, um, didn't memorize Alex's phone number. It doesn't matter anyway because I'm at the hospital with his butler Willard."

"What happened to Willard?"

"Some wild bats got into Alex's house and chewed up Willard. We came here in the ambulance. I think he'll be OK." Leslie sighed. "I'll get you Alex's number as soon as I can. All right?"

"Not really," Warren murmured under his breath before hanging up.

Crawford looked up from his papers. His eyes wore the cunning look of a hungry beast. "It sounds like you've gotten yourself into a jam," he said, smiling.

"Nothing serious." Leslie's eyes dropped to the fleshy mound of his neck. His carotid vessels hummed audibly, radiating a sweet smell. "Someone played a horrible joke on my family."

"Well, I don't find this paperwork amusing," Crawford said. "I don't have time for games."

Parched as her throat felt, Leslie had to smile. The joke suited Crawford perfectly, considering the way he ran his department. "I'm sure you don't," she said, humoring him. "May I ask you something?"

Crawford shrugged. "Go ahead."

"My memory came back. I recall the mistakes I made here, especially the one that caused Fitzpatrick's brain damage." Leslie lowered her head. "I'm sorry."

"Apologizing won't cure him. Do you realize that?"

Leslie nodded, rolling her tongue over her lips. Her thirst ignited a ball of heat in her stomach. "Thank you for giving me another chance."

She won't last long after I get through with her. Eyes on Crawford, she shivered at the words flowing like printed text from his head.

"Everyone deserves second chances," Crawford said in a voice oozing with concern. "There's a right way, a wrong way, and the Crawford way to practice therapy. Understand?"

"Perfectly." Leslie leaned toward Crawford's desk and inhaled deeply, relishing his sweetness. It was time to make her pitch. Maybe this talk might end in fun. "My eyes have become sensitive to light since my operation."

"Is that so?" Crawford sighed and glanced at his watch. "You ought to tell your doctor."

"I will." Leslie cocked her ear to the door, but heard nothing. "You once said you needed people to work the night shift. I'm volunteering for the job when my doctor nods his OK."

"Nights?" Crawford raised his voice. His eyes glittered like tarnished silver.

Leslie licked her lips. The reddish haze swimming around her made it hard to think. "I won't repeat my mistakes."

"You want to work nights?" The look of distracted surprise left Crawford's eyes. His cheeks filled with a dark, red color. "You think I'd let you work without supervision?"

Leslie did not answer. She was focusing on Crawford's scent that teased at her nostrils, teasing at the corners of her mind.

"You have nerve asking about night shift. I should have fired you long ago. Idiots like you shouldn't work without supervision."

Visions rolled through Leslie's head: Crawford as a little boy cowering from his father's whip. Tears streaking his pale face. *You idiot!* his father shouted. *You'll never amount to anything.*

"Oh, my God!" She stared at Crawford, awed by her vision's clarity. "Your father beat you and called you an idiot."

"What?" Crawford jumped from his chair, nostrils flaring, face turning purple. "How dare you question my personal life? Get out, before I call Security."

"I'm not finished yet." Leslie's voice sounded as if pebbles had lodged inside her throat. Hands locking Crawford's arms in a steel grip, she shoved him against the wall. His lips moved like those of a fish, issuing only faint croaks. She gazed into his terror-stricken eyes.

"You listen to me and listen good," she whispered in his ear. "If you had assigned the work load evenly and allowed me to practice dry runs on equipment, I could have avoided those mistakes."

Arms pinning his shoulders, Leslie sank her newly grown teeth into his throat. Crawford's legs kicked and drummed, but his struggles only excited her more. His life force warmed her stomach, soothing her thirst. Feeding on Crawford, an emotional vampire, served poetic justice. It was just the thing she needed.

Then her excitement faded a little. *You're sinking to his level. Mom didn't raise you that way.*

Leslie licked and swallowed, catching the blood dribbling down his neck. A rush of energy suffused her body with a glow. Mom had taught her differently, but Crawford had this lesson coming. Still, the thought nagged at her, that the end did not justify the means.

Crawford slumped to the floor. His heartbeat became erratic and his face turned chalky pale.

"Oh, no!" Leslie cried, horrified at the enormity of what she had done. Grabbing a tissue, she held it against his wound, stanching the blood flow. Her other hand formed a fist over her quaking mouth. Shame washed through her; tears flowed down her cheeks in rivulets. With a flick of her wrist, she locked Crawford's door.

Moments later, footsteps sounded from the hall. Crepe-soled shoes. Urgent knocking and doorknob rattling followed.

"Leslie?" Saunders called. At least the voice sounded like Saunders. Perhaps he saw her in the emergency room with Willard. "What's going on?"

The footsteps faded. Leslie leaned over Crawford, listening to his labored breathing. Seconds passed, and then sliding metal sounded from Crawford's bathroom. A window opened, and then, more footsteps.

Chapter 16

"Leslie," Alex shouted, sprinting to the basement. Its shelves and tiled floor appeared intact. Shoving aside the paneled door, he bolted downstairs to his bedchamber.

His green flannel robe lay in a heap on the mattress. Someone had torn open a trash bag, spilling its contents on the floor. He picked up the wineskin. Empty.

"Leslie!" he screamed, his voice floating up the stairs. He didn't expect her to wake so soon after her change. He scanned his basement. No sign of Leslie.

He ran upstairs again. Where was Willard? Gone on some errand? He'd rather that than find his servant torn apart by the bats. "Willard!" he cried, scurrying from room to room. "Come out and talk to me. The bats are gone."

Silence.

Looking down, he noticed scuff marks on his hardwood floor, followed by a trail of blood. The trail led to the bathroom in his den. Someone had broken the doorknob. Inside, blood pooling by the tub had congealed like paste.

Something glittered on the ceramic floor—a plastic name tag bearing a photo of a crew-cut young man. Underneath, the caption read, "Raymond Gilmore, First Alarmers."

"First Alarmers?" Alex gasped. "What were they doing here?"

With a long, agonized sigh, he concentrated on Willard. The image of Willard's scratched and bloody face materialized in his mind. He was lying in a hospital bed, tethered to plastic tubes.

At the telephone, he spotted a folded paper addressed to him in a voluminous scrawl. He snatched it up.

Dear Alex, it read. *Please come to Betsy Ross Hospital as soon as possible. Willard's hurt. My memory came back. Many things happened that I just don't understand. I need answers!*

After calling a cab, Alex shuffled outside, tears running down his cheeks. "Oh, Leslie, I never meant for you to face *undeath* alone."

****

At Betsy Ross's emergency room, Willard slept in a cubicle by the nurses' station, arms and face swathed in bandages. The needles buried in his left arm fed him blood and antibiotics. Alex tiptoed to the bed and nudged his shoulder. "Willard, wake up," he said. "We've got to talk."

Willard's eyes fluttered open. His face jerked, and he started shaking. "You better run. Those bats ripped your house apart and cut me real bad."

"Don't worry about the bats." Alex stared at Willard, willing him to compose himself. "Who brought you here?"

Willard's shivering subsided. His rasping breaths echoed through the ward. "Leslie found me in the bathroom. She came here with me in a police car."

"You mean ambulance."

Willard propped himself on his elbow and glanced around the ward. His face turned ashen. He sank against the pillows, groaning. "I guess. They want to keep me here a while. My nurse badgered me for an insurance card and got into a fight with Leslie over it. What does 'insurance' mean?"

"Insurance provides money to pay your hospital bills." Alex shook his head with a sigh. "I'll take care of it. Where's Leslie?"

"She went for a walk because the nurse upset her." Willard burrowed under the blankets, shivering. "The people treat her like dirt. She's got a look in her eyes, like you get before you go hunting."

Alex watched the hall uneasily, hoping that Leslie would emerge. She didn't. "Willard," he said, lowering his voice. "Leslie heals sick people for a living. She wouldn't hurt anyone. You know that, don't you?"

The scared, set look on Willard's bandaged face warned that he knew no such thing. "Who are you trying to convince?"

Alex paced around Willard's bed, eyeing the monitors and IV pumps. Hadn't Elliott warned him to expect the unexpected when Leslie completed her change? Tempers ran short at Betsy Ross, and Leslie bore the brunt of her coworkers' caustic tongues. Stress rang the dinner bell for the dragon, and sometimes the dragon turned the meekest person into a monster.

"Willard, get some rest," he said. "I'll find Leslie."

After scanning the hall, Alex hurried to the lobby. Where would Leslie go? The Forrest building? The Tower? Her thoughts no longer offered clues, since she became immortal. Instead, he'd have to think like Leslie.

Leslie yielded to her dragon, he decided, glancing at the grandfather clock. Who became her first? Certainly not a patient. Leslie carried tons of emotional baggage over people who'd died before their expected time. More likely, she went after a nurse or coworker. Perhaps she visited a patient floor to see how her new senses reacted to disease and equipment. But first, she'd go to the respiratory department to check the status of her disability pay.

With that thought in mind, he hurried to the elevators. Definitely the elevators, because Leslie seldom used the stairs. The car stopped at the first floor. When the doors creaked open, a honeyed scent called to him. Faint weeping—a woman's voice, and muffled footsteps called to him.

"Leslie?" Alex kept his voice low, opening and shutting doors. "Are you here?"

The sobbing continued, rising in volume. The aroma was strongest around a door bearing the nameplate "Daniel Crawford, RRT." Alex tried its knob. Locked.

"Leslie!" He banged on the door. "What's going on?"

No answer, except her weeping. Maybe Leslie confused his voice with Bill's, although Alex spoke with an accent. Given her panic, she might not notice the difference. He walked the hall back, checking each room, and noticed a cool draft blowing from the conference room.

Someone had left the window open. After lifting out the screen, he poked his head outside. Black rooftop extended across the adjoining building, ending at Crawford's office window. He wriggled through the opening and tiptoed across the roof. Using a penknife, he cut the screen and climbed into Crawford's private bathroom.

Craning his neck, he saw Leslie bending over two black-soled feet jutting from behind a mahogany desk. Crawford's feet. With his bushy eyebrows, lustrous, brown hair, and chalky, angular face, he looked like Kenworthy. The resemblance sent an alarm racing through Alex's spine, spreading to his nerve endings. Though he hadn't seen Kenworthy for over seventy years, Alex recalled his face as if he'd seen it yesterday.

Blood trickled from two puncture wounds on Crawford's neck, staining his shirt collar and blazer. His gray eyes looked glassy, like someone who'd overdosed on coca. His heart beat erratically, punctuated by Leslie's anguished sobs. Alex recalled Delia's first feed, when she turned on him in anger. Would Leslie hate him, too?

"Leslie," he began in a tremulous voice. "It's only me. I'm going to make everything all right."

Slowly, very tentatively, Leslie lifted her head. Blood dripping from her mouth congealed on her chin. Her pink silk blouse looked new, but something had torn it at the left shoulder. Her face had a spooked look. "You can't," she said. "Crawford's dead."

"Creeps like him don't die easily. Clear your head and listen for his heartbeat." Careful to avoid unexpected movement, Alex knelt by her side. "Hear it?"

Leslie nodded. "He needs a doctor. Will you help me move him to the emergency room?" Her voice heaved with silent weeping. "Please?"

Squatting, Alex laid his hands across Crawford's forehead and wrist. His skin was pale and clammy, but he had a good, strong pulse.

Hushed voices caught Alex's attention. Footsteps from the hallway. "Keep your voice low," he said. "I hear someone."

Leslie hiked Crawford's sleeve, exposing his watch. "Aw, shit!" she cried.

"Quiet." Alex gestured to the door.

"It's almost eleven. People are coming for shift report. That takes almost an hour." She gazed at her boss, assessing his condition. "Crawford's going to die."

"Crawford's out cold." Alex nodded, assuring himself. "After your peers leave, we'll take him to his car. In a few hours, he'll wake up with a headache and a score of bruises, and that will be it."

"You're not a doctor," Leslie cried tossing her head. Her thick red curls glimmered in the light. "He may have broken something."

Eyes regarding Leslie, Alex detected softness in her features that revealed grief and shock. The way he handled her now would determine her willingness to embrace her new life.

Getting up, he rushed to the bathroom for paper towels. After soaking them with water, he gently wiped the tears and bloodstains from her face. After pushing two chairs together, he ushered Leslie to one and sat in the other.

"Before I became a vampire, I treated injured soldiers," he said, rubbing her shoulder. To his surprise, she didn't pull away. "I set broken bones, treated stab wounds, whatever had to be done."

Leslie leaned against the chair back and sighed. "I believe it," she said with admiration. "I remember how caring you were with me when I first told you about my problems with work. You listened, really listened without judging. And when I got hurt, you stayed by my bedside. That means a lot. I can't imagine what a bright man like you sees in me."

Alex regarded Leslie, brushing back the hair that fell into her eyes. Her freckled face registered loneliness and nostalgia. "I'm not that brilliant. My knowledge came from reading minds."

"Reading minds?" Leslie sat forward, brushing Alex's hand aside. "Oh, shit, I read Crawford. That's when all hell broke loose."

She pressed her trembling hands over her eyes, as if trying to blot out the memory. "He said some awful things, and then it was like I saw images floating from him. Something about his dad mistreating him. It felt really creepy."

Her voice became fierce with grief, and fresh tears oozed from her eyes. "I blurted out what I saw, and he ordered me to leave. Then this thirst ... craving got into me, and I attacked him. You've turned me into a monster, Alex."

"I wish I had had time to explain immortality before I changed you." Alex gazed at Leslie and saw fear in her eyes. "You remind me of someone I knew long ago. A woman with heart. I love you, Leslie."

"You hardly know me," Leslie said in a quaking voice.

"Your life became an open book, and I soaked up every page, including the part about your learning impediment." Despair weighed inside Alex like lead as he noted Leslie's blank stare, a mixture of horror and surprise. "You must hate me."

"Let me ask you something." A steely note crept into Leslie's voice. "Did this change, or whatever you call it, restore my memories, including the killings and the attack on my coworker Fred?"

"It wasn't me." Loneliness sank through Alex's heart like arrows. He felt a chasm open between them. Already, she'd accused him of turning her into a monster. "I've bled dying soldiers, but I never assaulted anyone. Thirst for blood comes with this territory."

"Fred's attacker was husky like Crawford, but I never got a look at his face." The sharpness in Leslie's voice faded, but the sadness remained. "Maybe I can bleed animals. I've watched some vampires do it on television."

"In the real world, humans have certain enzymes that our bodies need, something that animals lack. I'm sorry that you found this out the hard way."

Alex cradled Leslie's face against his chest. The fact that she hadn't called him names offered hope, but he could not indulge in illusions. Maybe she was humoring him the way she'd humored Crawford during his tongue-lashings. "You're still the same caring person, with much love to give. Look at the way you saved Willard."

"Helping Willard meant the world to me." Leslie stood up and paced around the room. Her eyes regarded Crawford with an icy contempt. "When we got here, the sounds and smells jumped at me as if they were happening inside my own body. I wondered if my new powers could save lives. After Willard settled in, I played with the respiratory equipment to see how my altered senses would affect my job performance."

A dark look crossed her eyes. "The results seemed promising, so I asked Crawford about working the night shift. This abomination just happened."

Tears misted in Alex's eyes, blurring his surroundings. "I understand," he said. "I've lived this way for almost a century."

Leslie favored him with a subtle glance, and then her voice softened. "Maybe you did give me a way to work around my meager skills. But you've tied us together for an eternity. Why, Alex? We came from two different worlds."

Alex crossed the room and laid his hands on her shoulders. "I had no other means of saving you."

"I know that. Maybe I'm asking why I had the car accident and why Drusilla attacked me. God must be punishing me, that's why."

Alex gulped, tightening his clasped hands. "What god?"

"My religion only acknowledges one God." Leslie began pacing again, refusing to meet his eye, her black shoes clicking against the floor. "My negligence caused my mom's death. Her emphysema got worse, but I didn't push Dr. Saunders into seeing about a lung transplant. I failed to keep narcotics out of her reach. Warren and I found her dead, with an empty bottle of sleeping pills beside her." Her voice choked. "We tried to hide the pills, but one bottle, enough to kill Mom, made it into her room."

Alex's fingers folded into his palms, and his hands rested against his forehead. He pictured a well-dressed man blaming Leslie for her accident; the image had haunted him since his search for her. "Who called you negligent?"

"Gerry, my oldest brother." Leslie paused by the door, cocked her ear, then met Alex's gaze. "He should know because he is a prominent lawyer. He became my judge, jury, and executioner after Mom died."

"He had no right." Alex folded Leslie into his arms and kissed her forehead, her cheeks, and her shoulders. He longed to kiss away her pain. "Maybe your mother knew the end was coming, and she didn't want to prolong the agony."

"I let her down. That was worse than any mistake I made, even worse than my attack on Crawford." Her shoulders shook and the tears started running again. "Mom fought my battles in school, loved me unconditionally. She'd forgive my Apticom test scores."

An angle, Alex thought; *that is what I'll need to encourage Leslie's acceptance of her new life.* "Let's suppose you were talking to Mom now. What do you think she'd say to you?"

"That I'm being too hard on myself. She might not understand my bodily changes, but she'd want to protect me. But she was the one who needed protecting." Leslie gazed up at Alex, her tears glistening in the light. "When you read my thoughts, did you get the part about Dad giving Mom a black eye? Warren never forgave Dad for that."

Hands pressed against Alex's chest, she looked into his eyes. "I've forgiven Dad, but I've lost my heroine. I worked in an office before Mom died. Her death created a domino effect—my training in respiratory care and its complications, the fights with Gerry, the accident, and finally, Drusilla's attack."

"You don't know that." The strained look on Leslie's face mirrored the loneliness that had troubled Alex since his own change. "We have more in common than you think."

"Yeah, right." Leslie pulled away and stared at Crawford, as if she expected to find revelations. "Vampires can read mortals, so you read me."

Stepping behind Leslie, Alex wrapped his arms around her silk-sleeved shoulders and rested his face in her soft curls. "My lover Elizabeth drowned herself in the river when she thought I died in the war." He paused a moment, debating whether to tell her about Delia, then thought better of it. "Her body washed up on the Adrian shore."

"Oh." Leslie let out a small gasp.

"Losing someone to suicide isn't an easy pain. It doesn't get hard like a scab and go away so you can heal." Alex gave a bone-weary sigh. "Deep down, it makes a home, where it stays forever. Sometimes it's so soft and quiet you hardly know it is there. Next thing you know, it lays you back on your butt. Sometimes you wake up, and it's gnawing a hole in your heart."

Alex traced his finger along her cheek. "I won't insult you by saying that this makes what I did to you right. But I understand your loss. If you let me, I'll help you work through the pain."

Leslie stepped away and listened against the door. "My coworkers are finishing their reports. That's good." She looked Alex in the eye. "I wanted to confide in you before the accident. But people, including Gerry, said cruel things about my grades, and I didn't think you'd understand."

Leslie paused by a bookcase. She pulled out a text, glanced at it, then returned it to the shelf. "Dr. Saunders treated my mom. Did you know that?"

Alex nodded. "He told me that you trained in respiratory therapy after she died."

"I barely squeaked through clinical training. My counselor recommended that I change majors, but I wanted to help people like my mom. I thought that their blood tests or x-rays would contain special information that would help me make right decisions, in spite of my Apticom scores."

Leslie looked at Alex, her face sick with grief. "Instead, I made one mistake after another. Crawford never allowed tutoring. He lied about giving me a second chance. I was hoping to get my job back, but I blew my chances by attacking him. If he survives, he'll go to the police."

"You can convince Crawford to forget this attack ever happened by hypnotizing him," Alex said. "I'll show you how to feed without causing too much trauma. As for working, forget it. You need time to adjust to your new body."

"How will I pay my rent?" Leslie fretted, wringing her hands. "I owe fifteen thousand in school loans. *Undeath* doesn't exempt me from paying bills."

"You're right, it doesn't." Alex looked down at Leslie. "You'll stay at my house. My basement has a room that's shielded from sunlight. When we get home, I'll write a check for those school loans."

He pulled Leslie into his arms, pressing her hips against his groin. He planted a kiss on her lips, brief and intense. "I love you. Maybe ..."

"Alex, don't," Leslie cried, pushing him away. "I appreciate your kindness, but I can't love you the way you want. I'm afraid to love anyone because I don't know what to expect from my new body."

Her eyes fell toward Crawford. Crawford shifted on the floor and groaned.

"Part of me still thinks that I'm hallucinating. Another part loathes what I've become, and still another hopes I can use my powers to heal people and fight Drusilla. But mostly ..." Her voice saddened. "I feel like I did after my job orientation, when Crawford turned me loose in the ICU, expecting me to know all the new equipment. I need time to process everything."

"I'll give you as much time as you need." Alex knelt by Crawford again, but kept his eyes on Leslie. "I know how frightening the change can be, but please don't make hasty judgments."

"In other words, don't commit suicide." The words rolled off Leslie's tongue, smooth as oil. "I've used that don't-do-anything-hasty line on Mom many times. I'd never put my family through another suicide. If you find me dead, it's because someone killed me."

Like Hades. Alex shuddered. He wouldn't tell her about Hades just yet.

Crawford struggled to a sitting position. He rubbed his head. "Holy ..." He gazed at Leslie and Alex. "Why are you people here?"

Alex's eyes burned into Crawford's. "We're taking you to your car. You'll forget everything that happened here tonight."

"Happened ... where?" Crawford jerked his thumb toward Leslie. He mustered his administrator's voice, but a whine crept in with his arrogance. "That bitch tried to kill me."

164

"Relax." Lifting Crawford by the armpits, Alex prodded him to his feet. "You'd be surprised at how much punishment the body can take."

"Right." Crawford wagged his head. A glazed look clouded his gray eyes. "What am I saying? I should call Security."

"You'll do no such thing." Alex nudged him to the door. "When we get you to your car, you'll take a nap. Understand?"

Crawford's head bobbed, as if pulled by a puppet string. After glancing down the hall, Alex guided him to the elevators, with Leslie trailing at the rear.

****

"We've got a long walk through the tunnel," Leslie said when they reached the basement. "I'll get a wheelchair for Crawford."

"Crawford's a big boy. He can walk." Alex nudged Crawford in the ribs. "Isn't that right, Sir?"

Crawford wagged his head again and said nothing.

Alex focused toward the garage entrance, trying hard not to notice the blood on Crawford's clothes or his syrupy smell. Still, the thirst gnawed away at him. Hand grabbing Crawford's shoulder, Alex nudged him toward the glass doors.

"Wait a minute." Leslie tiptoed into the garage, then back into the hall. "The coast is clear. But someone will notice Crawford's scratches and the blood."

"Good point." Alex paused in mid-step and eyeballed Crawford, probing the recesses of his mind. "I get the feeling that Crawford antagonizes people."

Turning Crawford around, Alex stared into his eyes. "When you wake, Sir, you'll remember that you got into an argument with a patient, who then assaulted you with broken glass. You won't talk about it for fear of causing a scandal."

"I got into an argument," Crawford mumbled. "My patient ..."

165

"Move it." Alex gave Crawford another shove. "After you catch your nap, you can drive home."

Crawford grunted and staggered to his car. After sliding into his seat, he rolled to the side and passed out. Leslie watched Crawford a moment, then closed the door behind him. She followed Alex toward the street gate.

"The bats trashed your house," she said. "Did you see that?"

Alex patted her hand. "Don't worry about them."

"Don't tell me not to worry." Impatience crept into her voice. "They singled out your home."

Alex heaved an airless sigh. The fierceness in Leslie's eyes warned that she intended to dig until she uncovered the truth.

Leslie traced her finger along her lips. "Do many immortals live in Adria?"

"A few."

"Drusilla said that Hades judges the dead and sends the bad to this place called Tartarus," she persisted, "and that his bats spy on people like us. Did Hades send his bats to get us?"

"Let's forget Hades." Pulling Leslie close, Alex gazed at the moonlit sky. "Look at those stars. They shine like precious jewels. We can walk home and make it by sunrise."

"Good idea." Leslie lifted her fine eyebrows, giving him a wary look. "Now you can level with me. Something bad happened in Adria that may affect us, something that has to do with those bats."

"Let it go," Alex protested, though he felt himself weaken. "Don't look for dragons that don't exist."

"Willard warned me about the dragons," Leslie said. "He said that Hades hates vampires because they don't die, and that he sent those bats as a warning. Will Hades try to destroy us?"

Chapter 17

Leslie watched Alex's face, gauging his emotions as they glided, swift as beams of light, by the battered tenements. His green eyes became pools of silent tears. His face, white as an ice slab, spelled an infinite sadness.

"Alex, think," she said. "If Hades wants to destroy us, your keeping it secret won't stop him."

"Willard had it right." Alex's voice was a ghostly sigh. "My friend Elliott laid out the situation for me the night after I found you."

He's not a monster, Leslie decided, gazing at the star-studded sky. Not this sweet, caring man who didn't judge her by intellect. Falling in love with him could be so easy. But the memories of Tom shuddered through her mind. Tom used a gentle approach, too. When her learning deficit revealed itself, the temperature in her relationship with Tom cooled to freezing levels.

Suppose Alex made demands of his own that she couldn't meet? Demands aside, she understood little about her new body. What if the stress of lovemaking provoked her into killing someone?

Laying his arm across her slim shoulders, Alex drew her close. His sweet aroma told her that he'd fed some time before coming to the hospital. She lowered her eyes, not caring to look at the stains on his teeth.

"How much blood ..." Leslie snapped her mouth shut, trembling.

"Whatever satisfies your thirst." Alex rolled his tongue across his lips. "Never drink from a dead person. Blood from a corpse poisons our systems. It causes a slow, painful death."

Leslie shivered at her fear. "So your god wants us dead, sunlight will roast us, and tainted blood will kill us. Thanks for sharing, Alex."

"I'm not trying to scare you," Alex pleaded for reassurance. "Anyone could die when you're feeding on them. Back off when their heartbeat stops."

Leslie pulled away and faced Alex, eyebrows creased in a deep frown. "Don't ever use that word around me again."

Alex flinched, as if though she'd slapped him. "What word?"

"Die." Leslie gave him a hard, bleak stare. Her eyes became bleary with tears. "Nobody dies by my hands. Get it? NOBODY DIES!" Her shouts built in crescendo, trembling as the agony that had simmered inside released itself.

Her pace slowed, and Leslie noticed people in ragged clothes sitting on doorsteps. They stared at her and Alex with vacuous eyes. She tried to lower her voice, but the lump rising in her throat threatened to choke her. "I'll never eat supper with my dad again. Do you understand that? My mother must be turning over in her grave."

Alex's eyes misted with sadness. "What would you have had me do? You yourself said that your death would devastate your family."

"That's true." Leslie pressed her palms against her mouth, trying to still her quivering. "But this change took a lot from me. I already missed Easter. I can't go to Shelly's Memorial Day picnic or celebrate Warren's birthday in June. No more sunbathing or afternoon strolls in the park. You understand me?"

"Go ahead, say it," Alex blurted, fear and frustration edging into his voice. "You wish I'd let you die. I turned you into a monster, and now you hate me."

"No, Alex, you were practicing damage control. I hate Drusilla for forcing you into that position." Leslie thought about Willard and Drusilla, and the way they talked about Hades. Deity or no, Hades held power over the vampires. Something made him angry enough to send the bats to Alex's home. Angry enough to kill.

Whatever possessed her to run into the woods with a stitched-up head and busted ribs? It was like she'd opened the gates of Tartarus right there in Meadowood. "Damn Gerry!" she cried. "He started this by blaming me for Mom's death. I didn't make Mom swallow those pills."

They walked on in silence. Moments later, they headed down Sunset Lane, sheltered by the woods. Leslie listened to the squishing sounds as her feet sank into moss and grass.

"Maybe Gerry blames himself, too," Alex said at last. "You need time to grieve your humanity. The things you've endured ... your mother's suicide, the fights with Crawford and his staff ... are especially painful."

Leslie mulled this over, gazing at the sky's glowing field of stars. She couldn't help admiring their beauty, but beyond their glitter lay the unspeakable—Adria and its angry god. "I'm tired of having to watch my back," she said, looking up at Alex. "I think I can deal if my new body lets me do the things that make me happy. That means looking after patients and visiting my family."

"Visiting people or working shouldn't be a problem." Alex rubbed her shoulder, quieting her shivers. "But I can't let you do that now. If Drusilla finds out you survived, she may try to use your father or a patient as leverage."

Leslie nodded, dragging her fingers through her tangled curls. Drusilla had studied her at the cave, she recalled, reading minute details such as Dad's address. "What happens when she goes back to the cave and finds my body missing?"

"I don't know, but she won't find you at my house. Neither will Kenworthy. He thinks I'm dead."

"Why?"

"Twenty years ago I faked my death and moved here under my present name. If Kenworthy found out, he'd go after me in a heartbeat." Alex's voice faded, and for a moment, Leslie saw a tired, broken man cringing behind his brilliant eyes. "What can I say about Hades that you haven't already figured out for yourself?"

"I don't know." Leslie fell silent. Moments later, they came upon his house. Glass shards jutted from the window casements, glittering in the moonlight. The memories of the trashed living room sent cold tentacles shivering through her brain. She hugged herself, trembling at the doorway.

"We can't stay here," she said. "Hades will come looking for us."

Alex sighed. "If Hades wants to find us, he will."

"Not if we move, right?" Leslie persisted. "We could hide out in a different hotel every day."

"Leslie." The oily brightness of his eyes met hers squarely. "Our home guarantees protection that you won't find in any hotel. It's got secret passages and panels to block out the sun and discourage nosy people."

His voice softened and he pulled her close. "Elliott said that we may still have some time before Hades strikes."

"How much? A week? A year?"

"I don't know." Alex gazed at the rose-streaked sky. "If we don't go inside soon, the sun will fry us. This house won't protect us from Hades, but it's the best that we've got. Now will you come with me?"

"All right." Leslie trailed Alex to the basement, fingers pinching her nose shut, and feet dodging the bat droppings. At the hidden door, she watched Alex tug on the candlestick. She followed him into his chamber.

"We'll have to share," Alex said, climbing into the spindle bed. "I won't do anything that you don't want."

After fishing a blue nightgown from a trash bag, Leslie changed behind the metal door. She slipped under the spread beside him.

"Tomorrow night, I will show you how to hunt," he told her.

"Hunt?" A sob escaped Leslie's throat.

"Don't cry." Alex's hand stroked her shoulder. "Feeding grows on you. In time, you'll form your own personal communion with whoever provides the nourishment."

"Is that right?" Leslie snapped.

But Alex had already dropped off to sleep, one arm wrapped around her.

****

During the next few days, Alex replaced the furniture and windows, while Leslie scrubbed the floors. In between, he walked her through *Undeath* 101, teaching her how to hypnotize and touch minds, and how to lure potential providers of nourishment. Leslie went through the motions, but her heart ached for her family. She longed to visit Dad and care for her patients, instead of stalking people for blood. The grief nesting inside her spoke in a faint whisper until something small triggered it into a roar. Leslie made a point to avoid TV shows that centered on food and family gatherings.

Willard came home a week after his attack, face and arms covered with bandages. Changing his dressings and helping with his day-to-day care took the sting out of her grief. The prospects of going back to work motivated her to pay attention to Alex's instructions regarding her new powers.

About two weeks after her change, Leslie lugged her trash bags to a room upstairs with a pewter bed. Its baby blue spread and matching drapes reminded her of her father's house. Leaving the door ajar, she dumped the bags contents on the floor.

Her stethoscope lay in a mound of lab coats, pink scrub pants, and floral tops. Tom had her initials engraved into its bell before giving it to her as a graduation present. He'd paid a small fortune for her stethoscope and uniforms before things went sour. Putting the stethoscope to her ears, she moved it around her chest, but she only heard silence.

"Phooey," she muttered, tossing it into a trash can. "It's a piece of shit."

"People like us don't have heartbeats," Alex called from the stairway. Stepping into the room and over the clothing piles, he retrieved the stethoscope. "It looks expensive."

Leslie shook her head. "I don't want it."

Advancing toward Leslie, Alex cradled her shoulders in his arms. "Does it remind you of something at work?"

"No, it reminds me of some jerk I used to know." Leslie leaned her head against his silk-clad chest and watched the moon shadows danced across on the floor. "I'd like to go back to work. Crawford always needs people for the night shift."

"What?" Alex cried, stepping back. Blood from an earlier feed rushed to his cheeks. "I thought we agreed it wasn't safe for you to work."

"Drusilla won't know anything if I use an assumed name, the way you did to avoid Kenworthy."

"Do you realize what you're saying?" Alex's voice rose a notch with each word. "Your coworkers will call you by your real name. They despise you, and stress will aggravate your bloodlust."

Leslie averted her gaze, smarting from his rebuke. Why let her new powers go to waste, especially if they compensated for her learning deficit? "Feeding on those barracudas would upset me less than chasing after some innocent guy on the street. My coworkers would provide healthy ..."

"No, no," Alex cried, waving his hands. "You don't stalk your neighbors or coworkers. Why work at a dive like Betsy Ross? My investments alone earn more than enough money to keep us comfortable."

Tom had promised comfort, too, Leslie remembered ... a mansion and designer clothes. Those comforts came at a price that she couldn't pay. "I want to give respiratory therapy one last try," she said. "Drusilla used her powers to destroy. I want to use mine to preserve life."

"If Drusilla thinks you escaped, she'll look for you at the hospital." Alex's voice became a cold shiver in the night. "You'll need a good disguise to preserve your anonymity. Is that what you want?"

"I don't know." Leslie stared out the window, arms folded across her chest. "If Hades sees me use my powers to help people, he'll leave us alone." Her voice faltered. "Maybe he'll just leave us alone."

"One good deed won't impress Hades." Alex's voice softened, conceding compromise. "If you think it will work, go ahead, but use your real name. Since Willard's still feeling badly, we'll take a cab to the hospital."

"We don't need a cab." Leslie wagged her white forefinger. "I've got a driver's license, remember?"

Alex's angular face turned gray. "You're not driving. Our eyes can't take the glare from the oncoming cars."

"Bright light bothered my eyes after the car accident," Leslie said. "Before I assumed my present condition. I've got sunglasses."

Alex frowned. "I said that we're taking a cab."

Leslie shook her head and sighed. She also wanted to visit her father, but announcing her intentions would push Alex too far, and the resulting argument might aggravate her thirst.

"Let me use the sunglasses," she managed in a bleating voice. "Trying new things will help me understand my body."

"I bet they will," Alex mumbled. "OK, if it will make you feel better, you can drive."

****

The following Monday, Leslie got behind the wheel for the first time since she became a vampire. She drove Alex to the hospital. The moonlight flooded her surroundings with a pearly mist, broken only by the blacktop road.

Light pulsed from the head and taillights, but her sunglasses took the edge off their glare. Columns of trees rose up like shadowy stalagmites, bearing corpse candles at the end of each glowing twig. The swirling mist of light illuminated street signs and buildings miles away. Night had never looked so beautiful.

At the hospital, Alex climbed out of the car, hugging his leather briefcase. Leslie knew that he'd made appointments with Saunders and others at the hospital. "Alex," she said, smiling, "go have your powwow with your clients. I can talk to Crawford alone."

Alex set down his briefcase and gave her a censoring glare. "You've got this look that I don't like. What are you up to?"

Leslie cleared her throat. "I'm feeling rather thirsty. I was hoping to do something about it before meeting Crawford."

"Why didn't you say so?" The frost faded from his voice. He smiled. "Take all the time you need. I'll catch a cab home."

Leslie stopped in the ladies' room to check her make-up. She'd worn a white linen dress. Her mom had once said that wearing white made a good impression. Not that it mattered now.

At the office, Leslie felt machine-cooled air blast against her face. Crawford sat at his desk, head bent, hunched over a file. *Targeting the next scapegoat,* she thought, fists tightening around her purse.

"Mr. Crawford," she called. "May I come in?"

Crawford lifted his face. His skin had regained its ruddy appearance. Already, she heard his strong, steady heartbeat, the rush of blood calling to her. "Hello, Leslie," he said, smiling. "I see you're not limping anymore."

Leslie watched her boss, fearing that any minute he'd recall their last meeting and bellow for Security. But no sign of recollection crossed his face. Her eyes drilled into Crawford's, turning them to silver glaze.

His face broke into a crooked smile. "You look great," he murmured. "What can I do for you?"

After closing the door behind her, Leslie proceeded to his desk. "I heard that you need help on the night shift," she said, smiling. "Dr. O'Toole said that I can work part time."

"He said that?" Crawford arched his brows, but his eyes maintained their glassy look. "Can you give me a note?"

"Sure. Any time." Leslie smiled, knowing that she'd leave with something else besides a job. Crawford never raised his voice, not even when she unbuttoned his shirt collar.

The April air felt crisp against Leslie's cheeks as she walked toward the car, whistling to herself. She'd gotten a second chance. Let her skills fall where they may. She promised herself to quit if she saw anything like her previous failures.

About forty minutes later, she rode up Johnstown Avenue, her father's street. She drove with the windows open, savoring the floral and grassy scents. As she approached her father's home, a fetid, wet smell greeted her, the stink of things long dead, exploded by the gases of their own decay.

"Uh, oh," Leslie groaned. If she were human, she'd drive straight to a police station. Drusilla lived nearby, and she imagined the look on Drusilla's face when an officer came knocking on her door.

Don't involve the police, her mind screamed. *They'll get killed.*

Maybe, maybe not. Before telling anyone, she needed proof that Drusilla committed the murders. Maybe Drusilla kept scrapbooks or souvenirs from her victims. Alex said that some vampires did that. Once she found her evidence, she'd convince Warren and the officers to protect themselves. Hypnotize them, if necessary.

After glancing right and left, Leslie crept through a path, following the odor. She stepped over broken branches and twigs. Thorns snagged her shoulder, tearing her sleeves. Faint humming called to her, leading to what used to be an old well.

Squatting on her knees, she gazed into the well. Flies and beetles inside made the humming sound. They were swarming, forming a dark cloud over a woman who appeared dead—many days dead. Breaks in the cloud revealed blisters that wept greenish pus on her clothes. Maggots covered her eyes and streaked her face white. One hand lay stretched above her head, as if she were giving a blessing.

"Ugh!" Leslie grimaced. Of course, Drusilla had killed the woman. Killed and relished the act. Squinting hard, she saw something shiny and pointed in the dirt.

Whatever it is, I can't look. I can't go down there. As a human, she'd never dared to climb anything steeper than a stepladder. Yet there she was, kicking off her shoes and scrambling down the well, hands clawing the dirt and rocks. Climbing became as easy as taking a stroll.

Using a handkerchief, she grasped the shiny object. It was a knife. The foot-long blade was coated with dried blood. The initial "M" was engraved on its silvery white handle. Why would Drusilla use a knife?

Because Drusilla's cravings went beyond appeasing thirst. Drusilla became a sponge saturated with her victim's blood, gotten through pain and torture. Perhaps she'd taken drugs before her change, something that had warped her brain. *undeath* added to the destruction.

"Drusilla, I hope you rot in hell," she whispered.

After wrapping the knife in her hanky, she scrambled up the well and sprinted back to her car. It was time she leveled with Warren.

****

Leslie crept up her father's sidewalk, hoping that no one noticed her. She tried the door. It was locked, and she'd lost her keys during the accident. She didn't want to knock and startle her family, at least not yet. Instead, she pried open a screen and wriggled inside.

Gurgling respirations issued from the den. It was her father's labored breathing. Moonlight shone through curtained windows, dancing silvery shadows on the furniture. The smell of rotting tomatoes drifted from the kitchen. Moldy fruit. She grimaced at the dishes littering the sink, the food-crusted linoleum, and dirty shirts on the chairs.

While inspecting her surroundings, she mentally rehearsed what she'd say to her father and brother. At the stove, she happened upon a gallon-sized pot caked with tomato sauce. Maybe soaking it in hot water would dissipate its odor. With trembling fingers, she reached for its handle. The pot slid and clattered to the floor.

"Son of a bitch!" her father's slurred voice bellowed. "Who's making that noise?"

Moments later, light flooded the room, and her father stood at the doorway clad in his plaid robe. Wrinkled hands gripping his walker, he hobbled into the kitchen. His creased face turned ashen. His lips trembled as he struggled to get the words out. "Leslie, what ..."

"Daddy, I'm OK." Leslie hugged him gingerly, fearful that her strength would crush him. She held him away from her, gazing at the shadows circling his eyes. His pajamas swam around his bony frame. "You'd better sit."

"Warren said that you got into trouble," her father said in a thick voice. His shaking hands grasped hers. "Mother of God! You feel like a dead person."

"Thanks a lot, Dad," Leslie said, giving a soft chuckle. "You really know how to make me feel good. Where's Warren?"

"Upstairs, asleep." Her father hobbled to the stairwell. "Warren, wake up!"

No answer, except rustling bedsprings.

"Warren!" Her father thumped on the banister. "Get up!"

Silence followed a moment, and then a door upstairs banged open, followed by thumping footsteps on the stairs.

"Fucking aggravation," Warren muttered. "What's wrong with you, old—" His voice cut short as he met Leslie's gaze. "Holy shit!"

"Pretty soon, you'll wish you had holy water, too," Leslie said.

"It's not funny, Leslie," Warren said.

"Who's laughing?" Leslie asked, looking at her father. "Dad, you look sick."

"I feel awful," her father blurted. "I can't ..."

"He's got an upper respiratory infection," Warren cut in. He hitched up his wrinkled pajamas and rubbed his eyes. "We'd better take this outside, Leslie."

"OK. Dad, take care of yourself." Leslie followed Warren to the porch. "Where's Shelly and Gerry?"

"Gerry went back to New York, and Shelly's working." Warren stumbled outside and flopped into a lounge chair. His lips quivered. "The police are still looking for that killer. You shouldn't go out alone."

"The killer can't hurt me now." Digging into her purse, Leslie handed Warren the handkerchief-wrapped knife. "Take this to the police. I found it with another body."

Taking the knife between his thumb and forefinger, Warren got up and held it under a street lamp. "Where did you find this?"

"I smelled something funny in the woods. The killer dumped a body into a well about a mile down your street." Leslie paced up and down the slate walk, gazing at the azaleas. "I think it may be the same killer who attacked me. Her name's Drusilla."

Warren edged along the bushes, pointing his unsteady finger in her direction. "You ruined a good dress. Why, you look like a ghost. What happened?"

"It's hard to explain." Leslie leaned against the flagstone wall and regarded her brother. "Let me put it to you this way. I can smell what you ate for dinner. Beans and chili. Last night, Dad gave you hell about the friends you keep bringing home. Today, your boss yelled at you."

"What?" Perspiration glittered on Warren's chalky face. His voice wavered. "Since when did you become a mind reader?"

"Since Drusilla ..." Leslie's voice cracked. She tightened her clasped hands, dreading her brother's reaction. "Just tell me if I'm right."

"Yeah." Warren sighed and wiped his forehead. "According to Dad, I've turned his home into a cathouse. My editor's tired of hearing about dogs biting people. He wants a story about a person biting the dog. How did you know?"

"I can read people right down to the last time they went to the bathroom. For example, Gerry, who thinks his shit doesn't stink, but his farts give him away, drinks tequila for breakfast. Next time he visits, go check his suitcase. He keeps his booze stashed there."

"Hot damn!" Warren shouted. "Did I step into the Twilight Zone?"

"Maybe. I am still your sister Leslie, with the hopes, dreams, and baggage that came with my territory. But I've had to make major lifestyle changes."

"Such as what?"

"Altered senses, aversion to sunlight, and the need for ... how can I make you understand something I don't?" Leslie shifted her gaze toward the azaleas. "I'd better say it straight so you can protect Dad. Drusilla's a vampire, and ... and so am I."

"Is this supposed to be a joke?" Warren snorted.

"No." Voice shaking with sobs, Leslie described Drusilla's attack and her change. "Only sunlight and fire can destroy Drusilla. Look, I'll take the knife to the police, but I'm making sure they know the score. I'll hypnotize them, if necessary."

"Hypnotize who? Come on, Leslie, you're imagining things." Warren nodded, reassuring himself.

"Then how can you explain my instant recovery? My ability to read your mind?" Leslie's eyes, drenched with tears, met Warren's. "Now you know why I haven't called. The thing was, I only had one other option: death. You know what that would've done to Dad."

"Dad took your disappearance pretty bad." Warren smiled, striding toward Leslie. "Let me see your teeth. I'll prove that you're hallucinating. Come on, open your mouth."

"No," Leslie cried, backing away. "You won't like it."

"Only a look," Warren pleaded, as if he were humoring a child.

Leaning back against the flagstone bricks, Leslie parted her lips.

"Oh, my God!" Warren's eyes bulged like saucers. The self-assured reporter disappeared, replaced by a vulnerable young man afraid for his baby sister. "Who did this to you?"

"I told you, Drusilla," Leslie blurted, her voice tired and dusty. "She lives in this flagstone house surrounded by cement posts, right there in your woods."

"That monster!" Warren's shoulders shook. His gray eyes assumed a vacant look. Something inside Leslie shuddered at the sight of them. Once he'd gotten over the shock, he'd run to the woods and maybe get himself killed. "I blame Gerry. This happened because that pompous ass sent you running to the woods."

"Warren ..." Leslie's chest tightened as she strained to get the words out. "Something good came from this. My powers may help me with patient care. I also got my memory back. The night of the accident, I made a mistake that hurt someone very badly. This condition gave me a chance to set things right."

"It doesn't matter, you're still my sister." Warren's watery eyes radiated a mixture of fear, love, and anger. "I can't pretend to understand your condition, but I'd like to try. After the police catch this bitch, we'll go to Dr. Saunders. Maybe he can undo what happened."

"Saunders can't help me," Leslie shouted, raising her voice above his sobs. "We're talking the supernatural here. I'll handle the police. Just make sure you and Dad carry a lighter, something to frighten Drusilla. And for God's sake, keep this out of the papers."

"I will," Warren managed in a lifeless voice. "No one would believe me anyway."

Chapter 18

Drusilla glanced toward the door as she stood before the bedroom mirror. She wore a navy silk gown with spaghetti straps and a plunging neckline. Ken's favorite dress. Yet, something felt wrong.

"Drusilla," Ken bellowed from the living room. "Have you seen my knife?"

The sound of stomping boots over plush carpet followed. Ken wore them with his navy tunic and trousers, the same garments the soldiers had worn when they chased Drusilla through the market. She shuddered.

"Drusilla, answer me," he shouted.

Drusilla haltingly descended the stairs, her red curls swirling behind her. "What knife?" she asked in a small voice.

"My good platinum knife. My father carved his last initial on its handle." Ken rooted through his roll-top desk, yanking out its drawers and emptying their contents on the floor. "Son of Hades! Someone went through my things."

Drusilla covered her mouth, stifling a giggle. The night she'd stalked Claire replayed itself, pushing aside her fear. Watching the blood gush from Claire's throat had been fun.

"You think this is funny?" Ken kicked at the drawers. "My father used that knife during his coup against the Lyonessiens. It's all I have left of him."

"Oh." Drusilla's smile wilted, crushed by pangs of grief and loneliness. She'd longed for mementoes of her

182

family, but what little her parents gave her had been stolen. "I'm sorry."

"Watch yourself when you feed. Whoever's snooping through my drawers may find something suspicious." Ken shook his head. "If I catch that scoundrel, he'll be sorry."

Drusilla stared at his glittering eyes. "I saw your knife upstairs," she said. The lie came as easily as feeding.

"Upstairs?" Ken stepped back, utter contempt in his pose. "Why would I leave it there?"

"I'm not sure." Drusilla tried to force cheerfulness, but a high-pitched whine crept into her voice. "I think you were going to chase down the bats."

"I don't recall using the knife. How could I be so careless?" The ice melted from Ken's voice, and he let out a despairing moan. "At least, some stranger didn't get it."

Drusilla licked her lips. Though she'd fed earlier, Ken's tirade nudged her thirst into a bull roar. "Let's find some dinner. It will help you feel better."

"You've got that right." Ken's teeth shone in a savage grin. "Nothing soothes like the nectar of the gods."

Rapping sounded from the front porch. Probably someone trying to sell magazines. Definitely her next meal. Drusilla hurried to the door.

Two men in blue uniforms strode into the living room. One, short and stout, with a ruddy complexion and dark gray hair. The other, tall and stringy, with a mop of dark curls surrounding his mocha-complexioned face. With their guns poking from their holsters, they reminded Drusilla of Adria's soldiers.

"Good evening." Short-and-stout smiled a thin-lipped smile that didn't reach his dark eyes. "Are you Drusilla?"

"I'm Kenworthy Mason, her husband," Ken spoke up, his grin spelling naked defiance. "What do you want with her?"

"Police business." Reaching into his pants pocket, short-and-stout produced a wallet bearing his photo. "I'm Lieutenant Chase, and this is Detective John Hannon.

We're here to question your wife regarding two crimes. I'll ask her these questions at the Meadowood State Police Barracks."

Drusilla's eyes dropped toward Chase's fleshy neck. His throbbing vessel called to her, drowning out the sound of his voice.

"You have the right to legal counsel," Chase continued, sticking the wallet back in his pocket. "If you can't afford a lawyer, we'll provide one for you."

"Whoa, there." Ken smiled again, his voice oiled with good cheer. "My wife isn't going anywhere with you."

Detective Hannon cleared his throat. Digging under his shirt collar, he rubbed two scabs on his neck. "We could get a warrant for her arrest, Mr. Mason. With the evidence in our possession, it would be no trouble at all."

He glanced at Chase. "Lieutenant Chase insisted on bringing one. He would've gotten it if we had time to process the paperwork."

Chase shook his head and glared at his partner. Hannon saw the look, shuffled his feet against the rug, but pressed on. "Given the circumstances, I thought you should know."

Another look crossed Chase's reddening face. His heartbeat thumped loud and fast.

"You'd better explain those circumstances," Ken said ominously.

"We want to question Drusilla about the murder of Claire Benson and the attempted murder of Leslie Taite," said Chase.

"Who?" Drusilla gasped.

Ken tapped her shin with his booted foot. "Let me handle them," he whispered.

"Claire Benson and Leslie Taite." Chase's dark eyes narrowed. "Two reliable sources found Benson's remains in a well near Johnstown Avenue. Leslie Taite barely recuperated from brain surgery, when you, Mrs. Mason, proceeded to pulverize her. You're going to tell us those people mean nothing to you?"

"Yes," Drusilla shouted. "We just moved here."

"Is that right?" Chase produced a photo of a blood-covered knife. "Our sources found this weapon near Benson's remains. The one used to slash her throat, according to the autopsy."

"How did it get there?" Ken blurted.

"Does it matter?" Chase asked in a frosty voice. "We heard graphic details about your penchant for bloodshed."

"That's ridiculous." Drusilla looked at Chase's partner fixedly. He stared out the window and shifted his stance. "That knife doesn't even belong to me."

Another jab from Ken's boot followed. He smiled, his voice seemingly open and friendly. "She's right. It belongs to me. Someone broke into my living room drawers and stole the knife."

"Did they now?" Chase's voice oozed with sarcasm. "Leslie Taite claims she was attacked on the evening of April 10, 1995. Do you folks have an alibi?"

"Around eight p.m.," Hannon added, scratching his neck again.

"We have an alibi." Ken's silvery eyes radiated savage exultation. "My wife and I were discussing our portfolio with Roy Jacks, my financial manager. I can arrange for him to call you."

"In other words, lie for you." Chase paced around the room, staring into the corners as if he thought he'd find clues there. "One source claims that vampires attacked Leslie. I told myself that he was crazy, but funny thing..." He looked at Drusilla. "He had it right about your address and description of your home."

He started toward the door. "Come on, Johnny, let's see about getting that warrant. We're getting nowhere here."

Crossing the room in one leap, Drusilla snagged the detective by the shoulders and locked him in a tight grip. She forgot about Ken's warnings to use discretion with victims. She forgot about his order to remain quiet. She forgot about everything except the thirst which raged like a burning fire.

But the crack of Chase's pistol, drilling a bullet through the plaster, brought her back to reality. Ken lunged at Chase, angling for his throat. Chase's gun sailed across the room and clattered behind a radiator.

Wriggling under her grasp, Hannon flicked open a lighter and held the flame to Drusilla's face. "Warren didn't make sense," he whispered, defiant stubbornness in his eyes. "But Leslie was right when she read me the bill of goods."

Drusilla skittered backwards, releasing her grip. John flung the lighter at her and bolted for the door.

Bright tendrils of flame licked her dress's silky folds. Drusilla rolled on the floor, howling as searing pain climbed up her thigh. Had John aimed higher, the lighter would have hit bare skin. By the time she smothered the fire, Ken was disposing of Chase's body.

Scrambling to her feet, Drusilla raced outside. Where was Hannon? Probably somewhere in the woods. She picked up his scent from the trail and heard his shrieks for help. He ran like a hunted rabbit, but it only took minutes for her to catch up with him. She swung into his side, and pinned him against a tree stump.

"You should mind your own business," she said, staring at him raptly. Her teeth raked his throat. She relished the taste of his blood, and his twisting and jerking excited her more.

Moments later, he collapsed like a dead weight, and his heartbeat twittered to a stop. Later, his body would go to the mass grave in Ken's basement.

At home, Ken stormed around the living room, cursing to himself. What sounded like keys scraped against the rug. Eyes meeting Drusilla's gaze, he lifted a menacing fist, brandishing a metal chain. It dangled from his clenched fingers, trailing on the floor behind him. Drusilla remembered seeing one like it in the cave where she'd left Leslie.

"Ken, I eliminated John Hannon, or whatever he calls himself," she managed in a shaky voice. "No one will bother us now."

"No one?" Ken echoed in a deep-throated bellow. "Chase's superiors will expect his report. They'll come sniffing like wolves after their prey, asking about Chase and his partner."

He raised his chain-clad fist. "Sometimes, I use these chains to confine my sources of nourishment until I'm ready to sup. These chains also make great disciplinary tools."

Down the chain swung, biting into Drusilla's shoulders. Incredible pain shot through her spine. Screaming, she scuttled to the hall. "Why did you do that?"

"Because you couldn't keep quiet! I can tolerate foolishness from a fledgling, but I won't forgive disobedience or lies."

The chain tore into Drusilla's back. Hot, salty tears coursed down her cheeks. "What lies?" She sprinted through the library and ducked behind the slate table. "You told me not to deny my thirst."

"I also told you to leave Leslie alone." Ken heaved the table aside. Another swing of the chain slashed Drusilla's face. Something wet dripped into her eyes, blurring her vision. "You had plenty of panhandlers, criminals, people who wouldn't be missed. Instead, you chose Leslie. Worse, you took my knife without permission, my only family heirloom, and then lied about it."

"Leslie summoned those officers, not me," Drusilla told him.

"You expect me to believe that, given her injuries?" Ken cried with stunned surprise. "Leslie understands the concept of family loyalty and discretion, something foreign to you. You'd better pray that she survives."

He chased Drusilla through the hall, lashing out with his chain. Its metal links dug into her back, buttocks, and thighs. She slid on the trail of her own blood.

"Stop!" she pleaded, cringing in a corner like a trapped animal. "I promise to do better."

"Your ears are on your back." Ken smiled. "You only listen after a beating. So listen now, Drusilla, and heed me. If you go near the Taites and their officers again, I'll lock you in my courtyard before the sun rises."

"Don't do that, please ..."

Ken laughed, a raucous laugh sounding like rocks banging together. "You should return to the street and find your own shelter. Perhaps you'd like to sleep in a coffin like some vampires do."

"No!" Drusilla wept a high-pitched spate of sobs.

"No silk-lined casket for you," Ken crooned, his voice rough, yet caressing like a snake's tongue. "You'll share a pine box with someone's remains. The bugs and worms will feed on your bedfellow while you sleep."

"Ken, don't," Drusilla begged, edging toward the hall and its brass stairs. "I won't give you any more trouble."

She scurried up the stairs with Ken at her heels. Another lash of the chain pelted her on the back. Fresh bolts of pain passed through her spine. "One to grow on," he said, grinning. "I'll leave you alone now. When I come home, I'll let you know your sleeping quarters."

Drusilla raced into a bedroom and flopped on the bed, red hair spread over her face. Her fists pounded the mattress. Here she was, starving for love and a real home, while Leslie marshaled an army of supporters, including the officers.

It occurred to her that the detective kept scratching his neck. She had to wonder why. Understanding dawned, and she realized that his scabs were fang marks, and more important, that neither she nor Ken had inflicted his wounds.

Perhaps another vampire foraging for nourishment had stumbled on Leslie in the cave and taken pity on her. Would her wide-eyed innocence move this vampire to bestow her with immortality?

"Only one way to find out." Drusilla concentrated hard on the image of Leslie's face. "Talk to me, Leslie. What are you thinking?"

No thoughts emerged in her head. Drusilla dug and probed, but only saw blankness. Ken had explained to her that vampires could shield their thoughts from each other. Whoever had turned Leslie would wall her some place where Drusilla couldn't get to her.

Drusilla wondered how Leslie would approach hunting. She thought about Adria and how she'd gotten even with her slave bosses by draining them dry. Leslie had taken emotional abuse, as the New World called it, from slave bosses at Betsy Ross Hospital. Would the blood lust tempt her to go after them?

"Do I enjoy feeding?" Drusilla asked herself, laughing.

****

After bathing and changing into a sleeveless, pearl-gray gown, Drusilla helped herself to some cash from the roll-top desk. She called a cab to take her to Betsy Ross. At the hospital, the security officers gave her wary looks. One kept his right hand near his pistol. Another nodded in a chair, his bland face wedged between his jacket's folds. On closer inspection, Drusilla noticed a white bandage on his neck.

So Leslie turned this hospital into her own restaurant! With her new senses, Leslie could spot an enemy miles away. Drusilla tiptoed through the lobby and first floor. No sign of Leslie.

After taking the stairs to the second floor, Drusilla stepped into the children's ward. Women in white uniforms hovered at the desk. One patient, a girl who looked about ten years old, moaned softly. Drusilla gazed at the girl's tangled almond-colored curls, weepy eyes, and cast-clad legs.

Looking at the child's china-doll face, Drusilla saw herself at age ten, unmarked by grief or evil. But the fear lurking in the girl's eyes warned that her fall from innocence had already begun. Something inside Drusilla shuddered at the sight.

Perhaps the girl fell down the stairs. Perhaps Drusilla didn't want to know how she got hurt. The images slithering through her mind said that someone had beaten the girl. Weeping noiselessly, Drusilla fled the ward.

Later, she'd comfort that child and make her realities seem like bad dreams. First, she had scores to settle. She crept up the stairs to the third floor. After closing the door behind her, she heard groaning from the left hall—an older woman's cries.

"I'm sorry you need the operation," she heard Leslie's gentle voice say. "Dr. Saunders will refer you to a good surgeon."

"Dr. Saunders ordered a CAT scan." More choked sobs followed. "What if the cancer spread?"

Drusilla heard shuffling feet. Probably Leslie. "Margaret, I don't smell ..."

Margaret? Drusilla lifted her auburn brows. According to her New World visions, healers considered their patients guests. The one time she'd dared called someone's guest by the first name, she'd taken fifty lashes across her back.

"What I meant to say is, I think you'll get a good report. Dr. Saunders just wants to cover the bases. After you recover, you'll get on with your life."

Don't bet on it, Drusilla thought, smiling. *Accidents happen, and I'll be glad to arrange one.*

"I hope you're right." Margaret's voice came out a dusty croak. "I want this operation done and finished."

"I understand," Leslie said. Silence followed a minute, and then Drusilla heard fizzing noises. "I'll start your treatment."

A nurse pushing a cart looked askance at Drusilla. She gave the woman a withering look, then crept behind a stretcher to eavesdrop. The fizzing continued, sounding like hair spray. Leslie emerged from the room, walking without swaying. Her sapphire eyes, close-lipped smile, and the streaks of ivory skin under her rose powder confirmed Drusilla's suspicions.

"Leslie, I've got a surprise," Drusilla whispered in a soft, caressing voice.

Leslie spun around and glanced over her shoulders. Crouched behind the wall, Drusilla watched Leslie search the front desk and surroundings rooms.

"CODE BLUE, SIX FORREST!" boomed a voice overhead. "CODE BLUE, SIX FORREST!"

"Shit!" Leslie cried. She bolted to a rear exit.

Giggling noiselessly, Drusilla tiptoed to Margaret's room.

Chapter 19

Shoulders bent, arms clutching his briefcase, Alex shuffled up his sidewalk. He spent his evening going through his clients' portfolios, advising whether to buy or sell. By now, Leslie had gone to the hospital. She'd said something about working a half-shift.

He heaved a sigh, hating it when Leslie took orders from any mortal. Watching Leslie go to Betsy Ross, where Drusilla could get to her, left him with an uneasy feeling. But Leslie didn't seem afraid. Sometimes, he caught her smiling to herself.

Walking into his den, Alex shed his gray tweed blazer and plopped before his computer. He scanned his radio for soft music he could listen to while he sailed through the Internet. The networks allowed him to process his cash and stock transactions through the night.

A newsflash intruded on his concentration. "Drusilla Mason, accused of the murder of Claire Benson ..."

"Now what?" Alex started in his chair.

"... Lieutenant Roger Chase and Detective John Hannon allegedly visited Mason's premises, but they failed to return to the station. A search turned up their cruiser in the bottom of Meadowood Lake, but no sign of the officers."

"Oh, no!" Alex buried his head in his hands and snapped off the radio. He only knew one potential informant: Leslie. He guessed that the officers tried to apprehend Drusilla with conventional weapons and were killed.

Deciding that he wouldn't get any further work done, he logged off the Internet. He paced through his house, asking himself why Leslie involved the police.

About three o'clock, he heard shuffling footsteps on the sidewalk. The front door banged open, punctuated by harsh sobbing. Leslie emerged from the hallway, her blue eyes wide and vulnerable as a doe's.

"Alex." Her voice sounded tired and distant. "Drusilla killed my patient. The woman needed a part of her lung removed."

"What … who?" Alex stopped his pacing mid-step. White-faced and tearful, Leslie looked badly frightened.

"She had cancer in her lung, but they caught it early. She could have made it if …" Her voice exploded with hoarse wails. With trembling hands, she pulled a crumbled paper from her scrub pocket. She handed it to Alex.

"Leslie, what happened?" Alex cried, cursing himself silently for allowing her near the hospital.

"The charge nurse and I found the patient dead. Someone drained her dry and jammed this note inside her gown."

Alex spread the note on his desk between his splayed fingers. "Your father will die next," it read in bold block letters.

Sinking into his chair, he uttered a grief-filled sigh. Leslie had once said that she couldn't think under stress, but he never realized what she meant until now.

"What did you tell the officers?" he asked quietly.

"I gave them the knife I found by one of Drusilla's casualties." Leslie wiped her eyes with a hanky. "I won't lie for Drusilla or myself, Alex. Warren took my change bad, but at least he knows the truth …"

"No, Leslie!" Alex groaned, covering his eyes. "You told Warren, a newspaper reporter, of all people?"

"My brother deserves the truth." Leslie squirmed at the alarm in his voice. "He said he still loves me and wants me to help with Dad's care."

"Is this supposed to make me feel better?" Alex shouted. "Warren's gone into denial. What made you send those officers into Drusilla's trap?"

Leslie winced. "They didn't go in blind," she said in a weepy voice. "I hypnotized an officer named John into believing the truth. He was planning to fight Drusilla with fire. I read his thoughts for myself."

Alex propped his elbows on his desk, massaging his temples. "Well, guess what? John and his partner are missing. Your plan failed. Even with fire, humans can't match vampires' speed and strength."

He shook his head, brows drawn down. "Know what really hurts? You disobeyed me because you hate me for turning you."

"Oh, dear." Leslie paused by the desk, her face thoughtful and troubled. "I never thanked you for rescuing me, did I?"

"Well, don't feel obligated." Anger seeped into his voice. "Obligated, a 64-cent word for doing something you hate, like respecting my wishes."

"What wishes?" A puzzled, hurt look crossed Leslie's face. "Alex, aren't you listening? Drusilla's going after my dad."

"You brought this on yourself." He crossed his arms and stood, meeting Leslie's hurt eyes with hardened eyes. "You smile at me, but heaven forbid if I get too close. I told you to steer clear of your dad's house, the police, and the hospital. But you insisted on rushing back to work. Worse, you involved two officers, innocent men with families. Now, see what has happened."

Leslie looked back at Alex, arms hugging her leather purse against her chest. "How dare you accuse me," she said coldly. "I can't sit back while Drusilla goes on her killing sprees."

He shook his head, not quite believing what she said. He knew Leslie might grieve her lost humanity, even despise him, but he never counted on her involving the police. No fledgling had ever done that. "You don't involve innocents who can't defend themselves. Like those officers."

"You sound just like Tom and Gerry. Maybe you all

went to the same school." Leslie edged toward the door, her eyes brightening. "When you talked love, I knew I was headed for trouble. You think I'm so rotten? Fine, I'll move in with Dad, where I can keep an eye on him." She bolted outside.

"Leslie, you can't stay there," Alex cried, tearing after her. "His house isn't sun-proof."

"I'd rather roast than take your abuse." Leslie hopped into the car. By the time Alex got to the driveway, she'd sped onto Mill Road, spraying a cloud of dirt.

"Leslie!" he cried, his wail echoing down the street. Muffled footfalls followed him. Slipper-clad feet. Willard limped from the porch, dressed in his plaid pajamas and robe.

"Willard." Alex gave him a stern look. "Shouldn't you be resting?"

"You and Leslie shouted loud enough to wake the dead." Willard sounded annoyed and disappointed. "How come you sent her away?"

Alex let out a harsh sigh. "Leslie wanted to leave."

"No, you forced her," Willard said reproachfully. "People at the hospital yell at her the way you did. I know because I saw it. She ran because she associates you with people who treated her badly."

Alex leaned against his garage door and looked at Willard. "You watch too many talk shows. Why do you care?"

"Her father should stay here with us," Willard said. "I wouldn't mind looking after him. It's the least I could do after Leslie saved my life."

"Oh, Willard." Alex rubbed his forehead. The agony of a thousand knives sank through his heart. "Leslie's had it with me."

Willard cleared his throat. His feet dragged against the pavement. "If you go to her father's house and offer our help, she might forgive you."

****

A cab brought Alex to Christian's home. His own

195

car was parked in front of the Taites' garage. Two lights glimmered in the windows by the front door, assuring Alex that Leslie's father was still awake. He leaned against the doorbell.

Creaking noises followed. Glazed eyes nested inside a wrinkled face peered through the door's peephole. The door opened.

"Hello, Alex," Christian said in a bleary voice. Dressed in a flannel bathrobe, he hobbled to the living room and eased onto his sofa. "Is everything OK?"

"No," Alex said regretfully. "Where's Leslie?"

"She's in the bathroom, crying." Christian sighed. "Something about a murder at the hospital. Warren went there to cover the story."

"Anything else?"

Christian coughed, spewing a foul-smelling breath. "She asked if she could sleep in my basement, but it's got bugs and mice. I can't let her sleep there."

Alex knew about that basement all right. Leslie had once complained that mice got in through the cracked stones lining the foundation. Those cracks would filter in deadly sun rays. "I agree," he said softly.

"What's wrong with my children?" Christian asked in a shaky voice. "Each night, Warren comes home, cock-eyed drunk. He and Leslie ramble on about the living dead. Horseshit! You're either alive or dead."

The bathroom door banged open. "We're talking about the border between life and death, Dad," Leslie called from the hall. "Maybe Alex can explain better. He thinks he knows everything."

She shuffled into the room, her eyes pools of tears. "If you're going to dump on me again, save it."

Eyes misting with tears, Alex gazed at Christian's pale face and vacuous eyes. Leslie had tried to tell her dad the truth, but he'd refused to understand. "Leslie, your father should stay with us. Drusilla can't get to him there."

"You think I can't look after my own father?" Leslie's eyes flashed with indignation. "I'm not going anywhere with you."

"Can you watch him every second during the night? Can you guarantee protection for him while you're asleep?"

"Drusilla sleeps when I sleep," Leslie said petulantly.

"It doesn't matter. She'll hypnotize a mortal into doing her work." A sob crept into his voice. "Can you forgive yourself if something happened to your dad?"

Leslie regarded Alex with distrust, hands resting on her father's shoulders. "Who's going to watch Dad during the day and cook his meals?"

"Willard. He offered."

"You people have enough trouble," Christian spoke up. "I'll spend a few days with Gerry. His house has burglar alarms."

"The alarms won't stop Drusilla," Alex said with finality. "She knows where you live, and she'll find Gerry's address."

"Please stay with us, Dad ... at least for a few days." The longing in Leslie's voice was more obvious than ever. "I'll call Warren on his cell and let him know. Maybe he can lay low at a hotel."

"OK." Christian shrugged. "You know where to find my clothes and medicines."

****

On the way home, Leslie's father sat in the front seat. Alex sat in the rear, wedged between two paper bags filled with clothes and Christian's walker. Christian made small talk, complaining that the damp weather hurt his arthritic joints. Except for an occasional nod, Leslie drove on in stony silence.

Willard greeted them at the door. He'd changed into corduroy pants and a sweatshirt. Leslie glanced at the sky, then hurried inside. "Willard, thank you," she murmured, ushering him to the kitchen.

Alex gave Christian a tour of the first floor. "If you

make a left through that hall, you'll find a bathroom. But ..." his voice faltered. "The bedrooms are upstairs. The best my first floor can offer is my sofa or reclining chair."

"Relax." Smiling, Christian took a seat in the reclining chair. "My doctor doesn't want me to lie flat, so this chair will do nicely."

Alex peeked at his grandfather clock. After assuring himself that he still had some time before daylight, he sat on the sofa facing Christian. "Maybe tomorrow night, Leslie and I will think of a way to stop Drusilla."

Christian's eyes darted toward the kitchen. "Maybe you two will also stop fighting," he said in a measured, quiet voice. "I certainly hope so. She can't take it."

Alex shifted on his sofa and said nothing. Christian's set jaw and determined eyes reminded him of the way Adrian travelers circled their wagons during a Lyonnesien raid, circling them around a campfire to shelter their children. Sick as he was, Christian still felt compelled to protect his daughter. Alex supposed he could hypnotize Christian into silence, but he decided instead to let Christian have his say.

"I felt the tension between you two," Christian continued in a sad voice. "She came to my house bawling the way she did the day she and Tom broke their engagement."

Alex leaned back, shoulders sagging against the cushions. "Don't worry about us. Leslie and I had this thing, that's all."

Christian let out a slow breath, coughing deeply. "You call it a thing? Trust me, Alex. Leslie will call it a fight." He spoke without rancor or sarcasm.

Probing Christian's mind, Alex saw an image of an ailing man who anticipated death soon and feared for his daughter's happiness. "I told Leslie not to involve you or the police in our problems. She didn't listen."

"Let me tell you something," Christian said. "Leslie and her mother share a stubborn streak the size of Pennsylvania. Her *undeath*, or whatever you call it, won't change her personality. Sometimes you have to count to ten."

Alex started, surprised that Christian had opened up so readily. "Maybe I should have counted to a hundred."

Christian laughed a dry laugh of commiseration. "Someday, you'll have to count to a thousand. When my wife got into her stubborn moods, I never bothered counting at all. I said and did whatever crossed my mind." He raised his pale, wrinkled forefinger. "You don't want to repeat my mistakes."

He let out another harsh cough. "I don't mean to interfere, but I'm getting weaker every day. I've got to say my piece before it's too late."

A tear slid down his cheek, pooling at a crease in his skin. Alex sensed a profound loneliness, a gnawing pain that had eaten at Christian for years. "Go on," he prodded.

"When my wife got a bee in her bonnet, she wouldn't budge, no matter how much I yelled. I tried to bully her into doing things my way. More than once ..." His face drained of color, but the glint in his eyes hinted of a man determined. "I left bruises. Black eyes. Eventually, I broke her spirit and she stopped caring. During her emphysema, she forgot to take her medicines. On purpose. You understand me?"

Alex nodded, shivering at the cold feeling rushing through his limbs. He thought about Leslie's sobbing face, her curls drenched with sweat, her trembling hands.

"My wife swallowed a bottle of sleeping pills because of me," Christian blurted. "Now Warren hardly speaks to me, but I can't take back those years."

In his mind's eye, Alex saw Delia's ashes in the garden. He shifted his gaze, hoping that Christian wouldn't notice his own tears. "I understand more than you think."

"Then maybe you can figure out why Gerry attacks Leslie." Christian's spidery hands shook. "In case you didn't know, he's a lawyer. You'd think that with his schooling, he'd understand what Leslie tried to do for her mother. Instead, he blames her for everything."

Alex swallowed hard, fighting back more tears. *I've got news for you, Pop,* he thought. *Your oldest son broke Leslie's spirit long before Mom's death, leaving me with the pieces.*

"Things never came easily to Leslie." A far-away look crossed Christian's eyes. "When my children were learning to ride their bikes, Leslie always stumbled on the corners and skinned her knees."

"I bet it hurt to watch her try," Alex said.

"It did. I don't know what will become of Leslie after I'm gone." Christian's voice broke. "Look after her, Alex. Please?"

"I promise to try." Alex heaved an airless sigh. *If she'll let me.*

"Go easy on Leslie," Christian advised. "She's painfully aware of her shortcomings, and bullying will make things worse. She'll put on a tough front, like my wife did, even laugh off your temper flares. But inside, it's killing her, and one day ..." He clapped his hands. "Poof! You get my drift?"

Alex nodded gravely. "I'll keep what you said in mind. Thanks, Dad ... I mean, Christian."

Christian grabbed his hand and smiled. "You may call me Dad. I consider it a sign of respect."

Alex glanced at the clock again and stood up. "I'd better let you get some sleep. I'll get you a blanket."

By the time he returned, Christian was snoring. Alex spread a cotton blanket over him and headed to the basement.

In the chamber, Leslie appeared to be asleep, curled in a miserable ball, her mouth and nose pressed against the wall. Propping his elbow against the pillows, he smoothed the hair that had fallen in her eyes.

"Leslie," he whispered, longing to kiss away the hurt. "I'm sorry I said those awful things to you. I'll find a way to make this up to you."

Chapter 20

At the hospital, Leslie learned that immortality did not shield her from the stress of heavy workloads. Her beeper dogged her like a miserable boss. She was setting up a 7200 ventilator for someone having emergency surgery when harsh whistling issued from its compressor. After placing a "do not use" sign on the front panel, she wheeled the machine back to the storeroom.

Soft-shoed footsteps sounded from the hall. The door whispered inward. It was Diane Bradly, a co-worker and newly appointed charge therapist. "What's wrong with the ventilator?" she asked, her eyes arching slightly.

"Air compressor leak." Leslie reached for another ventilator. "I'll call Engineering when I get a chance."

"Did you run an E.S.T.?"

"I didn't have to." Leslie sighed and looked away, hating to admit that the ventilator's E.S.T. troubleshooting program looked like Greek. "That leak made enough noise to bust an eardrum."

Diane snapped on the ventilator and hooked up a test lung. Silence followed a moment, and then the harsh whistling started again. Diane glared at Leslie, her blonde brows knitted together and green eyes narrowed. "You stupid, stupid girl," she scolded. "This vent needs new tubing, that's all."

"I know bad tubing when I hear it," Leslie said between clenched teeth. She listened hard, just in case. She found herself smiling at Diane's sweet smell and pounding heart. "It's coming from inside the air compressor. Run your E.S.T. if you don't believe me."

"It's not funny, Leslie." Diane stepped toward Leslie. "If your stupidity didn't cost Fitzpatrick his life, I'd feel sorry for you."

"What?" Leslie gulped. Her throat felt bone dry.

"Fitzpatrick's wife signed the Do Not Resuscitate papers today. The doctors disconnected him from the vent and let him go." Diane's eyes narrowed. "I wouldn't let you touch my dog."

Stepping away from the ventilator, Leslie looked up at Diane. She'd come to work armed with witty comebacks, but fantasies of blood-drinking distracted her and she forgot her lines. Another smile played on her lips.

"My God!" Diane's face reddened. "You think his death is a joke."

"No, Diane, you're the joke." Leslie's eyes focused on Diane. "For the record, I don't trust you either, but I'd love to have you for dinner."

Duties forgotten, Leslie jumped on Diane like a cat. They tumbled on the floor, with Leslie's fangs seeking and gaining purchase. Wedging Diane against the ventilator, hand yanking her blonde hair, Leslie sucked gently from her throat.

After Diane's struggles subsided, she lay slumped against the 7200's side panel, hands flopping on the linoleum. Leslie rose to her feet, wiped her face with a damp towel, and straightened her lab coat. She relished the sweetness lingering inside her mouth until her eyes took in the mess.

Blood ran in long crimson trails down the ventilator's white side panel. It trickled from Diane's throat punctures, staining her pink scrub shirt, and plopped in fat drops on the floor.

"Shit!" Leslie glared at the ventilator. The emergency patient still needed a functional machine. Her log sheet listed a stack of overdue breathing treatments, and she also had Emergency Room coverage. Any second, she expected someone to barge into the storeroom and draw their own conclusion.

Hypnotizing Diane would not clean up the evidence. Fists gripping towels and peroxide, Leslie scrubbed the stains while listening to Diane's heartbeat. It was fast and erratic, but still strong. She expected trouble, counted on it, when Diane assumed her new position, but she promised herself to ignore Diane's comments. The promise became meaningless when her thirst erupted into an ugly flare.

Poking her head out the door, Leslie sighted a wheelchair by the elevators. The hall appeared deserted. "Get up," she ordered, hoisting Diane by the armpits.

Diane let out a tired, little groan and collapsed against Leslie's chest. Leslie propped her in the chair, covered her with a sheet and wheeled her to the elevators leading to the Forrest garage, Diane's favorite parking spot.

"You're a bitch," Leslie whispered in her ear. Images flashed through her mind: Diane and Crawford going at it in bed; Diane complaining about Leslie and Fred; Diane pushing for extra vacation time. "I know things about you that would stand out on Betsy Ross's bulletin board. Like how you slept your way to your current job."

She parked the chair by Diane's car. Digging through her pockets, Leslie fished out the keys. "Sleep well," she said, easing Diane into the driver's seat. "Think about what I told you."

At the storeroom, Leslie grabbed another 7200 and rolled it to the Intensive Care Unit. A stench like rotting vegetables wafted from the ICU's rear cubicles. It meant that death was visiting the respective occupants. Three weeks after returning to her job, Leslie taught herself to diagnose illness by a patient's scent, heartbeat, and breathing. One look from Leslie soothed the most agitated patient. Last week, she'd detected a life-threatening heart arrhythmia before the monitor showed abnormalities. The cardiologist involved had cited her for an "astute assessment."

But her thirst lurked in the background like a wolf circling a campfire. The other night, an intern asked when she'd pull another Fitzpatrick. He paid for his insult with a contribution to the Leslie Taite Blood Bank. The week after her rehire, she had two run-ins with Diane's friends during shift report. Ditto deposits.

What made her thirst spiral out of control? Drusilla hadn't left any more gruesome surprises, and for the moment, her father was safe. She contemplated asking Alex to explain the bloodlust, but the expectation of trouble nagged at her like a festering sore, especially after their fight.

Last night, Alex tucked her father into the reclining chair. The affection between Alex and her father moved Leslie to tears, but his reaction to the officers' deaths had frightened her. So she withheld any questions regarding her change, lest she provoke Alex into another blow-up.

She dreaded thinking about the repercussions should she and Alex part ways. It meant buying a house with a sun-proof basement and hiring someone to run her day errands, something not easily done on a respiratory therapist's salary.

Though she hated to admit it, even to herself, Leslie had fallen for Alex. She loved spending evenings with him, watching television, dancing at good clubs, and swapping stories about their past. Some deeper part of Leslie sensed that he resented her working, though, and their fight had opened a chasm between them. Since then, she'd cried herself to sleep every morning. At night, she consoled herself with crimson nectar, obtained from any worker walking the halls alone.

Just as Leslie sat at the desk to chart, Fred scurried in from the hall, panting for breath. "Leslie, we've got trouble," he murmured. "Diane went home sick."

"Did she?" Leslie swallowed hard, wincing at the dryness, as if her throat had turned to sand. She tucked her sheets into her lab coat pocket. "Why?"

Fred blotted the sweat from his pudgy cheeks. "She said something about a stomach virus. Jim told me to cover her assignments. All my treatments are late."

"Damn!" Leslie leaned against her chair and groaned. She'd never considered the rippling effects of her attacks, that is, overworked therapists and under-treated patients. "I'm sorry, Fred. What can I do to help?"

"If you do the vent checks, I'll finish the treatments." Fred breathed a sigh of relief. "Could you check out Robert McGrath, room 120? His nurse called me twice for stat breathing treatments on him."

"Albuterol?" Leslie rooted through her pockets, confirming that she had the vials. "Let's go."

Loud wheezing shuddered from room 120. At least, it seemed loud from where Leslie stood at the nurses' station. She inhaled deeply, anticipating a rancid stench, but she only detected sweat and body odor. This left her shaking her head. "What's wrong with him?" she asked.

"They think it's pneumonia," Fred said. "He's had this cough for weeks."

"I see." Leslie stepped inside the room, eyeing McGrath closely. He looked to be in his late fifties. His dark hair flopped against his white pillow case. Deep crescents in his pale cheeks accented his emaciated appearance.

"Hello, Mr. McGrath," she said, walking to his bedside. "I'm Leslie from Respiratory Therapy. What's wrong?"

With gagging breaths, McGrath coughed blood-tinged phlegm into a paper cup. "It's this bug. I can't seem to catch my breath."

"Can you lean sideways? I'll listen to your lungs." Leslie placed her stethoscope against McGrath's back and chest. Wheezing and rubs screamed in her ear, loudest around his left lower lung. She recalled hearing those same sounds from lung cancer patients.

Backing away, she motioned Fred into the hall. "I'll be back, Mr. McGrath, after I speak with your doctor," she said, forcing cheerfulness into her voice. "Fred, let's go."

At the desk, Leslie yanked McGrath's binder from the revolving chart rack and flipped through its dog-eared pages. "Fred, I think McGrath has a tumor."

"What?" Fred's mouth gaped like a goldfish. His sneakers skittered against the linoleum. "The x-rays didn't show any tumor."

"X-rays lie." Leslie gazed at the progress notes, thinking about the way she'd fretted over reading x-rays, until Saunders explained that certain diseases didn't show themselves on film. "Who's his doctor?"

"Saunders," Fred said. "He's down in Emergency. Want to page him?"

"I'll talk to him in person," Leslie said, scurrying to the exit. "Don't worry; I won't forget your vent checks."

At the Emergency Room, Saunders sat at the desk, typing into a computer. Clad in his black tweed pants and pale blue shirt, he almost looked like Alex. His rosy cheeks contrasted with Alex's translucent complexion. More to the point, Saunders never blasted her like Alex did, even after a glaring error. Instead, he drew a diagram of where she went wrong. He even volunteered to write the letter that green-lighted her return to work. He was one of her few friends.

"Leslie," Saunders called, waving his hand. "What's wrong?"

"Nothing," Leslie mumbled, fighting back tears.

A troubled look crossed Saunders's face. "You look upset," he said in a low voice. "I thought that changing shifts gave you a fresh start."

She managed a smile, but her eyes brimmed with tears.

"Leslie?" Saunders stared at her, tension edging into his voice. He snapped off his screen. "What happened?"

"I'm OK." Leslie advanced toward the desk, eyes burning into Saunders's. "It's just that since my car accident, watching people suffer really gets to me."

"That's understandable. You went through a major trauma."

"It's getting a little easier." Leslie focused on Saunders, pushing all thoughts about Alex from her head. "Robert McGrath has a tumor in his left lower lung. He needs a bronchoscopy and biopsy."

"McGrath's had trouble shaking his cough." Saunders sighed, rubbing his temples. "But his chest x-ray showed a left lower lobe infiltrate, indicative of pneumonia. Besides, he doesn't have a smoking history."

Leslie propped her elbows over the countertop, chin over the computer, and eyes bearing into Saunders. His eyes became dull and vacant. She hated manipulating him, but she was trying to save McGrath's life.

"Infections smell like garbage," she said. "McGrath doesn't smell, but I heard a harsh wheeze on expiration, like an obstruction blocking his air. I've heard this sound from lung cancer patients."

"Lung cancer?" Saunders's half-lidded eyes blinked, and he glanced at his hands. "I'm a doctor. I go by test results. Where is this coming from?"

"My head injury affected my senses," Leslie told him. "I can smell infections and hear a pin drop a mile away."

Saunders's eyes widened. "Did you speak with Dr. O'Toole about this?"

"Bill, I consider this a gift." Leslie maintained her intent stare. "Just factor my senses into your decisions when I recommend treatments or tests. McGrath needs a biopsy. Pay attention to his left lower lobe." Leslie averted her gaze.

Saunders rose from his chair, rubbing his eyes. "Wait ... I've been woolgathering. Did you say something about a tumor?"

"Robert McGrath's wheeze is getting worse, especially on the left side," Leslie said. "I thought he might have a tumor."

"Good thinking." Saunders pulled a leather booklet from his back pocket. He flipped through the pages. "I can schedule a bronchoscopy tomorrow morning if McGrath consents to it."

"He will," Leslie smiled. "He feels awful."

****

Before heading back to ICU, Leslie went to the hospital courtyard for her break. She sat on a wooden bench by the gate, watching the moonlight dance on the grass and topiaries. Security guards strolled about, most of them armed. Sometimes they provided nourishment. Leslie remembered feeling the butt of one man's gun pressing into her stomach while she fed on him.

"Paper tigers." She laughed softly. "Their guns are useless."

"You've got that right," whispered a voice from the shadows. It sounded like her own, except for the European accent.

Seconds later, Drusilla limped from behind a rose bush. The moonlight illuminated the sequins and beads on her ivory gown. Leslie found herself gagging on the stink of spoiled meat. Red, fiery curls swirled around Drusilla's parchment pale face.

"Bitch." She hissed, lips wrinkled in a snarl. "Those bats should have ripped you to pieces."

"But they didn't." Arms folded across her chest, Leslie mustered as much arrogance as she could, though the sight of Drusilla's bloated pupils chilled her to the bone. Yet, some deeper part of Leslie salivated at the thought of going toe-to-toe with Drusilla. Maybe immortality had increased her fear threshold.

Drusilla marched forward, her bloodstained teeth shining in a gruesome smile. "Call off the police now," she ordered. "Otherwise, your father will die next, then your siblings, your friends, even the person who created you."

Fists braced against her hips, Drusilla propped her sandal-clad foot against a bench. Her knee poked like a bone between satin folds, exposing cherry-red skin.

So John used his lighter after all. If only he'd aimed higher. The memory of Alex's scolding made Leslie want to cry. Instead, she burst into high-pitched giggling. Every time she tried to say something, she exploded with fresh laughter that sounded like screaming.

"What's so damned funny?" Grabbing Leslie's left arm, Drusilla shoved her toward a bush. Leslie plopped into a pile of soft leaves.

"Want to know who created me?" Leslie laughed again, holding her side as she struggled to her feet. "Kenworthy found me at the cave. He changed me because he wanted me to live."

Drusilla shook her head. "No, he would have drained you dry."

"Kenworthy feared that my death, among others, would upset your god Hades." Leslie didn't know what made her mention Hades, but she thought it sounded convincing. Somewhere, fear hid behind Drusilla's narrowed eyes, wild grin, and clenched fists. One slip would give it away. "He warned me to use discretion when feeding because Hades's bats watch everything we do."

Drusilla's face contorted in rage. "Ken would tell me if he'd changed you."

"Maybe he didn't get around to it." Leslie hugged herself, suppressing a shiver. How far dared she go to provoke Drusilla? At this point, she was flying blindly. "After I regained consciousness, Kenworthy and I made love."

Thoughts of Alex sprung up from nowhere, and Leslie felt tears in her eyes.

Drusilla's mouth worked convulsively, then broke into a hideous laugh. "Some other vampire made love to you, then dropped you like a hot coal. You look like you're going to cry."

"Ken dropped me after I spoke to the police." Leslie concentrated on Drusilla's eyes. "He was great while our fling lasted. Think, Drusilla. I've never gone to Adria on my own. Only one vampire besides us lives in Philadelphia. Someone had to turn me."

"Maybe Ken wanted to teach you a lesson." A smirk curled at the corners of Drusilla's mouth like dog-eared paper. Her pupils, dark as marbles, mirrored the sidewalk lights. Her voice hissed like an axe swinging through the air. "Just remember that I can hurt your loved ones."

Fear sent its claws shivering through Leslie's body. She glanced toward the pay phone near the hospital's glass doors. She needed to warn Warren. Like yesterday.

"Kenworthy is furious with me," she managed after a pause. "But he respects my brothers' connections with the police and fears that hurting them will draw unwanted attention."

"Ken said no such thing!" Drusilla cried, stamping her foot. Her ruby lips worked into a snarling grimace, and she snorted.

"If you think I'm lying," Leslie said, "ask Kenworthy."

Drusilla backed away. "You'd better believe I will," she muttered, before slithering into the shadows.

After Drusilla's footsteps and scent faded, Leslie raced to the phone. She dialed Warren's beeper. "Please call back," she begged silently before hanging up.

Moments later, the phone rang. Leslie snatched up the receiver with trembling hands. "Warren, we've got to make special arrangements for Dad. Drusilla threatened to go after both of you."

"Did she?" A long, skeletal sigh echoed through the line, followed by Warren's quaking voice. "That doesn't surprise me."

Leslie pictured Warren's face. She heard men's voices from the background. Police officers.

"I think that bitch broke into Dad's house. I found Mom's good china in pieces, our glasses, our dishes ... this house is a mess."

"Oh, no!" Leslie huddled against the phone, trying to force calmness into her voice. Drusilla would continue her vendetta, even if Hades himself warned her to stop.

"Warren, Drusilla knows we've fingered her."

A long, deep gasp followed. "I thought you and Officer Hannon ..."

"Hannon went after Drusilla with a lighter." Leslie's voice quivered and her eyes pooled with unshed tears. "He got himself killed. You'd better leave town before she gets to you."

Chapter 21

"Leslie's changed, Alex," Bill Saunders said, looking up from his financial statements. He reached for his calculator. "She seems more confident."

Reaching behind him, Alex cracked the window. The damp breeze felt deliciously cool against his cheeks. A smile touched the corners of his lips. "In what way?"

Bill raked his fingers through his moist, wavy hair. "Before her accident, Leslie used to second-guess herself, but now ..." He furrowed his brows, as if something important lurked in the back of his mind, something that he couldn't quite recall. "She can diagnose someone's illness just by looking at him. One of my patients had an awful cough, and she swore that he had a lung tumor. I did a bronchoscopy and found a malignant tumor the size of a cherry. Thanks to Leslie, we caught it in time."

"What do you think gave her confidence?" Alex asked, still thinking about her haunted eyes and plaintive voice.

"Maybe she had an epiphany after the accident. Near death experiences can do that to people." Bill leaned against his chair, arms folded behind his head. "Maybe she just needed a friend. Personally, I think Dr. Wolf, or whoever did her Apticom tests, got their degree from a Sears catalogue. I told Leslie to get another opinion. She isn't slow; her learning processes are different, that's all."

Alex turned from the window and massaged his throat. The disquiet that had nagged him lately, a feeling of something not quite right, mushroomed. "Then why question her success?"

"A second opinion might help others like her," Bill said. "She refused, and it's her call anyway, but ..."

Alex stiffened his back against the chair.

"It seems that aggressiveness came with our new Leslie. Crawford, Diane, and their clique used to badger her, sending her to the ladies' room in tears. Now, they all cringe when she shows up at their station."

"I see." Alex forced calmness into his voice, but he trembled at the alarms going off in his head.

"Leslie threatened to sue them," Bill continued, his rambling voice tinged with unease. Alex sensed that he'd left something out, something that eluded his conscious memory. "But Diane and Crawford don't scare easily. Did you say anything to them?"

Leaning against the desk, Alex gazed at Bill's neck. No bandage or fang marks. He affected a long, agonized sigh. "OK, you've caught me," he said, forcing sheepishness into his voice. "After Leslie made her threat, I called Crawford, masquerading as her lawyer."

"So that's it." Bill threw back his head and howled with laughter. His edginess was gone. "That's brilliant. For all his bravado, Crawford is a gutless wonder. I wish I'd thought of that myself."

A beeping sound cut into Bill's laugh. He glanced at his pager. "Duty calls again, but I expected this one."

Alex stood up, allowing a weak grin. "Then you'll keep this between us?"

"Your secret will go to my grave with me." Bill chuckled.

"Good. We'll talk later," Alex said, heading to the door. *That was close,* he thought, shuddering.

At the lobby, an anemic-looking officer patrolled the desk. Gauze bandages covered his throat. Alex stared at the man, probing his thoughts, but saw no sign of recollection. With a sick feeling, he concluded that the tension at home had goaded Leslie into a feeding binge.

Leslie didn't have duty tonight. Her father said that

213

she planned to move him, but he didn't know where, and Leslie wasn't volunteering information. She clammed up on most subjects after Alex reamed her out for going to the police. Now was his chance to assess the damage. He headed toward the elevators.

Head lowered, he crept through the respiratory therapy offices. He saw people in pink uniforms at the conference room table. One of them, a blonde, wore gauze on her throat. The bearded man beside her had scab marks below his chin. In the ICU, three nurses lingered by the station. One kept yawning and dragging her feet. A glance at the crusted sores on her neck told him why.

Maybe Alex wouldn't live to confront Hades. The victims' precise wounds would alert some vigilante smart enough to rule out human monsters as suspects, clever enough to figure out the necessary weapons. Somehow, he'd have to make Leslie understand the importance of discretion.

****

Rain came down in torrents during the cab ride home. The driver slowed, blinded by the storm. Deafening thunder exploded overhead, punctuated by lightning bolts. *Hades is preparing his attack,* Alex thought, shivering. *Innocent mortals will die in the crossfire.*

Shuffling up his driveway, he found his house cloaked in shadow. A rosy fragrance wafted from his living room. Leslie's scent. She lay on his cream-colored sofa, face buried in a paperback.

"Leslie, we have to talk," he began, taking a seat in the chair facing her. "This silent treatment ..."

"Talk?" Leslie sat up, hugging her floral print robe around her. Her blue eyes blazed like pilot lights. "What did I do now?"

Alex's fists tightened inside his pockets. *Count to ten like Christian advised. One, two, three ...*

"You have no idea how much your accusations hurt. I used to hate Gerry's visits. His plane would get in from

Buffalo late at night, and just when I'd fallen asleep, I'd hear him bellowing from the kitchen. It got so ugly, I packed my bags and moved." Leslie slammed her book on the cushions. "Do you remember the time I found Fred bleeding in the alley? I told Gerry about it. He glared at me and said, 'That's right, you rescue strangers, but you let your own mother die.' If you're still looking to rake me for those officers' deaths, save it."

"I'm sorry." Alex shifted in his seat. He covered his ears, longing to blot out the sound of his anger and Leslie's muffled weeping. "Before you met me, you had no exposure to the supernatural. I forgot that."

"Damned straight you forgot." Leslie's voice rose to a shrill pitch. "Know what makes this so sad? I thought we shared something beautiful. But you expected me to blossom like some flower; now you're stuck with withered leaves."

"Leslie." Alex squirmed in his chair. Understanding dawned, and he saw that Leslie's career struggles were only the tip of her nightmares. "I never expected anything but love."

"Really?" Leslie said pointedly. "You made it clear that my developing instincts didn't suit your timetable."

"I never compared you to a plant gone bad. That's an awful thing to tell someone."

"I've heard it before," Leslie said in a weepy voice. "Tom said that to me when he called off our wedding."

Alex paced around the room, eyes on Leslie, and tried to think of a way to get through to her. "I can't comment on the past, only on what I see now. Bill told me that you diagnosed his patient's tumor. You saved the man's life. That should make you proud."

"Tumors cause the lungs to make squealing noises when a patient exhales. I can smell infections and hear the slightest variation in heartbeat. You've turned me into a healer. A twilight healer." Leslie sighed. "If only bloodlust didn't enter the equation."

"I understand." Straining his ear toward the hall, Alex made out snoring, a sign that Willard had gone to sleep. "Where's Dad?"

"Drusilla broke into Dad's house and left it a shambles." Leslie sniffled and wiped her eyes. "I moved him because she might find our address during her raids at the hospital. It's highly unlikely, given her scrambled brain, but possible. Dad and Warren are staying with Shelly in Chester County."

"If Kenworthy wants to find them, he will." Alex paced around the cherry wood coffee table, licking his lips. "Like I said, you lack exposure to the supernatural. So if I see you walking into a trap, I should holler. Right?"

Leslie shrunk against the cushions. Her blue eyes darted around the room. "Just get to the point."

"I've warned you not to stalk neighbors or coworkers, but you left your marks on Diane and a few others. Bill noticed how they've changed toward you and he's asking questions. I covered for you this time."

"I knew that Bill would suspect something," Leslie said in a subdued voice. "I should level with him."

"What?" Alex felt his muscles tighten.

"Lying spreads like cancer." Leslie spoke with a strange kind of serenity. "It has to stop."

Alex clenched his fists inside his pockets. At this rate, he'd have to count to a thousand. "Some things you don't tell people. In Adria, people would burn your house if they even suspected you of consorting with vampires."

"We're not in Adria. Where I come from, certain illnesses mimic vampirism. My doctors treat those cases with respect."

Alex shook his head. "Bill can't handle *undeath*."

"He'll keep it together if he sees me using my powers to save lives." Leslie's huge eyes pleaded for understanding. "Bill knows more than anyone how much patient care means to me. When he's ready, I'll tell him in my own way."

"In other words, you'll gloss over the blood craving." Alex drew a long, weary sigh. He didn't know whether to laugh, cry, or scream at Leslie.

"Warren knows about my diet. He still loves me. Why not Saunders?"

With a weary shrug, Alex sat heavily on the sofa beside Leslie. "At best, Saunders might think you've got a serious medical condition. He'll try to keep it confidential out of obligation, but his fear will show, and Gerry will bombard him with questions. Suppose he caves in and lets the truth slip?"

"Gerry would ban us from the house." Leslie lowered her eyes. "He might even try to destroy us."

"My point exactly." Alex took Leslie's hands in his. To his relief, she didn't pull away. "You've got to keep a low profile and abstain from coworkers. We don't want police on our trail."

"I can't help it," Leslie wailed. "No matter how many miracles I work, my coworkers see me as the slip-and-fall therapist. The shouting starts, my throat gets dry, and then I'm feeding on someone."

"I told you that stress aggravates bloodlust. Can't you work at another hospital where people don't know your past?"

"No other hospital is hiring now," Leslie said in a weak and watery voice.

"And so we have the dog chasing its tail." Alex shook his head. "Would it help if I brought you nourishment?"

"Yes, it would." Leslie smiled. "Some of the stress might go away. By the way, I think I've silenced Drusilla."

More alarms went off in Alex's head. "What did you do to her?"

"Drusilla and I got into it at the hospital courtyard. She threatened to attack my family. I lied and said that Kenworthy turned me and would protect my relatives."

"Oh, Leslie." Alex pulled at his hair with trembling fingers. "Tell me you're joking."

"Who's laughing?" Leslie asked innocently. "I told Drusilla what I knew about Hades, and that Kenworthy made love to me. She got this look like I get after Diane hassles me, and then she took off like a shot."

"That's nice," Alex murmured, massaging his temples. "You've ignited a loose cannon. She'll bulldoze her way through a mall, leaving a massacre in her wake."

"There you go again, accusing me," Leslie cried, jumping up. She strode to the stair steps and leaned against the wooden banister. "Your explanations about the supernatural sound like Greek. You tell me that Hades hates killers, but when I try to stop one, you yell at me."

Her tearful face swam in the shadows, pale as paper. "You want me to understand my bodily changes? Explain them as you would to a six-year-old. If you can't, then leave me alone."

Another wall went up, and Alex felt the chasm between them expand. He understood that her mother's death and career failures made her sensitive, but understanding something and knowing how to act were two different things.

"Maybe I should draw you a picture," he said in a quavering voice. "It's time you met my friend Elliott."

"Elliott?" Leslie echoed feebly.

Alex glanced at the grandfather clock. "He lives in Adria. You'll have to cross the border between your world and Adria. We'll wait until sunset tonight because Adria's time zone runs six hours later than ours."

"You're taking me to that squalid place?" Tears fell down Leslie's face, and she wiped her finger across her cheek. "Why, Alex? Drusilla tortured me there. I get it. You're angry at me for baiting her, so you're punishing me."

"No, Leslie, I'm trying to save your life. What good will my loving do if you don't understand the dangers?" Alex drew in a deep breath. He marched to the sofa. "Over here, we have your past; Gerry hounding you, your hassles at work, and your broken engagement."

Alex stepped up to the banister, close to Leslie. "Over here, we have Adria, your need for blood, and Hades watching us like a hawk." He made wiping motions with his hands. "Your past no longer applies."

"Oh yes, it does," Leslie said coolly. "Because my feelings haven't changed."

Alex's eyes brightened. He willed back his tears and mustered patience into his voice. "Elliott warned that bringing you into my world could lead to heartache. My world regards vampires the way yours does terrorists. If you listen to him, he'll explain so you understand." He clasped Leslie hands in his. "Will you please come with me to Adria?"

Leslie leaned against the wall, fist pressed against her lips. "OK," she said in a faint voice. "One visit."

"Good." A wan smile surfaced on Alex's bony face. "We'd better take nourishment before going to bed. Making the crossover requires energy."

****

When Alex opened his eyes, he shook Leslie's shoulder. "Wake up. We'll have to move."

Leslie yawned and rubbed her eyes. She smoothed out her thick curls. "Do I wear anything special for this trip?"

"No jeans, no pants." Alex watched Leslie for skittishness and darting eyes, signs that she might change her mind about going. "Women wear long-sleeved dresses to their ankles. Nothing transparent or low-cut."

Leslie nodded, hurrying to the door. "I'll find something."

Alex's green eyes followed her to the stairs. Her troubled face had the air of a woman who'd realized she'd lost her purse. But her soft voice indicated willingness to listen, and he'd settle for that. He donned a bright green tunic and trousers.

He found Leslie in the living room, dressed in a maroon gown with a lace collar. Its wrist-length sleeves and flowing skirt met his specifications.

"Gerry made me wear this for his wedding, so I won't care if it gets dirty." She smoothed out her dress. "What happens next?"

"Take my hand and concentrate on a door."

"Which door?" Leslie glanced around the room.

Alex looked at the clock. "Imagine any door standing in front of you. It could be wooden, glass, any material you want. If you focus hard enough, you'll see this door, a gateway to Adria."

Leslie started to shake. She gazed at Alex with frightened eyes. "I find this rather creepy. Will you hold me?"

"Sure." Alex folded Leslie against his chest, chin resting atop her head. "I could concentrate for both of us, but it's better if you try."

Moments later, Alex's door appeared before him. He guessed that Leslie saw hers, given her burst of trembling. "It's OK," he whispered before ushering her through the exit. "Nothing can hurt you here."

Outside, a full moon overhead spread puddles of light on the dirt road, two horses corralled to a post, and stray travelers passing on foot. Leslie's eyes flickered back and forth. Her arm tightened around his waist.

"Horses?" she cried. "Drusilla said that Adria had no modern conveniences, but I thought she was blowing smoke."

"She had it right. Adria's time runs five hundred years behind yours. Picture your world in the 1500s, and you've got Adria." Alex lifted his gaze toward the mountains ahead. "We should get there in an hour."

"Get where?" Leslie shuddered with uncertainty.

"The Athyr Mountains." Alex folded his arm around her, savoring the feel of her bosom against his chest. Under more pleasant circumstances, he might have taken her somewhere private. "Try to relax. People here consider you the danger."

"I doubt it." Hands linked with Alex's, Leslie stepped over fallen branches and followed him up the path. "Why couldn't we drive across the border?"

Alex gazed at the lumpy grass and gnarled trees. He burst into laughter. "You'd terrify the natives. Besides, why ruin a good car?"

"Because this place gives me the creeps." Leslie rubbed her arms and glanced backwards. "Why is it so cold here?"

"Adria's seasons run opposite of Philadelphia's. Winter's coming."

"Everything about this world is backward."

They walked on in silence, passing through a battlefield. Mortally wounded soldiers lay in the dirt, their sweetness blending with the smell of wild flowers. Alex found himself literally inhaling blood from one soldier. When he finished, he looked up and saw Leslie feeding on another. Blood ran down her chin.

As they resumed their journey, a wind blew eastward, chasing the floral scents, and replacing them with a horrible, burning odor. Alex happened upon a forest of skeletal trees, their charred branches swaying in the breeze. His crepe soles slid through ashes and grass with the consistency of hay.

"I don't like this!" Leslie cried, clutching his tunic sleeve. "What are we looking for, anyway?"

"A temple." Alex pulled Leslie close. "Elliott's home."

As the burnt trees thinned out, he saw what used to be the temple—a pile of rocks nested in charred timbers. His cry came and died in his tightening throat.

Kneeling between the bleached stones, Leslie sorted through the blackened wood splinters. "This is awful," she said. "Who'd burn down a temple?"

"Maybe some vigilante. Maybe worse." Alex let out a harsh sob. Poking between the ashes, he found an opening barely wide enough to accommodate an adult, and cracked, cement stairs. "These steps lead to Elliott's apartment. Stay close to me."

Without another word, Leslie crept down the stairs behind Alex, hand gripping his shoulder. Black soot coated the tunnel's walls. The rugs and furniture had roasted to ashes. The white-veined marble floor had burned pitch black.

"Oh, God!" Leslie's bulging eyes took on a glassy sheen. Her arms clasped over her chest. "You think Elliott escaped?"

"I certainly hope so." Alex pressed on through the ashes.

At Elliott's quarters, the brass door had been torn from its hinges and dumped aside. Hand linked with Leslie's, he forced one foot before the other into the suite.

Elliott's expensive table and embroidered chairs lay in charred wood stumps on the floor. Alex shuffled through the crumbling timbers, followed by Leslie, until he reached the bedroom. The brass bed and silk canopy appeared intact, but blackened splinters littered the soot-covered floor. A charcoal skeleton dressed in Elliott's sterling white robe lay in the bed, staring at them through empty pits.

Chapter 22

Drusilla's gown refused to stay in place. Every time she climbed a flight of stairs, its skirt slid up her thighs, wrinkling at the waist. By the time she reached the fourth floor, it looked like something fished from a clothes hamper.

Patient wards loomed ahead, obscured by metal doors. She only needed seconds to figure out which workers were Leslie's friends, and minutes to eliminate them. But a skeletal finger of terror crept up Drusilla's back at the thought of even approaching anyone connected with Leslie. Having infected Leslie with immortality, Ken would include her friends under his umbrella of protection. One word from Leslie, and he'd get out his whipping chain.

Fear and frustration combined, Drusilla tugged at her dress, cursing low enough so that no one would hear. Her pumps had scuffed its silk hem. It didn't matter; she hated the dress because Ken bought it. "You bloody monster," she whispered. "May Hades damn you to eternal misery in Tartarus."

Faint groaning invaded Drusilla's thoughts. A child's sobs. Tiptoeing down a side corridor, she found herself in the children's wing. Beeping machines, scratching pens, and hushed voices assaulted her ears, but Drusilla focused on the voice calling to her—the girl wearing casts to her hips. She lay inside a corner room, weeping in her pillow. Shiny metallic balloons and stuffed animals surrounded the bed, everything a child wanted, except the most important people – Mamma and Papa.

Moved to tears by the girl's loneliness, Drusilla stared into her reddened eyes. "What's the matter?" she asked gently.

"My legs hurt." The girl wept. "No one can find my nurse."

Drusilla brushed back the moist curls falling into her eyes. "I specialize in finding lost nurses," she said, smiling. "My name's Drusilla. What's yours?"

"Robin."

"That's a pretty name." Grabbing the sheet, Drusilla wiped the moisture dripping from Robin's face. "Do you live nearby?"

Robin nodded. "My mom and step-dad just bought the house behind Little Flower School."

Although Little Flower School meant nothing to Drusilla, the image drifting from Robin's head—a battered, wooden row home facing a beige brick building—came through crystal clear.

"I know Little Flower." Drusilla watched Robin's brown eyes. She'd seen enough fear in her own mirror to recognize Robin's spooked look. But tonight, Drusilla would help Robin sleep in comfort, at least for a while. "What should I tell your nurse?"

"That my legs ..." Robin shifted under the covers, and some of the fright left her voice. "They don't hurt so much now."

That's right. Drusilla mustered a penetrating stare. *Imagine your pain as the tide going out. Soon, it will go away completely.* "Sometimes your body hurts more when you're upset. Don't you think?"

"I guess." Robin blinked her eyes.

More images flooded Drusilla's consciousness—Robin cringing behind a threadbare sofa. A bearded man with a cherry-red face pushing Robin down broken stairs. Her step-dad, Robin called him, because her real dad had gone to Heaven. Heaven? Tears trickled down Drusilla's face as Robin's memories played across her mind. Whatever that meant, her daddy had left Robin at the mercies of a glorified slave boss.

"Robin, I'm going to make your problems disappear," she whispered. "Soon, very soon, you'll feel better."

Running her tongue across her lips, Drusilla headed to the lobby. "Beige, brick building," she murmured. Outside, she gazed up the street, surveying the cars and run-down apartments. "Where would that be? Never mind, I'll take a cab."

It only took moments to get to the school. A dilapidated house like the one in Drusilla's vision beckoned from across the street. She crept toward its open front window. Inside, a rat-faced man with a beard the consistency of mashed spinach sat on a couch. He chugged down something—ale, she guessed, judging by its yeasty odor. Coffee and ale stained his jeans and white T-shirt. Reading his thoughts gave the rest of the story. Mommy had gone to work, leaving Robin alone with this wolf. When he drank too much, he got mean, and his meanness put Robin in the hospital.

Fury surged through Drusilla, and she shook with anger at her own parents as well as Robin's. She eased herself through the window and leaped into the living room. The man jumped from the sofa, still clutching his bottle. His eyes bulged and his face bleached bone white. He let out a scream as Drusilla's teeth snagged his throat.

Warmth slid over Drusilla as his gushing blood chased the loneliness and heartache that she'd felt earlier. When his heartbeat stopped, she tossed him aside like a rag doll. Perhaps Step-dad's death would give Robin a chance at happiness. Better yet, she'd let Leslie take the fall. After looking right and left, Drusilla scrambled out the window.

On second thought, she decided to keep quiet. Lately, it seemed, Ken invented reasons for whipping her. Last night, she went hunting without telling him, and paid for her indiscretion with ten lashes of the chain. Hades help her if he found out that she trashed the Taite home.

She guessed that Ken wanted her to leave so he could marry Leslie; but her poverty of funds and relatives made her his captive mate. Nursing children like Robin offered a decent income, but she could barely read and write, let alone treat complicated injuries. Either she'd sleep in a pine box or she'd steal the money to buy a shelter. Dread swept through her like a frosty wind, and tears pooling in the corners of her eyes ran down her cheeks.

Miles later, Drusilla turned left and headed up Broad Street, a major thoroughfare that led to newer buildings. Blue and red neon lights caught her attention—a sign saying "Neptune's Orchard." Fake trees and grass surrounded the white brick tavern and its tinted doors. After wiping her face, she shuffled up the marble steps.

Drusilla glanced at the sky. The stars' position promised six more hours of darkness. Plenty of time to kill. Besides, while Drusilla was cleaning her wounds from his last beating, Ken informed her that he was leaving for Adria for a few days to settle a property dispute. After blotting the fresh tears spilling down her cheeks, she took a seat at the slate bar.

"What do you want?" a bartender called, raising his voice over the blaring music.

"Red wine, any brand." According to Ken, vampires could handle wine in small sips. With drink in hand, Drusilla watched blobs of humanity float by, men in dark suits and women wearing beaded silk dresses. No one looked her way.

Sitting erect on her stool, Drusilla spread her hands across the bar. Her ring, a carat-sized diamond, glowed under the rainbow lights. Ken gave it to her after she became a vampire. She'd loved wearing his ring, but now, its cold, glittering stone seemed to mock her. With a burst of fury, she hurled the ring to the floor.

"Whoa there, Leslie!" a man's voice called behind her. Drusilla straightened up and started. Except for the music, a quiet came over the place.

The speaker, dressed in a brown gabardine suit, propped his hand against a stool, widening gray eyes focused on Drusilla. Rust colored, fine hair surrounded his mustached face. "Sorry," he said. "I mistook you for someone else. You look rather upset. Do you think tossing your ring will solve your problems?"

Drusilla gasped, realizing that she was crying again, and lowered her eyes. "I guess not."

"Could you use a friend?" he asked.

"I could, except ..." Drusilla shook her head and gazed into her wine glass.

Reaching down, the man retrieved the ring and handed it to Drusilla. "Every problem has a solution."

This is getting deep, Drusilla thought, probing the stranger's head. He was a thirty-five-year old history professor who lived alone. Once, he gave Leslie a diamond ring, and took it back after their final argument. *I envisioned you as a blossoming rose,* the words flashed through her mind. *Instead, you withered into a dried up weed.*

"I'm Tom Brent," he said aloud, "and you are?"

What name should she give him? Certainly not her own because the police were looking for her. "Tabitha," she said, smiling her tight-lipped smile.

"Want me to drive you home?" he asked.

Drusilla bore her eyes into Tom's, reaching into his soul. His eyes became glazed silver, and a dreamy look crossed his face. "Yes, please. I live off Johnstown Road in Philadelphia."

"I know Johnstown Road," Tom said absently. He led Drusilla to his car, a four-door parked near the entrance. "You're new to this area, aren't you?"

"I grew up in a town near Athens, Greece." Drusilla settled into the navy velour seat. She told him about her life on the farm, changing the location and names, and omitting the gruesome details of her jobs. "My parents made me leave when I turned fourteen, so I took a job cleaning houses."

Tom's eyes clouded. "That's awful. Do you ever see them?"

Drusilla shook her head.

"I can't imagine supporting myself at fourteen." Tom's voice saddened. "Unfortunately, you can't choose your parents. How did you survive?"

"I almost ..." Something—intuition perhaps—closed Drusilla's mouth. She felt his kindness seep into her soul, but confiding too much might scare him. "The gods looked out for me," she said, smiling thinly.

"I only know of one God, but I'm glad you made it."

"Trust me, there's more than one." Drusilla shuddered. "You want to watch out for Hades. He's dangerous."

"Hades?" Tom's eyes lit up like candles, and he broke into a grin. "I'm a Christian, but I've got many books on Greek mythology. I'd be glad to loan them to you." He laid his hand over Drusilla's. It felt warm and comforting. "I hope that America treats you well."

At home, Drusilla invited Tom inside, finding him approachable and easily hypnotized. She threw fresh logs into the fireplace. After lighting a rolled-up newspaper, she tossed it onto the logs. The flames flickered a moment, then died.

"Allow me," Tom offered, reaching for another newspaper.

Moments later, the fire crackled, twirling its shadows across the marble floor. The fireplace faced the door, its slate mantle extending across the rear wall. Ken had once bragged that he'd used it to cremate victims, but tonight, the fire set the stage for a romantic tryst. It hadn't crossed Drusilla's mind, until now, that she could love New World men.

Still hypnotized, Tom followed her upstairs to a bedroom. Drusilla slipped off his blazer and unbuttoned his shirt. He cradled her against his chest, pressing her ear against his thumping heart. She held him gently to avoid breaking bones.

"You're a beautiful woman," he whispered. "I'd love to show you America."

His body melted into hers, and Drusilla savored the feel of his warm skin. She never heard the door creaking downstairs or the heavy boots on the stairs.

The bedroom door banged open. Fists clenching his chain, Ken charged inside, his face contorted with rage. "Bitch!" he shouted. "Slut! How dare you bring your lover into my home?"

"Why do you care?" Drusilla snapped. "You've got Leslie."

With wiry hands, Ken lifted Tom by the shoulders. Tom's feet bicycled in mid-air before he soared through the room. His back crashed against the wall, jarring his dreamy face into a look of terror. Faint croaks escaped his quivering lips. Hugging the scarlet cover around her, Drusilla scooted to Tom's side. "Let him go," she begged tearfully. "He's got an important job, and Hades will avenge his death."

Frowning, Ken stared at the trembling young man at his feet. "A lowly teacher won't attract public notice, and your friend considers Hades nothing more than a fictional character." He licked his lips. "Besides, I haven't had dinner."

Stabbing pain flashed through Drusilla's head as he yanked her by the hair. Seconds later, his teeth burrowed into Tom's throat, trailing blood like ribbons down his naked body. Tom flailed with his arms and legs, unable to free himself from Ken's steel grip.

"I thought you were looking for more trouble, so I came home early," Ken said, cradling Tom's lifeless body in his arms. "Think twice before bedding down with another man."

"Why didn't you leave Tom alone?" Drusilla's voice came out in loud, choking sobs. "He would've taken me off your hands."

"I don't need any mortal's help to get rid of you." Ken carried Tom's body toward the stairs. "I should have gone after Leslie."

"I knew it," Drusilla screamed, fists balled inside the blanket's folds. She flew into the hall after Ken. "You went and bestowed Leslie with our powers."

"What!" Ken flipped his arms, sending Tom's body crashing down the stairs with sickening thumps.

"That's right, bastard." His startled look fueled Drusilla's rage. "She's one of us now, thanks to you. I saw her leftovers stumbling through the hospital."

"Leftovers?" Ken's voice softened. "If Leslie experienced the craving, she'll understand me. Maybe she'll even welcome my advances."

"Don't act so innocent," Drusilla said through clenched teeth. "You know that she ran to the police."

Bending over, Ken gathered Tom into his arms and marched toward the fireplace. "You're not making sense."

"Just answer me this," Drusilla cried. "How did it feel to make love to her?"

"I will not dignify that question with an answer." Ken's voice chilled like ice. "Obviously, beatings haven't taught you anything, Drusilla. Maybe watching your lover's cremation will."

Pausing before the fireplace, Ken dumped Tom into the fire. The flames shot upward, devouring Tom's skin. Within minutes, his clothes blazed to ashes. His charred, skeletal hands bounced in the air, as if he were waving goodbye.

"Ken, stop," Drusilla pleaded, rushing to the door. She had to get away, even if it meant sleeping in a cemetery. Cold, muscular hands snagged her shoulders. Ken shoved Drusilla against the wall. "No one crosses me, not even you."

"I hate you!" Drusilla cried, fists beating against his chest. Ken stood immovable as a block of stone. "I hate you."

"Do you?" Ken crooned softly. A stranger might have mistaken his cheerful tone and shining eyes for goodwill, but Drusilla knew better. She gazed toward the door.

"Do you really hate me?" Ken asked.

"I didn't mean that." Drusilla swallowed hard. "As one of Adria's former governors, you know best."

"If you really believed that, you wouldn't have betrayed me," Ken said in a cold voice. Drusilla's head bobbed up and down.

Ken's lips twisted into a crooked, evil leer. "Since you love this man so much, you shall spend eternity with him." He burst into raucous laughter.

Flexing his arms, he scooped Drusilla against his chest. "Let me go!" Drusilla screamed, kicking and thrashing. She was strong, but no match for Ken's Herculean grip.

Standing before the fireplace, he shoved her face up into the fire. Horrible searing agony licked up her back. She writhed and howled against the scorching flames engulfing her body. Ken's hideous laughter echoed in her ears as the darkness swallowed her.

Chapter 23

Leslie froze at Elliott's bedside, hand pressed against her mouth, stiff as a statue. His ivory linen gown reminded her of the vestments priests wore at church, but his blackened skull, pitted eyes, and nightshade grimace chilled her. Charcoal bones poked like twigs from his gown's flared sleeves and hem. With trembling fingers, she grasped his foot. His bones crumbled into ashes on the silk sheets. She screamed, recoiling slightly.

"What happened?" she asked in a low voice.

No answer, except for Alex's choked sobs. He knelt by the headboard, face buried in Elliott's robe folds.

"Alex." She tiptoed to his side and rested her hand on his shoulder. "Did your god, did Hades do this?"

Alex's eyes, filled with sadness and grief, regarded her fixedly. "Only Hades can fry people without burning their clothes. Do you understand the need for discretion now? Innocent people might get hurt."

"With visual aids like these, how could I not?" Leslie's eyes swept the room. She noticed letters and drawings of bats on the wall. "You loved Elliott like a father, didn't you?"

Alex nodded. "Elliott predicted that you'd have trouble understanding our life; I thought he'd make things clearer for you." Taking Leslie into his arms, he brushed the soot and ashes clinging to her hair. "I made a mistake bringing you here. No woman should see this."

"I've seen worse when I pulled emergency room duty." Reaching up, Leslie caressed his face. Alex looked fearfully old, fearfully used, the way she'd felt after her mom's death. "Besides, you didn't know."

"Hades will burn out my house, too. Our house, because I dragged you into this." Leslie felt his dead gaze on her, his tears dripping into her hair. "He'll damn us to eternal misery in Tartarus."

"You don't know that." Leslie backed away, only dimly aware that she'd begun to cry. The thought that Hades might be a demon occurred to her, but the idea implied sinister meanings that she couldn't face. She followed Alex through the blackened hall. "Did the other vampires ever use their powers to help people?"

"All of them killed and robbed their victims, except Elliott," Alex said in an odd, slow voice. "He earned his living selling paintings. Hades wants to destroy us all, Leslie. He doesn't care about our motives."

"Hades might make an exception in our case," Leslie said. "If the bats tell him everything they see, he must know that I'm using my powers to become a better therapist. He knows that you gave Willard a home, rescued me, and looked after people's investments. As a god, he's capable of mercy, right?"

Alex's thin lips quivered. Tiny sounds came and died in his throat.

"Right?" Leslie persisted, gazing into his watery eyes.

"*Mercy?*" Alex let out a long, choking sob. "You call what he did to Elliott *mercy?*" At the stairs, he cupped the ashes in his hands and let them run through his fingers. "You call this destruction *mercy?*"

"It doesn't make sense." Leslie trembled at the terror leaping in her throat. "In my church, even murderers can seek forgiveness if they're truly sorry." She shuffled up the steps.

Outside, the moon hung over the mountain pines, pushing through their branches like silver. Blasts of frosty wind slapped at her cheeks.

"Leslie." Alex laid his arm across her shoulders and

drew her close. "Don't confuse Hades with the God of Christianity. Your God makes allowances; Hades does not. Think of Crawford at his worst."

Leslie felt her mouth draw down slightly. "If I sued Crawford for harassment, I would've gotten my tutoring. Fitzpatrick would have survived."

"Fitzpatrick?" Alex echoed in a sharp voice. He rubbed his eyes. "What does he have to do with this?"

"I'm not sure." Leslie wrinkled her brows, digging for the seed of an idea that had materialized in the tunnel. The noxious, stale air made it hard to think. "The other night, Fitzpatrick's doctors took him off his respirator and let him go. He died because I was so busy worrying about Crawford that I couldn't concentrate on my work."

"And later, you lost your humanity," Alex added, defensiveness creeping into his voice.

Leslie stopped in mid-step, squaring her shoulders against a tree. "I stopped feeling human after my mom's drug overdose."

"You mean that?" Alex stepped and turned his head. His wide, green eyes settled on Leslie.

Leslie gazed at the moonlit sky, watching its shadows cap the tree tops like snow. "The first time you kissed me, you partook of me, like someone receiving a sacrament. No man ever loved me that way. But the idea of drinking your blood frightened me. If I understood that exchanging blood would join us, I might have gone along with you willingly."

"We'll never know, will we?" The skepticism lingered in Alex's eyes.

"If I'd learned to fight my own battles, that exchange might have ended in a warm bed instead of some smelly cave." Leslie met his gaze, her eyes resolute as steel. "With my lesson in assertiveness in mind, I think we should approach Hades or ask some other god to intervene for us."

"Leslie, don't!" Alex cried in a quaking voice. Tears glistened in his drawn cheeks like exclamation points.

"You're all I've got. If you get within ten feet of Tartarus, Hades will burn you alive. The other gods fear him."

"OK, I'll stay close to home. But Hades won't destroy us just like that. I don't want him to, so he won't. Because if he does ..." Leslie leaned against Alex, sobbing into his velour shirt. "It's not fair. Animals of prey tear humans to ribbons, but Hades leaves them alone."

"I know." Alex patted her shoulder. "It's not fair at all."

Leslie lapsed into silence, listening to the sound of twigs crunching under their feet and the birds cackling in the air. She felt the specter of death circling them like a wolf moving in on its prey. After the crossover, its eyes continued bearing into the back of her neck, watching and waiting.

At home, deep breathing and snoring echoed from the living room. Willard lay in the reclining chair, hands cradling the remote switch. He'd fallen asleep watching a movie.

Alex stared out the window, its linen drapes billowing around him. Watching him from the door, Leslie marveled at his wiry arms and legs, his fine features, and she felt bittersweet emotions—love mixed with sorrow.

"Alex." Even his name sounded sweet, like the cinnamon coffee she used to drink at her family gatherings. He turned toward her, his face mournful, and held his arms out to her. Leslie moved into his embrace, moaning softly as he kissed her forehead, cheek, and the hollow below her chin.

"Let's go upstairs," he whispered huskily.

Leslie gazed toward the steps, feeling excited and at the same time terrified. She longed to spend hours lying naked in his arms, but feared that the sexual tension would arouse her thirst again.

"Let's make the most of the time we have. I love you, Leslie."

Leslie couldn't answer; she merely nodded. He stroked her thick, fiery red curls, and she felt his gentleness seep into her soul. She followed him up the steps. At the landing, she pulled him close, fingers gripping his shirt. "I love you, too," she said, bursting with ecstasy.

Alex led her into the blue room and began removing her clothes. For the moment, Leslie forgot about the night's horrors. Nothing existed for her now, except Alex and the passion they felt for each other.

After Alex's clothes joined hers, he positioned her on the blue spread and lay beside her. His gentle caresses and endearments made Leslie long to join with him. Moments later, his body melted against hers. Leslie felt her passion burning like blazing embers as he mounted her. She cried and groaned with pleasure, hands splayed across his back.

Alex murmured her name over and over, and stiffened as her body and soul exploded in a cry of passion. She saw no approbation or condescension in his eyes, only genuine love. After his release, Leslie nested against his sinewy chest, fingers entwined in his silky, wavy hair. She would have joined his world long ago for such unconditional feelings.

Dawn was lighting the sky outside when she and Alex headed to the basement. She had only moments to think before her vampire day-sleep dragged her into oblivion, but it was long enough. She didn't realize true love only to have the jaws of death snatch it from her. No, she would plead with Hades to spare them. Even if it meant groveling on her hands and knees. And if Hades condemned her to hell in Tartarus, Alex's love would sustain her forever.

****

Leslie woke in Alex's arms. She feared that any second, Hades would send blasts of fire into their home. But it didn't happen. Instead of charred wood and cinders, she made out their familiar wall panels and spindle headboard. Giving a sigh of relief, she winced at the horrible, burning sensation.

Alex's eyes fluttered open. He planted a long, lingering kiss on her cheek. "I really enjoyed myself," he whispered.

"So did I." Leslie pressed her face against his chest. "I wish we could go to some island and forget Hades."

"I wish we could, too," he said, tracing his finger along her chin. "You sound like you swallowed a bucket of sand. Feeling thirsty?"

"That's putting it mildly." Leslie sat up reluctantly, hating to break the embrace. She put on her floral print robe. "Guess I'd better do something about it."

In the living room, Willard sat by the television, eating dinner. "Leslie," he said, looking up. "Warren called. He took your dad to the hospital."

"What?" She paused by the banister, hand gripping the stair post. "Did Drusilla hurt Dad?"

"No." Willard scratched his ruddy forehead. His eyes seemed far away. "Warren said that your father has ammonia."

"Pneumonia," Leslie corrected him. "Which hospital?"

"Betsy Ross." Getting up, Willard paced around the table; hands shoved into his jeans pockets. His fretful eyes and scarred face made him look like a beaten, elderly man. "I'm sorry. Your father treated me like a real person."

"He liked you, too." Leslie turned toward Alex, still clad in his robe. "To hell with Hades. I've got to see Dad. Like yesterday."

"Not until after you feed," Alex said. "You can't think clearly when the bloodlust is on you."

"Tell me about it." Leslie shivered. Her throat felt desert dry. She massaged her neck. "I've got to work tonight, too."

"Can I visit your father?" asked Willard.

"Sure," Leslie said, hurrying up the steps.

****

On the way to the hospital, Willard stopped the car at a seedy bar on Broad Street, where Alex and Leslie scouted donations for their respective blood banks. They found donors—a gang of young men looking for a good time.

At the hospital, Leslie's father lay in ICU, arms hooked to IVs. Probes attached to his chest monitored his heartbeat and nasal prongs fed him oxygen. His white hair seemed thinner and drier. A wet, putrefied stench wafted from his bed, sickly sweet and decayed sour, like moldy fruit.

Warren stood at the bedside, fingers hooked around his leather belt. His face glistened with sweat. Shelly sat in a leather chair by the bed, eyes focused on her father. Her red face told Leslie that she'd been crying.

Leslie laid her hands on her father's. "Hi, Dad," she said in a cheerful voice. "What happened to you?"

"Bad cold." Her father coughed a wet cough. One hand gripped the top sheet, the other clutched his chest. "I can't breathe ... can't swallow."

Leaning forward, Leslie listened against her father's chest. His lungs whistled long, harsh notes, and she felt each note shudder through her ears. "A breathing treatment will help," she said. "I'll ask Dr. Saunders to order one."

****

"Been there, done that," Warren said. "This husky, blond guy gave Dad a breathing treatment, Albuterol, I think. Said he works with you."

"Fred Mayes." Leslie gave a sigh of relief. "Thank God."

"Who's Fred?" Shelly asked, squirming in her chair.

"My good buddy and coworker. Warren, Shelly, I brought some friends." After making introductions, Leslie shifted her gaze between Shelly's weepy face and Warren's granite eyes. "What's going on?"

"You shouldn't have come," Shelly blurted, recoiling slightly. "Not with that woman chasing you. What if she shows up here?"

"Shut up!" Warren shouted, his voice dangerously close to tears. "I told Leslie to come. You don't like it, too bad."

"Not again," Leslie whispered, huddling close to Alex.

Alex drew his protective arm around her. "I won't let you go through this one alone."

Perching by Dad's bed, Willard leaned against the side rails and chattered about baseball. A smile crept toward Dad's ashen face. He might have laughed, but instead, another explosive cough left him gasping for air.

"Shit, we've got too many people in here," Warren mumbled, waving toward the door. "Leslie, come with me a moment."

Leslie squeezed Alex's hand. "I'll be right back."

She followed Warren to the floor's closet-sized kitchen. Head bent and back toward the microwave oven, Warren sighed. "Dr. Saunders said that Dad might need a ventilator. We're talking the long haul, as in months."

"Oh, dear." Leslie fought back her sobs. She'd heard her father's worsening cough, smelled the decay that followed him like a dark cloud, despite repeated rounds of antibiotics. Still, his crisis came on so fast. "Did Saunders say what caused the pneumonia?"

"Aspiration." Warren traced his finger along his cheek scar. "Shelly hid some grapes in her refrigerator. Somehow, Dad found them. He ate them and aspirated one. Gerry knows and he hasn't said boo. If this happened on our watch, we'd hear about it."

"I know." Leslie folded her arms across her chest, fists clenched. She fought back the tears and sobs welling up inside. Why couldn't Hades leave her alone? Why couldn't he understand that right now, Dad needed her?

"Gerry wants heroic measures," Warren said. "CPR, a ventilator, the whole nine yards. I can't see putting Dad through that torture."

Leslie glanced down the hall. "What does Dad want?"

"He never said." Warren mopped the sweat from his forehead.

"Unfortunately, I never read his thoughts on it either," Leslie said. "If I can get Dad in a lucid moment, I'll ask him his wishes and we'll take it from there."

Squeaking footsteps sounded from the hall leading to Dad's room. It was Willard. "Alex wanted to talk with Shelly alone," he said, ducking into the kitchen. "He said he'll get her to lighten up."

"I ought to sell tickets to that one," Warren snorted. "Willard, thanks for looking after Dad."

"I'd do anything for Leslie." Willard reached for a plastic cup and held it under the ice dispenser. Clattering sounded as the machine sprayed water and ice cubes. "Those bats cut me real bad, but Leslie saved my life."

"I believe it. The problem is that no one else in our family does." Warren's eyes moistened. "I'm heading back, in case Shelly loses it with Alex. Coming, Leslie?"

"In a minute." After Warren left, she turned toward Willard. "Willard, I've got more bad news. Hades destroyed Alex's friend, Elliott."

"He what?" With a startled gasp, Willard dropped his cup, spraying the linoleum with ice chips.

"We went to Adria last night and found Elliott's skeleton in his bedroom. Hades burned out all the surrounding apartments."

Willard's lips trembled. The images filtering from his head betrayed an unspoken dread, something pertaining to a dark palace and trees. With shaking hands, he filled another cup. The cup dropped again. Water and ice splattered the sink, his dungarees, and Leslie's lab coat.

"I told Alex that changing you would make Hades angry," he shouted. "I told him!"

"Keep your voice down." Leslie glanced out the door. The hall appeared deserted. After closing the door behind her, she continued. "I'm going to try to persuade Hades to spare me and Alex."

"He won't listen," Willard blubbered. "He'll burn you."

"Shh." Willard's darting eyes and wavering voice warned that he was going to be no help at all unless she hypnotized him. Eyes burning into Willard's, Leslie held a finger to her lips. "My father needs me alive. Do you understand that?"

Willard's head bobbed up and down, voice whimpering.

"I get this feeling that you know where to find Tartarus."

"You can't go there," Willard said in a loud whisper. "Hades will burn you."

Leslie gulped, trying to push back her terror. "Hades will destroy us if I keep silent, so I have nothing to lose. Right?"

Willard glanced toward the hall. "Alex will never forgive me for telling you."

Leslie cradled Willard's scarred chin in her hands, her eyes smoking into his. "He won't find out because you'll forget our talk when you leave this room."

Willard's voice came out in short rasps. "Make the crossover in the ravine where you had your accident. Turn until you're facing the Athyr Mountains. Head toward those mountains, and you'll pass a cemetery. After the last row of graves to your left, you'll see cracks in the ground. Tartarus lies under those cracks."

Leslie's eyes widened. "How do you know all this?"

"Before I worked for Alex, I fought for the Adrian army. We used to bury our dead in that cemetery. Sometimes we heard screaming from below the ground. One night, I saw smoke coming through those cracks."

Leslie suppressed a shiver. "I heard those cries when Drusilla brought me to the cave."

"You want to watch yourself going to the underworld." Reaching into his jeans pockets, Willard handed Leslie two silver coins. "After your descent, you'll have to cross a river, and you'll need these for the ferry."

Leslie gasped. "How did you get these?"

"My grandmother gave them to me. She was a seer. She learned all about Tartarus by communicating with spirits." He gulped his water and looked out to the hall. "Alex always blamed my nervous condition on the war. The war didn't scare me, those cries did."

"I believe it." Leslie touched his arm. "What did your grandmother tell you about Hades?"

"Hades wears black, and he lives in an obsidian palace. You'll see ghosts dancing through fields filled with black poplars." His voice saddened. "Whatever you see in Tartarus is bound to be unpleasant. You understand that?"

"I do." Leslie tucked Willard's coins into her leather purse. "Believe me, I do."

****

The night dragged on, with people weaving in and out of Dad's room. Leslie never got her chance to discuss what measures he wanted taken. Around midnight, his oxygen saturation dropped, and he lost consciousness. Dr. Saunders ordered Fred to put him on a ventilator.

Afterwards, Leslie asked Crawford for time off because of her dad. Mesmerized by her spell, he granted it without question. At home, Alex followed her like a shadow. He relented after Leslie said she needed a few hours alone with Warren. No one questioned her when she left the house the following evening.

Grabbing a canvas bag, Leslie packed her maroon gown and two liters of day-old blood she'd filched from the hospital bank. After getting behind the wheel, she breathed a silent prayer that she would come home alive. The drive to the scene of her accident went without a hitch.

After pulling over to the shoulder, Leslie changed into her gown and drank the blood. She gagged on its bitter taste. Though it had clotted to the consistency of dried paste, it left a pleasant moistness in her mouth. She then slid down the ravine.

Leaning against a thick trunk, Leslie took in her moonlit surroundings. She faced a tree that had split, dented by her car. In her mind's eye, she saw her car skidding to the shoulder, its wheels lifting as it rolled down the ravine. She heard the sickening crunch of metal tearing into tree bark. She longed to take back that night, to make Hades's threat and the other dangers disappear.

Every time something goes wrong, you crumble, she imagined Gerry saying. *If you see a problem, fix it.*

The trouble was, Gerry's courtroom experience never included dealings with demon gods and alternate worlds. She thought about the days when she and Mom took extended trips. Usually, they went to the Atlantic City casinos. She used to love walking through the hotels' glittering halls, admiring their paintings and crystal chandeliers. In her mind, she pictured a brass door lined with twinkling lights, like the kind she'd seen at the hotels.

A brass door materialized before her and swung open, its rainbow lights casting reds, greens, and blues on the grass. Hugging herself and shivering, Leslie bolted through the doorway into Adria's dimension.

Now surrounded by a maze of boulders and trees, she hiked up a trail that led toward mountains. The trail rounded toward a slope, and she found herself trudging past row after row of markers, battered stones with a foreign script. Every now and then, she noticed fresh flowers at a tombstone.

Loud keening reverberated from underground—a cacophony of cries sounding like people being tortured mercilessly. The noise was loudest around a deep, dark crevice hidden beyond the last row of graves. A bony hand of terror wrapped its fingers around Leslie's throat and squeezed. Soon, she'd face the being responsible for the tortures behind those cries.

What made her think that he'd listen to her pleas for mercy? She knew she should expect a horrible death. But Alex made it clear that a bad death was forthcoming, no matter what she did. Maybe Hades, sensing her ignorance to Adrian customs, might cut her a break. Maybe her world's inventions and achievements might impress him enough to stall her execution. *Wishful thinking,* her inner voice whispered.

With a deep shudder, Leslie rubbed her arms and walked toward the fissure.

Chapter 24

With her sneaker-clad feet wedged between the stones lining the rim, Leslie peered into the fissure, feeling like a pallbearer staring into a grave. Black grass sprouted from the pit's muddy walls, without rocks or protuberances to serve as footholds. She thought about Alex and the way she'd lied to him. She squeezed her eyes shut and shoved herself down the fissure.

Compacted soil under the mud slowed her ride at first, and then ... nothing. Down, down, down, she slid. She heard her screams echo through the abyss. After moments that seemed like hours, she crash-landed onto a pile of boulders and splintered rocks. The stones sliced through her body like knives, their sharpness digging into every part of her body. Sprawled on her back, eyes squinting skyward, she made out a patch of moonlight.

As her head cleared, Leslie realized that she hadn't landed on a rock pile. Instead, she found herself lying on a mound of human skulls and bones. The bleached skeletons, one dumped on top of another, stretched ahead as far as she could see. Swallowing hard, she struggled to her feet. Her superficial cuts were starting to close, but her dress had ripped to shreds. Bone chips poked from her wavy hair and tattered clothes. Her bag lay wedged in the rubble.

Listening hard, she made out a trickling sound. Running water. She headed toward its source, and moments later, happened upon a river. In the distance, a man with silvery hair and beard rowed a boat made of woven reeds. He parked it alongside the black-grassed shore where she stood. Ghostly figures ambled toward the boat like passengers boarding for a trip.

The captain stared at Leslie with shrewd, calculating eyes. Her back ached terribly. Other dangers lurked here, hidden ones that Alex and Willard didn't know about; but the prospect of convincing Hades to spare her and Alex motivated her to ignore her pain. She forced one foot before the other toward the boat. With trembling fingers, she placed one coin into the captain's gnarled hand.

Listening to the sound of her gnashing teeth, Leslie shivered toward her seat. The shadowy figures on board twittered among themselves like bats. One figure looked her way, but said nothing. Eyes focused ahead, she watched the captain take his oar and row across the river.

Harsh wails sounded behind her, punctuated by splashing. A man bobbed his head above water, waving and shouting for help. Two bats circled him, their ruby eyes following his moves. One of his hands missed three fingers. His blood turned the water rusty.

Leslie scanned the boat for a flotation device or something to throw at the bats, but the cabin offered nothing, except the wooden benches attached to its sides. The shades whispered to each other, but did not acknowledge the swimmer. The captain kept on rowing without answering his cries. He pulled up beside a rocky strip that led to another black grassy shore.

An iron fence, ornate with curlicues, surrounded this shore; its gate sported a gargoyle face. At the gate squatted an enormous dog with three heads, each one uglier than the next, gnawing what she hoped was raw beef.

Leslie felt someone's eyes on her. Turning around, she saw a woman wearing a crown of rubies exiting the gate. Her cool mint gown contrasted with the glinting auburn highlights in her braided hair. With her high cheek bones and willowy figure, she looked like Shelly's double.

The ghosts descended from the boat. Hugging her ragged skirts, Leslie walked in file with them. The dog looked up, slobbering and snarling, then scarfed down his meal. "Shelly?" she called timidly. "Is that you?"

Whirling around in mid-step, the woman gazed at Leslie with disbelief. "You can't stay here," she cried, the pitch in her voice matching Shelly's. "Go back before he kills you."

What was Shelly doing here? Perhaps Leslie didn't want to know. The devastation in the woman's voice spoke of something traumatic, like maybe a lethal encounter with Drusilla.

"Shelly, listen carefully," Leslie said. "Hades wants to kill me, no matter what. But Dad needs me alive. You know that, right?"

The woman regarded Leslie intently, but her expression implied sorrow. "I'm not your sister," she said. "Leslie, you are Leslie, aren't you? I'm Persephone, Hades's wife. Phetheus, his bat messenger, spies on you and tells Hades everything he sees. They don't know I can overhear. I understand your plight. My husband won't, though, and there's no convincing him."

"Husband?" Leslie echoed, arching her eyebrows. She never expected Hades to have a spouse, least of all one who might become an ally. "Can you make him see why I had to come here?"

"I couldn't make him see why I didn't want to be here." Persephone's lips trembled, and her eyes brightened. "Hades forced my hand in marriage, condemning me to live in this Underworld, far from my mother. He ignored my pleas to go free. I've begged him many times to go easy on his prisoners. He never listened. If he sees you now, he might not let me take you above ground." She glanced up the black, grassy slope. "Go back now, before it's too late."

"It is already too late." A towering, muscular figure swathed in yards of black cape glided toward the gate.

"Captain, what is she doing here?" he demanded, pointing toward Leslie. "Those shades belong here. She doesn't."

Leslie's scream came out a barely audible croak. Her throat felt like sandpaper. This had to be Hades.

Eyes glancing in her direction, the captain climbed off his boat and spoke to Hades in hushed whispers. Hades nodded at each shade walking by, like a teacher counting student heads. After he finished, his black eyes fell on Leslie, glowering like burning coals.

"You, there," he said in a stern voice. "No one visits Tartarus without being summoned. Give me a good reason why I shouldn't destroy you."

"Hades, stop this." Persephone hissed. "Phetheus told you about this girl's sick father. Must you continue your vendetta?"

"Silence, woman," Hades said in a low voice.

Persephone rolled her eyes. "Not in my lifetime."

"You don't have a lifetime," jeered Hades.

"Details, details," she sniffed.

Leslie gazed at Persephone and the shades that waited to get inside Tartarus. "If your bats gave thorough reports, you must know that Alex and I use our powers to help people. My senses alone enabled me to save two lives. I was hoping that you'd let us live."

"I am a god," Hades cried, clenching his fist. "My rages are not to be assuaged, nor my decrees nullified."

Persephone shot him a disdainful look.

What kind of god, Leslie wondered? *Demon? Angel? Perhaps a fallen angel, judging by his dress and dark surroundings.* She folded her hands, trying to still her shivering. "Lions, tigers, and other beasts of prey stalk in my world. They eat and kill people. The Supreme Being lets them live because they fit in with His master plan."

"That sounds well-rehearsed." Hades maintained his hostile glare, but some of the fire left his voice. "Did Andrej tell you to say this?"

"No, I learned about God as a child." Hushed murmuring erupted among the shades. Leslie raised her voice. "I respect your power, but my religion only acknowledges one God. And I don't know anyone named Andrej."

"Sure you do," Hades said. "He assumed the name Alex to protect himself from Kenworthy. That I understand. But hiding behind your skirts, sending you to Tartarus to plead for mercy makes him lower than a snake."

Leslie brushed the wisps of red curls from her eyes. She gazed at the shades, who were listening to the conversation with fascination. The glint in Hades's eyes and his crafty smile warned that the difference between the right and almost-right answer would send her up in flames.

"Alex warned me not to come here," she said after a pause. "If he knew I did, he'd lose it."

"You deliberately disobeyed his orders?" Hades cried with stunned surprise.

"Alex isn't my father. I've only got one father, and right now..." Leslie gulped, fighting the sobs building in her throat. She wiped the tears spilling from her eyes. "He's got pneumonia, and the doctors don't expect him to recover."

Hades advanced toward her, staring fixedly with his dark eyes. "You think that weeping will change my mind?"

"My tears have nothing to do with you." Leslie's voice trembled. "My father's staying at the hospital where I work. I've made enemies there who might do something to hasten his death."

A subtle look crossed Hades's square face. "Why would they do that?"

Leslie gazed into Hades's shiny eyes, wondering if he were reading her mind, but his blank expression offered no clues. "Before I became what I am, I asked for tutoring on certain procedures. My boss refused to give it. He said I was incompetent and unable to learn. I didn't push the issue because I feared that I might lose my job. Because of this fear, my mistakes antagonized people.

One patient died needlessly, leaving behind a wife and two children."

"Perhaps it was his time to die."

"No." Images of Fitzpatrick swam before Leslie, forcing her to put aside her terror. In a halting voice, she described Fitzpatrick's CAT scan and the mishap with his ventilator. "Loving Alex and becoming a twilight healer have taught me to love life," she finished. "Many patients die because the human eye can't spot symptoms until the disease has progressed too far. With my new powers, I can save those people. I know I can."

Hades leaned against the gate, bushy eyebrows furrowed. His voice saddened. "If what you're saying is true, your situation presents complications."

"I tried to tell you that," Persephone said, sniffing again. "You never listen."

"Leslie's telling the truth, great Hades," said the shade watching Leslie. He spoke in a silvery voice. "I'm Raymond Fitzpatrick, the one she's talking about."

A shadowy figure in white stepped forward. Leslie didn't recall his voice, but his pale face, cadaverous cheeks, and crusty lips were etched in her memory. "My Master won't let me rest until I've completed unfinished business," he said. "That involves you, Leslie."

Fresh tears flooded Leslie's eyes. For the moment, she forgot her reasons for visiting Tartarus. Her shoulders shook as she turned toward Fitzpatrick. "I'd give anything to take back what happened."

How could she explain, let alone justify something which cost someone's life? "During your test, your nurse screamed words at me that didn't make sense. Her shouting made it hard to think. I tried to move your ventilator to give your tubing enough slack. It didn't work." She sank to her knees, shoulders trembling. "I don't expect you to forgive me."

Persephone stepped toward Leslie's side. "If your mother was here, what do you think she'd say about this?" she asked gently.

More tears slid down Leslie's cheeks. "This happened because of my mother's death. I let her die, and since then, nothing has gone right." Between sobs, she described her mother's illness, the drug overdose, and the fights with Gerry. "I chose my occupation thinking that I could help people like Mom."

"In other words," Hades said in a pained voice, "your brother, a mere mortal, blamed you for her death, and you think that helping the sick will ease your guilt."

"Yes." Turning to Fitzpatrick, Leslie said, "For what it's worth, I'm sorry."

"People say that the comatose can't hear, but I heard everything during my CAT scan, including the remorse in your voice." Standing before Leslie, Fitzpatrick rested his hands on her shoulders. His fingers, though chilly, eased her shivering. "You've carried this burden for months. Isn't it time you let it go?"

The other shades murmured among themselves. Some wept. Hades did not cry, but his eyes shone with brilliance. "He's right. Your compassion and love for your parents could have earned you a seat in the gods' court. Instead, your guilt sentenced you to *undeath*. How can I forgive your condition when you can't forgive yourself?"

"I don't know," Leslie said in a broken, tired voice.

"Perhaps you could show her by example," Persephone said, smiling.

"Let Leslie go," Fitzpatrick begged, "so that she and Alex can get on with their lives."

"I wish I could," Hades said. "But allowing undead to thrive will only court disaster."

"Not in this case," Fitzpatrick said. "Leslie's tragedy and mine happened, in a way, because of the hostility she endured from her peer workers. Her demeanor alone tells me that someone condemned her long before she became my therapist. This act of mercy coming from you would prove to Leslie that she deserves forgiveness. Just this once, great Hades, let her and Alex go."

Hades stepped closer, his cape shimmering in the darkness, and looked down at Fitzpatrick. "Even someone of my temperament is capable of mercy, especially when I can teach a lesson." Turning toward Leslie, he waved his hand toward a black, grassy trail. "I have a proposal for you, the outcome of which may determine your survival. Come with me."

A proposal? Feeling intrigue mixed with terror, Leslie wiped her eyes and followed Hades. Keening of tortured souls echoed from an abyss to her left. Hades led her through a desert where a skeletal man lay gasping for air. His hands clawed at the sand, reaching toward a creek just inches beyond his fingers. After the desert, they plodded through black boulders into what looked like a castle made of obsidian bricks. Inside, he ushered her through a marble hall into a room furnished with an oblong table and chairs. Everything inside was black—the slate walls, the crystal chandeliers, even the candles sitting in their glass holders. Leslie stared wide-eyed at the ebony throne.

Easing into his throne, Hades motioned her to sit. Flapping wings sounded above her. A bat circling around the room perched on the throne, behind Hades's shoulder. Leslie tucked her hands under her thighs, trying hard to suppress a shudder.

"My bats won't hurt you," Hades said, smiling.

Willard's face, torn and bleeding flashed before Leslie's eyes. "My doctors and I saw these bats at the hospital. Will they try to hurt my dad?"

"If your father dies, it will be because of his illness." Hades looked at her steadily. "Do you know what brought my creatures to your world?"

"Alex said that you use them to spy on vampires." Leslie leaned against the table, hands folded. "Was their attack on Alex's house and his butler meant as a warning?"

"I think of it as my calling card." Hades smiled a crooked grin. "My bats also held a ceremony to restore your memory. Sometimes they transfer memories from one human to another to ease someone through mishaps like yours. When the parties die or become immortal, the bats return to undo their work."

"I suppose you've read my life?" Leslie covered her trembling mouth. Of course, Hades read her life history, including the fights between her parents. He probably knew when she'd taken her first step.

Hades arched his brows a moment, then burst into laughter. "Your world doesn't acknowledge the supernatural, does it? You're still overwhelmed by your own powers."

Leslie nodded, unable to speak. If she were still human, her cheeks would have turned scarlet.

"The events leading to your change of life, shall we say, intrigue me the most." Hades's voice grew somber again. "Your people's indiscriminate killing left orphans, widows, and homeless. I will end these crimes by going after their source. You helped my cause by destroying Drusilla."

"How?" Leslie stared at her towering host with bulging eyes. "I didn't even touch her."

"Kenworthy did the actual killing, but you set the stage by telling her that he made love to you. Drusilla flew off in a jealous rage and turned on him. No one turns on Kenworthy and lives to tell about it. He roasted her alive. Besides, Kenworthy wanted Drusilla out of the way so he could be with you."

"What?" Rubbing her temples, Leslie leaned back against her chair. "What does Kenworthy want with me? I never met him."

"Kenworthy has admired you from a distance and fantasized about making you his love slave," Hades told her.

"I suspect he'll approach you soon. You know him in an allegorical sense because you work for his dimensional twin."

"Crawford?" Leslie gasped, shivering.

"Yes." Hades sighed. "If you had thought clearly, you would have sought other employment."

"I found out about Crawford the hard way."

"I know. Kenworthy, like your superior, can't get enough power." Hades's face darkened. "Having money and the governor's position wasn't good enough for him. That scoundrel seduced my wife and bragged about it. He told everyone that he and Persephone shared this great love."

"Love?" Leslie ignored the phantom voice whispering that Hades's cruelty may have forced Persephone into Kenworthy's arms. "That man destroys everything he touches."

"Tell me something I don't know." Hades's words rumbled forth like a funeral dirge. "Two hundred years ago, I burned out Kenworthy's home, hoping to consign him to a slow, painful death. My plan almost worked."

"Almost?" Leslie looked down thoughtfully, then up at Hades again. His willingness to explain took the edge off her shivering. "How did he survive?"

"A town seer cast a spell to make him immortal," Hades said in an acid voice. "Since then, he has preyed on innocents and taught his followers to kill. I've bode my time for centuries, hoping that some mortal would figure out a way to destroy him. But I can't wait any longer. Do you see why?"

Leslie nodded, shuddering again. "More than once, I've stumbled on Kenworthy's casualties. But Alex doesn't act like a typical vampire. He fished me from a car wreck, paid my debts, sheltered my dad ..."

"And now, you're smitten with him." Hades shook his head, exasperated. "Unfortunately, Alex is no moral giant. Did he tell you about Delia?"

"You mean Elizabeth."

"No, Delia."

Leslie brushed back her dirt-crusted hair. "No," she said in a small voice.

"You seem to love this man," Hades observed in a dry voice. "Don't you ever question him about his past?"

Leslie shifted in her seat. "If Alex wanted me to know something, he'd tell me."

"Some things you have to ask." Hades took a deep breath, sounding like wind blowing through sand. "Alex met Delia a year after Elizabeth died. Delia had copper hair and a beautiful, fair complexion. She'd planned to marry someone else, but Alex was determined to have her. He hypnotized her, literally forcing her to become a vampire."

His eyes glowered like smoking volcanoes. "Delia hated drinking blood and being separated from her family. Three weeks later, she walked into the sunrise."

Leslie squeezed her eyes shut, trying to reconcile Hades's version of Alex with the man who loved her now. Colors floated in sickening patterns underneath her lids. She opened her eyes again. "Why are you telling me this?"

"So you can understand the nature of the beast. How would you feel if Alex forced his way of life on you?"

Leslie scratched her head. "I can't say because I lost my humanity the night my mom swallowed those sleeping pills."

A look crossed Hades's face—awe close to horror. "Doesn't it matter that Alex has ruined someone's life?"

"Yes," Leslie said, squirming in her chair. "But neither Alex nor I can go back and fix it."

Hades regarded Leslie like a scientist observing a specimen. His eyes glittered like gemstones. "Like I said, some things you have to ask," he said patiently, "because the past explains his present behavior. He made a life in the New World to escape Kenworthy. He fears that you might try to destroy yourself because he remembers Delia. He warned you to avoid Tartarus because he knows I'll fry him on sight for what he's done."

Leslie nodded, stunned to silence. The thought of

Alex robbing Delia's humanity turned her skin to goose-flesh. Still, it happened over a century ago. "Alex has carried this guilt too long," she said after a long pause. "Do you think we should show him a way to forgive himself?"

"Very well put, Leslie." Hades smiled. "I'll consider your request if you and Alex can stop Kenworthy."

Leslie's face jerked. Swallowing hard, she met Hades's piercing gaze. "You want *us* to eliminate Kenworthy?"

"You will," Hades said steadily. "If I do it, my fires will hurt innocent bystanders. Destroy him, Leslie. Use whatever means you've got."

Chapter 25

Leslie slumped in her chair, fingers gripping the table edge. Outside, shrieks of mad fear and agony came through the open windows. The screams rose and fell, punctuated by a deep-throated growl, and then the cries stopped. She felt her body tremble like a wire.

"You've become very quiet," Hades said dryly. "Perhaps you're not equal to the task?"

"Not at all." Leslie gulped, still horrified at the prospect of crossing Kenworthy. "Alex and I can figure out something."

"Good," Hades said, smiling. Getting up, he stared at an hourglass mounted on a black rock. "You should return to your world now. Morning has broken, but I'll hold the darkness until you cross the border."

With a wave of his hand, he motioned Leslie to the door and pointed to the black, grassy trail. "Stay on this path until you reach the upper light. It should take you an hour. Then you can make your crossover."

"Thank you," Leslie murmured, willing back her urge to protest. She counted herself lucky to leave alive.

While she trekked up the gloomy path, the screams started again. The inky darkness concealed the surroundings from ordinary people, but Leslie's night vision saw torn limbs scattered on the blood-streaked sand. Figures crawled about, searching for missing arms and legs. She pressed forward, eyes focused on the ground, not caring to step on or into the body parts.

After making her crossover, she found herself at a shopping mall. Its blue painted sign read "Lawndale Center." Rain came down in torrents, drenching her shredded clothes. The lot appeared deserted, except for a few stray cars.

She glanced at her watch. Its face had shattered. Looking toward the sky, she counted fifteen stars peeping between the clouds. Alex tried to teach her how to tell time by their position, but his explanation never made sense. "The hell with it," she muttered, heading to the street.

Moments later, she spotted an approaching truck. A sixteen-wheeler. She waved her hand. The truck squealed to a halt. A burly man poked his head out the cab's window. "Need a ride, miss?"

"Yes, please." After climbing into the cab, Leslie scanned the dashboard's clock. The digits "4:00 a.m." stood out in bright red. She concentrated on the driver, trying hard to ignore his sweet scent. His eyes assumed a vacant look. "I must get to Mill Road before sunrise."

Pink and lavender ribbons of dawn streaked the sky by the time Leslie shuffled up Alex's driveway. She tossed her soggy sneakers into a trash can by the garage. The hardwood floor chilled her bare feet. The house felt cold. Rainy spring nights in Philadelphia left dampness on everything. Inside, Alex paced his living room, eyes glued to the windows. Tears ran down his bone china cheeks, and black shadows circled his eyes. Shadows under a vampire's eyes meant that he was overdue for a meal.

"Leslie?" Alex started. Running to the door, he pulled Leslie into his arms. "I worried that you'd gone to Adria and gotten yourself killed."

"I spoke with Hades," Leslie said in a tired, wavering voice. "He said he'll consider sparing us if we bring him Kenworthy."

Alex backed away, his thin lips and shining eyes glaring with disbelief. "This isn't a joke. You look like hell."

"I'm not laughing." Leslie walked to the basement door,

rubbing her arms, trying to ease her chills. Her throat ached with the sensation of dry cotton lodging in her windpipe. If only she'd gotten fresh sustenance instead of stored blood. "I ruined my clothes when I fell into the pit."

"Pit?" Alex echoed, following her down the steps. "Where's the car?"

"I parked it on Sunset Lane, near the spot where I had my accident." Leslie backed against the secret panel, cringing at the sharpness in his voice. "Tartarus was a nightmare. I saw a three-headed dog, skeletons, and then Hades and I talked in his palace. I even met his wife."

"Persephone?" Alex let loose explosive epithets in a foreign tongue, his face turning the color of cement. "You went to Tartarus after I asked you to stay away?"

"I went there to plead for our survival." Leslie yanked the silver candlestick, desperate for rest, anxious for the night to end. The panel slid open, revealing the stairwell to their sleeping quarters. "Raymond Fitzpatrick and I made our peace. He and Persephone stood behind me when I approached Hades."

"So why are you shaking?" Alex followed Leslie down the steps. "The way you trust strangers before listening to me shows how much you hate my world."

"My name isn't Delia!" Leslie cried, gagging on the dryness that threatened to suffocate. After bolting through the metal door, she flopped into bed.

"What?" Alex grabbed Leslie's shoulder, turning her toward him. "Who told you about Delia?"

"Forget it." Leslie's voice cracked, and tears pooled in her eyes. "I'm too tired and thirsty, *Andrej*."

"So am I!" Alex shouted, his emerald eyes glowing fiercely. "I went all night without feeding, waiting for you, and ... why did you call me Andrej?"

"Never mind." Leslie swallowed hard, pushing back the lump in her throat. "Let's finish this discussion to-night. After we hunt Broad Street."

"Who told you about Andrej?" Alex persisted, his fixed gaze warning that he wouldn't back down without answers.

"Hades said that Andrej was your original name." Leslie buried her face into the rose print pillow, sobbing. "He told me that you forced yourself on some woman named Delia. You've carried your guilt all these years, and now you love it like some sickly old relative. How can you expect me or Hades to cut you any breaks when you haven't forgiven yourself?"

Without waiting for his answer, Leslie pressed her face toward the paneled wall, weeping, until her day-sleep plummeted her into nothingness.

When she woke hours later, Leslie went upstairs to take a bath. She scrubbed her body hard, erasing the debris and soot, longing to wash away her pain. After donning beige pants and a sleeveless floral top, she padded to the living room, where Willard and Alex were watching the news.

"Willard, I'm taking a cab to visit Dad. Warren will be there, and I'll catch a ride with him later to pick up the car. You're welcome to come with me, but ..." She cleared her throat. "I have to do something along the way."

Willard nodded with his usual stoicism. "What about Alex?"

Leslie regarded Alex's posture. Legs crossed and arms folded. Soon, he'd twist himself like a pretzel to cling to his guilt. "Alex is staying home so he can look after his old friend."

"Alex?" Willard folded his calloused arms over his chest. "Did you yell at her again?"

"Never mind." Alex leaned back, his arms sagging in the cushions. "I don't pay you to ask questions."

Leslie couldn't help wincing at Alex's sharp voice. "Hades said that people should ask questions," she said, looking at Willard. "So ask away."

"You spoke with Hades?" Willard gasped, his lips quivering. "How come you're still alive?"

259

"Before my car accident, I made an error which cost a patient his life," Leslie said. "He died just before my trip and came with me to Tartarus on the same boat. Hades heard about my mishap and decided to show me how to forgive myself. He set an example by letting me live."

"Sometimes the gods do the unexpected to teach their lessons," Willard said somberly. "Did you get what he was trying to tell you?"

"Maybe Alex and I can learn together," Leslie said. "Did you know that Hades has a wife? Kenworthy tried to seduce her, and now Hades wants him dead. He said he'll consider sparing Alex and me if we go after Kenworthy. But Alex refuses to cooperate."

"I never refused anything," Alex protested.

"I can tell by her look that you yelled." Willard cast Alex a reproachful glance. "Now she's afraid to ask for your help." Turning to Leslie, he said, "Why should Alex learn forgiveness?"

"That's for him to ..." A shrill ring of the phone cut into her voice. "I'll get it," she said, snatching up the receiver. "Hello?"

"Leslie?" Warren's broken, tired voice floated through the wires. "Dad's not doing well."

Leslie's hand tightened on the receiver. "What happened?"

"He had another stroke." A long pause followed. "His oxygen levels dropped, and Saunders upped his ventilator settings."

"I don't believe this." Warren's anguished, haunted voice pierced Leslie's heart. The anger she'd felt toward Alex faded. "Does Gerry know?"

"Gerry knows, and he wants heroic measures," Warren said. "Saunders will meet with all of us in an hour. Can you come to the hospital?"

"Sure," Leslie mumbled. She hung up the phone, sobbing. Family meetings at the ICU meant that death was imminent.

Alex jumped to his feet. The defensiveness escaped from his voice like air let out of a balloon. "What's wrong?"

"Dad's getting worse." Leslie buried her face in her hands. "Hades warned that Dad might die of his illness."

Alex rushed to her side, holding out his arms. This time, Leslie did not pull away. "I'll help you destroy Kenworthy. But now, Dad needs you. We'll get dinner on the way to the hospital."

****

At the ICU, a horrible smell wafted from her father's room, causing Leslie to grimace. He lay limp in bed, breathing tube poking through his milk-pale lips. Running to the bedside, she drained his ventilator's water-filled hoses. "Dad," she whispered, nudging his shoulder. "I love you."

Her father's eyelids fluttered like window shades. He coughed, setting off a chorus of ventilator alarms. Alex gazed warily around the room, his eyes twitching. "Look!" he cried, pointing to the ventilator.

A bat perched by the flow sheets, staring at her father with its ruby eyes. It shot a glance toward Leslie, then soared around the bed and out the window.

"Oh, shit." The putrid odor was heavy in Leslie's nostrils. She shifted her gaze, fighting panic, and inspected her father for gashes and bites. There were none. "Hades promised that his bats wouldn't hurt Dad."

"Let's not tempt fate." Alex banged the window shut. "Where are the nurses when you need them?"

"I don't know." Scurrying toward the station, Leslie spotted three nurses at the desk. One of them, Ruth, a member of Leslie's Hate Club, wore thick gauze around her left forearm. *I bet she tried something funny with Dad. Then one of those bats swooped down and nipped her.*

Sharp whistling jarred her to attention. Warren stood by the metal doors, jerking his thumb toward the hall. "Leslie, Dr. Saunders is waiting in the conference room."

"OK." Motioning to Alex, Leslie hurried down the tiled hall, with Warren behind her. "What about Shelley and Gerry?"

"Shelly's boss ordered her to work overtime, and Gerry had some emergency meeting with a client." Warren's angular face reddened. "Bullshit! He couldn't care less about Dad."

With Warren at the lead, they filed into the ICU's conference room. Leslie sat beside Alex, facing Warren. Saunders took a seat by the blackboard, a chart spread out before him.

Elbows braced against the table, he wiped the sweat from his forehead. "I consider you guys family," he said regretfully. "I'll do anything I can for Christian."

Leslie's head drooped and tears came to her eyes. Alex shoved his chair close and draped his arm across her shoulders.

"Christian has developed adult respiratory distress syndrome, a complication of his pneumonia. His chest x-ray showed white-out lungs." At this point, he stood up and grabbed a piece of chalk. He drew a rough sketch of the lungs on the blackboard, and then colored them white. "The fluid inside would impede his air ..."

Leslie tuned out his words, not needing to hear more. In plain English, adult respiratory distress syndrome, or ARDS, as the staff called it, meant that someone's lungs went on vacation. Permanent vacation, in many cases. Worse, her father's age and multiple strokes counted against him.

"I don't mean to bore you with medical jargon," Saunders continued, "but you need the facts in case you'd want to make him a no-code."

Warren leaned forward, stripe-sleeved arms folded on the table. His eyes brightened. "Does no-code mean no CPR?"

"It means that if his heart stops beating, we'll do nothing to revive him. It's a decision that only you can

make, but_...." A long pause followed, and Saunders looked |
each person in the eye. "All family members must agree. I
understand that Gerry wants heroic measures."

"He doesn't know the latest score," said Warren.

"Call him," Saunders said. "Christian's poor oxygen
intake could cause brain damage and impair his quality of
life."

Quality of life. Leslie used to cringe at that phrase
during Mom's flares with emphysema. It sounded like a
trumped-up excuse to quit when the doctor tired of his
case. But her father needed a miracle. More than once,
she'd cared for young adults in vegetative states, compliments of ARDS. Hands gripping Alex's, she rested her
head against his shoulder. "Do you think CPR could save
Dad?"

"It might revive his heart," Saunders explained. "But
the longer it takes, the more brain cells will die. That's
why many post-code patients have flat-line electroenceph-
alograms."

"Meaning absence of brain-wave activity?" Leslie
stared at the blackboard, now cluttered with Saunders's
diagrams. Saunders nodded.

"We consider those patients dead, even though they
have a heartbeat," Saunders told her. "You've seen such
cases, haven't you?"

Memories of previous cardiac arrests swam before
Leslie's eyes. She'd seen such cases all right. After revival,
the pupils became fixed and dilated, and the skin turned
waxen. Yet the beating heart imitated life. *This imitation of
life could fool vampires.*

At that thought, she sat up ramrod straight.

Alex rubbed her back. "Take it easy," he whispered.
"I won't let you go through this alone."

"Give it to me straight, Doctor," Warren said. "You
think Dad will end up a vegetable?"

"I can't answer that." Saunders let out a ghostly
sigh, his green eyes brightening. "There's always a chance,

however slim, that he'll come out of this. Talk this over amongst yourselves, and call me if you have questions." He stood up and headed to the door. "In the meantime, I'll continue antibiotics, supportive measures, whatever it takes to turn things around."

"OK." Warren shook his hand, as did Leslie and Alex. "Thanks, Doctor."

After the door closed behind Saunders, Leslie turned toward Warren. "Dad's independent," she said. "He won't want to spend months lingering on a ventilator."

"You've got that right." Warren paused at the blackboard, eyeballing Saunders's drawings. "None of this shit makes sense. But when I look at Dad, I see a man in agony. I'd better sign the DNR papers and keep it quiet."

"Please do." Leslie leaned against Alex, relieved that a decision had been made. "Alex, you didn't hear anything about those papers, right?"

Alex smiled and kissed her on the cheek. "What papers?"

"I'd better scram," Warren said. "I've got an interview to cover tonight."

Leslie watched him scurry down the hall, sneakers whispering against the linoleum. "Flat-line electroencephalogram," she said.

"What's going on?" Alex asked, rubbing her shoulder. "Your eyes lit up like Roman candles when Bill mentioned the EEG."

Leslie stared out the window, twirling her red curls around her finger. "I figured out a way to get Kenworthy."

Chapter 26

Leslie's father died three nights later while she, Alex, and Warren kept vigil. His flickering heartbeat heralded his death, but she didn't expect what came before his passing.

After midnight, he lapsed into a coma. Though the ventilator provided one hundred percent oxygen, his skin turned dusky and his chest muscles grunted with each intake of breath. He died within minutes, but it seemed like hours. Leslie held his limp, swollen hand against her face, weeping.

Alex handed her a box of tissues. "You gave Dad your best," he whispered. "No one can take that away from you."

"No one in the family loved Dad the way Leslie did," Warren said, blotting his reddened eyes. "Seeing Dad like this makes me think about Mom."

"Like Alex said, we gave him our best." Sniffling, Leslie wiped her eyes. She tried to remind herself that extraordinary measures of life support only prolonged suffering, but the tears kept flowing. "You did most of the work, keeping his house and hiring his nurses."

"Listen to her, Warren." Alex tightened his grip around Leslie and cocked his head toward the door. "You'll save yourself nightmares and years of ..."

A bellowing sound from the hall cut into his voice. Gerry was giving Dr. Saunders the grandfather of tongue-lashings. "Oh, Lord." Warren covered his eyes. "Here it comes."

Gerry burst into the room, tears streaming down his face. His swollen eyes focused on Leslie and Warren, and he jabbed his stubby finger toward their father's body. "Both of you, look what you've done! You should feel ashamed for putting him into this dive."

"Dad had adult respiratory distress syndrome," Leslie said. "Given his other problems, he didn't have a prayer."

"What did you tell Saunders?" Gerry asked abruptly.

Warren jumped up from his chair, eyes blazing. "What the fuck do you care? You never showed for any of the conferences."

"Saunders said that he made Dad a DNR with the understanding that I'd consented," Gerry said, his voice smoking with fury. "I never agreed to let Dad die. When I finish suing that incompetent, he'll dig ditches for a living."

"Money, money, money." Warren shook his head. "You never stop, do you?"

Waves of anger washed over Leslie, leaving her throat parched and dry. She stood up. "Gerry," she said, staring into his eyes. "Leave Dr. Saunders alone."

Gerry looked at Leslie intently. His lips trembled. "I guess I will, for now. Saunders will get his friends to lie for him. That doesn't take away your responsibility for Dad's death."

Gentle hands tugged at Leslie's arm. "Leslie, don't," Alex whispered. "I'm taking you home."

"Let me finish shutting Gerry down before he causes more trouble," Leslie said in a broken voice.

"People will realize that someone manipulated Gerry, and they'll ask why. Besides, Warren has his own plans for Gerry."

Leslie gazed at her brothers. Gerry's thin-lipped frown and narrowed eyes warned that any effect from hypnosis wouldn't last. Already, Warren was waving his fists and moving toward Gerry. It wouldn't be the first time he and Gerry settled their differences with a fistfight.

"OK." She followed Alex to the elevators.

At the lobby, she studied him, realizing that they'd quarreled a lot lately. "Alex, don't ever leave me," she blurted, bursting into fresh tears. "I know that my trip to Tartarus and other things upset you, but I'll try to do better."

Alex's lips quivered. "Oh, Leslie," he murmured.

"What's wrong?" Leslie asked.

"Nothing. I'm just following some advice that a wise old man gave me." Alex smiled, folding her into his arms. "I don't expect you to change, even when you rattle me. I don't expect anything from you except love. You've got me, Leslie. You'll always have me."

Leslie nestled in his wiry arms. His gentle touch and voice took the edge off her grief. "I couldn't lie down and die without pleading our case with Hades. Do you understand that?"

"Of course, I do." His grasp tightened. "When you're ready, we'll go after Kenworthy."

****

Leslie couldn't make it to her father's funeral, a noon service, but the evening before, she attended the viewing. Each night, she laid flowers at his grave in Meadowood Cemetery. She insisted on going alone in case Kenworthy approached her. After each visit, she drove past Kenworthy's house, hoping for a chance encounter. Then she'd use his alleged infatuation to her advantage.

Instead, she only saw the meadow surrounded by woods, a flat silvery sheet in the moonlight. The house appeared deserted. Either Kenworthy was lying low, or he'd set up shop in another state.

The following night, while weeping over her parents' tombstones, she heard velvety soft footsteps. A pungent smell wafted from the street, and then she felt a hand on her shoulder.

"Who died?" asked a man's voice. Crawford's voice, with a thick accent.

Lifting her fine eyebrows, Leslie made out angular

features, silver eyes, a crop of chestnut hair, and thin lips. The stranger looked like Crawford. He even wore a black, businessman's suit like her boss.

"My name is Kenworthy." The stranger smiled. "I believe we've met."

"Oh, shit!" Leslie scrambled to her feet. She never counted on Kenworthy surprising her. She kept her voice low, not daring to provoke him. "I saw you in Betsy Ross's alley, feeding on my coworker."

"I realized that you cared for him so I spared him." His lips curled into a crooked smirk. "I couldn't hurt someone close to you."

"I appreciate your kindness," Leslie said in a small voice. Looking down, she noticed the mud stains on her orange slacks and sneakers. She backed against her father's marker, shivering.

"You shouldn't wear trousers." The intensity of Kenworthy's stare sent tentacles of fear through her heart. "A woman should dress like a woman, don't you think?"

"I guess so," Leslie mumbled, stepping behind the tombstone. She could run, if necessary.

"I don't mean to castigate your choice of attire." Kenworthy's voice softened, but his eyes wore the look of a cobra waiting to strike. "You've lost someone dear to you."

"My father died of pneumonia."

"I'm sorry to hear about that." Kenworthy affected a sigh, but his glaring eyeballs made Leslie feel like a mouse gazing into the jaws of a lion. "Where I live, pneumonia takes the young and old. It creeps up on you like a specter in the night."

"If Adria had antibiotics ..." Leslie clamped her mouth shut, trembling. That monster couldn't care less about medicine, and she knew it.

"Don't stop." Kenworthy's eyes shone like silver. "You seem like an intelligent woman."

He sure knows what buttons to push. Leslie smiled, hoping that she looked calmer than she felt.

"Very intelligent," Kenworthy repeated, his voice laced with sugar. "Drusilla said that you became one of us. I assume you've heard about me, none of it good."

"I form my own opinions," Leslie said through clenched teeth.

"Do you?" Kenworthy reached out and smoothed the collar on her lace blouse. Leslie cringed at the feel of his icy fingers digging into her skin. "You convinced Drusilla that I turned you. Your story made her angry enough to have an affair behind my back. Allow me to congratulate you."

"Thank you ... I think." Leslie swallowed hard. "I was trying to distract Drusilla because she threatened to destroy my family."

"She can't hurt you now," Kenworthy said. "I find you very attractive. Besides, you've got a lawyer and newspaper reporter for brothers. Hurting any of you would draw unfavorable notice."

Leslie nodded, brushing back her thick curls with shaky fingers. "You sure did your homework on me."

"I'd consider it disrespectful not to." Kenworthy smiled, his pointed teeth glistening in the moonlight. "Hades destroyed most of my people, including Elliott. Perhaps you and I can share hunting territories. I'm sure that we can reach some agreement."

And if we don't, his steely eyes and crooked smile said, *I'll make you an offer you can't refuse.*

"You can't control Drusilla." Leslie said. She hoped that faking ignorance about Kenworthy would spare her the agonizing fate that Drusilla suffered. "When the cat's away, the mice prey."

"I destroyed this particular mouse," Kenworthy said in a matter-of-fact voice. "She fed without discretion, taking officers and public dignitaries, and left her kills where people could find them."

"Why did she kill?"

"Sometimes your thirst won't let you quit until you've drained your source." His voice was flat and deathly cold. It made Leslie feel as if someone had slapped her with a bag of ice. "You'll find that out one day. So tell me, Leslie, how do you like our vampire world?"

Leslie gritted her teeth, hating to share her feelings with this snake. Too much enthusiasm rang false; too little made her look unworthy of his respect. "Fifty-fifty," she said after a pause.

"Fifty-fifty?" Kenworthy threw back his head and laughed. "Most people either hate our life or embrace it."

"My parents raised me to help, not hurt people," Leslie said. "I treat people with lung disease for a living. Drinking blood goes against my background. Because I can't go out during the day, I hardly see my family."

Kenworthy stepped forward, his voice oozing with snake charm. "Something made you find *undeath* worth living."

Leslie backed away as Kenworthy inched closer. "Certain mechanical deficiencies almost cost me my job, but my new senses compensate for what I lack in ability. Darkness looks like living color. My strength allows me to move equipment and patients, and protect myself on the street."

Kenworthy draped his arm across her shoulder, pressing his leg against hers.

"Most of all, I value the *freedom*," Leslie added, wrenching from his grasp, "gained with my new powers."

"My, aren't we touchy," Kenworthy said with mock wonder. "I thought you wanted companionship."

"I don't like being pawed by strangers," Leslie said hotly.

"You said you liked your new senses," Kenworthy protested. "The sex act will thrill every nerve and take you to heights of ecstasy never known by humans."

"And of course, you can't wait to show me." Leslie laughed, a nervous giggle. "I'm saving myself for the right man."

"You mean the one who turned you."

Leslie brushed back her hair with shaky fingers. She'd have to invent more lines than a con artist to fool this pig. "A woman saved me because I reminded her of her younger sister, but then, you wouldn't understand familial love."

"I understand more than you think," Kenworthy said, "because Drusilla took my knife, the only thing I had left from my father. It had a platinum handle. He used it in battle."

"Platinum?" Leslie stared across the graveyard, thinking about the well. "Does it have the initial 'M'?"

Kenworthy nodded. "Drusilla lost it when she went hunting, and the police found it. They badgered me with questions about Claire Benson's murder, forcing me to reason with them."

Leslie mustered a smile, but her fists clenched in her pockets. "You only get one father and you should have something that belonged to him. If you want, I can get your knife back for you."

"I don't expect you to risk attracting the officers' attention," Kenworthy said, seemingly touched by her offer.

"Don't worry about it." Leslie waved toward the street, where she'd parked her car. "I can convince an officer to let me into the evidence lab. If you behave, I'll drive you to the station myself."

Kenworthy's gray eyes widened. "But you've got such sensitive eyes."

"I can drive if I wear sunglasses." Leslie rooted through her purse and pulled out her glasses case. "Let's go."

****

"What's wrong with you?" Alex cried hours later, when Leslie told him about her encounter with Kenworthy. His face turned dusky and his neck muscles tightened like ropes. "You let that beast get into our car!"

Leslie shrugged. "The station was too far to walk."

"What were you thinking?" Alex railed; his fury was passing, and fear was now arriving. "Kenworthy can fry you or lock you some place where the sun can get to you."

"Hades expects us to hand him Kenworthy, remember?" Leslie said in soft, measured tones. "I'll need Kenworthy's trust to put my plan in motion."

"What plan?" Alex leaned against the mantle, green eyes smoldering like heated embers. "I don't like Kenworthy touching you. What if he rapes you?"

"He won't if I get his respect." Leslie smiled. "You should have seen his look when I gave him the knife. It was like I'd given him a million dollars."

"I still don't like it." Alex paced around his living room. "Hades sent you after Kenworthy knowing we'd get killed."

Leslie stood before Alex, looking him in the eye. "If Hades wanted us dead, he would have destroyed us by now. Will you calm down and listen?"

She lowered her voice. "Do you remember what Dr. Saunders said about flat line EEG's? Such readings mean brain death. I think that blood from a brain dead patient would poison people like us, but Kenworthy doesn't know that. Betsy Ross gets a lot of these patients; perhaps I can trick him into drinking their blood."

"Maybe." Alex laid his hands on Leslie's shoulders. "What happens if Kenworthy feeds and your theory about brain dead people happens to be wrong?"

"He'll walk away with a warm stomach, and a certain god will get angry." Leslie shuddered, still thinking about Kenworthy's unsettling stare. "Alex, this is the best chance we've got at beating him. I'll offer Kenworthy a meal to prove my goodwill. He won't know the blood's tainted until it's too late."

Alex sagged against the mantle, rubbing his forehead. "I really hate the idea of you going near that man."

"I really hate the idea of frying in Tartarus." Slowly, Leslie walked toward Alex and kissed him on the cheek. "Don't you think we've earned the right to live?"

"Of course, I do. Whatever happens, Leslie, just know that I never meant to bring you into this nightmare." With a deep sigh, Alex turned on his heels and shuffled up the steps.

"Wait!" Leslie cried, feeling her heart sink. Was he giving up on her? "Where are you going?"

"I'm looking for a decent disguise," Alex said in a flat, resigned voice. "You don't think I'd let you do this alone, do you?"

****

Weeks passed. Kenworthy began visiting the hospital. He waited for Leslie in the courtyard, joining her every time she went on break. He bombarded her with sexual invitations, promising expensive jewelry and other "fringe" benefits.

At work, Leslie scanned the computer for patients with flat-line EEG's, people who'd survived cardiac arrests or massive head injuries. She got a hit during her rotation in ICU. Her list of patients included a young man named Steve who'd smashed his head in a motorcycle accident.

"Hello, Steve." She walked into the cubicle. "I'm Leslie."

"Skip the introductions," a nurse said, looking over from the monitor. "Steve's got a flat-line EEG. He's gone."

Leslie gazed at the patient. He smelled slightly rancid, but his heart pumped with a steady beat. His mustached face looked like that of a porcelain doll. Blood oozed from the bandages covering his head.

"Why are we keeping him?" she asked.

"His family wants to donate his organs. Dr. Jamison will meet with them tomorrow."

"I see." Leslie checked his ventilator in silence. After she finished her rounds, she glanced at the wall clock. It was almost one a.m., Kenworthy's visiting hour. She could set her watch by his "surprise" arrivals. After assuring herself that the floor nurses were occupied, Leslie walked to a phone and dialed Alex's number.

"I've got a brain-dead patient," she said after he answered.

Alex let out a startled gasp. "Where?"

"The ICU." Leslie glanced toward the window facing the courtyard. Already, she saw Kenworthy's black-suited figure seated at a bench. "Kenworthy's outside. I'll tell him that dinner's waiting."

"Stall him for fifteen minutes," Alex said in a tense voice. "I'll distract the nurses before he reaches your floor."

"Make it quick. Kenworthy's salivating like a dog in heat."

After combing her hair and applying fresh makeup, Leslie proceeded to the courtyard. She found Kenworthy sitting near the rose bushes. "Hello," she said, smiling and taking a seat beside him.

"You look better every time I see you." Kenworthy gave her a ghoulish grin that she guessed was meant to be engaging. He edged closer and pressed his thigh against hers. "I'd like to take you home with me."

"My shift doesn't end until six," Leslie said, her back stiffening.

"Since when do mortals dictate your hours?" Kenworthy gave her a wounded look. "You and I could have something good."

"You don't know me that well," Leslie said, forcing cheer into her voice.

"I know plenty," Kenworthy said. "We'll work well together. Your job will provide a beard for our night activities."

"You think so?" Leslie laughed. "Did Hades tell you that, or are you trying to impress me?"

"Both." Leaning forward, Kenworthy brushed his hand against her left cheek. "My connections would surprise you. Did you know that I used to govern Adria?"

"No, I didn't." Another lie, but these days, lies came as easily as drinking blood. Leslie smiled. "Perhaps you can share those connections with me over dinner."

"Dinner?" Kenworthy arched his bushy brows and frowned. "Who will supply the nourishment?"

"I will." Leslie glanced around the courtyard, but it appeared deserted. "Where I live, a person cooks dinner for someone they want to know better. Since neither of us can handle table food, I'm offering a young man who's hurting badly. His parents don't expect him to recover, so they won't question his death."

"You'd offer me a patient?" Kenworthy's eyes bulged. His shocked look faded, replaced by a grin. "I never refuse nourishment, so lead me to dinner."

Leslie jammed her twitching hands into her scrub pockets. "Follow me to the loading dock," she said, forcing coolness into her voice. "The lobby is crawling with officers. I'd better find you a uniform in case someone asks questions."

Hands clasping Kenworthy's, Leslie led him to a cement deck. A combination lock secured its doors, but she'd convinced an officer to give her its combination weeks ago. She walked Kenworthy down a tiled corridor to a freight elevator. At the first floor, she spotted a door marked "Resident." She wriggled its knob. It was unlocked.

"Sometimes the doctors keep spare uniforms here," she said, nudging open the door. Inside, blue scrubs and lab coats lay piled on a chair by the bed. "Put this on," she said, tossing him a scrub uniform. "We're going to the ICU."

"What's the ICU?" A dazed look crossed Kenworthy's eyes.

"A place where the badly injured and sick go," Leslie said, before stepping out to the hall. "I'll wait for you outside."

Moments later, Leslie ushered Kenworthy to the ward. His silvery eyes took stock of his surroundings. He grimaced. "I'm not feeding on sick people. Their blood tastes like acid."

Leslie glanced toward the station. Two nurses leaned over the desk, heads folded in their arms, appearing to be asleep. She thought she detected a musk smell—Alex's scent. She held a finger to her lips. "Steve was healthy as a mule before his accident," she said, prodding Kenworthy toward Steve's room.

"In Adria, vampires feed on dying soldiers. I know because one of those soldiers provided my first meal. Think of the ICU as your battlefield, and Steve as a soldier with healthy blood."

Kenworthy walked toward Steve's room, inhaling deeply. His grimace faded, and he laughed a hideous laugh, sounding like rattling bones. "Maybe I should come here all the time."

Leslie felt her fingers curl into claws. She longed to assault Kenworthy with a lit torch. Instead, she scurried into the room to silence the heart monitor and ventilator alarms. "I'll stand lookout in the hall. Enjoy."

After scanning the ward for visitors and seeing none, Leslie watched Kenworthy approach Steve's bed. His eyes shone like glazed stones. After whispering something into Steve's ear, Kenworthy bent over his neck.

Hands rubbing her arms, eyes shifting between the hall and desk, Leslie listened to the soft sucking sounds. The noises cut short, and Kenworthy let out a deep-throated howl.

Chapter 27

Kenworthy's scream rang out again, a cry of inhuman anguish and mad fear. Leslie whirled around. Blood trickled from two puncture wounds on her patient's neck, but his heart still beat, aided by the respirator and IV medications. His eyes focused vacantly at the ceiling, unaware that a 200-year old vampire was withering at his bedside.

The excitement fled from Kenworthy's eyes, chased by disbelief and shock; yet still, he screamed. Creases broke out on his face. Thin lines spread at his chin. His lips turned flabby, and his face grew loose around the bones in his cheek. His hands twisted and contorted, until they resembled those of a very old man.

Leslie stepped backward, glancing at the window parallel to the bed. The doors behind her burst open, and Alex came running into the ward.

Outside, heavy wind began to blow—only it wasn't wind; it was flapping of wings. She had time to watch Kenworthy's withering hand claw the bed rails, time to hear the monitors beep in the other patients' rooms. She saw Philadelphia—its battered tenements, abandoned buildings, a bruise-colored sky ... and then bats everywhere, more than she'd ever seen before. Philadelphia was turning into an immense bat cave.

It looked like Tartarus. How could she escape a second time?

Alex's white-sleeved arms cradled her shoulders, and she knew she was still in Philadelphia. "Let's go," he whispered. "His destruction will complete itself."

"What about the nurses?" Leslie glanced sideways toward the open door. In the ward, the two nurses remained slumped over the desk. "Suppose a security guard comes in to check? They've got keys to every room."

"The nurses will sleep peacefully. I made sure of that before you and Kenworthy got here. I also hypnotized the officers and confiscated their keys."

Leslie peered toward the station again. Despite Kenworthy's bellows, the nurses didn't stir. "We'd better stay," she said, shaking her head, "and make sure nothing goes wrong."

"Andrej!" Kenworthy spat out. His fingers jabbed at the heart monitor. "Leslie, how? Why? His heart still beats. *What have you done to me?*"

"You supped from a dead man," Leslie said coldly. "The machines keep his heart going because someone needs his organs."

Outside, the rustle of bats grew to a roar. The decrepit buildings, the streets, and the sky had disappeared, replaced by a gray and white curtain peppered with glittering fangs and shiny red eyes. Leslie recognized the bats as Hades's messengers. She heard chewing noises, the bats gnawing the outside screen, when Kenworthy slammed the cubicle's glass door shut.

Chittering issued from the door. Kenworthy, now a withered, ancient man, wove spasmodically toward her. Flakes of skin fell from his twitching arms in a gruesome rain. "Stop it!" he shouted, waving his fists. "Whatever you're doing, stop it right now."

Alex stood, back pressed against the wall, shaking his head. He burst into triumphant laughter. "Come on, Kenworthy," he said, pulling Leslie close. "Leslie's only finishing what you started years ago, when you locked me in your courtyard."

Standing by Alex's side, Leslie watched the screen outside the window fall away. The bats were now working on the window itself. Already, she heard creaking, the sound of its hinges coming loose.

Still screaming, Kenworthy wobbled toward the bed. He clawed through his pockets and brought out a cigarette lighter. His eyes, sunken deep inside his head, became glazed silver.

"You want me dead, Andrej?" he croaked, and Leslie saw the skin around his face crack, revealing tufts of gray flesh. "Both you and your lover are going down with me."

"Kenworthy, no!" Leslie shuddered at the phantom voice warning that it was too late to run. She glanced between Steve's bed and his machinery, hoping to find something that would distract Kenworthy. The ventilator was still pumping oxygen into Steve's lungs—one hundred percent oxygen. A lit match could cause an explosion.

"That's right, fire and oxygen make a deadly combination," Kenworthy shouted. "This lighter used to belong to your friend, Officer Hannon. I carry it for insurance."

"Kenworthy, don't." Alex threw his body in front of Leslie. He kept glancing toward the window.

"Don't what?" Kenworthy looked toward the window and let out another blood-chilling shriek.

Splintering sounds came from the window. The glass panel popped open, and dozens of twittering bats swarmed into the cubicle, followed by dozens more. The ventilator alarms went off as the bats clawed at its tubing. Somewhere there was a crash as the heart monitor exploded. A clattering of syringe boxes falling to the floor. Metallic clangs—the sound of bats blundering into the ventilator and IV pumps.

And still, Leslie heard Kenworthy's screams.

"Leslie, run," Alex shouted, grabbing her arm.

"If we open the door, those bats will be all over ICU," Leslie cried, pulling from his grasp. "Besides, I've got to check the ventilator."

279

She felt the room close in on her as she tunneled through the bats to get to her patient. She cringed until she realized that no bat touched her the entire time. They'd come for Kenworthy, but she gagged on the stench of bat dong. Around her, she heard the clatter of falling equipment and the tinkle of broken glass. Kenworthy kept on screaming, his cries blending with the twittering of the bats, creating Tartarus right there in the ICU.

While she fed her patient oxygen with a plastic bag, Kenworthy collapsed, his bony hand still gripping the lighter. His skeletal arms flailed at the bats, but his final attempt at bravado fled, replaced by horror and understanding.

"No!" he screamed. "Hades will never get me."

Leslie understood what was happening. Kenworthy would not die an ordinary death. He would not ride the boat across the river Styx like most Adrians did after they died. Instead, the bats would escort him directly to Tartarus and his final judgment. "Grab him," she cried. "Take him to Hades."

Leslie looked at her patient. His heart still beat with a steady rhythm. Bats lit on his bed, but did not attack. They also perched on her shoulders and Alex's, waiting and watching. The other bats closed in on Kenworthy, grabbing his clothes, his arms, and his legs. Within minutes, he disappeared under a pile of gray wings and sharp teeth. But Kenworthy would not check out without a fight. His arms thrashed, causing the horde of bats to shift, revealing a hideous sight.

Kenworthy was disintegrating alive. His eyes and cheeks sloughed away, leaving behind a skull. Bits of flesh clung to his bones. His scrubs shredded to tatters. Naked ribs poked through his crumbling skin, but still, he screamed.

The bats shifted again, and then their wings flared and beat. The thing that had been Kenworthy, now a decomposed 200-year-old vampire, rose in the air in a blanket of bats. The blanket moved across the cubicle through the open window.

Still feeding her patient oxygen, Leslie craned her neck toward the window. Alex stood behind her, arms wrapped around her, looking over her shoulders. The bats lifted Kenworthy up to the top of the tenement buildings. She thought she heard a high-pitched scream from those buildings. The other bats streamed from the room, funneling toward Kenworthy, forming a grayish, man-shaped patch. The patch moved over the buildings until it blended in with the sky.

"We cut that one real close," Alex whispered, leaning his face against hers. "But Kenworthy cannot hurt us anymore."

"I guess not." Leslie glanced toward the station. The two nurses still lay keeled over their desk, fast asleep. Later, she would wake them for their next patient rounds. "I wouldn't want to be in Kenworthy's shoes when he reaches Tartarus. Do you think his death will satisfy Hades?"

"I pray it does," Alex whispered. "For both our sakes."

Chapter 28

Hades stood on the river Styx's grassy shore, gazing toward the upper light. Tonight, Phetheus had told him, Leslie planned her move against Kenworthy. Hades expected his messengers to return with Ken's body at any moment.

As he gazed at the darkness over the river Styx, whispering footfalls sounded behind him. It was Persephone, dressed in her ruby-studded ivory robe. "So now you've got another soul." Persephone stamped her slipper-clad foot. "You've sent Leslie into a trap, knowing she'll get killed."

"What soul?" Hades asked, half-listening for twittering bats. "Leslie went willingly."

"You gave her an ultimatum: deliver Kenworthy or die." Persephone kept her voice low, but her eyes burned with fury. "You knew that Leslie was no match for Kenworthy."

Hades sighed. "You don't know what you're saying."

"Don't I?" Persephone's blue eyes locked with his in heated combat. Hades dropped his eyes and looked away.

"Why can't you let Alex and Leslie get on with their lives?" Persephone continued, her voice softening.

Hades reached his black-sleeved arm toward his wife. "I must make their survival contingent on bringing Kenworthy," he said, trailing his fingers along her wrist. To his amazement, she did not recoil. "Otherwise, he'll go on killing people and school others to do the same. Do you remember how he roasted Drusilla alive? In the end, he'll do the same to Leslie and Alex."

"I hear that he loves Leslie," Persephone said mildly.

"The lover you knew no longer exists." Hades felt the familiar rage stirring again, but he mustered calmness into his voice. "When I set fire to Kenworthy's house, the smoke got to his brain. It made him crazy and dangerous, even before he became undead. Tonight, Leslie plans to poison him. I sent my messengers to her hospital to ..."

He paused in mid-sentence to listen. He thought he heard distant humming punctuated by a man's scream. "My messengers are coming. I believe they've brought me Kenworthy. If not, I'll go after him myself."

****

A man-shaped, grayish patch soared over the river, and screams echoed through the abyss. A pile of wings, red eyes, and sharp teeth lit on the grassy shore. The bats scattered, leaving behind a skeleton covered with flaky skin and tufts of gray flesh. Yet he screamed piercing shrieks, flailing his spidery arms as he rolled on the grass. Even in the man's present condition, Hades recognized him as Kenworthy, his old rival.

"Did you have a great time?" Hades jeered, sending out two bolts of blue to the man's bony toes. He laughed as the man writhed between the scattering sparks. "Did you enjoy yourself?"

"Don't do this," Kenworthy begged, clawing at the grass. "Don't let me ..."

"Suffer?" Hades laughed. "You expect mercy when you've shown none to your victims?"

"Persephone?" Kenworthy rasped. "You can influence your husband. Tell him to go easy on me."

Hades looked at his wife warily. Her eyes were open and alert, but the contempt for him was gone.

"My husband tells me that you kill," she said in a disgusted voice. "I don't see how anyone can excuse a cold-blooded murderer."

"Bloodlust is the nature of the beast," Kenworthy gasped. "The thirst demands that we kill."

"Does it?" Persephone looked at him with steady eyes. "Why should I believe you?"

Flapping of wings sounded, and Phetheus soared from the darkness and lit on a rock. "Don't listen to his excuses," he said. "Kenworthy would have destroyed Leslie and Alex if the other messengers and I hadn't stopped him. He was going to set her hospital on fire."

"That doesn't surprise me. Well done, Phetheus." Hades watched his wife, bracing himself for a sarcastic remark or lifted eyebrows.

Instead, she gave Kenworthy a withering look. "Kenworthy, what have you done to Leslie?" she demanded.

"Leslie poisoned me with a dead man's blood," Kenworthy said in a gravelly voice. "Then she summoned the bats. That witch doesn't deserve to live."

"Kenworthy, I sent the bats," Hades said. "Leslie was following my instructions. You only have yourself to blame."

"What are you saying?" Kenworthy asked in a low voice. "Talk to him, Persephone."

Persephone shook her head. "I can't help you."

Kenworthy's hands dug at the grass and sand. "Why is this happening to me? I don't understand."

"Yes, you do, Kenworthy," Hades said. "You don't want to believe that Leslie poisoned you. You think you're indestructible"

"That's not true." Kenworthy twisted and squirmed on the grass. "I took people who wouldn't be missed. Please don't let me die."

"Murder is murder, but you made your point about mercy," Hades said, nudging Kenworthy's ribs with his sandal-clad feet. "Eternal rest would be too merciful."

He roared in delight. "For every death you caused, you'll suffer a death—200 years worth of deaths, Kenworthy, and you'll suffer every one of them." Smiling, he turned to Phetheus. "See to it that Minos chains this animal. Then you and your friends can work on Kenworthy at your leisure."

"Consider it done," Phetheus said, before taking off. Hades turned away and trudged up the path, feeling Persephone's eyes on his back. He expected another harsh scolding, but right now he didn't care. He was trying to decide whether or not to spare Leslie and her lover. Leslie's face wore a frantic, haunted look when she talked about her mother and her desire to heal people. He'd become well attuned to this expression, having seen it in his own mirror enough times after his exile from Olympus.

Like other vampires, Leslie preyed on people. More than once, his messengers caught her manipulating people for her own profit. Still, Leslie restrained her bloodlust better than most vampires. He contemplated giving her an easy death, but he feared he would destroy her gift of healing.

Sighing wearily, Hades went to his palace to nap. Sleeping on matters seemed to make things clearer. Persephone followed him to their bedchamber.

"You surprise me, Hades," she said after a long pause.

Hades grunted. "Don't I always?"

"I mean it. As god of the dead, you love it when people die and come here. Yet you sent your messengers to rescue Leslie."

Hades grunted again, louder this time.

"If I didn't know any better," Persephone said, smiling, "I'd say this means you plan to spare her and Alex."

"Let it go, Persephone," Hades muttered.

"I went to know your plans," she said, looking at him appealingly. "You like Leslie, do you not? Why?"

Hades looked at Persephone and sighed. Her false politeness was gone, replaced by sincere interest. "She reminds me of you," he said at last. "Stubborn and willful, but she loves her mother the way you love yours."

"Yet you let her go," Persephone said. "Why then do you insist on keeping me here?"

"Because I love you," he said. "Maybe I was wrong to kidnap you, seeing how you love your family and the upper light. But what's done is done." His voice saddened. "If I could give you a daughter, I'd want her to be like Leslie."

"I believe it," Persephone said quietly. "I see now that you're trying to make peace with Leslie's condition. But before you can forgive anyone, you need to forgive yourself." She walked toward him and laid her hands on his tense shoulders. "A good teacher follows his own instructions."

"This isn't about forgiveness. Leslie misses her parents dearly. If I let her live, she'll never see them again."

"She'll have Alex," Persephone persisted, almost begging. "Leslie will go to any length to save someone she loves."

"Even if it means making others like her. But humans weren't meant to live as agents of the afterlife. When they do, someone pays a price."

Persephone sighed. "Maybe we can save that question for another time. Leslie embraces her new life because it enables her to follow her chosen calling."

"Maybe I should let fate be her destiny. She spoke of her God and His master plan." He settled under the rose-colored blankets. "I need time to think about this."

Persephone slipped into bed beside him. For the first time since their marriage, she kissed his cheek. Her lips felt like warm honey. "I can see that you genuinely care about Leslie," she whispered. "I'm sure you'll make the right decision."

After drawing the covers, Persephone nested beside Hades, with one arm draped over his chest. He pulled her close and rested his face against her cheek. Even as he drifted to sleep, he still saw Leslie's haunted look in his mind's eye.

Chapter 29

People's nightmares—their real tragedies as opposed to hallucinations of sleep—end at different times. Leslie's nightmare ended at two in the morning when the bats carried Kenworthy off to Tartarus. It ended in a patient's room at Betsy Ross Hospital, where she had endured other tragedies.

Leslie was still feeding her patient oxygen. The nurses remained fast asleep at their desk. Alex watched them as he stood near the white and black ventilator which was no longer white and black. It was now gray with bat droppings.

Leslie couldn't help staring around the cubicle. The window side took the brunt of the assault, but the bats left the entire room in ruins. The plaster walls had splintered and were caked with blood and manure. An IV pump lay on its side, its panel cracked. Plastic syringes were scattered amidst a battlefield of dead bats, their wings caught in the heater's air vents. The moonlight sent sprinkles of light from the heart monitor's broken glass, illuminating the bats ruby eyes.

Leslie looked up at Alex. "I've got to replace the ventilator," she said. "Do you feel comfortable bagging?"

Alex nodded and shrugged.

"I'm only asking because I could get us both into trouble by asking an untrained person to give life support." She giggled nervously. "Not that anyone would care after seeing this mess."

"You've got that right." Alex reached for the resuscitator. A fearful look crossed his harrowed face. "Do you blame me for any of this?"

"If you're looking for blame, Gerry sells the ticket to that ride." Leslie stripped the soiled ventilator and rolled it toward the hall. "Kenworthy's gone. That's all I care about."

After replacing the ventilator, Leslie surveyed the cubicle again. She scrambled around the bed, retrieving syringes and righting the IV poles. "These pumps are shot," she said, looking at Alex. "I'll have to wake the nurses. They'll want to move Steve to another room and call Maintenance for repairs. We'd better dummy up and let everyone make their own assumptions."

"All right." Alex sighed. "No one would believe the truth anyway."

Leslie looked out the open window again into the night. A bat flew in from the darkness. It perched on the window sill, eyes on her and Alex.

"Thank you," she blurted, trembling.

The bat twittered and nipped the side of her cheek.

"*Ow!*" Leslie looked at Alex with shocked surprise. "What's wrong with that creature?"

"I think you already know."

Leslie did not reply, but she thought she could figure out the answer. Hades hadn't yet decided whether or not to spare her and Alex. He sent another bat messenger to watch them, and its report would influence his decision.

"We're talking good behavior, right?" Leslie stared at Alex, eyes wide, hands going to her throat. "By which standards? Adria's laws? Christianity? How long will he watch us?"

"I don't know," Alex replied. "I honestly don't know."

****

Leslie did not have long to wait for Hades's decision. He appeared in Meadowood Cemetery three weeks later, while she and Alex visited her father's grave. Dressed in a conservative black suit, he looked ordinary, except for the luminescence that radiated from his onyx eyes.

Looking upon this extraordinary being from a distance, Leslie understood why artists adorned paintings of gods with bright auras. Maybe some part of them knew that these gods actually existed. Still, she had to wonder how Hades figured into her God's master plan.

"Your world has its Higher Power and Adria's time dimension has theirs," Hades said, as it though reading her thoughts. "But your skepticism doesn't surprise me."

"Guess so." Leslie folded her arms across her chest, shivering. Hades's decision affected her fate, and she didn't want to antagonize him.

Hades circled a row of tombstones and stood next to Alex. "Leslie loves you," he said. "She all but pleaded with me to spare you in spite of your crimes."

"Leslie!" Alex gasped, stunned. His eyes misted with tears. "You did that for me?"

"I did it for both of us," Leslie said quietly. Turning to Hades, she said, "Fitzpatrick taught me to forgive myself. I hope I can share my lesson with Alex."

Hades heaved a great sigh. "Your people's greed for blood has broken up families, made children orphans. The less vicious vampires spare their victims, but they still control people. Even you, Leslie. My messengers informed me of the miracles you worked, but you used your powers to intimidate humans, too."

Leslie tightened her clasped hands, staring at Hades in awe and fear. "Have you made a decision?"

Hades looked down at her with a peculiar combination of love, sympathy, and reluctance. "No vampire or other unworldly creature should walk this earth. But alas, the theory that you expressed before has merit—your Master feels that you have your place in the scheme of things."

Hades gazed at the tombstones, a look of infinite sadness on his face. When he turned toward Leslie and Alex, he continued. "You and Alex performed bravely, bringing me Kenworthy, and so you shall live to fulfill your destinies. But Leslie, immortality means that you'll never see your parents again. I hope you've considered that in your decision to pursue living."

Leslie looked up at Hades. Comments about Mom and Dad always brought tears to her eyes, and now the grief washed fresh through her heart. "Alex's love made me want to live," she said. "Besides, saving people from their illnesses means the world to me."

"Point well taken," Hades said sadly. "But I suspect in the years to come that you'll wish that I'd destroyed you." He cast his gaze toward the clouded sky. "One day, you may find yourself at a crossroad, and the wrong turn could lead to disaster. Think carefully before you make any major decisions."

Hands pressed against her lips, Leslie watched Hades turn away and slithered into the shadows. "What was that all about?" she asked in a trembling voice.

"I don't know, but he let us go free." Rushing forward, Alex clasped her into his arms. "You risked your life on my account. I can't begin to tell you what this means to me."

Reaching up, Leslie smoothed back the wisps of hair from his eyes. "Alex, you taught me to love life, and I plan to stick around. You've got to remember that Delia and I come from different places. Maybe one day, you'll believe me."

"I believe you now." Taking Leslie's arm, Alex walked her through the cemetery to the street. "But we haven't heard the last from Hades. His mercy comes with strings attached."

Leslie nodded solemnly. She understood that favors from an underworld god came at a steep price. Then again, maybe the price had already been paid.

As they got into the car, thunder rumbled overhead and rain splattered the windshield. Leslie paused, hands gripping her keys. The slick road ahead reminded her of

Fitzpatrick and the night she'd totaled her car after his CAT scan. Again, she saw her car bob over the guard rail, plunging down the ravine, and smashing into the tree.

"Whatever happens, I promise to love you forever," Alex said, eyes shining like lit candles. "My soul will become one with yours. I wanted to give you a church wedding, but a civil ceremony will have to do."

Leslie leaned over, cradled Alex's face in her fingers, and kissed him ardently. "A civil ceremony sounds great. I promise to love you beyond forever."

His hands cradled her face, fingers stroking her hair. "Let's go home, so we can cement our commitment."

Cranking the engine, Leslie nodded and smiled. Home sounded like a great idea.

About the Contributors

Barbara Custer:

Barbara lives near Philadelphia, Pennsylvania, where she works full-time as a respiratory therapist. When she's not working with her patients, she's enjoying a fright flick or working on horror and science fiction tales. Her short stories have appeared in numerous small press magazines. She's published *Night to Dawn* magazine since 2004.

Other books by Barbara include *City of Brotherly Death* and *Steel Rose*, plus novellas *Close Liaisons* and *Life Raft: Earth*. She's also coauthored *Alien Worlds* and *Starship Invasions* (both now out of print) with Tom Johnson. She enjoys bringing her medical background to the printed page, and then blending it with supernatural horror. She maintains a presence on Facebook, LinkedIn, Twitter, and The Writers Coffeehouse forum. Look for the photos with the Mylar balloons and you'll find her. You can contact Barbara at barbaracuster@hotmail.com. Visit her at:

www.bloodredshadow.com
www.facebook.com/barbara.custer
https://twitter.com/NighttoDawn1
http://barbara-custer.livejournal.com/4528.html

Teresa Tunaley:

Originating from the UK but residing in the Canary Islands for the last 10 years, freelance artist Teresa

Twilight Healer

Tunaley devotes time to her love of art and painting. For more than 30 years she has been doodling with pencils and dabbling with watercolors. More recently she has been painting traditionally in oil and creating large canvasses full of color and life. Sometimes she uses a more modern technique using software such as Photoshop, Corel Draw and Paint Shop Pro to produce her creations for online publications.

During her art career, she has produced countless illustrations, book covers and paintings. Along with published stories and poetry, she can be credited with award winning cover art and illustrations for author stories. Her work can be seen online and in print across the UK, US, Canada and Europe.

In May 2011, she opened a new Exhibition in Puerto del Santiago (Tenerife, Spain) entitled Tutto per la vita (All for the life). She has over 30 works on show and is hoping to be selected to participate in the Capitals annual Art Festival. Should she win, there will be invitations to exhibit her work in a whirlwind trip across Spain and Italy.

Touching and spectacular "has been the inauguration; Tutto Per la vita" Some thirty of their works appeared, giving you a journey to Spain, Africa, America, Japan and Thailandia. The work was intense with feeling, in full color and textures, where figures, landscapes and moments will leave the visitor with a memory of a magical trip."

Jose Francisco Morales
Comisario de la Exposicion (Tenerife)
http://www.artesigloxxi.org
I like to think that I am very versatile in my choice of subject matter - my new surroundings provide the inspiration for me to paint on a daily basis and the fact that others may enjoy my work gives me the confidence to continue.
Website: www.artstopper.com

www.ingramcontent.com/pod-product-compliance
Lightning Source LLC
Chambersburg PA
CBHW050710180626
46814CB00002B/371